Praise for Threatened Loyaltiees

Loved it!!!
This is the second book by JF Ridgley I have read and I really enjoyed both of them! I read a lot and most of the books I read are about the Roman empire so I am pretty well versed in the era. This author's books belong up there with Simon Scarrow.

—N.M. Cox

Puts the "Roman" in Romance
Apologies on the cheesy title, I couldn't help myself. …
I'd recommend it to fans of Roman historical fiction wholeheartedly.

—Amazon Customer

Well done.
Ridgley has woven a wonderful tale. Love, identity, rebellion, intrigue, and adventure in ancient Rome. Well-executed plot and engaging prose. Very infrequent, minor editing quirks that are easily overlooked and forgotten.

—Layla

Threatened Loyalties

JF Ridgley

OTHER BOOKS AND STORIES BY JF RIDGLEY

Historical Fiction
Vows of Revenge
Birth of a Bully

VULCAN'S WRATH SERIES
Threatened Loyalties
For the Family

AGRICOLA SERIES
Red Fury – Revolt
Chrysalis

Contemporary Romance
Love Backwards
18 Wheeler

To Joe
Thank you for believing in my dreams.

CHAPTER 1

ALEXIUS'S GAZE VENTURED down the night-filled street littered with garbage and trash shifting over the stones. Sons of Dis and Jupiter, he did not want to do this. Messalina could be anywhere. She knew how dangerous Herculaneum's streets were this late at night.

He could not believe that Didius, Messi's father's master slave, had actually climbed over the dividing wall between their houses to beg him to go find her. "Please, before the dominus returns home, or he'll beat me and sell me. I am too old, young dominus. Please."

It was not like her father to threaten an old trusted slave. However, it was not like Messalina to sneak out either. There was no logical reason for her to do that other than to see Hector—*that interloping piece of dog dung. If this has anything to do with him, I will kill that spawn of a slave's whore.*

A brisk February wind whipped through the street as he wondered how he was supposed to find his betrothed out here. Not an easy task in Herculaneum, even during the day.

Alexius flung his legion cloak over his back and checked his dagger in his belt. In the two years he had been in Britannia with Agricola, Messi had gone from an ugly duckling to a regal swan. Everything had changed but her attitude toward him. She still despised him. Especially after he had nicknamed her Medusa. Now that he was back home, he was determined to redeem himself in her eyes.

However, I could not if she is lying dead in some alley.

Alexius stepped out of his doorway and into the shadows. Entry torches over doorways guttered in the wind. Clouds hung heavy in the evening sky, thick with the smell of rain.

Earlier that day, his mother had mentioned something about Messi being upset over her friend Rosa for not answering her letters. So maybe she had received word that Rosa had returned home. Well, that was a good a place to start. All he had to do was cross the street to Balbus's house, wake up the door slave, and ask.

Frustration escaped with a heavy sigh as Alexius strode the twenty paces across the street. After bruising his fist on the hard-oak door, a pair of sleep-filled eyes appeared in the peephole.

"Is the domina Nonia Rosa present?"

"No, dominus."

"Then, has the domina Messalina Claudia been here tonight?"

The eyes glared at him. "No. Certainly not at this hour, dominus!" The small flap snapped shut, jolting Alexius back on one leg. He stared at the closed peephole. If Messi was not there, then where in Hades was she?

Hector's?

Fury burned in his veins as he stepped from Balbus's stoop and heard footsteps behind him. He wheeled about, dagger drawn. The face hidden in the shadow stopped his hand. "Fosco? What are you—?"

"You didn't think you are searching for the young domina alone, did you?" His personal slave stated as he joined him by the stoop.

"I guess not," Alexius said and let out his sigh of relief. Sliding the dagger back into its sheath, he asked, "You have any idea where Messi could have gone?"

Fosco shrugged. "Hector's been banned from her house. Could she have gone to his house, maybe?"

Alexius fingered the dagger's hilt. "She had better not."

Marcus, Rosa's brother, had informed him that Hector had been stupid enough to request that her father to grant him Messalina's hand in marriage. It would be like that fucking idiot to try to steal her away. By the gods, Messi was his and he was not giving her up this easily.

The night shadows lurked around their feet as he and Fosco marched toward the corner of the block. Wind clashed in the intersection, gusting as if to stop them. Like a guiding light, silver moonlight spotlighted the Corinthian crowns of Hector's entry.

This time Alexius let Fosco hammer on the door, setting off the guard dogs inside. An eternity passed until the peep-hole opened and another set of sleep-filled eyes appeared. "Yes, dominus?"

Alexius stepped closer. "I want to speak with Hector."

"Neither are here, dominus. Father and son remain in Rome, not to return for another week."

Alexius studied the slave's eyes. "Is the domina Messalina Claudia here?"

"At this hour? No!"

Alexius stepped closer. "If you are lying, I will have—"

"Jupiter's throne, I haven't seen her!" Once again, the small window clipped shut, leaving Alexius staring at wood.

A sense of foreboding shrouded Alexius as he returned to the corner that led to Herculaneum's main shopping district. Whiffs of over-cooked chowders, rank odors of ale and rotten wine assaulted the restless air. Sounds of dice tumbling from cups mingled with cheers and laughter that grew louder with each step they took toward the busy tavernas.

An odorous shadow appeared from a black alley and held up a wooden cup. "Denarius, young dominus, so I can eat today."

"Have you seen the domina Messalina Claudia tonight?" Alexius asked the beggar.

The man drew back into the hovering darkness. "I… No. I…I haven't seen her." He glanced nervously up the street. "I haven't seen anyone." The bowl lifted again. "Please, I haven't eaten for days."

Alexius motioned to Fosco to deliver a coin. "If you do see her, find me, and you will eat for a month, I assure you."

"Yes, if I see her. Yes." The coin dropped into the cup with a dull thud. "May the gods bless your election, young dominus." The beggar clutched the bowl to his chest and withdrew into the darkness.

Alexius moved on. *Yes, my fine election.* That thought also snarled through him. He had never expected to come back from Britannia to start working on his election into the Senate. He scowled into a narrow alley of angry dogs and unconscious drunks. That was not supposed to begin for at least five more years.

However, Balbus, his father, and Messi's father had managed to obtain Vespasian's approval for him to run for an early appointment to the Committee of Twelve. And if that was not enough, they had arranged his appointment to Gaius Pomponius Beastius's financial committee. Alexius growled into the next dark alley as he recalled Messalina's father boasting, "Gain Pomponius's approval, and your appointment is done."

Never once had anyone asked me what I wanted.

Fosco approached a group of men lounging outside the taverna to ask about Messalina.

"Yes. She's up there. I just finished fucking 'er."

"She's with someone else now. You'll have to wait your turn. Line's a long one."

"No, she ain't, you ass. Saw her about an hour ago. Goin' that way." The drunk pointed down a narrow alley thick with smells of urine and garbage. "Or was it that way?" He acted unsure.

"The young domina Claudia, yes. Saw her earlier. Went home, she did. One of her slaves came for her," another assured.

Wanting to bash their lying faces, Alexius studied the number of vagrants that seemed to be multiplying in the street like hungry rats. He scanned the area for any sign of Messalina, as female laughter, giggles, grunts, and groans plummeted down from the second stories, nothing like a struggle or rape.

Thunder rumbled the ground beneath their feet. The night patrols, the Vigils. Where were they? Not here, obviously, Alexius thought.

That was another situation that he had found himself in. The retired centurion Flaccus had been thrilled that Alexius had volunteered to act as tribune and help patrol Herculaneum's streets at night. Only, he had not volunteered. His glorious father had done that masterful work for him.

All he wanted since his return was to workout at the palestra and go hunting. Just relax. But not now. It was all he could do to not bash something.

Once again, the shifting moonlight broke through the black clouds. In that instant, Alexius saw something white like a beacon bobbing through the filthy bodies. It nervously turned, revealing a glimpse of Messalina's face in the brief light. The urge to strangle his betrothed exploded with a sense of relief.

Alexius pressed toward her. However, a mass of filthy bodies suddenly spawned between them. Hands reached out for offerings or grabbed at his cloak, his wrist, his arm.

Alexius slapped, shoved, and punched them away as he fought to keep her in his sight. When Messi darted into a dark stairwell of an apartment building near the corner of the main street, anger coiled in his veins.

Men went down, falling over the street curbs where he and Fosco tossed them. At last, they both barged into the stairwell and he pinned Messalina's lush body against the stairway wall. "Messi, what do you think you are—"

An arm clamped around Alexius's neck as a knifepoint pierced his cape and pricked his flesh. "Let her go if you wish to live, dominus."

From the corner of his eye, he glimpsed another knife at Fosco's throat, rendering his slave useless. "The vigils are coming," he said, hoping they were. "I called for them."

A deep-throated chuckle sounded in his ear. "They're busy at the moment. We made sure of it." Fragrances of rancid wine and garlic drifted across Alexius's face. "I'm not repeating this again, let her go, dominus."

Every way to get rid of this man flashed in Alexius's mind. However, he would have to risk letting go of Messalina. "She stays with me."

"Then you die with your slave."

Messalina jerked against him. "No. Please. No. Alexius, I am safe. Let me—"

"I am not leaving you, Messi." Alexius bit his bottom lip as the knife pressed deeper. He studied the delicious depths of her brown eyes. He had to release her to get rid of this fool with a knife.

Light burst down the staircase as a door opened. "Domina?" The shadow of a man appeared from the corner apartment and started down the stairs. "Felix, what's going on?"

"He stopped her, Zeno. Want me to kill the fool?" The arm tightened around Alexius's throat.

Balbus's premier charioteer rushed down the steps. "Let him go."

The knife retreated.

When Alexius stepped back enough to breathe, Messalina bolted toward the charioteer. "Zeno, I don't know how Alexius found out. I told no—"

Alexius grabbed her wrist, stopping her. "Messi?"

Messalina jerked her hand away. "Let me go, Marcus Galerius Alexius."

"No. Let me take you home."

"No. You have no business being here. You go home."

Alexius endured her glare, sharper than the knife's point. Dis and Jupiter. He was only trying to protect her. And damn near had himself killed doing so. "No."

"It's not what it seems, young dominus. Come," Zeno waved them to follow him to his apartment. He halted and glanced back. "Felix, allow no one else, even if it means killing them."

Alexius turned to Fosco who was rubbing his neck and glaring at his captor. "Go tell Didius she is with me and return with the litter."

"Yes, dominus."

Messalina ordered her heart to still in her chest as she ventured into Zeno's small apartment. Warmth from a burning brazier erased the chill of the night. The fragrance of simmering cherry-wood blended with the soft rain now pelting down on the roof tiles. Thunder rumbled softly.

Her father would kill her if he knew she had come to a slave's apartment. However, Zeno had sent a message about Rosa and promised she would be safe if she came. Hope and concern for Rosa had driven her to sneak away.

She passed a large bed by the door and sat on the bench nestled beside a wooden table that butted up to the stairway wall. Alexius crossed the room as if he owned the place and leaned against a window frame, folding his arms over his chest hidden by the legion cape.

Messalina glared at him as he intently studied her with a laser blue gaze. First, her fanatical father had restricted her to the house like a child. Now, Alexius had the gall to come after her, pretending to protect her. *As if he cared.* How did he even know she had left? She melted with the answer… Didius, of course.

The thud of the security bar dropping across the door jerked Messalina's attention to Zeno. He crossed the apartment to the brazier. He stood slightly taller than Alexius and was more muscular in the arms. But not the shoulders. Unlike Alexius's short brown hair, Zeno's curly black hair fell in thick coils down the back of a short green tunic.

Zeno turned from the brazier. "Rosa told me I could trust you, domina. Can I?"

"Of course, Zeno."

He looked at Alexius and waited for his answer.

"I am only here to see she does not get hurt. That's all I care about."

Messalina wanted to laugh. He was as trapped in this betrothal as she was. If she were out of his life, his parents could arrange a betrothal with a girl who did not reminded him of the gorgon Medusa.

"Do you know anything about my Rosa?" Zeno pleaded, eyes filling with worry. "Domina, I have to find her."

My Rosa. What did he mean by that?" Messalina's thoughts flashed as to why she had risked her father's fury… Rosa, her very pregnant friend who had gone missing for the last three months.

Her throat closed with the fact. *The baby.* She remembered feeling it moving beneath her hand as Rosa spewed her fury that hot September day. *"Messi, we are going to run away before Papa marries me to…."*

But, before Rosa could finish, her father had bolted in the terrace sunroom, with his fist crumpling Hector's letter requesting a betrothal with him instead of Alexius. Hades' entire wrath erupted just then, and Rosa had snuck away before she could tell her anymore. It was now February and the baby…

Bona Dea! She realized that Rosa could be in labor… right now. And the father of that child stood before her. Messalina dropped her head into her palms.

Rain cascaded off the roof as Alexius drew from the wall, worry blatant on his face as Zeno squatted in front of her. "What? What is it, domina?"

Messalina stared at the slave's worried face. If Balbus knew Rosa carried a slave's child, her father would have killed her, which would explain why Rosa never answered any letters.

But, no. Just that afternoon, her mother had babbled on about Rosa's wedding with Pomponius which had been set in March. Messalina's heart leaped in her chest. That could only mean Rosa was alive. She had to be.

"Domina." Zeno's calloused hand touched her wrist. "Tell me, please."

Messalina startled at the unfamiliar touch. "First, I have to know, what do you know?"

Zeno melted back on his haunches. "That my Rosa wants to go with me to my homeland and become my wife. We had it all planned. Now, I don't know where she is."

Across the room, Alexius rolled his eyes and slumped back against the wall.

No matter how much she despised him, Alexius should not know any of this. It could cost him far too much. "Alexius needs to leave."

His gaze shot across the room. "I am not going anywhere without you."

She glared at her betrothed as he seemed to sprout roots against the window. After all the years of growing up together, she knew how stubborn Alexius could be. More stubborn than a goat. A herd of goats.

Zeno fell forward on his knees. "Domina, I just need to find her so we can leave."

"You are a fool if you do." Unflinching, Alexius perched his hands on his hips, lifting his cloak out like wings as Zeno rose to his feet. "Balbus will have every legion in the Empire after you. And may the Gods forbid what he would do when he finds you."

Gazes locked. "Once we get back to my homeland, no one will find us."

"Enough money loosens tongues. And I assure you, Balbus will spend every ounce of gold he has to find you."

Zeno's hands slid over his head. "I can't leave her to marry Pomponius." He stepped back, hands out. "Rosa begged me to take her away. I can now."

"She can't travel."

Both men tore their attention to her. Messalina met their questioning gazes. Every sane part of her told her it was a mistake to say more. However, the words simply poured out of her mouth.

"She is pregnant."

As if hit by the fact, Alexius whirled to the wall and braced himself against it. Zeno slumped to the floor. "Tell me it's not his." He looked to the bed. "No. I don't care if it is. I don't care. I just have to get my Rosa—"

"It's not…his."

Alexius looked back over his shoulder at her, as Zeno stabbed her with his attention. "It's mine?"

Messalina nodded.

Joy flashed on Zeno's face. "I know women who will care for her. Hide her." He fell to his knees and clutched Messalina's hands. "Domina, where is she?"

She blinked with disbelief. "Zeno, I thought you could tell me. That's why I came."

"I don't know!" Zeno growled as he rose to supported himself with his arms against the wall.

Alexius left his window and crossed the room. "Are you sure she is pregnant, Messi?"

She looked into his serious blue gaze. "I felt it move."

"And you are sure Zeno is the father?"

She nodded as her hand curled to keep from rubbing her cheek where her father had slapped her that same afternoon. Alexius did not need to know about her father's tirade that had ruined Rosa telling her everything. "She told me she was going to run away and that Pomponius was never going to touch her. That's all."

Alexius sat down on the end of the bench and stared at the floor. A thick silence filled the apartment. His familiar fragrance, woodsy spice, very pleasant, floated over her. Whatever he had done in Britannia had made him more serious. He seemed more…responsible, unlike before he left. Had his heart really changed? Not likely.

"When is she due?" Alexius asked. The intensity of his gaze intruded. Zeno lifted off the wall, focusing intently on her as well.

"Now."

CHAPTER 2

ZENO STRUGGLED TO the bed and slumped onto it, dropping his forehead into his hands. *Rosa. His child. Their child. By the gods.*

"Does Pomponius or Balbus have any idea about you and Rosa?" the young dominus asked.

Zeno shook his head. "No. We were careful. We only saw each other when Balbus was away in Rome." He looked to the ceiling. "Rosa came to the practice track, demanding I let her ride around the track. I told her that her father wouldn't approve. But she said he wasn't there to deny her. As a slave to her house, I had to take her out."

Zeno remembered every moment of that day and every day since. Rosa laughing as he galloped the team of horses around the practice track with her beside him, shifting against him so easily. He studied the two attentive gazes—Roman gazes—and wondered if he should say any more.

But Rosa had trusted the domina Messalina, so he continued.

"After that, she came every day her father was gone." Zeno pinched the bridge of his nose to stop the tears. "She started bringing friends, so it would appear that it was simply an outing." He looked at the young domina who was no longer the ugly duckling as she had been. Beauty had finally kissed her. Still, his Rosa was more beautiful than all the goddesses. "Remember, domina?"

Alexius turned, stunned. "You? You rode in the race chariots?"

A blush rose over Messalina's face. A timid smile appeared. "A few times. It scared me, so I just went along and watched."

"It was safe, dominus, I promise you," Zeno assured the young patrician. "The trainer couldn't refuse because Rosa paid him enough to keep his mouth shut."

A wave of stupidity seared through Zeno. He stood and paced across the room. "Like my Rosa said, we should have left then. She had saved enough to pay for everything. She had even drawn up my manumission papers to get us to Armenia. She said no one would challenge them once there." Even though he couldn't read, he remembered the feel of freedom in his palms.

"But I had to win another race. Another damn race. Then, I would have had enough to buy my own freedom… freedom that her father had promised."

Shut his eyes as the memory returned of Balbus calling him into the triclinium before his clients. "Zeno, Zeno, come. I have something to tell you." Every step he had taken had been carefully placed, as if at any moment a gladiator might appear from a side room to execute him.

No matter how the man had tried to appear cheerful, Balbus's gaze remained deadly, calculating, and cold. "I want my clients to see how I reward such achievement because you have done well, Zeno. So, I wish to reward you for your victories in the Circus Maximus. From here on, I will grant you one fourth of the winnings to apply toward purchasing your freedom." His ringed hand had waved between them, glinting in the candlelight. "The more you win, the sooner you are free."

Zeno remembered how he had dropped to his knees before everyone. "I will win for you, dominus. More than ever before. I promise."

Hatred wheeled Zeno around. He slammed a fist against the wall. "If he's hurt her, I'll kill him."

Alexius shrugged. "You are as good as dead if you do."

Zeno sprang from the wall, wanting someone to pummel. The young dominus would do. Messalina's voice cut through the tension.

"She is alive. I know that."

Zeno jerked his attention to the young domina.

Her rich brown gaze flickered between the young dominus and himself. "Volasennia is planning the wedding. She's telling everyone."

"To Pomponius?" Alexius asked, curious.

Messalina nodded.

Zeno couldn't breathe. He started pacing the room like one of the lions caged in the amphitheater. "I can't let her." He stopped as another reality struck him like a fist. "The bastard will expose my baby. I know he will." Tears jerked from his eyes. "I'll kill him. I'll kill them all if they touch her or what is mine."

The young dominus spoke, "Remember, Zeno, Rosa still lives."

He looked over at the young Roman seated ever so calmly on the bench. Their gazes locked again. "You're right, dominus. It's not too late. I could find her, and we can go now. Yes."

"Balbus will be looking for you to do exactly that." The young dominus shifted on the bench, resting an arm on the table. "Right now, I would assume Rosa needs a reason to keep living more than anything else."

His mind couldn't accept what he was hearing from this Roman. Let Rosa go to that fat fool? Let them expose his child to the wolves as if it were fodder?

"Alexius is right." Messalina stood. "If Rosa knows you are coming for her, she will find some way to stay alive."

She was offering a fragment of hope; hope that he would hold his Rosa again. Hope that came with sacrifice. His soul. Zeno ran a desperate hand over his head and started pacing again. "I don't care what happens to me. But I can't let her marry Pomponius."

"You have to let this wedding happen." The young dominus let his hand rest open on the table. "Or you will be useless to Rosa."

Zeno's throat closed. What he meant was Rosa had to go through with the wedding. No. He couldn't let that happen. Rosa hated the fat senator more than he did. "How would either of you understand? I'm nothing but a slave to you. But never to my Rosa. She's my life! I love her. I can't let this happen."

The young dominus stood. "Think, Zeno. Yes, you are a slave. But if you allow Balbus to torture you or sell you—or both—you will destroy Rosa and lose all chance at saving her."

Zeno scrutinized the Roman standing before him. The boy had become a man in these few years and now spoke with authority the empire granted him. It cut like a knife. His insides were being torn out of him. "What about the baby?"

Alexius's gaze deepened with pity. "Let the gods decide that, Zeno."

A deep silence permeated the room as the rain drummed overhead and thunder shook the walls. Zeno studied the two before him like possible enemies, like possible friends. He didn't know. "I need to get a message to Rosa to wait for me. But how?"

The young dominus shrugged. "Maybe I—"

"Alexius, no." Messalina gripped his arm. "You cannot be any part of this. Not with your election."

Alexius stared at her. The corner of his mouth lifted. "I already am, Messi."

"No. All you have done is discourage Zeno from doing anything that could hurt him or Rosa. That is all."

Zeno barely heard their quarrel as his world crumbled. He didn't care how, or who got Rosa the message to wait for him. He twisted a round silver pendant bearing the image of a racing chariot from his neck, the one that Balbus had given to him after his last win in the Max.

"Here, domina. Here! Use this. Get this to my Rosa." His hand trembled as he held the necklace out. "Tell her I will come for her. Tell her I love her. Just wait."

Messalina reached for the pendant, but the young Roman pulled her hand away. "Messi, you know the laws as well as I do, and you know you have as much at risk as well."

CHAPTER 3

ROSA WADDLED ACROSS the inner garden surrounded by a portico supported by white marble columns. Thunder rumbled in the darkening, wet afternoon sky. Eels and fish frantically darted through the water in the long, narrow impluvium lined with rain-drenched boxwoods and six, life-sized, bronze statues of young maidens.

She meandered through the massive collection of statues of great men that Sulla's wife had tucked against the muraled walls. She stopped at the blue-striped lounger where she spent her hours reclining, napping, or reading near Zeno's great-grandfather's bust—Zeno of Sidon.

Your father looks like your grandfather, as you will, she thought to the baby instead of speaking aloud. Ears were everywhere. *You will share the same black curly hair and rich hazel eyes, the same slender nose, and lips, Baby Paullus. In addition, you must remember that your grandfather was known for his wisdom, just as your father is known as the best charioteer in all of Rome. Why, just today, I heard the slaves say that your father won again.*

The night before, she had heard talk among the slaves that Zeno had raced in the Circus Maximus. Therefore, he must be alive. Rosa rested a hand on the statue's base. *Please, King Zeno, I ask that your gods protect your sons and help us return to Armenia. Please, Jupiter Optimus Maximus, hear my prayer.*

She walked out to the impluvium pool and tossed grain to the eels rushing to her for their daily offering. Her reflection rippled in the water, displaying a round, plain-faced girl with wide-set green eyes. She was not stunning like Messalina, who had become so beautiful this last year. Messi could walk down the street and young men would stare at her in awe. Once one even tripped over his feet while gawking. Yet, Messi refused to believe she had changed, insisting that they were making fun of her, whispering *Medusa*, as Alexius had so despicably nicknamed her.

Rosa grinned at her reflection. Zeno thought she was prettier than Messi, more beautiful than all the goddesses on Mt. Olympus. Her smile faded. He had to come for her soon. The baby was anxious to be free of its confinement. Contractions had already started.

Rosa returned to the lounger and melted into the plush cushions. She pulled the thick velvet drape over her swollen legs. She had to get a message to Zeno…or to Messi. However, getting a message to anyone was impossible because her father had ordered everything brought to him first.

Her father, Marcus Nonius Balbus, had only one true desire in life—to elevate the family of Nonius before all of Rome. In public, he exemplified the essence of congeniality. At home, he was harder than the fine marble that adorned his house. And Marcus Nonius Balbus expected everyone in his family to elevate this facade with absolute submission.

She could not do that anymore, not since he expected her to marry Spurius Pomponius Bestius. This final expectation had destroyed the few shreds of what remained of her loyalty and had led her to Zeno.

However, one thing was certain—if her father knew Zeno was Paullus's father, he would have already made Zeno's death a horrendous spectacle for everyone and enjoy every moment of doing so. However, Zeno still lived.

Oh, once he learned of the baby, her father had tried to beat Zeno's name out of her, as her mother and her witch of a grandmother watched. That day roared back to Rosa's memory…the day when all the gods had turned their backs on her…all except for Jupiter, the one god powerful enough to stop even her father.

"Father, you called for me?"

He sat at his dark, teak desk like a god himself, drumming his fingers on the surface. He glanced at his mother—the witch—who stood in the corner like a black-draped statue.

When she had entered the atrium, his fingers froze and hung like claws. Then, he motioned to the cross-legged chair before him. "Nonia Rosa, sit."

She sat, folding her hands protectively over her baby, and watched as her father came around the desk to sit on its polished corner. Before he spoke, he adjusted a fold of his gleaming senatorial toga that had slid down his arm.

The entire family knew he was never without his mark telling the world—no, reminding the world—that he, Marcus Nonius Balbus, was no longer a descendent of a slave now a freedman. He was a senator of the great Roman Empire, as well as a personal friend of Vespasian Caesar.

He leaned forward, resting his forearm across his thigh. "Is there something you should tell me, Nonia Rosa?"

She had studied his aristocratic face weathered from serving with the legions in Crete. His intent gaze was dangerously dark and deliberate. "No, Father. All is well."

He smiled the cold calculating smile that had given her nightmares. "Are you sure?"

An ominous sound of thunder rumbled as the clouds darkened the atrium. She glanced at the busy fountain and the plants waving in pots set around the raised impluvium. She remembered her sudden fear. *He could not know about the baby. Not unless Carena told. Nothing about her slave girl had changed. No torture covered her flesh.*

"Yes, Father. I am sure."

"When was your last blood flow?"

Her heart stopped. "Two…weeks ago, I think."

"Are you certain of this?"

Carena had dipped the rags in chicken's blood. She nodded.

His hand had crashed across her face, sending her and the chair sprawling to the floor. Pain shot like lightning striking through her back. She scanned the columns for help from someone, anyone. Her mother stood in the doorway, frozen like a statue. The old witch remained statuesque in the dark corner. Nothing breathed but wind blustering downward through the opening in the ceiling.

Her father had set the fallen chair upright and lifted her by her hair, dropping her into it like a piece of trash. "Don't lie to me, Nonia Rosa." He shoved a cloth filled with blood over her nose and mouth. Its stench made her gag

"Explain this, Nonia."

"It…it is my last cloth."

"It is blood from a chicken." The words came from the dark corner, from the witch.

He smeared the foul cloth over her face. "Is it?"

"Yes."

"Then, you are pregnant?"

She twisted away to glare into his deadly gaze. "Yes."

"Tell me who!"

"Never."

Again, he knocked her out of the chair and across the marble floor. She had slid into the nearby column, driving her shoulder into her spine.

"Tell me!"

Lightning struck through the opening in the ceiling, filling the room with piercing, white light. Shards from the fountain had exploded everywhere, slicing her face and arms. Thunder boomed against the walls, deafening her, followed by a downpour of rain falling into the atrium pool. Two ceramic medallions crashed beside her head.

For one glorious moment, she saw her father sprawled on the floor. He rubbed his hand over his face and stared at the crimson streaks on his palms. Then he rose like a demon. "Tell me his name or I will—"

"No! Nonius! It is a sign." The old witch bolted from her corner to stop him. "Jupiter protects her!" The witch's bun now hung like silver snakes over her shoulders. Her gnarled hands reached for her son. "Listen to me, Nonius. Please."

Balbus tossed the old woman aside and stumbled through fragments of the atrium fountain. "Tell me his name!"

"Nonius, no! Do not do this! Jupiter has spoken!" The old woman clutched her son's rain-soaked toga.

As he slithered out of the soaked wool gripped by his mother, her father's face had contorted with rage. His teeth bared like a rabid wolf, ready to tear flesh. "I want the bastard's name! I want him dead!"

A slave boy cleared his throat. "Domina."

From the couch, Rosa watched the rain spewing out through ceiling drain spouts like narrow waterfalls cascading over the eels and into the impluvium.

"Domina! You are expected in the library."

Fear swept through her like a cold whirlwind. "Who asked?"

"Your father, domina."

"How long has he been here?" As if it mattered how long her father had been there.

"They just arrived, domina."

"They?"

"Dominus Sulla and your father."

Even though the witch had protected her, Marcus Cornelius Sulla had saved her from her father. He had arrived shortly after her grandmother had thrown herself over her body to stop her son.

Sulla convinced Balbus to send her away to his villa, away from the city's eyes and gossip until the baby was born. Sulla had even talked to Pomponius and assured him that everything would be fine. He would see to it.

No doubt, Sulla agreed with her father that Baby Paulus should be exposed. The only thing that had kept her alive these last few months was the hope that Zeno would come for her. Glancing desperately at Zeno of Sidon's statue, Rosa tossed the blanket aside and stood. She had to stay alive until then.

Wooden shelves full of scholarly scrolls wrapped the small library's interior room like comforting arms. A brazier simmered by the doors where Rosa's feet halted. Its warmth drew out the fragrances of parchment and ink. The polished marble floor reflected the two loungers occupied by Sulla and her father.

Her father's gaze darkened the room. "Nonia, sit."

Her feet refused to take a step further. Like always, the smell of his exotic oil nauseated her, as did his presence. "I do not feel well."

Sulla's wife, Agrippina Fluvia Pulcher sat in one of the two rattan chairs placed across from the men. Agrippina adjusted the light green stola over her legs and looked toward the door. The array of curls arranged around her face accented her large brown eyes and refined features. "Nonia, come. Join us. Please."

Sulla motioned to the empty chair next to his wife. Sulla's manner seemed pleasant and comfortable. Still, Rosa wondered about the gesture. There was flint in his steel-gray eyes. He was taller and had more regality in his left hand than her father could ever possess. However, he was a mysterious man, a chameleon of sorts.

She eased into the empty cushioned chair and felt Agrippina rest her hand on Rosa's arm. "I will stay if you wish," she said softly.

"Please." She did not want to be alone with these men.

"Nonia," Balbus said, rising on one elbow from the couch cushions. "Pomponius has forgiven you for your ignorance. Look at me, girl, when I speak to you!"

As ordered, Rosa lifted a cold glare to her father.

"Fortunately, he still agrees to the marriage."

She dropped her attention to her fingers as they knitted over the baby.

Balbus sat up right. His glare burned from the lounger. "I am told the baby is due any time. Is that true?"

Words had dried in her throat. Tension in the room thickened.

"Agrippina?" Sulla asked, the tone of his voice urgent.

"I believe so, yes," his wife answered, her gaze darkening toward her husband.

Rosa had not been in their villa long before she discovered there was no warmth between Sulla and Agrippina. As gentle as Agrippina seemed, she was the force in the villa. No one challenged her, not even her husband. While Sulla brought his name to their marriage, Agrippina had brought the money. Therefore, Sulla could not afford to divorce her because she would bankrupt him. Having borne him one son who was now grown, she had only stayed in the marriage out of respect to her family's name and because Sulla left her alone—facts Rosa had gleaned from the slave gossip.

Balbus cleared his throat. "Pomponius, of course, will not accept the child in his house. Therefore, unless you tell us who the father is, it will become a slave. Is that what you want, Nonia Rosa?"

Rosa looked at her father. If he knew who the father was, both the child and the father would be dead before nightfall. "I will not marry Pomponius."

"Oh, yes you will, you little fool. Or you will be damned from my sight. I will see that—"

"Rosa, there is another option," Sulla said, stopping Balbus with a raised hand. "I promise that if you marry Pomponius, your child will remain here—alive, of course." Sulla met her gaze fully while her father frothed.

"As a slave?"

Sulla nodded. "I will have it adopted by one of my freedmen, if you wish it."

Rosa glanced at her father. "If I refuse?"

Balbus settled back in the cushions, flexing his fingers. "Then you will be sentenced to a public death, for I will not forgive your stupidity. Of course, we expect the man who gave you this bastard will try to save you. I assure you that I will see that he begs to die."

Rosa forced herself to remain passive even though her heart had risen to her throat and stopped. "He doesn't know."

"But he will, Rosa. I will see to it the Empire knows." Her father smiled without humor. "In fact, I would prefer this to Sulla's offer."

Lies! She knew how her father loved a grand display of his dedication to the law. However, it would never appear at the cost of his family's image. Rosa's stomach heaved chunks of beef stew over the mosaic flooring.

Sulla gagged. "Slaves!" Slaves all but tumbled through the door. "Clean this."

Her father's face turned white and then green as both men raced out into the fresh air. Agrippina motioned for a cold rag to brush over Rosa's face. "It will do you no good to fight them."

"I hate him! I wish he would die."

"I understand," Agrippina whispered. "I truly do, Rosa. Nevertheless, do this for your baby." She wrapped Rosa in her arms. "I will do all I can for you and your child. However, I need you to tell me who the father is so I can."

Zeno's name lifted to Rosa's lips, but refused to come out. She studied the depths of Agrippina's warm gaze then looked away. Her stomach dry-heaved. Time. She needed time. She needed a friend. "I need Carena. I need her. Bring her to me and I will do as they wish, Agrippina."

CHAPTER 4

"MARCUS GALERIUS ALEXIUS Victrix!" Alexius had no more than stepped into the formal garden to join his father and his clients when he heard his name. He turned around to a short, middle-aged man in a brown tunic with gold trim covering his thick torso. The man's calloused hands clasped both of Alexius's ears and pulled him close for a robust greeting kiss to both cheeks.

"Querito Mannius Tidius," Alexius said after being released from the man and enfolded the older man in a bear hug. "Where have you been, my friend? You weren't at my gathering to welcome me home."

Tidius pulled back. "Illyricum, my boy," he said enthusiastically. He scanned Alexius. "By the looks of you, your time in Britannia was most enjoyable." He leaned in. "Were the Britanni women as good as I've heard?" His jovial brown eyes danced with expectation.

Alexius burst aloud with laughter. "Better, Tidius. Much better," he answered, lying. He knew little of the Britanni women. His time had been spent tied to Agricola's heels.

"Ah, then you must tell me more about Britannia," Tidius said. The short man stretched an arm across Alexius's shoulders. "Should I consider taking my ships to Londinium?"

"I promise you that it is a venture well worth your money," Alexius answered.

They strolled toward Galerius's newest statue of a drunken Hercules basking in the golden morning. His father noticed them and broke away from his group of clients. "Tidius, my friend, where have you been?" Both men hugged and broke with jubilant smiles.

"My apologizes, Galerius, for not making your welcome home for Alexius. I see he's a man now and no longer a boy."

Both men turned to Alexius. "He is nothing but a pride to my eyes, Tidius, and a song in my heart," Galerius said with a beaming smile. "I praise the gods that he has been returned to me." His father straightened his shoulders to brag further. "And he has been granted permission to begin his run for senator this September."

"So I hear!" Tidius pounded Alexius's back. "Such a thing is a gift of the gods. With certainty, Alexius will only bring more honors to your name. Why, only yesterday, he was a pest on my galley, worse than a maggot."

"Don't speak too quickly," Alexius said. "I have not been to your galley yet, Tidius."

The short man chortled. "Come any time. I have great news and cargos for your future father-in-law, as well as delights for your future wife."

"Your news may draw this maggot sooner than you may wish," Alexius said, hoping the gifts might help soothe Messalina's wrath.

Tidius looked at Galerius. "Then, I can presume that the wedding is still planned for September?"

"Sooner, I say, for my purse's sake," Galerius huffed. "If imperial taxes aren't draining it, it is Aurelia's planning. Come. You will not believe what Alexius brought his father from Britannia."

The men meandered off, leaving Alexius to thoughts of marrying Messalina. He had left for Britannia with the image of a gawky, bug-eyed girl, with frantic curls springing about her face set on a pudgy body. He had returned home to a regal goddess with forever-long, silken curls of mahogany draping over satin shoulders that was colder than snow and a doe-eyed gaze sharper than any spear in the Empire. He had felt every stab of its last night in Zeno's apartment. He just hoped he could change all that.

"Such sobering thoughts, dominus."

Alexius turned to the leathered face of the centurion who, in a very short time home, had become more of a friend than a burden. "Flaccus? What brings you?"

"You, my friend," Flaccus said, leaning against the statuary base of Hercules. "I need you with the vigils tonight."

"What is it?"

"There was a fight last night that left three of the vigils at home."

Ah, yes. The one Felix mentioned—at knifepoint. Alexius remembered the sharp prick of piercing his cloak and Messalina squirming against him.

"In case another bunch of fools decide to cheat at latrunculi," the centurion continued. Flaccus scanned the garden and then looked at Alexius with even more concern. "There's something else I need to talk to you about. Will you be there, Alexius?"

He had planned to spend the afternoon with Marcus at the Palaestra to work out and glean what he could about his sister Rosa. Then, he had planned to spend the evening with Messalina in an attempt to thaw the frigid chill between them. However, the worry in this soldier's eyes said that whatever concerned the retired centurion was important.

"Certainly, Flaccus."

After the clients had left with his father, Alexius directed his steps toward the Palaestra, the one place he had been seeking since he had returned home. He strolled through the vaulted entrance decorated with painted stars of red, green, and white and then through the colonnaded portico muraled with scenes of the various competitions: discus, javelin throwing, wrestling, boxing, foot races, and his sport—swimming.

"Reach! Reach!" … "No, get his arm under him" … "Again. Do it again."

Sounds of commands greeted Alexius from the long, green playing field confined within the surrounding stonewalls. The field was a cacophony of wild cheers and frustrated failures as the boys rid themselves of winter fat and prepared for the coming competitions. At the far end, a row of umbrella pines provided a respite for weary contenders who sprawled about the grass.

Of course, center field was the swimming pool, and he had owned that sport. The pool cut through the grassy field like a white cross only wide enough for two swimmers to race. A fountain shaped like a five-headed hydra sprayed water in the intersection of the short narrow pool and the main pool. At the end of each outer corner spewed more fountains that anointed the victor and those who followed. Alexius remembered the feel of those simple fountains spraying him as he slapped the marble first.

"Brings back good memories, doesn't it, dominus?" Fosco asked, as he also gazed at all before them.

"Oh, so well, Fosco. Oh, so well."

At the far end of the field, in all his naked glory, stood Rosa's brother shoving a younger victim into another narrow pool full of water and fish.

'He who loses, gets dunked with the fishes.' Obviously, the motto still reigned. Alexius remembered being dunked a few times. However, he also remembered dunking more. It was good to be home.

"Alexius!" Marcus jogged across the grass toward him, ignoring the other nude boys who were taunting the one trying to climb from the pit. They met under the shade of an umbrella pine full of cooing doves.

Alexius grinned. "Gone fishing again?"

"Not me, my friend," Marcus said, glancing at his competitor who was now pulling others in with him. "Who gets to feed the fishies next? You? Dare you challenge this victor?"

Marcus laughed. "Most definitely."

"And he who feeds the fishies, buys lunch as well."

Alexius began stripping down as Fosco begin working on his shoulders like a fretting mother hen. Practice everywhere stopped as competitors gathered around the swimming area to watch the unplanned race.

He and Marcus bent into a starting position before the end of the longer pool, waiting for the grinning swim coach to chop his hand through the air. Lurching into the water was like the first soar of an eaglet caught in the cool drifts of wind. Alexius's arms became wings stretching for air and then cooled through water. The familiar rhythm of breathing came instantly, filling his lungs with life and the thrill of living.

Marcus matched him stride for stride as Alexius plowed for another inch of water, kicking for more distance. Around him, voices yelled, urging him on. He was not going to become fish bait. Not today.

One of the fountain's five hydra heads spewed water over his back as he reached through the water toward the one remaining fountain waiting to anoint him once again. Alas, his hand slapped stone and lifted him from the water like a leaping dolphin. Another slap hit stone a millisecond later, and Marcus lifted from the water to stand beside him. Both bent over, gasping for air as the coach lifted Alexius's arm in victory.

Jubilant hands fell on Marcus, dragging him kicking and fighting to the narrow pool, where they dropped his friend with a magnanimous splash. Alexius watched with satisfaction as others were shoved or pulled into the frolic.

The following hours filled with new faces and familiar coaches as the routine of learning new moves and forgotten holds in sandy wrestling pits returned quickly enough. His time with the legions had paid off well. The long marches had been good for the short race. Weapons practices and games helped with the javelin throws. All concerns about elections, Pomponius's finances, and even Messalina were forgotten.

Marcus met him under the painted stars. "I know. I am buying."

"And I am hungry."

People, busy about their day, greeted them as they strolled toward Marcus's house. Insults and laughter flowed with little mercy until they halted before Marcus's door. Their mirth melted, replaced with a frigid chill.

All those years growing up with Marcus, memories of entering Balbus's house never changed. The visit lasted as long as the earliest escape as possible. No joy nor excitement ever played in this house, not ever.

The door slave greeted them with a proper welcome and stepped back, allowing Alexius to follow Marcus toward the atrium, each hoping to remain unnoticed to the private entrance to Balbus's thermae. Their steps quickened like childhood thieves.

Marcus's grandmother, Viceria, called out from the terrace garden. "Marcus. Come. Pay your respects."

Like guilty schoolboys, they both halted. Familiar dread coated Alexius's insides as he obediently followed Marcus into the garden that was thick with fragrant spring blooms and early herbs.

All their years growing up, Alexius remembered this woman continually cording wool and lecturing Rosa and Messalina about their responsibility to uphold the family's honor. During which, he and Marcus would make boyish faces behind the woman's back and escaped outside to their pirate's nest in the ravine beyond the terrace wall.

Every child in Herculaneum still called the Viceria, "The Witch." Something never spoken to her face. Ever. Obviously, the elderly woman had failed to change that image. She remained thick bodied and draped in black wool. Her square face, with its jutting stubborn jaw and thin lips, remained unyielding as ever. The old woman's silvery-brown hair had always been pulled back in a tight bun that made her harsh, brown eyes severe enough to frighten even the real Medusa.

"Alexius," Viceria called curtly. "I wish to see you." She handed the wool combs to the awaiting slave and sat up in her chair set under a palm tree.

"Domina, good day." Alexius bowed respectfully as Fosco backed to the nearest wall and dropped his gaze to the floor.

A faint smile turned the tight edges of her lips. "I am glad to see that you returned safely. I hear nothing but credit to your family, which merits you well in my eyes."

"Thank you, domina."

"You do plan to continue into in the path of your father, I hear."

"Yes, domina, I look forward to it." He would have said the same if she had asked if he intended to fly Apollo's chariot for a day.

Her hardened face softened as much as baked mud would in a delicate shower—very little, but a little no less. "I commend you, Marcus Galerius Alexius. Would that my grandson be as respectful and accept the opportunity his father has provided for him."

"I am sure he will, domina," Alexius stated, knowing such would never occur in his friend's lifetime.

"Marcus?" The old woman almost smiled. "I fear not. The boy still dreams of Greece, Plato, and that idiot Zeno."

Zeno? Surely not the Zeno Alexius was thinking about. It had to be some philosopher Marcus had found to infuriate his father.

Marcus stiffened next to him. "W-we'll be in the th-thermae. S-since I'm s-such an em-embarrassment," Marcus stuttered.

Alexius looked away to swallow his laugh. Marcus was still feigning a stutter, which incensed his parents and his grandmother. The woman waved them away and returned to carding wool.

They scurried off like good boys to Balbus's personal thermae that was attached to the house. It was open to only selected members of the community who continually kissed Balbus's ass or held a high enough position in the Senate to threaten Balbus's stature. Fortunately, the name of Marcus Galerius stood in that latter position.

"I hate that bitch," Marcus mumbled as they entered the changing room. "I wish she would die."

"I fear she will live forever," Alexius said as he let Fosco remove his tunic. "I find it unbelievable that they still believe you stutter."

"If they knew otherwise, I would have been beaten senseless." Marcus glanced at the attending slaves. "And they will not tell, because I will kill the one who does. Besides, they enjoy the charade as much as I do."

They sat on a hot bench before the simmering rocks and gleaming bodies of men sitting in silent suffering. Sweat quickly rose through pores and trickled down flesh. There was, now, an edge to his friend, brittle and sharp like an agitated animal trapped in a cage.

Alexius barely had the picture of Messalina in his mind when Marcus bolted to his feet and left. He followed his friend into the more temperate room with a large pool and dived in behind Marcus. The cooler water washed the sweat away. They lifted out of the pool at the same time and sat on the ledge.

"C-come on, Alexius." Marcus pointed to the two empty loungers by the wall of windows that looked out at the pebble beach. Brilliant waves grappled at the shoreline like greedy fingers, only to slip away and try again.

"Go on. I'll join you in a minute." Alexius plunged back in and took his time swimming across the pool again. Some of the men stopped to congratulate him for his early appointment, asking about his election, and what plans he had. He answered and joked with each man, knowing that in the future, he could be working with any one of them.

By the time he left the pool, Marcus had food waiting. Lazy sounds of waves along with the soft scents of seaweed and fresh fish drifted in through the open windows. Alexius sighed and sank onto the opposite lounger beside the wall where he had once drawn his ugly image of Messalina. By the gods, he wished he had never drawn that.

Growing up knowing he was the only kid betrothed, and betrothed to the ugliest girl in Herculaneum, had been mortifying. His friends continuous taunting drove him to save face by drawing this insult to her that had resulted in creating the nicknamed of Medusa after that.

He remembered laughing when Messi went crying to her friends. Regret flooded over him. He deserved every ounce of Messalina's fury and somehow, he had to make amends and convince her he was sorry. "Your grandmother—"

"The witch?" Marcus corrected as he took cheese from the food tray. Another slave presented a goblet and poured chilled wine.

"She mentioned Zeno," Alexius said, reaching for a biscuit. "Was that your father's chariot driver?"

Marcus shook his head and rested back on the cushions, closing his eyes. His face became sublime. "Zeno, the Greek philosopher who founded stoicism about three hundred years ago, before Seneca." He ate. "As Zeno says, 'we can only determine how to play the part of life given us.' Therefore, I shall play stubborn and stutter until they allow me to study in Greece. After that, I will miraculously recover." Marcus lifted his goblet as a toast and did not wait for Alexius to honor it before he drank.

Alexius relaxed and ate, knowing Marcus wanted nothing more than to study with the Greek philosophers. Once, his friend had said he wanted to study law and would have gladly entered the Senate, providing that his father stayed out of his pursuit. However, Balbus controlled everything he touched.

Broiled shrimp rolled in capes of spinach, small bowls of garum, olives, and carrots lay on small tables before them. Alexius feasted. He had never considered not following his father and agreed that Rome needed men to deal with issues of the legions, the courts, the taxes, and laws. That way, the rest of the Empire could continue working and living in peace. Rome expected this of him, and he wanted to contribute all he could, just as his father had.

Yet, if anyone discovered that he had helped a slave escape with a senator's daughter, the embarrassment would destroy everything his father had ever done for Rome. In addition, his own future would be nonexistent. Alexius's mind stymied, food clotting in his throat.

He studied the view outside the window. Waves slumbered ashore. Seagulls drifted in the air. If this accusation were ever proven after he was elected, he could be appointed indefinitely to some miserable outpost like Judea—without Messalina ever being allowed to join him. His stomach twisted, presenting another wave of nausea.

However, if helping Zeno and Rosa redeemed him in Messalina's eyes then he had no choice but to embrace the risks. He would just have to make sure no one learned of it. Alexius made a silent plea to Felicitas and Venus to favor him, dribbled wine on the floor, and then rested back in the blue cushion.

"Did you hear," Marcus asked, "that Father's finally bartering Rosa off to that rich son of a whore for more power in Rome?"

"He will kill her the first time he mounts her."

"Ah, however, the fat boy will bring influence and wealth to the house of Balbus. Therefore, for father's sake, it must occur." Marcus popped a shrimp in his mouth. "I pity Rosa. I do."

"I do too. In more ways than just that." Alexius reached for his goblet of wine. "When is this occasion going to happen? Do you know?"

"Fifteen March, I think."

Alexius sipped wine as the fact sank in. That would leave Zeno no time to get Rosa away. He breathed a sigh of relief. However, the wedding date had been set, so the baby must have been born. The liquid pooled in the back of his throat. He coughed to clear it. "That soon?"

"I guess it is, is it not?" Marcus popped an olive into his mouth and gazed outside the window.

They ate silently for a while.

"Is she…excited about any of this?"

"Rosa? I think not. However, does it matter to our illustrious father that she hates him as I do? But, what do I know? I haven't seen her since September." Marcus reached for his wine. "Mother said she is with a sick aunt in Capua." He chuckled. "I never knew I had an aunt living there."

Marcus lost himself in the wine as Alexius looked out through the warbled glass at the fishermen and people strolling about the beach. Apollo was driving his sun chariot back to Olympus as the day set.

By every god he knew, he wished Rosa had not gotten pregnant. He wished Pomponius would go broke. He wished Balbus were not so powerful. He wished he had not been so horrible to Messi and that she wanted to spend the rest of her life with him. In addition, he wished he had not promised Flaccus that he would help with the vigils. All wasted wishes.

Marcus smirked across the food. "So, have you found out about Hector and your betrothed?"

"Yes. And if you think anything of your friend, advise him to leave Messi alone." Alexius glared across at Marcus. "She is mine."

He laughed. "Oh, I will certainly tell Hector. The question is…will he listen?"

"He had better." Alexius downed the wine in his cup. "Why Messi would give that fool the time of day."

"You mean, why would Messi choose him over you?" Marcus asked. "I will tell you, if you promise not to pummel me into this cushion."

Alexius nodded.

"Sappho and a healthy bit of Ovid."

Alexius stared at Marcus. "What do they have to do with this?"

Marcus dropped a shrimp into his mouth and puffed up into the great orator. "'How could I change towards you who are so beautiful? Let the man be the first to make the approach and entreaty. Give her a cause, an excuse.'" He gave a theatrical wave of his hand. "'Of course, I love you. But if you love me, marry me…' give or take a few words and adjustments."

"Messalina listens to that shit?"

"Avidly, so I hear. They all do. I also know how well Hector does expound." Marcus feigned a lover's death upon being struck by Cupid's arrow. One dead eye popped open. "Hector has seduced many with these honeyed words and is a very proficient actor."

That evening, Alexius's leather cuirass, helmet, and gladius were unbearable because of the time spent free of these entrapments since leaving Britannia. Patrolling with Flaccus and the vigils had started almost as soon as he had returned home.

As their small group of vigils meandered through the dark streets and alleys filled with boisterous laughter and unfriendly arguments, he had furthered his misery by simply by asking of this Ovid character. Then the night had become an evening of them man's ditties of lust and love, expounded from the younger men as they strolled.

"'Read my book and results are guaranteed. Technique is the secret,'" one quoted with theatrical enthusiasm.

When one finished, another began. "'Corrupt her with promises, corrupt her with prayers. If she's willing, you'll get what you want'."

"'You'll sit right beside her without let or hindrance, so be sure to press against her wherever you can…'"

"May the gods have pity if Sempronus survives the night," Alexius muttered to the centurion.

Flaccus agreed and announced, "The next idiot spouting off his mouth gets my fist down his throat, "taking as many teeth as I can." Little good that did—the fools simply kept out of reach and continued clipping off more ditties.

They stopped at a rowdy bar filled with sailors and freemen willing to gamble what little they had on dice. He and Flaccus left the younger men at one table and found a table with a game board of latrunculi glued to its top. A plump, dark-haired slave girl approached, carrying two mugs of ale and a box of playing pieces. "You wish either or both?"

"Both," Flaccus said and began placing a line of flat black stones across the board. "I'll take black," he said as Alexius sat across from him.

"So, you want the advantage," Alexius asked after taking a drink. It slid down his dry throat with ease.

"Of course." The centurion grinned up at him. "Tonight's pay?"

Alexius nodded. The game began.

His attention to stone pieces walled out the sounds of boisterous talk and laughter mixing with fragrances of sweat and day-old soups. Two mugs later, he caught the last of Flaccus's black stones in the corner with what remained of his white ones. "I believe I see a mandra before me."

Flaccus huffed and toasted back. "I don't know how you did that, but with a mind like yours, I would follow you in any legion."

"There is no centurion I would rather have in my legions than you, my friend. Nor win a night's pay from." He meant every word.

In the few nights with Flaccus, Alexius had acquired a tremendous respect for the centurion. He was what all soldiers should aspire to—loyal to Rome and willing to defend the Empire against anyone who threatened its foundations. Alexius wanted the seat in the Senate to protect such men.

Another girl placed a round of drinks on the table. Flaccus lifted a glass and toasted him. "Oh, did I tell you also, the winner pays for drinks?"

"No."

They laughed.

Alexius watched the glee melt from the centurion's face as he leaned closer. "I've heard things, Alexius."

Alexius scooped the playing pieces into the box, setting them aside, and then crossed his arms to lean in closer. "What?"

A group of men staggered too close. Flaccus drank from his mug and kept his gaze on Alexius. After the men swaggered on, he set his mug on the edge of the game board and leaned forward again. "A few nights ago, a soldier, released from the III Augusta, bought me a few drinks."

"The legion stationed in Crete?"

"The same." Flaccus toasted Alexius but failed to drink. "The fool bragged that it would be the Augusta and Cyrenaica legions who will be choosing the next emperor for Rome."

"Next emperor?" Disbelief swirled in Alexius's mind. "Next Emperor? Vespasian does not appear ready for the Ferryman."

"Then you know what that means, Alexius?"

It was no joke. "You mean an assassination?"

Flaccus nodded.

Alexius leaned closer. "Or was he just wishing?"

The soldier shook his head. "I laughed at him and asked why a sane man, an honorable soldier of Rome, would want a new emperor." Flaccus met Alexius's direct gaze. "For land. Someone's promising them premium land grants outside the city."

"Vespasian has already granted them land."

"I know. But only shit holes."

Alexius stared at the sober face before him. A million ideas of what he should do raced through his mind. None seemed valid, because there was no evidence to prove the accusation. "Someone is lying. Who?"

Flaccus shrugged. "I wanted to know that too, but he went upstairs. Looked for him around the city. No one's seen him since, not even the whores."

Alexius stared at the gameboard and then looked up. "I am going back to Rome soon. I will check into the records and see what I find about those recently released from the Augusta."

"Good. Let me know what you discover."

"'Corrupt her with promises, corrupt her with prayers. If she's willing, you'll get what you want.'" erupted in the taverna's newest drinking song.

CHAPTER 5

"TOMORROW. I PROMISE." Not even a note from him to explain why he had not come. Alexius's promises still rang in Messalina's ears. Fury consumed her as she walked down the street toward the shopping areas.

Oh, he had seemed truly concerned about Zeno while they were in his apartment. But then, after Alexius had brought her home in his litter. It all changed the instant her father barged out of their doorway, yelling for an explanation for her not being there when he got home.

It had stunned her that Alexius calmly lied and apologized for not informing him that he had asked her to join him for dinner with a friend. And of course, her father had instantly mellowed to a mutter.

The sincere sound of Alexius's voice still echoed in Messalina's mind as she stood in the city's main street near the massive columns of the Forum's four-way arch. Slaves were busy arranging the festival garlands to Mars and Juno in the nearby basilica. Clear skies, white clouds, and fresh breezes stirred the fragrances of mint and the various flowers used to make the streamers.

Shockingly, she had pleasantly endured Alexius riding beside her in his litter when they had returned from Zeno's apartment. Fortunately, at least, he had not looked at her as if she were Medusa. He had even called her his swan, which had made no sense.

She had started to smile at the memory, but Zeno's pendant shifted beneath the neckline of her yellow tunica, reminding her of what she had agreed to do for Rosa. Desperation sank in deep.

Unfortunately, that following morning, her mother had seen the pendant, the moment she stepped inside the sunroom, and was elated over such an elegant gift from Alexius. Messalina had no choice except to let her think Alexius had given it to her. Yet, what would her mother think when she gave it to Rosa…if she ever managed to see Rosa. She would deal with her mother's fury later and adjusted the dark green palla over her shoulders as she walked on.

That morning during the women's time in Balbus's thermae, murmurs regarding Rosa's wedding had flowed deeper than the water. It nearly choked her. As much as she needed to see Rosa, as much as she wanted to help her and Zeno escape with their baby, as much as Alexius's scorn burned her veins, she did not want Alexius involved. He already knew too…

A daisy floated under her nose. "Innocence for the most beautiful," whispered into her ear. "I have missed you, Messalina."

She swirled around, her heart suddenly dancing. "Hector!"

Messalina gazed into the cherubic face beaming at her. He was so adorable with his sandy brown hair glistening in the sun. His hazel eyes simmered like warm honey.

"When did you return home?" she asked, wanting to throw her arms around his neck.

"You mean from my prison," Hector corrected with a glorious smile, "which has kept me from you. Making each day, a day without sun. Just seeing you makes my soul dance and the day ever more glorious." He drew closer. "Are you still being watched?"

"Yes." She glanced at Didius and Niki, her personal slave, walking toward them. Nothing she could say would override her father's threats of beating and selling any slave who let her near Hector.

"How long will you be able to stay this time?" she whispered as she appeared to study the vases in the nearest store.

"Not long." He glanced at Didius approaching like a guard dog. "Messi, I have to see you. Meet me tomorrow in the theater gardens, during the play. Can you be there?"

"I will be there." She would find a way.

Hector's gaze caressed her as Didius stopped beside her. "Domina, do you need help?" the old slave asked, casting a warning glance at Hector.

"No, Didius. You may go."

The old slave stepped back with a nod and stood there, waiting for her like a pillar of marble.

Even with the shutters closed and the drapes drawn, morning crept into Alexius's bedroom like a thief. Like nearly every morning, his family expected him to join them for prayers in the garden lararium to honor their family's gods. However, his entire body ached from the afternoon in the Palaestra and walking the city streets all night with Flaccus. To further his misery, what sleep was granted to him, had been endured with vivid dreams of being tied to a column and tortured while Hector spouted Ovid ditties to Messalina and dogs chased Vespasian.

Groaning, Alexius slowly eased up, dragging his feet from the warm covers. He dropped his forehead into his hands, grinding his gritty eyes with his palms. He had to see Messalina today because Fosco had informed him Hector was back from Rome. He had to tell her what Marcus had told him. Not that it was much. However, it was enough of an excuse to see her. He struggled down the back staircase, still hearing Ovid in his brain. "'If she's willing, you'll get what you want'."

His father and mother stood before a crowd of drowsy slaves gathered along the walls near the lararium. Alexius joined them as his father turned to the statue of Venus and the funeral masks of the Galerius's fathers to begin the morning rituals and prayers. Alexius closed his eyes and automatically went through the procedure so routine that he could not remember how he ended up asleep on the terrace lounger in the gazebo.

"Dominus."

Alexius finally looked up at Fosco.

"Your father goes to the basilica today and wants you to join him."

Would it ever end? Just leave me alone. Alexius closed his eyes again, feeling the warm morning breezes and soothing sound of waves float over him. The fragrance of wisteria drifted in the air. He leisurely inhaled the scent and managed to ask, "Why…does he need me?"

"I have no idea," Fosco said as he motioned for another slave to bring Alexius's white election toga and tunic. "He doesn't often ask you to join him, so I would assume it must be important. But as a slave, I know nothing."

"Alexius! Praise the gods!" His father left the group of clients milling restlessly about in the enclosed atrium lined with black walls and elegant mosaics and hurried to greet him. "We are late. Where were you?"

"On the terrace. Late for what?"

"Never mind. We need to go now. They are expecting us at the basilica."

His father's clients taunted him while they paraded together down the city streets as he had the night before. Alexius sighed as he walked amid the morning greetings from the differing storekeepers and customers who were busy with the day's commerce. Galerius acknowledged each person with a radiant smile, a wave, or a pat on the shoulder as he passed.

Alexius joined the salutations with a growing sense of pride. This was what he had wanted—to earn such people's respect and honor for his family because they knew the house of Galerius cared and wanted to help make their lives better.

He focused on each person until he noticed Zeno's man Felix. Alexius's stomach lurched as he remembered the man on the stairs, threatening his life. Why was he helping Zeno and Rosa, when doing so could cost his family so much? The answer came as simple as a drop of sweat—Messalina.

The accepted revelation left his white election toga laying as heavy over his body as a full water bucket. "What is going on this morning?" Alexius asked as he adjusted the wool bearing no purple stripe over his shoulder.

His father grinned as if protecting a secret. "I want you to meet our new curatore. I think you will like him."

That was why? He could meet him later at some dinner party. Yet, when his father's group reached the basilica, Alexius immediately recognized the new curatore and smiled. *Marcus Cornelius Sulla.*

Sulla's son, his mentor, and long-time friend stood in the center of a group of city administrators and senators vying for his attention. This man, this friend, had taught Alexius everything: how to out swim everyone, how to out wrestle anyone in the Palaestra, and had erased all concerns about pursuing a senatorial appointment. Alexius smiled with delight.

"Marcus Galerius Alexius," Cornelius announced. He burst through the thick circle of senators and joined Alexius and his father. "You survived Britannia, I see."

"And you, my friend and favorite of the Flavians, are our new curatore? Amazing." Alexius answered as they hugged, pounded backs, and then stood back admiring each other.

"You mean the Flavian's favorite mule." Cornelius draped a possessive arm across Alexius's shoulders and drew him toward the garlanded entrance crowned with full-sized bronze statues of a four-horse chariot driven by Apollo.

A crowd followed on their heels as he and Cornelius led everyone into the huge chamber, passing the two new statues of Balbus and Marcus riding on horseback…the one that Marcus swore he would destroy one day. Alexius noticed Rosa's statue among those of Balbus's family along the far wall.

Dread returned. Alexius blocked his mind to it. "Now that you are his favorite mule, what are you to accomplish for the emperor?" he asked.

"Write reports about the problems plaguing Campania," Cornelius said with a laugh. "Therefore, I am no more than a scribe."

"A well-paid scribe, I am sure," Alexius added with a taunting grin.

Cornelius stopped beside the wooden steps up to the stage. His eyes twinkled with humor. "True. Now, I must begin earning it. You and your father will join me for dinner this evening. Yes?"

"We would love to," his father chimed from behind.

Alexius smiled in agreement while his plans with Messalina wilted once again. Tomorrow. He would see her tomorrow after the ceremonial parade. "Certainly."

"And bring that future father-in-law of yours," Cornelius added as he strode up the steps and past the bust of Vespasian to the waiting ivory chair.

From where Alexius stood behind the last row of seated senators, but before the citizens, he observed Herculaneum's new curatore claim the room. He sensed the power that the respect granted a man who claimed to be nothing more than a scribe as it filtered through the crowd. Admiration flooded over Alexius. By the gods, he wanted this. He wanted...

Something nudged his hand. He looked down to see Felix standing near his shoulder, pretending to listen to the curatore. The slave pressed a folded note into Alexius's palm.

Alexius's insides froze as he read Zeno's note. *I need to see you. Z*"

"City magistrate, is that expense shown in the records?" Cornelius's voice seemed to fill the hall.

Alexius jerked his attention back to the proceedings as a short rotund official stepped toward the stage and began expounding about Vespasian's taxes. "Where?"

"The stables." Felix pulled back and disappeared.

CHAPTER 6

MESSALINA NOTICED ALEXIUS as the theater crowd drew back to make way for the parade of Galerius's clients. Obviously, Alexius had not seen her or had pretended not to. He would never embarrass himself in public and recognize her. No. Not Medusa.

People shifted and moved closer toward the theater entrance. She saw Hector disappear through the archway to the men's section as she inched forward with her mother. Her heart lifted and fluttered like a moth near a flame. *At least, he had come to be with me.*

As Ovid said in his writings, she and Hector were doomed to endure the punishment of gazing at each other, pulling ears, brushing one's cheeks, or licking lips as signals of their love. However, she was sick of doing this. Even so, she was not even sure it was love she felt toward him. Whatever it was, it was better than anything she felt with Alexius.

To Alexius, everything else was more important than she would ever be. And, Hector had risked everything to be with her, even her father's wrath. That had to mean something.

Well, she was in no mood to play Ovid's insidious little games. Her nerves were rankled enough as it was. She needed time with Hector to get Alexius out of her mind, and, there was the possibility that he knew something about Rosa. After all, he was as close to Marcus as Alexius ever was.

Damp afternoon breezes nudged at the thick scarlet curtains hanging across the front of the stage. Musicians tuned instruments. Stage crew adjusted for the forthcoming play as women quickly filled their balcony section shaded with a blue and yellow canvas. Messalina and her mother settled on the front bench. Below them, the first four cushioned rows, reserved for the senators and city officials, remained empty.

Rosa's mother Volasennia, and sister Nonia Prima settled into their exclusive stage seats in the private cubicle directly over the stage like goddesses.

Messalina adjusted her blue palla over her arms. She wanted to march up to Volasennia and demand to be told where Rosa was. However, no one could enter in Balbus's balcony unless invited.

"Treats, domina, for you?"

Messalina turned to the strange vendor holding out warm, honeyed almonds contained in a parchment cone. The fragrance smelled delicious, but she shook her head.

"For your beauty, I give you this one. It is special," the vendor said and placed the cone in her hand. His calloused fingernail scraped across the loose piece of paper on the end of the cone.

"Thank you," Messalina said and peeled the note away.

"In the garden after the first play. H."

Thunder boomed from the bronze drums in the orchestra pit, jolting every nerve in Messalina's body. The curtains dropped, and an actor dangling from a crane swung across the stage with a city backdrop. As he pretended to fly, he shot fake arrows at the audience.

Hoots and insults from the few plebian men echoed from them as a nude female dancer swirled onto the stage. The cupid acted stunned to see her and motioned to be lowered quickly to the stage. She tried to flee, except the crane kept bouncing Cupid before her until the audience rolled with laughter. Including Hector sitting in the citizen section below the women's section.

Her mother gasped with laughter. "This is delightful, Messi. I am so glad you wanted to come today."

Messalina glanced at the stage in time to see Cupid groping the girl. "I did not expect to see this."

"Oh, they are just being silly." Her mother turned her attention back to the stage and was soon laughing again, oblivious to Hector nodding toward the entrance. A moment later, he rose to leave.

"Mother, I need to go to the lavatory. I cannot wait another second. Besides, this is boring." Her mother frowned and started to rise. "Mama!" Messalina snapped in a whisper. "Mother, I am not Antonia."

Her mother's face became serious. "Should I trust you, Messalina?

"Yes, of course." *You should not.*

Messalina kept her face calm. She had just lied to her mother. It hurt, deep in her soul. However, her parents refused to understand how she felt and never would relinquish control over her life. That left her no other recourse than to lie and sneak about.

Vendors hawking everything from treats to toys were busy outside the arched exits near the garden walkway lined with blooming oleander brushes. Niki saw her and hurried toward her. "Domina, you're not to—"

Messalina grabbed the girl by the arm. "Niki, you say anything, and I will tell Papa about you bringing me Hector's letters."

Panic flooded the girl's face as she stepped back.

A wave of filth coated Messalina's insides as she hurried along the walkway, empty of all except pigeons and sunshine. She hurried past a thick tall pine tree, feeling terrible, despising herself for threatening Niki when a hand grabbed her wrist and pulled her into a niche of dense white oleanders.

Immediately, her arms circled around her captor's neck as familiar lips found hers, stunning her senseless. Joy burst inside her, shredding all reasons for guilt. "You are the most beautiful flower in the garden," Hector whispered as he coated her neck with kisses, leaving her skin rippling. "You are nectar more precious than honey. You are my swan."

Swan? Something flinched inside her. She struggled to gain some room between them to think. "Wait, Hector. Wait."

However, his lips kept nibbling at her neck, biting her ear, trickling closer to her lips again.

"Hector, stop. Please."

His lips glided up her neck to her emerald earring. "Can a bee wait to taste a flower?" He continued his onslaught.

She shoved away, breaking his grip around her waist. "Please, Hector. I want to talk."

He slumped back on one foot. "About?"

"Us. Everything."

A condescending smile oozed over his lips like rancid oils. "Why? When my mind spirals with the merest thought of you, taste of you?" He started toward her again, looking way too eager.

Escaping, Messalina stepped back toward the walkway. The afternoon sun danced in the blond curls encircling his soft pinkish face. As he stroked her arm with his hand, his hazel gaze made her feel like a specimen. Being there with him made no sense. Something had changed.

"What vexes you, my beautiful swan?"

"Do not call me that." Being compared to a gorgon was enough to live with. She did not need another lie in her life.

"Why?" Hector stepped forward, clasping her wrists. "I assure you no one will find us, my precious swan."

"I said not to call me that."

He shrugged, hands up in submission. "All right."

She noticed his voice had lost some of its silk. He drew her toward a bench cloistered with pink blooms. "I know about Rosa. I know where she is. I wanted to tell you."

Joy exploded in her heart. "You know where she is?"

"Yes." Hector drew her down on the bench beside him. "Marcus said she was with her aunt in Capua."

A cloud darkened the glow sweeping through her. "There is no aunt in Capua. She is…"

"However, she has returned," Hector said cleverly. He leaned close to kiss her cheek. "Her wedding is set after the festivals."

She already knew that from her mother's chatter. Messalina drew away. If Rosa was home, then she could give her Zeno's necklace. Maybe even tell Zeno. She had to know more. "Is she here in Herculaneum?"

He shrugged and clasped her hands to kiss the top of her knuckles. "I dream of nothing more than escaping with you and making you mine." He drew closer, leaning further to kiss her mouth.

She pulled away as a wave of nausea flooded over her. "You do? You truly do?"

He blushed. "One day with you is a lifetime of joy. One moment. One breath."

Her heart lurched to her throat. Did she really want to run away with him? "Where will we live? What would we do?"

Again, he lifted the back of her left hand to his lips and kissed each knuckle. "We will live in Rome, in a rental apartment until your father realizes what a success I will be. Then, when I become a famous playwright, I will buy you everything you ever dreamed of."

Unpleasant images of Rome's apartment buildings in Subura flashed in her mind. The people there were rude. Her thoughts shifted to what she would leave behind. The elegance of her home. Family. Freedom to shop for what-ever pleased her. But she knew her parents would never forgive her for running away with Hector. Actually, they would disown her. She was certain of that. Nor would she even be allowed to come to her sister Antonia's wedding or…or be there when her brother Claudius left for his tri-bunius. Suddenly, all those events seemed important. Her heart sank into the grass at her feet.

"What worries you, my swan?" Hector cradled her jaw as he kissed her cheek.

She jerked from his touch as if stung. "I said don't call me that."

Nothing felt glorious about being with him. Nothing felt right about anything anymore. Not with Hector. Not with Alexius. Nothing.

"Nothing…worries me." Another lie.

She turned and looked directly into those pleading hazel eyes. "Hector, you know if we leave without Papa's approval, he will disown me. He will never give us my dowry."

His hands flinched, even though he smiled beautifully. "Do I care, my—love."

Her dowry. In that instant, she knew that was all she meant to either of them. Alexius or Hector.

Fury surged through her, as Hector possessed her mouth. She struggled to free herself from his tongue plunging between her lips. She tried escaping but failed. His arm held her. One of his hands stroked beneath her gown and along her thigh. "I cannot part with you."

"Hector, Stop. Please." She wished she had never left the theater.

"Messalina," he breathed, "I am drawn to you. I want to explore you as bees want to explore flowers. I love—"

"Love?" Marcus's intrusion bolted Hector to his feet, leaving Messalina teetering precariously on the concrete bench.

"Marcus? Wha…what are you doing… here?" Hector glanced nervously as she grappled at her fallen palla and jerked his gaze back to Marcus. "I…I thought you were in the basilica with—"

"Obviously, I am not." Marcus's gaze lowered to Messalina. A sneer coated his lips as he stood there stoically wearing a cream-colored tunic belted around a dark blue toga resting on his shoulder.

He leveled a gaze, as lethal as his father's, on Hector. "Alexius had best not know of this, now should he? Not if you want to live, Hector."

She jerked the damn palla over her shoulders and stood. "Alexius has nothing to do with this!" Messalina snapped. Actually, she did care if Alexius knew. Why, she didn't know.

Marcus's condescending smile itched over her skin like a rash. "You know as well as I do that there will be nothing left of your lover if Alexius learns of this encounter, Messalina."

"Hector is not my lover."

"Oh really? Then why allow him to shove his tongue down your lovely throat?"

"I was curious." Another lie.

Marcus's eyebrow rose in doubt. "Well, I am sure Alexius would be happy to satisfy any curiosities you may have, Messalina." He studied Hector as if he were a stinkbug.

Hector snarled and looked away

"Come, Messalina." Marcus offered his hand to her. "I will walk with you back to the theater. I believe your mother just left, looking for you. She and Niki are, shall I say, talking. We will say you were with me." Marcus led her toward the garden entrance. "And that I led you here to discuss whether your father will allow you to lead Jupiter's chariot in tomorrow's parade. Father is asking your father as we speak."

CHAPTER 7

ALEXIUS WON'T COME. Why would any citizen come to the aid of a slave, especially a young dominus running for office? Zeno brushed the hand over the black haunch of the lead stallion tied to the corner of the box stall.

The air was thick with the fragrance of horse, hay, and clean straw. The stallion shifted and slapped Zeno across his face with its black tail. He laughed and kept grooming its haunch as his thoughts continued to ramble.

Why would Alexius risk even being seen with him? Why would the young dominus care whether Rosa married Pomponius or ran away with him? What did he care?

A thousand times, he wished he'd listened to Rosa. They would be safe now. And just knowing Rosa carried his child cut through Zeno like a knife, adding yet another wound to his gut. He'd said prayers to his mother goddess Anahit to take care of Rosa and the baby. Still, he couldn't sleep nor eat. Even the horses sensed a change in him.

Zeno's hand resting on the stallion's rear curled into a hungry fist. He had to admit that Alexius was right about

Balbus. The man would pay every denarius he had to have every Roman hunting for them.

A grin eased across his lips. But he knew the legions would never find them once they were in the Caucasus Mountains that surrounded the Gregham Sea. That was his home, his people. They would be safe there.

He'd given up ever seeing his mother and sisters again, but Rosa had reignited that desire. She had begged him to describe what he remembered, images he thought he'd forgotten.

He told her that when as a boy, he'd tossed stones into the clear mountain waters made from the many rivers that fed that nearest sea. Each image returned as vividly as if he could touch them: the lush, tree-lined mountains capped with snow, the colorful ducks, and delicious trout in the streams, the leopards and panthers that roamed the forests.

His had described his richly painted home and his mother's gardens of herbs and foods. He told her of the laughter that filled the air each day as they worked, played, ate, all shared with travelers in need of rest or a meal.

He was only eight when the Romans came. His father had sided with the Parthian kings. When the kings lost, everything his father had achieved had been burned, taken, or destroyed. Zeno remembered his mother screaming as Romans raped her and his sisters, and then killed his father and two older brothers.

Then, the Romans had dragged him away, leaving his mother and sisters to die with the memories. He would never forget the cold blade of fear slicing through his young heart as the soldiers beat him into submission on the galley. Those bruises never healed.

Every pore in his body now wanted to take Rosa back and show her what a loving family could be like. He wanted to give her what she deserved. She was a good girl, a kind girl. A girl his mother would easily love. A girl he loved and wanted to protect as his woman, his wife. Rosa was all that. She was perfect. She was pregnant.

Zeno collapsed against the stall wall, dropping his head back on the wood to stare at the tiled ceiling and whispered a prayer. "Aramazd, master of all gods, creator of heaven and earth, protect her and our child. Aramazd, more powerful than the Romans' Jupiter, wiser than their Minerva, bring us home."

The barn manager's voice rang down the stable hall. "Dominus Marcus Galerius Alexius, what brings you to our stable?"

He came? Zeno reached out to the horse's shoulder to steady himself. That night in his apartment had given him hope that maybe there was one patrician who would help. Yet, the risk for Alexius, if he did, could be devastating to the young dominus. There was another risk—that the young dominus would expose everything. As Rome expected every citizen to do.

So many things flooded Zeno's mind, a thousand pleas for help. He needed answers and he had no one beyond Felix to trust. Should he trust Alexius?

"I heard the Blacks were here," Zeno overheard Alexius say. "They have won me a lot of money at the Circus Max. I would like to see them up close."

"Don't see any problem with that, dominus. Zeno is with them. Nobody else can handle them."

Alexius's laugh sounded closer. "No one handles any of the teams like Zeno. He is here, you say?"

"Yes. Zeno!" The barn manager barked.

Zeno glanced up at the stallion. Its ears flattened and the animal's eyes darkened as the barn manager approached the stall. "Hush now, Vahagn, this is important."

The horse snorted and lashed his tail in response.

Zeno ran a soft hand along the stallion's side as he walked out. "Yes, dominus," he said submissively, dropping his gaze to black hair that dusted the golden straw at his feet.

"The young dominus wishes to see the black team," the barn manager announced.

"I will prepare them, dominus." Zeno shifted his gaze from the leathery manager wearing Vahagn's long scar across his face and studied Alexius. Curiosity lingered in the young patrician's blue gaze. "Would the young dominus care ride with me on the track?"

The curiosity exploded into brilliance. Alexius turned to the barn manager. "Would that be possible?"

Zeno grinned. "Only to breeze them today."

The barn manager glared at the restless stallion lurching at the rope. "You're their trainer. You do as you wish." He turned to Alexius. "Watch that one. He'll kill you."

"Get on," Zeno said. He moved to the side of the heavy training chariot, making room on the floorboard. Alexius tossed his white toga to his personal slave and stepped onto the chariot with the enthusiasm of an adolescent.

The horse handlers released the reins when Zeno nodded and let the team jerk forward at a walk. Alexius rode at ease beside him, not gripping the chariot handles as Rosa had the first time she rode with him. Zeno focused on settling the team instead of who was riding beside him. "Hold on," he ordered.

Alexius rested a hand on one handle as Zeno snapped the reins and the horses broke into an easy canter. He zigzagged them across the track, in long slow circles, and then brought them down to a walk again, letting the team snort and toss their heads.

"That's Vahagn, the lead horse," Zeno said with a nod. "They follow him. Amanor and Vanature are the power. That's Nane. She is my watchdog. I know when anyone is coming along side. She trusts no one except her brothers." He laughed. "And she can outrun all three." Nane snatched at the bit and tried to break into a canter.

"Where did you come up with those names?"

"Gods from my homeland," Zeno answered, letting the team trot. The chariot jerked rhythmically along. "Vahagn is like your Hercules, the god of thunder and lightning. Vanature is hospitality and bountiful hosts. Amanor is the god of a New Year and yields. Nane is the goddess of war." He serpentined them down the track's center and pulled them to stop. Zeno glanced at Alexius. "You have time?"

"For this, I have all day."

"Open the gate," Zeno called to the attending slaves waiting by the rail. "We're going for a run."

Alexius laughed as Zeno released the horses into an easy gallop along a dusty road stretching across a field bursting with early spring flowers and busy butterflies. Hawks soared over the silver olive trees and flowering fruit trees. All around them stalwart pines rose like gods from the ground. Nothing was said, just absorbed.

Zeno's mind floated to Rosa and the day he had kissed her by the oak tree they had just passed. The memory tore at what was left of his heart. Unconsciously, his fists tightened, and the horses slowed before he could master his thoughts.

"Want to drive them?" Zeno asked.

Alexius's eyes widened as the answer spread into glorious smile. "By the gods, yes! I have dreamed of this chance. I certainly never expected to ever touch their reins."

Zeno placed the reins properly into Alexius's hands. "Now, all you do is tighten the finger to which ever horse you want to direct. Lean forward and release the reins if you want them to go. Draw back to slow down."

Nane broke into a canter while her brothers trotted out of time. Zeno could see they sensed the new driver. "Tighten Nane's rein a bit more."

Alexius drew her rein tighter, and the mare eased back with her brothers. Soon, the chariot was jostling along easily. "Do you take people out like this very often?" he asked.

"If they come with enough money, we take them out."

"I paid no one anything."

Zeno rested a hip on the chariot's grips. "You didn't have to."

Alexius tightened the reins. "Who comes usually?"

"Kids, but never with enough money." Zeno smirked. "More daughters than you realize. They don't have to pay as much."

"Messalina?"

He shook his head. "She came that one day because of Rosa."

Alexius let the horses break into an easy canter. The sun warmed the back of Zeno's tunic as he watched Alexius experiment with the team, slowing, releasing them, and swerving them to the sides of the road or around an approaching cart and driver.

It was easy to see that the horses trusted Alexius. From that alone, Zeno felt he could as well.

Alexius drew the team to a walk. Vahagn and Nane responded, dragging Amanor and Vanature down with them as the two horses tossed their heads in frustration. A deep sigh released beside him. "By the gods, Zeno, racing this team has to be unbelievable."

"Oh, it is, dominus. It is." It was all that kept his sanity. "You're lucky. They're in a good mood today."

They laughed and rode silent for a while. Zeno looked to another tree of memories. "You're expecting me to let her go to that fat fool, Alexius. I can't."

Alexius failed to say anything as he drove the team off the road and into the tall grass. The horses snatched for treats as they meandered over grassy lumps. "I cannot imagine what you are going through, Zeno. But if you attempt to do anything now, you are dead, and she gains nothing."

Vahagn lifted his head to the distant mountain and snorted. Nane pawed the ground as Amanor and Vanature twisted in the harness.

"Better get them back to the road," Zeno said, motioning with his hand.

Suddenly, the horses bolted, jerking wildly at the chariot, barely giving Zeno time to grab the chariot's front handles and lurch back into place.

Alexius grappled helplessly at the reins. After a few jolts, he managed to hand Zeno the leather strips that slid between Zeno's fingers as if sinking them into a bucket of water.

If they choose to run, then run they would—at his command. "Hold on!" Zeno yelled as he whipped the horses into a full gallop. Once on the road again, manes lashed straight back as the horses found their stride and ate ground.

A victorious laugh exploded beside him. Glancing quickly, Zeno saw Alexius's face filled with the thrill he knew with every race.

As team began to tire, Zeno lashed the reins over their haunches, pressing them on until a white lather saturated each horse. Only when they passed the backside of a deep crater lake did he slow them to a walk. He glanced at Alexius and asked what he already knew. "You all right?"

"By the gods, yes." Alexius chuckled nervously. "What happened back there?"

Zeno shrugged. "They've been restless lately. Don't know why." He relaxed the reins as the horses' mouths softened on the bits. "What did you think?"

Alexius's smile was radiant. "I will never forget this day." He leaned against the chariot's side, suddenly serious. "Now is not the time to escape with Rosa, Zeno."

Zeno watched Nane's ears twitch forward and back. "I'll kill Pomponius if he hurts her."

"After they are married, he will likely forget about Rosa. He will have what he wants. Balbus too, for that matter."

"What about the baby?" There was pain in his voice when he spoke.

"Only the gods know, Zeno." Alexius gripped a handle with one hand and seemed to see whatever Nane was watching. Nothing.

Zeno studied the horses briskly trotting in time. He would never hold their child unless they ran away. He'd never see Rosa's belly full. He'd never see her nurse his child.

The horses felt the sudden tension and sporadically cantered. He brought them all down to the walk again.

Alexius's coming had sprouted hope in his heart like an unwanted weed that was yet dying. "Does Rosa have my pendant, the one I gave the domina Messalina?"

Alexius rested against the front of the chariot. "I do not know, Zeno. There has been no time to talk to Messi." He looked up, his gaze a dark blue. "However, I know Messi will give Rosa your pendant when she has the chance."

The stable drew closer. "We leave for Cremona next week," Zeno stated as the handlers took hold of his team."

"For how long?"

"Six months."

"Good." Alexius nodded to the horses. "Things should settle by then."

"You mean the timing would be better?"

They stepped off the chariot for the handlers to lead the team away.

"Please, dominus, give Felix any message I should know about. That's all I ask."

Alexius looked deliberately at him. "And leave Messi out of anything further. This is between you and me now."

CHAPTER 8

"GALERIUS, MESSALLUS, AND Alexius, welcome. Come in," Cornelius said, waving at the slaves to finish washing their feet so everyone could retreat into the atrium. Other slaves accepted the men's togas, leaving everyone in comfortable tunics and house sandals.

Sulla's son draped an arm across Alexius's shoulder. "Alexius, I am honored that our soon-to-be senator has granted us one evening of his time," Cornelius smirked.

"I thought that spending time with the Emperor's chosen curatore could be advantageous to anyone's election," Alexius said, hoping Fosco got his message to Messalina this time.

"The rumors are all to your favor, so I hear," Cornelius said as they walked. "Even Vespasian seems anxious to see you elected. He showed me your commendation letters from Agricola. Impressive."

"Thank you." Alexius noted the strange new bracelet on his friend's wrist. "What is this? A bracelet made of hair?"

"That it is, Alexius. Given, to guide me through a maze of ledgers." Cornelius grinned as he withdrew the obvious prize.

"As Ariadne gave Theseus in the Minotaur's maze?" Alexius asked.

"Exactly that, my friend."

"And who is she?"

"None of your business, at least for now." The smile on Cornelius's face had grown to obscene proportions. No woman had ever accomplished such a feat with Cornelius, though many had tried. Sulla's son had remained elusive of marriage, something Alexius once envied.

"After the council meeting this morning, I noticed you were gone?"

"I had the opportunity to race Balbus's blacks."

"Then I do not blame you for going. I would have called the session closed and joined you."

The small group began adjusting themselves in the triclinium, filling the dining couches. Cornelius sharing the honorary couch with Alexius. "Maybe you can before they leave for Cremona," Alexius said as he reached for a boiled egg."

"When is that?" Cornelius asked, motioning for wine.

"By the end of the week, I think."

Cornelius nodded. "I will talk to Balbus about it."

Alexius managed to smile in return even though the mention of Balbus deflated every pleasant thought of the afternoon.

Cornelius turned to his guests. "Relax. Enjoy yourselves." He nodded to a lute player to begin. Slaves scurried to wash hands, present napkins, place and remove food trays on table and continuously fill glass goblets with wine.

"Now, tell me, Messallus, are the buildings in Herculaneum as bad here as in Pompeii because of the earth quaking?" Cornelius sipped wine, ready to listen to Messalina's father.

"Well, there has been much damage," Messi's father, said with a shrug. "The top level of the apartments at the Palaestra are no longer safe, so no one is allowed to live there…for now, at least. We have Balbus to thank for seeing to the damages."

Cornelius munched on a curried carrot stick. "I will tell Vespasian that Balbus is taking good care of Herculaneum. He will be glad to hear his friend has dealt with the problems as usual. Unfortunately, in Pompeii, the magistrate seems to have trouble even seeing the floors swept."

Galerius shifted elbows and accepted a filled wine goblet. "Isn't Holoconassis magistrate?"

Cornelius shrugged. "Yes. However, he is in Delphi, soaking his gout in the waters there. Cossus Labinus is overseeing his responsibilities, since he is the second magistrate."

Galerius and Messallus smirked. "Then, no wonder Pompeii is still falling down," Galerius said, after sipping his wine. "The man is a fool."

"Agreed. I have had one too many dealings with the man myself," Messallus said. "Never again."

"Enough of what plagues Campania for now," Cornelius said with a wave of his hand. "I am sponsoring the games for Tabilustrium this May. Will you all join me in Rome?"

"Certainly," Galerius said after sipping his wine.

Cornelius turned his attention to Alexius. "You will be in Rome, shaking as many hands as you can find, I am sure."

"I believe that is the plan," Alexius said. "As well as trying to understand Pomponius's reports." No matter how much he would enjoy attending the games, that would only mean more time in Rome, more time away from Messalina. However, maybe she would come to the games. He would talk to her about that—eventually.

"It was unbelievable when I heard you were placed on the Committee of Twelve," Cornelius said. "I thought you would wait and relax before getting so involved with politics."

Alexius cast a dubious glance at the two fathers. "I would have preferred to do so. However, I was not asked."

"Balbus arranged it," Messallus said through a full mouth. He washed the remainder down with wine. "As good a start as any for the boy."

"Hardly a boy." Cornelius lifted his wine cup for a refill from the passing slave. He looked over at Alexius. "What is your impression so far?"

Alexius sat his glass down on the table and glanced at the attentive expressions before him. "It seems to me that more money flows out of Pomponius's ledgers than flows in."

"That is typical," Galerius said with a chuckle.

Alexius looked at his father. "And, I fail to find where it all goes. Neither can anyone else."

"I am sure he blames it all on the Flavians," Messallus huffed.

"Everyone does these days," Galerius added, spearing a chunk of simmering pork.

"The legions need that money," Alexius said a bit more bluntly than he should have. "Agricola was forever struggling to keep the soldiers in supplies. Even if it was necessary to pay for it out of his own pocket." Nights of watching Agricola pace his tent returned to his memory.

"Nor, does the money just show up as Pomponius says it will. No one seems accountable for anything."

Cornelius studied him while swirling his wine. "Maybe there needs to be an investigation into this."

"Someone should," Alexius said, before realizing that if Pomponius thought he had anything to do with such an investigation, he could forget ever being elected or even living long enough to marry Messalina.

Silence blanketed the table as everyone inspected the food trays and decided on which sauce to enjoy. Messallus speared small chunk of pork with the sharp end of his spoon and dipped it in the honey sauce. "I recently heard a rumor that the III Augusta wants larger land grants now."

"Well, I would expect that out of them," his father chuckled. "They would even entertain the idea of choosing the next emperor."

Alexius choked on a pickled beet.

Cornelius nodded. "His Excellency would tax the rats if he could, considering that when he came to the throne, the treasury was empty. Even Titus questioned the latrine tax." He held his glass up for more wine. "I have told Vespasian that he allows too many to get away with men insulting him like Domitian, who is forever starting rumors against Titus."

Messallus shifted position on his couch and asked, "Does Titus still want to marry that Jewish mistress?"

Cornelius grinned. "He does, which is to my advantage."

"How is that to your advantage?" Alexius asked as he adjusted his arm over the couch cushion.

"You will see if you come to the games."

"Yes, Rome has done well by Vespasian," Galerius said, wiping his mouth with his napkin "And I fear, Cornelius, you are right about his sons. However, this nonsense about

African legions wanting more land grants and choosing a new emperor is surely rumors."

"Those rumors have reached here," Alexius said, eating a honey-coated dormouse. "Flaccus met a retired soldier from the III Augusta who said the same thing. The man bragged that it would be the Augusta and Cyrenaica who will soon be choosing the next emperor for Rome."

Cornelius set his glass down. "Do you know his name?"

Alexius shook his head.

Alexius walked across his second-story bedroom lost in total darkness. Even the nights owned him and failed to let him sleep. It had rained briefly, leaving the air heavy with evening fragrances. He stared down at the black throbbing bay swelling with waves.

As he and his father had prepared to leave for Cornelius's dinner, his mother had informed them of Rosa's wedding day. He wished it were his and Messi's wedding instead. Just thinking about his election, Pomponius, Zeno, and Rosa's wedding, his family's reputation, and Messalina caused his insides to twist and churn.

Something on the terrace next door caught his attention. The moon broke from the suffocating clouds, revealing Messalina leaning over her railing looking at the same throbbing black waves coming in from the bay. She bent down, out of view, and then stood up, holding something wiggling in her hands. Antonia's puppy licked Messalina's face, her chin, and her throat. A night breeze carried the sound of a delicate giggle to his window.

Envy penetrated every pour of his body as she put the wiggling puppy down on the terrace tiles and looked out to the throbbing sea again. As if he had called to her, Messalina turned and looked up at his window. The moonlight illuminated her face, lighting it like a candle. His breath caught in his chest.

He bolted from the window and raced down the back steps to the terrace, dodging the furniture. He stepped on a plant's vase to lift him high enough over the wall dividing their terraces. "Mess—"

The space was empty.

CHAPTER 9

A COLD WAVE SPLASHED onto a dozing young boy holding the end of the rope that was tied to his fishing cage resting beneath the waves. Ruso gasped awake and looked around his small boat in a stupefied daze. The distant cliff appeared to be vibrating against the sky.

"Another tremor?"

The waves were reversing, making them collide with each other. He pulled the cage into his small boat. Empty again. Another pitiful day for fishing. For the last year, nothing seemed right. The weather, the fish, the crops, even the animals were unpredictable.

But, the one thing he did know was that his stomach was growling, and he was tired of living off nothing but black bread, cheese, and water. He should at least be able to eat some of the fish he caught. But they destined for the rich patrician's tables.

As he opened his food pouch, he noticed Balbus's private galley working its way away from Herculaneum's pier toward Sulla's private pier. A short distance by galley but not by road. Curious, Ruso set the cage aside and began easing his small boat closer.

Many summer days had passed since private galleys collected at the foot of Sulla's cliff. He remembered many parades of sedan chairs and litters zigzaging up the trail cut into the cliff's side to the villa overlooking the bay like Olympus itself. That had been a year ago. Lately, things had been quiet…until now.

Carena? He saw her on the galley's poop deck and froze. He drifted closer and his heart sank to the wet boards below his bare feet. He'd never see her again if she went to Sulla's villa. "Please," he pleaded to any god listening. "Not to Sulla."

One side of the oars disappeared inside the galley as the other bank of oars turned into the dock. Waiting slaves scurried about as they draped ropes on stanchions and pulled the galley ever closer. The ramp shoved down from the deck to the pier and three men in casual togas walk onto the pier, laughing. He heard Sulla call to the Carena. "Come on, girl."

Rosa stood and placed her hand on her back for support to shuffle toward the slave girl appearing on the villa's terrace. Her huge belly made every step difficult. "Carena, you are here. I've missed you."

"Domina! I've worried about you. Are you well?" Carena asked meekly.

The truth—no, Rosa thought. However, eyes watched. "I am fine, Carena. Just fine." She slid an arm through the girl's and led her toward the seawall. "How is Messi? Is Alexius back—?"

"Rosa, we have fulfilled our side of the bargain," her father announced. "Before that slave steps any farther into this villa, you must fulfill your part of this arrangement. Now greet your betrothed like a proper bride."

Pomponius waited beside Balbus. Sweat drizzled from his baldhead as if he had climbed every step up to the villa instead of being carried in a litter. His gaze rose with disgust once it set on her huge belly.

Rosa stiffened, letting Carena step behind her. She swallowed the rising bile and lifted her chin to do what would be the hardest thing in her life. "Pomponius Beastius, I welcome you."

"Nonia Balba, I greet you as well," Pomponius said. A smirk appeared on his tiny, tight-lipped mouth. "Come, Nonia. Show me this splendid villa that I have not seen for ages." He offered his arm.

This was for her baby…Baby Paullus. She had no choice but to accept the offer. But soon. Very soon, everything will change. It must.

The tour of Sulla's villa was endless, fielded with a million questions about the decorations and how she occupied her time. They strolled along the grand peristyle that seemed as large as Herculaneum's forum. Bushes and flowers of every kind surrounded the center pool long enough for swimming laps. Statues added to the magnificence: young wrestlers, a bronze deer, a jumping piglet balancing on one-foot, bronze busts everywhere, a sleeping faun hidden as it would be in the wild, and Hermes resting on a rock.

"Sulla a most generous host, is he not?" Pomponius asked.

"Yes, of course," she amiably lied to the attentive ears.

"Where, in all of Rome, could more splendors exist except in Nero's palace?" Pomponius announced grandly.

He leaned close to Sulla following closely in their heels. "The Flavians had best not hear of this, or you will find it stripped of its beauty."

"My intention was for it to remain hidden," Sulla said. "However, I believe I am entertaining the emperor here in June. Is that not true, my friend?"

"Yes," Balbus said as he adjusted his toga on his shoulder. "Vespasian is coming to Herculaneum in June. During this illustrious visit, I believe that your wife is planning an auction here. From what I see, I am sure you could contribute to it."

"Vespasian will take it from me one way or another," Sulla replied. "And what are the generous donations going for?"

Balbus huffed. "For whatever Volasennia sees fit. Most likely it will be for the theater."

They had finally reached the end of the formal garden that basked in the spring sunlight. Rosa hesitated by a white marble bench near the bronze figurines of two naked wrestlers poised to grab each other over thick bushes of rosemary. No one had given her an ounce of concern, even though she had stumbled twice. The smell of Pomponius's garlicky sweat and sweet body oil nauseated her. "I would like to rest."

"My dear, I have heard so much about the rotunda," Pomponius pleaded expectantly. "It is this way, is it not?"

With her hand pressing into the small of her aching back, Rosa waddled on. She led the way into the woodland walkway lined with thick brushes that were broken only by small trails leading back into private sitting areas. They had no more than found the whitewashed hut that pumped water into the villa than Pomponius decided to return once again.

Fortunately, the men seemed content to stroll slowly along the ornate portico decorated with murals, ornate woodwork, and windows pulsing with cool breezes. They stopped inside the small inner garden with busts of Agrippina's favored philosophers.

"Tell us, Rosa, about these men," Pomponius said in an airy tone.

She knew nothing except the story behind Zeno's grandfather, which she would never share. "I know nothing about them."

"All this time, and you have not been the least bit curious?" Pomponius asked, grinning at Sulla. He sighed as if disappointed. "Well, then show me to the library. I hear that is quite extensive."

Rosa could barely put one foot in front of the other. A gladius blade seemed to be twisting deep into her back. Once in the library, the odorous man released her to sit down. A tight pain stretched across her belly. Panic tore through her. It was too early to be going into labor. She had to get away to her room.

"I...I feel dizzy. May I leave?"

The men glanced at each other over a scroll taken from one of the shelves. Sulla's gaze rested on Pomponius who spoke. "Yes, Nonia, you may go. I will leave it to Sulla to show me the baths. You will be joining us for dinner? Yes?"

"If you wish it," she whispered and reached for Carena. She was there.

Rosa struggled to her bedroom, feeling the walls closing in on her. She whimpered as another contraction drew across her abdomen.

"Domina, what is it?"

Rosa waved the other attending slaves away and motioned Carena to close the door. The delicate thud of the latch allowed her to sag onto the bed. "The baby…is coming." Another contraction gripped her. "Not yet, little one. Please. There is so much to do."

Rosa grabbed Carena's arm. "The chest, there." She pointed to the vanity. "Bring that to me."

Carena retrieved the jewelry box and returned in a flurry. Rosa emptied it in her lap, her hands trembling, and pulled away a false bottom. Another contraction mounted, freezing her in place. She gripped the slave girl's arm. Slowly, the misery passed.

"Domina, please, let me get someone."

Rosa shook her head. "Get that bag."

Struggling through the pain, she pointed at a red velvet bag laying on the vanity. Another wave stretched over her belly with crippling force. "Quick. Hurry, Carena!" Sweat burst across her forehead as she tried to breathe.

Carena claimed the velvet bag, her face white with worry. "Domina, the baby is coming. Let me get help."

"No! No. Not yet." Rosa rested back onto the pillows of her bed and waited until the contraction subsided. Taking a deep breath, she gazed deeply into the frantic eyes of the slave girl. "Listen to me, Carena. I need you. Please. I need you."

"Yes, domina. I'll do anything," the girl said, kneeling on the floor.

Rosa dug into the bag for a roll of parchment as another contraction threatened. "The jewelry. Take it. Hurry. Put it in the bag with your papers. These are manumission papers for you. Everyone outside Herculaneum will honor them."

Carena failed to move. "B-but domina, why? You need me."

"I need you to do this."

A strong contraction arched through her back. Rosa bit her lip to keep from crying out until it passed. For a moment, the contraction released. "Take my baby before they kill him." Tears burned in her eyes. "Do you understand? Save my baby, Carena. Please! Do this."

"How? I...I..."

Another contraction twisted through her. They were coming too quickly, too quickly. "Messalina. Go to Messalina. She will help. She will know what to do. Tell her. Do not let..."

Rosa gasped as water burst, saturating the bed. "Please, do not let them kill my baby!"

"The father—?"

"Carena, by the gods." Rosa's eyes opened with panic. She grabbed for the girl's hand. "Do not let me say his name. Please! Not his name."

"It's coming, domina!"

"I know. I know. Find a way, Carena. Promise me."

"Yes, domina. Yes, I will."

Rosa gasped back into the cushions. Another contraction mounted, this one stronger than any before. Nausea threatened.

Where does Agrippina find all these statues?" Pomponius asked as the men strolled back through the atrium overlooking the formal garden. Gleaming polychrome marble reflected every detail in the room. They stopped at the foot of a statue of the goddess Athena. "Anywhere she can," Sulla answered with a frown. He waved to recline on the three golden couches fanning out to the glorious view of the garden now shadowed with the early darkness. "Relax and enjoy."

Damp sea breezes rustled the white sheer draperies hanging at each side of the opening. Oil lamps reflected on the polished marble floor as slaves scurried about, filling goblets and setting trays of food on the ivory tables.

Pomponius reclined to Sulla's right and Balbus to his left. "Delicious wine. Surrentum?" Pomponius said, lifting his goblet in a toast.

Sulla nodded as he took a drink. "Found it in Stabianum not long ago."

"I thought I recognized it," Balbus replied. He reached for a stuffed oyster. "I prefer it to Massicum."

"I do as well. Yet, this is exceptional," Pomponius said as he studied Sulla. "This year's grapes fail to promise much of anything. I wonder why?"

"The weather has been horrendous." Sulla reached for a boiled egg slice. A slave waited. He looked up. "Yes, what is it?"

"Dominus, the girl, she is in labor."

Sulla flicked his finger to leave and glanced at his guests. "Well, the walk must have done her good."

"As I figured it would," Pomponius remarked quite happily. He dipped shrimp into a garum bowl. "It helped my other wives deliver."

Sulla shifted his arms to look at Balbus. "Should I keep the child as promised, or do you prefer that I turn the child over to the gods?"

A stuffed oyster halted midway to Balbus's mouth. "If Jupiter chooses to protect Rosa, then he can see to the bastard as well. I want nothing of it. You, Pomponius?"

Pomponius huffed as he set his goblet on the table and reached for an egg slice. "The girl holds nothing for me other than as something that joins our influence over the Senate. We have much to look forward to. Do we not, Balbus?"

"Yes, Pomponius," Balbus said, offering a toast across the food table. Three goblets rose and three men sipped as one.

"Sh-h, now. Being early born and so fragile, you wouldn't have lasted long on the garbage heap,'" Carena whispered as she stole deeper into the dark forest, praying her domina was right, that she was free. She stopped to draw back the flap that covered the newborn's face. "You're mine now. I'll take care of you." She now had enough jewels to buy anything Baby Paullus needed.

The restless bundle in her arms fought the blanket and the tight arms that clasped it. "Don't fret, little one. They don't want you, but I do. Ruso will help me take care of you. He and his father will know what to do."

Something snapped a tree branch as it moved closer. Carena squatted down to hide, except the black furry dog found them. It licked her face and then sniffed at the baby's blanket. "Help us, please. I need to get away. Where do I go?" she asked the intent brown eyes.

For a minute, the dog studied her and then turned, glancing back as if to make sure she followed.

"I'm here," she whispered.

The dog led her to a small wagon path and disappeared in the brush.

"Thank you." Carena felt tears fill her eyes as a long wolf-cry carried in the distant shadows. "Maybe Mars protects us, Paullus."

She stole quickly along the narrow black pathway, feeling fear tremble through her. An early gleam of dawn grew on the horizon. They would start looking for her soon. For her, not the babe. They would think some animal had already taken it. She had to find somewhere to hide.

Thick scents of smoke drifted to her nose, drawing her footsteps toward a faint glimmer of an oil lamp gleaming in a window of a small hut. A dog started barking and the hut door opened. "Hush, Hercules. Who's out there?" A man called out. "Show yourself, or I'll let the dog have ya."

A baby wailed inside the hut. Baby Paullus answered with his own misery. "I hear you. Step into the clearing now. I won't hurt ya."

Carena forced her legs from the tall brush and stared at the bony man who wore nothing except his loincloth. His white hair gleamed in the early morning light. He was her only hope.

"May the gods bless your house, dominus," Carena said as she walked closer. "Please. We need shelter."

The man was leathery and worn thin with hard labor. "What is it you have there? Come. Let me see." His face bore the marks of a wealth of miseries, yet his voice sounded kind.

"Please. They left him on a dung heap for the wolves. He's so hungry."

"Exposed was he?" he asked, his voice turning sharp with anger. "Not the first from there. Not the first. Bring it in. We've a babe ourselves." He stepped back to the door and held it open. "You'll be safe here. My girl will tend the babe."

The following days proved the man was true to his word. He'd hid her beneath the flooring when the slave hunters came searching for her. After they left, she made sure the farmer found a gold ring with a pink sapphire near the chicken feed, as if the gods had blessed him. Which is exactly how the man explained it.

Carena smiled as she squirted more milk from the restless goat. She and her Baby Paullus were safe for now.

CHAPTER 10

AN EXCITED THRONG of onlookers clotted the streets of Herculaneum, cheering and waving at whatever pleased them. Baskets and pockets brimmed with flower petals to throw as the parade for Jupiter passed. Everywhere ribbons of garlands draped the streets, the forum, and temples like gifts.

A rainbow array of spring flowers of every kind and fragrance blanketed a team of oxen hitched to Jupiter's golden chariot. One bull bellowed his indignation, while the second bull placidly slept though the complaints. Neither animal exhibited the same excitement that thrilled through Messalina's veins.

As Marcus had said, Balbus had requested that Messalina be one of the girls to lead Jupiter's chariot through the festival parade. How could her father refuse the high priest of the Temple Augustalus? Her father had grumbled incessantly thereafter, "Daughters of respectable families should never dance in front of the city like common plebes!"

Nevertheless, here she was. She knew from past parades that she would dance along the Decumanus

Maximus-Herculaneum's main street, past the Palaestra where her brother spent most of his time with his friends, encircle the city blocks, and return to the Forum. She was already breathless with excitement.

Messalina giggled with Alana and Florina, the two other girls. Their faces may burst if they smiled any broader. All three wore loose gold tunicas that came just mid-calf. They were to dance about while swirling ribbons at the crowd.

Florina was about to ask her a question when a pink rose floated before her face. Hector suddenly kissed Messalina on her neck before she could face him and fled as he had from the garden bench.

Unlike then, her heart failed to dance at his attentions. Instead, questions arose. Why? What had changed between them? Was it the way Hector feasted on her as if she were syrup? Or had she simply grown tired of hearing him laude her beauty? Beauty she did not possess.

Trumpets sounded and her concerns melted as they followed the rest of the parade. The fragrant air pulsed through the thundering drums, clarion trumpets, and the cacophony of cheering crowds.

Her task was to see that the gods were pleased with Herculaneum's celebration being held in their honor. She was to dance to please them. Therefore, dance, she would, swirling the gold ribbon through the multi-colored rain of flower petals already fluttering through the air like silk feathers.

The parade inched down the street and turned at Zeno's apartment, where Hector stood, his face glowing with pride. Messalina swept her ribbon at him. His smile became brilliant and then faded.

She twirled on her toes, only to find Alexius across the street, his glare searing at Hector. She swept the ribbon at

Alexius as if to punish him. Their gazes met and a magnificent smile emerged, one she had never witnessed before. It sank over her to her toes.

She slid her gold streamer across Alexius's sky-blue tunic. The sound of his laughter rose above sounds of clarion horns and thunderous drums, sending her heart soaring to the cloudless sky.

Alexius followed her, weaving in and out of the mass of people and managed to wash her mind of Hector. As much as she tried to taunt the on-looking crowd, the ribbon seemed to have a mind of its own. No matter where Alexius stopped, it found him. Until the end of the parade, she had forgotten of all else other than tormenting him. Hector had vanished not only from the crowd, but also from her thoughts.

Alexius worked through the people departing the street, feeling as if he had danced the entire parade with Messalina. She had become his siren, and he had become Odysseus as he hurried toward her. At least a thousand lashes had swept across his tunic in an exquisite torture as was watching Messi's lithe body and long silken arms dance in time with the drums.

"Did you see the size of Jupiter's bulls? Were they huge or what?" Claudius asked as he tried to keep pace with Alexius.

"They grow them bigger in Britannia," he grumbled.

"No! Impossible."

Alexius made his way around a large clump of people that suddenly blocked their way. Nothing was keeping him from being with Messi today. Nothing. He measured out his arms to full length.

"Britanni bulls are this wide." A passerby dodged him to keep from being knocked upside the head.

Claudius stumbled. "No! Not that big."

To his further delight, two girls called to Claudius to join them, and fortunately Messi's brother disappeared with them.

"You exaggerate, I am sure." Messalina's voice whipped Alexius around, only to find his betrothed standing behind him. Her skin glowed from dancing just as Alexius imagined it would be if they had just made love.

"Not for a moment."

Mesmerized, he watched her absently toss that wealth of hair over her shoulder. There never was a more beautiful girl anywhere in Rome. He plucked a rose petal from her hair just to feel the silken strands. "A keepsake for the most beautiful."

Messalina accepted the offering, smelling the sweet petal. For a brief second, she looked at him through mink-thick lashes, igniting every desire in his body.

"Messi, I have wanted to see you all week. Believe me, I am sorry."

"Have you been held captive?" she asked from behind the flower petal.

A grin eased over his lips. "In some ways, yes."

"Alexius," Messallus bellowed, as he and Octavia hurried toward them, pride dripping from their faces. "Was this not the most magnificent day for a festival? Wasn't my daughter the most beautiful?"

"That she was—the most beautiful," Alexius said, bending to kiss Octavia's cheek in greeting. Antonia tugged at his tunic. He picked Messi's sister up and felt her legs surround his waist. "Pity to the girls when you dance in a parade, Toni."

Antonia playfully pouted. "Why?"

"Because, like your sister, all eyes will be on you, making the other girls unseen and jealous." He glanced up to see if Messalina had heard him. She had. She was blushing with an attempt at a scowl.

Alexius handed Antonia to her father. "Would you mind if Messalina and I went for a walk?"

"Of course not." Messallus said, waving dismissal with his hand. "Take her, Alexius. She is yours."

She is yours.

Her father's remark throbbed in Messalina's brain like a tumor. She was not going to be anybody's property. Hot fury coursed through her as she stormed away from her parents, away from slaves, away from everybody.

"Where are you going?" Alexius asked, following in her wake.

Messalina halted, suddenly realizing that she was in the theater gardens again, just inches away from where Hector had snatched her into his arms. The memory itched with disgust. "I am not your property." She hurried on.

"Of course not." Alexius clasped her arm, wheeling her around just as Hector had. "And you never will be." He let go and stepped back, unlike Hector. "Unless you want to be."

His taunting gaze rankled her, as did the familiar oleander bushes behind him. "And I do not. Thank you."

"I didn't think so," he said, faking disappointment.

Alexius's comment melted her resolve to be angry, leaving a grin in its wake. Yet she turned to continue her escape and set an unrelenting pace, even though her legs felt like noodles.

"I got to ride with Zeno and his team of blacks before they left," Alexius said, catching up with her. "It was unbelievable."

"Is that what kept you away? Horses?" she asked while maintaining her pace. She remembered her day riding in one of those chariots. She had thought Rosa had lost her mind. "Did you like it?"

"Unbelievable. He even let me drive them." Alexius motioned toward a bench like the one she wanted to forget. "Messi, I can explain what has kept me away. Please. Can we sit here and talk?"

She stared at the bench, remembering Hector's pathetic attempts to strangle her with his tongue. She shook her head. "I would prefer that we go some other place else, more private?" she asked. They needed to talk about Rosa, the wedding, and Zeno.

Alexius looked around. "Where?"

Insanity ruled the day. Nothing in Herculaneum would be private. Their houses had guests. The streets clamored with celebration. The theater gardens were filling with people even now. An idea flashed in her mind. "Do you think Felix would mind if we used Zeno's apartment…to talk?"

They left Fosco and Niki talking with Felix at the foot of the stairs as Alexius followed her up the steps to Zeno's apartment. It was just like the night he had found her in the stairwell to the block-long hall.

Nothing had changed in Zeno's apartment, except that the window shutters were now closed. The bed, cold brazier, and the table butted to the wall remained undisturbed.

Alexius closed the door, halting her study of the small apartment. His woodsy clean fragrance assaulted her, tripping her heart as she stopped on the thick wool rug and turned. "Alexius, the wedding is tomorrow."

"I know." His gaze caressed over her as he let go of the door handle and rested his hand on the bed's post.

Messalina blocked her mind from the thoughts of Rosa and Zeno making love only inches from where Alexius's hand lay. "That means the baby has been born," she muttered.

"And it means Rosa is still alive." The corner of Alexius's mouth lifted slightly with assurance. "Messi, Rosa is strong, or she would have given up before now."

Messalina studied his expression while her heart punished her ribs. "But how can she marry a man she hates?"

Alexius walked to the same window where he had been before and leaned on the window frame. "She has no other choice."

"Alexius, somehow, we—no, I have to stop it." Messalina walked toward him as if the distance would make him agree with her. "I don't trust what Pomponius will do to Rosa."

He pulled away to run his hand through his hair and turned to her. "You cannot stop this wedding, Messi." "Let me get the pendant to her."

"No." She studied his face, features sharpened only by the shadows dancing in the room. "Alexius, I can't let you become involved."

"I already am." His gaze darkened with concern. "I talked to Zeno on the chariot. He is going to wait for a better time."

"Alexius. You shouldn't be." She touched his wrist. "They will only think I am a stupid girl worried about her friend, which is true." She moved away to stop the trickle of warmth surging through her.

He brushed her face with his fingers. "Messi, you have to think of Claudius and Antonia."

Her gaze locked with his. He was right! If anyone discovered her involvement in this, her parents would never find Antonia a suitable husband in all of Rome. In addition, Claudius would become a merchant like their father, instead of following Alexius's path into the Senate. And Alexius and his family could lose even more. She could not let that happen to either family. But Rosa's life was at stake.

Their gazes fought until he lowered his lips, brushing hers like a warm, sweet breeze. Messalina's mind vanished as his hand eased into her hair, covering her ear, muffling all sound except her heart thundering in her chest. She melted into him, drowning in the security of his arms.

She had no more than surrendered when the floor lifted beneath their feet. The shutters broke open, filling the room with brilliant sunlight. Frantic screams pierced the air outside as something somewhere collapsed. Stronger tremors bashed the apartment door against the wall.

"We have to get out of here," Alexius swept her up in his arms and raced down the bucking stairs to the street filling with the terrified crowds.

Then, the tremors stopped as quickly as they had started. Screams silenced. People studied each other for the certainty that it all had been real, not imagined. A donkey brayed in discontent, and life ebbed back into celebrations.

Chapter 11

SEAGULLS FLOATED IN a pristine sky just beyond the terrace wall of his house where sapphire waves sloshed onto the lazy beach just beyond Balbus's thermae that separated him and the distant sea. Brilliant fragrant flowers bloomed in a multitude of pots lining the terrace rail.

Yet, for Alexius, the day was dark and stormy. He would give anything to go back to the apartment instead of attending Rosa's wedding. The moment returned when he had kissed Messalina in Zeno's apartment, which had brought another onslaught of fantasies, along with the need to hold and protect her.

The festival had continued with demands from both families that lasted well into the night, talking of the tremors, the parade, his election, their future. Three times last night, he had walked to his bedroom window, hoping to see Messalina on her terrace again. If she had been there, he would have scaled the dividing wall just to hold her in his arms.

Now he stood on his father's terrace with both families milling about in the gardens. They were alone but not alone.

"I can't do this," Messalina said, spearing her forehead into his chest. Her fingers clutched the sides of his white electoral toga.

He entangled his hands beneath the wealth of curls cascading down her sun-warmed back and held her even closer. A strand of hair blew across her face as she looked up. He brushed the strand aside and drew the pendant from beneath her white tunica. "Then, let me, Messi," he whispered.

She shook her head. "No. I can't let you. I will find some way to get the necklace to Rosa." She started to draw away.

He drew her back into his arms and set his chin rest on her hair. The delicate fragrance of lilies drifted to him, one he could drown in. "If asked, tell them I bought this for you at the Circus Maximus."

She nodded against his chest.

Something tugged on his toga. He looked down at the interruption and saw Antonia holding the Britanni puppy he had brought from Britannia for her. It was almost too big for her to hold now. "We have to go," Toni said.

Alexius looked beyond the terrace breezeway and saw both families waiting in the glassed-in solarium. "Tell them we are coming, Toni."

Their fathers led the way up the street. The mothers followed, busily gossiping about the wedding. Slaves scurried behind Claudius and Antonia, leaving Messalina and Alexius trailing along at their own pace. Each step was like dragging stones behind her.

The man walking with her, whom she wanted to hate, was making that impossible. She knew what Alexius could do in a heartbeat, because he had done it a thousand times. He could destroy her with nothing but one word: *Medusa.*

She knew she should never trust him. Yet, the man she thought she loved with her life had become repulsive since Alexius had returned. She did not want Hector even touching her now. She glanced at Alexius. His soft blue gaze met hers, causing her to trip on an unseen stone. When he caught her, his strength both thrilled and frightened her.

"Messi, are you all right?"

"Yes." That was a lie. All she was certain of was that she wanted to choose the man she would spend her life with, knowing for certain that he wanted to be with her. And he liked being with her. He, in fact, wanted to be with her.

A haunting realization chilled Messalina like ice. Not only did she not know what direction her own life was taking, she was helping her one true friend do the same. What difference did it make that the daughter of a patrician loved a slave? Zeno and Rosa deserved a chance to be happy. At least, they were in love.

On the other hand, could Rosa be using Zeno to get away from her father and this marriage with Pomponius? Was she that desperate? Actually, yes. However, Rosa was unlike her father who excelled at using anyone to further his purposes.

This was more than just getting the message to Rosa that Zeno still loved her and was coming for her whenever possible. She was involving Alexius in something that could destroy his dream of becoming a senator and helping Rome. She was possibly ruining everyone's lives by this. The weight of an elephant crushed her stomach. She had to think of a way to keep Alexius out of all this.

A new idea struck in her brain. There was another way. Yes.

A meager sense of assurance filled her as their small parade merged with other families standing outside the temple to the Immortal Augustus. Beneath the imperial statue's gaze, people chatted and milled around his fountain and the statue of Hercules. Sage and mint burning in an outside altar filled the air with their cleansing fragrances.

"Alexius!" Alexius turned, taking Messalina with him. Marcus hurried through the crowd toward them, a devious grin lurking on his face. "I wondered when you two would get here."

Messalina's heart stopped as Marcus drew Alexius aside to whisper something. He leaned down to listen to something from Marcus and smiled. Then, they both looked across at her. It was happening again. The ancient chill of being humiliated enclosed around Messalina because Marcus had always been part of this little game that Alexius played. The blood in her body inflamed.

"Messalina! There you are," her mother called as she shoved through the gathered crowd. Her mother came to a frustrated halt. "Maybe you can talk some sense into Rosa, because if that fool girl does not stop bawling, she'll faint."

Panic led Messalina on her mother's heels through the blaze of sun gleaming through the temple's main chamber where a life-sized statue of Augustus beamed beneath the open ceiling supported by four pillars. Nearby, Balbus, Sulla, and Pomponius chatted and laughed. Balbus wore his golden garments as High Priest of the Temple Augustalus. The other two wore identical senatorial togas that Alexius wanted to wear one day.

These men held, twisted, and used their power as slaves used water, something Alexius would never do no matter how he felt about her. With all her heart, she wanted him elected because Rome needed him.

Women were pacing the outer room in the rear of the temple. Volasennia bolted from the group and charged at them, fury flooding her. "Today of all days. Rosa's crying is enough to fill the Tiber. You have to put a stop to it. Somehow, you have to, Messi." Rosa's mother draped an arm over Messalina. "You must talk some sense into Rosa. The ceremony is about to start."

Everyone moved aside as Messalina eased into the suffocating room. A shaft of light from a narrow window on the far wall poured down onto Rosa lying on the cot. This was not the jubilant girl that Messalina remembered reclining on the terrace couch that summer afternoon. All Messalina saw was a starved victim whose only signs of life were the gasps for air and the delicate whimpers of abject misery.

"Rosa?"

Rosa gazed around the small room. The thick perfumes of the mothers and daughters whispering to each other beside the opposite wall suffocated her. Then she heard Messi's voice call her name. Rosa turned to the sound and saw the only other reason she had not taken her life by now. She had to see Messi one last time before refusing to marry Pomponius.

There was no doubt that her father would kill her this time. She did not care anymore. She was already dead. Every day that passed without word from Zeno had finally drained all hope of ever being free. Of ever being loved. And she had to know if Carena had found her and that Baby Paulus was alive. Messalina would know.

"Oh Rosa! Rosa!" Open armed, Messalina charged toward her. "You are alive. I have written you a thousand letters. Prayed to Diana to protect you. She answered my prayers."

In an instant, Rosa felt the warm flesh of Messalina's hands and life surged into her, a life she no longer wished to endure. "They would not let me write you." Rosa said and glared hatred across the room to where her mother watched by the single doorway. "They read everything."

"It doesn't matter now," Messalina said, her voice quivering. "You are here. Everything will be fine…no wonderful."

There was too much pleasure in her friend's voice. "It can't be wonderful, Messi. Before the entire pantheon of gods, I will refuse to say any vows to Pomponius. I do not care what Father does to me now. I just had to see you one more time."

"No! Rosa! Please. You have so much to live for, so much to make you happy."

That was impossible. Rosa stared at Messalina as if she were a stranger, a lunatic, someone willing to betray her. Why? "I never thought—"

Panic flooded Messalina's face as she grappled to pull something from her tunica. "Look, Rosa. I…I bought this…for you." She shoved a pendant toward her as she dragged her hair free of the ribbon. "It…It is for you. I…I bought it here in Herculaneum. You remember when we told our dolls that horses would bring them happiness? Remember, Rosa? Horses. Rosa, they will come and bring you happiness. It will come."

Rosa's gaze froze on the pendant. She remembered dragging the image of the charioteer over Zeno's bare chest. She remembered teasing him with it and not letting him take it from her. She looked up at Messi, letting the questions sear in her gaze. *How, Messi? How did you get this? Why?*

Messalina gathered the ribbon and pendant in her palm and shoved it toward her. "Here. It is yours. For your happiness, Rosa. Happiness for your future. Your future is coming. You will be happy again. I promise."

Volasennia stepped closer with cloyingly interest in the pendant. Rosa dropped it into the thick folds of the wedding tunica. The act turned the woman's attention sharply to Messalina. "You bought this here in Herculaneum?"

"Yes. I did. I forget where." Messalina nodded too quickly. "A long time ago." She looked at Rosa, hope swimming in her gaze as she attempted to smile. "When we were children playing with our dolls, we talked about how Pegasus would bring us happiness. Remember, Rosa, how we told our dolls that. You remember, don't you, Rosa?"

Messalina was begging her to remember something that never had happened. However, they had, more than once, covered each other's lies so many times to keep one another from getting in trouble. It seemed instinctive to do it now. "Yes. I had forgotten. It was so…long ago.

Everyone smiled and nodded as if they remembered telling their dolls the same ridiculous story. Tears welled in Messalina's eyes as she clutched her wrists. "Rosa. You have to live. For your family, Rosa. They need you…to do this."

Her father and mother could go to the lower pits with Hades for all she cared. Rosa looked back at the girl she once believed to be her best friend. Somehow, she knew Messi's gaze was begging Rosa to read her mind.

Family? For your family. Rosa gasped. *Zeno! Baby Paullus! That was her family.*

That unspoken bond between lifelong friends told her she was right. Every fiber in Rosa's soul resisted. The thought of Pomponius so close to her, touching her, was beyond revolting. The fact that her father would win and gain his prize only added to the horror.

There had to be a reason why Zeno would allow her to marry Pomponius? She studied Messalina's pleading gaze. Was Zeno wanting her to wait for him? If so, they could find Baby Paulus and escape. Was that his message?

A spring of hope trickled through the desert of her soul, feeding a fragment of life in its wake. "Yes, for my family." Rosa swallowed her heart. "For my family."

Messalina's face glowed with joy. "Yes, for all of them, Rosa."

The invention had its instant effect on suffocating room. Her mother's gaze sparkled with relief and victory. The women sighed, and the room instantaneously filled with happy chatter. Hands clasped. Voices laughed.

The room buzzed as slaves prepared for the horrid ceremony. Rosa forced her feet to the floor and stood. Hands worked to smooth the wrinkles from her saffron-colored stola, fussed with the six braided coils that her grandmother had arranged that morning.

The old hag—the witch, appeared in the small room, her black stola cloaking everything with its perpetual gloom. Her hard-angry gaze burned in her eyes as she scanned what the slaves had finished. "Bring her. The men are waiting."

Alexius noticed Pomponius standing near the center of the temple columns amid a thick cluster of senators of the Collegium of Augustalus, Sulla, Balbus, his father among them.

Apollo's rays beamed down on their senatorial togas as if trying to match their power and presence.

Marcus snarled beside him. "Do they not look just like Rome itself?"

They did. He hoped that one day he would wear that prestige as successfully as his father wore his. With the political race going as well as it was, after the elections in September, he could well be so honored…as long as no one found out about Zeno.

Balbus moved regally before the chamber that contained a smaller statue of the Great Augustus. His golden robes glinted in the sunlight. "Citizens of Rome, in the name of our true protectors of our land, I welcome you," he announced to the world. "This glorious day I wish you to join me in celebrating the joining of that which makes Rome great—a man and a woman. For it is he who protects us. It is she who cares for us. Spurius Pomponius Bestius, come forward and join me before the gods."

Pomponius smiled and departed his gleaming group. He waddled up the steps to stand beside Balbus. Alexius studied the man who bothered him like a rash. He was always too coy and confident.

Memories of that first day in the tabularium in Rome when the fat senator introduced him to his chamber. "Ah, my boy, you'll come to understand all this in time. It has always been done this way forever, my boy." Pomponius had continually called him "my boy." Never had anyone in the legions referred to him as 'boy.' Respect thrived there. Never with this man. All were minions beneath his great weight.

Volasennia and Octavia interrupted Alexius's thoughts and joined the growing crowd of onlookers. A collective gasp swept the room when Rosa walked in from the side room, clutching Messalina's arm.

For a moment, Alexius thought he was witnessing the arrival of a ghost, a lemur dressed in a yellow tunica. The flaming orange veil crowned with marjoram seemed more than Rosa's body should carry. The procession stopped at the foot of the two steps to the sacred alcove. A long silent pause filled the temple as Rosa halted at the first step, as if she were to climb an immense barrier. Pomponius opened his palm to accept his bride's hand and waited until Rosa finally placed her hand in his.

As Pomponius drew Rosa up the steps. Balbus motioned them to a wide, fleece-covered bench, and then walked inside the rear alcove. The squeal of a piglet soon filled the temple.

Alexius would have gladly exchanged places with Pomponius if Messi would change with Rosa as well. His thoughts turned their own wedding day. Why did they have to wait until September as the auguries had commanded?

Quiet moments passed before Balbus reappeared, smiling. Names were stated and vows spoken, during which Alexius imagined Messalina saying to him, "To whatever family you belong, I belong. Where you go, I go."

Balbus offered a grain cake to the bride and groom. Everyone knew it symbolized the gods' giving of grain, the husband providing for his wife, and his wife accepting his care. Pomponius took a bite and handed it to Rosa.

A breathless few moments passed before she nibbled from the grain cake in his hand. Alexius thought of the three pomegranate seeds that Persephone had eaten—the three seeds that kept her with Pluto for three months of the year, and a man she also hated. Two clerks hurried forward for the signing of the contract.

Alexius turned his attention back to Messalina, her gaze never leaving the marble flooring at her feet. His attention jolted when the hall erupted with applause and yells of, "Feliciter!" "Talasio!"

The contract was signed, and the deed done. Balbus waved his arms for the crowd's attention. "Come one and all. Help us celebrate the joining of our houses." The man strode through the crowd like Caesar himself, making an aisle for the wedded couple to follow. Pomponius smiled victoriously as they passed. Rosa's gaze remained on the floor as she followed, her hand resting on his fat wrist.

Everyone gathered behind them, cheering and tossing nutmeats at the bride and groom as the two settled on Pomponius's huge litter garlanded with rosemary and white roses. It took twelve bearers to lift the litter and carry it along the Decumanus Maximus to Balbus's house.

Messalina failed to turn when he approached. She failed flinch or even seem to be breathing when Alexius found her staring at the crystal water flowing into the temple fountain. He saw that the ribbon was no longer on her neck, which answered his first question. Their parents waiting restlessly nearby, as the crowds followed the wedding litter through the jubilant streets. "Messi, they are waiting for us," Alexius said, touching her arm.

She jerked away. Tears lingered in her lashes like diamonds as she looked up at him. He tried to read the depths of her gaze. "Does Rosa know?"

She nodded.

"Then she will be fine, Messi." If she survived the wedding night.

The instant Pomponius reclined next to her in the litter, odors of garlic clashed with the thick fragrance of his sweet oils. "Well done, wife."

Rosa felt the litter strain as the slave bearers heaved it off the ground and looked at the blob of fat beside her: his narrow pig eyes, his jostling triple chin, and his soft pink lips. "I will act as such. Nothing more."

He laughed as he fingered the ribbon holding Zeno's pendant. "This must be magic. Let me see it."

Rosa withdrew from his touch. "It is only a gift from a friend."

He clutched the pendant before she could pull it from his palm. "As your husband, I shall determine what you wear. Do I have to tear it from your neck?" He tugged at the ribbon. "Let me have it."

"It is nothing except a childhood memory." Removing Zeno's pendant was like ripping skin. She could not let him take it from her. It was all she had of Zeno. Panic tore through Rosa's body. "Please. I will do anything. Please. Let me keep it."

"Anything?" He smirked as he fingered the pendant. "We will see about that."

Messalina endured people besieging both her and Alexius all the way to Balbus's house, chattering about their forthcoming wedding and his election. Of course, his all-important election.

Alexius talked as if he were looking forward to each occasion. The arm he placed around her waist tightened as he smiled brilliantly when the taunts of marriage came his way. However, he was in public, before those who would be electing him to office. How else would he act, as if anything other than becoming a future senator?

Her thoughts coiled in her stomach. How could Rosa walk out of that temple as wife to a man she hated? How could the world be so cruel to those so innocent? Alexius deserved the same, a woman who wanted to share his house and his heart—which she did not. Nothing of which mattered to either set of parents.

Those facts played in Messalina's mind as the guest line inched into Balbus's house. Finally, Messalina heard the tinkling white discs oscillating innocently between the atrium's red marble columns. Late afternoon breezes drifted in the room as they always had all those years of growing up with Rosa.

She and Alexius moved through the vestibule into the burgeoning sunlight beaming down on a new fountain that dribbled into the impluvium. Alexius placed his hand at the small of her back, sending tendrils of possessive warmth surging through Messalina.

She fought the desire to melt into his touch. He was doing all this for show. Because everyone expected it of him. She considered pulling farther away. However, the crowd pressed them closer as they approached the greeting line

"Good afternoon, Alexius," Balbus said. A dangerous sparkle lit the man's gaze. "Messalina, Volasennia told me what you did for Rosa today. We appreciate it."

Messalina wanted to scream at him for what he had done for the sake of power he did not need. "You have no idea how wonderful it was to see Rosa. I have missed her." She looked down the receiving line for Rosa. "Where is she?"

Volasennia grimaced beside her husband. "I am sorry, Messi. Rosa suddenly fell ill after the wedding. She has been given something to make her sleep. Unfortunately, her strength will only last long enough for her to say her goodbyes."

"May I visit her, just for a short bit, please."

"Not today. However, you can, in Rome," Balbus interjected. "Of course, after your wedding and as Alexius gains his first step into the Senate." He turned to Alexius. "I will enjoy seeing you there."

"Thank you, dominus." Alexius's hand on her back urged her toward Pomponius sweating in the cool spring air.

"Alexius, my boy, welcome." The man smiled as a slave swabbed his face. "And Messalina, so lovely. You are a lucky boy, Alexius, to gain such a prize. Your families arrived long ago. I was wondering if you were coming or had chosen to find time to yourselves."

Alexius granted the senator a proper smile. "We knew the line would be quite long with blessings to you and Rosa and so, took our time arriving."

"Already, I see that you are wise to such gatherings. It will see you well in Rome," Pomponius said, opening his palm. Zeno's pendant dropped, dangling from the ribbon and swaying lazily from the man's first finger.

Messalina's gaze froze on the pendant. Yet, Alexius never so much as flinched as the senator continued. "What a thoughtful childhood gift for my bride. A good luck pendant so I hear. I have to ask, where would Pegasus take her if he came for her?"

Alexius flinched beside her while she stopped herself from yanking the pendant from the man's hand. "I am sure it would be where she would regain her strength

"Well, she was quite delighted to have it," Pomponius said as he coiled it into his palm and handed it to the slave behind him.

"Hopefully, it will grant her the luck it brought me at the Max," Alexius said with a casual nod.

By the gods. She had forgotten to tell Alexius that she had changed their story. Messalina's heart sank as Pomponius smirked.

"Well, Alexius, I am surprised you would give it away before you claimed enough votes for the election."

Messalina felt Alexius's hand stiffen against her back as he smiled down at her. "I assure you Messi is all the luck I will need for that." He urgently glanced behind them and sighed. "We are keeping you from your guests and wish you both much happiness."

They moved into the busy crowd of guests milling about like bees. People approached wanting to discuss Alexius's election, and ask how he liked working in Rome. They assured him that he had their vote already. Alexius was the epitome of gratitude as he moved her through the guests to the terrace wall overlooking the river tumbling from the hills to the bay.

"Messalina," her mother called out. Her parents hurried through the crowd toward them. "Alexius, would you mind if we talk with Messalina alone for a moment?" Messallus sternly asked and gripped Messalina's elbow to draw her away.

"Certainly. I will get us something to drink." Alexius had barely stepped toward the terrace's impluvium when Balbus and Volasennia stopped him.

Messalina jerked her attention away from Balbus and Volasennia stopping Alexius to ask him something. Their private conversation floated toward her. She heard *pendant* mentioned.

Her own parents drew in even closer. "Messalina, why in the world would you give Alexius's gift to Rosa?" her father demanded in a hushed tone. "How could you do that to him?"

"Father, Rosa needs it more than I do. Alexius…"

She saw Balbus rest a hand on Alexius's shoulder. "That is interesting, Alexius," Balbus said. "I had a that specially made for Zeno, exactly like that one. It is curious that you say you bought it at the Max."

Alexius nodded. "From a vendor."

"Messalina, will you please listen to us?" Her mother's voice jarred her attention back to her parents. "He will think you didn't want it."

"He says I am his luck now."

"Messalina, don't be ridiculous," her father huffed. "That was a very expensive silver pendant."

"Yes, I know." It was hardly a child's pendant as she had pretended it to be. Fear curdled in her stomach. She should not have changed the story and not told Alexius. It was all wrong now. All wrong.

"A vendor? At the Max?" Balbus asked, withdrawing his hand from Alexius's shoulder. "Why would a vendor have an identical pendant?"

Alexius shrugged. "I only know that I bought it after one of the races."

"Messalina," her mother seethed, "you told Rosa that you bought it here in Herculaneum when you were a child. You never did such a thing. And telling her some story about Pegasus and luck. Why would you make up such a lie?"

Messalina's heart thundered in her chest as she met her mother's hard gaze. "That was not a lie. I wanted to remind

Rosa of that story, knowing she would understand, I mean, so the pendant will mean more to her."

"Balbus, it cannot be the same one you gave Zeno," Volasennia assured her husband. "Messalina said she bought it here in Herculaneum."

Balbus looked at his wife with a million questions. "That's impossible."

Messallus noticed people slowing to gather gossip. "We will discuss this later, Messalina," he growled."

"Yes, Papa." Out of the corner of her eye, she saw Alexius glance curiously her way.

"Well, yes," Alexius said stiffly. "It is strange that that I would have found a copy of it."

Messalina saw Balbus and Volasennia study Alexius and then each other and walk away. At that same moment, her parents moved away through the peristyle, whispering to each other.

Alexius claimed two wine glasses from a passing slave and walked nonchalantly toward her. He handed her one, as if nothing at all had just happened, as if such scrutiny were a daily occurrence. As if people changed stories all the time.

He sipped the wine, studying the crowd, smiling at any who passed them, nodding. "What did you tell Rosa?"

"I forgot to tell you. I am sorry."

"Just tell me what you told her."

Those passing saw nothing, but he was livid. Messalina could feel it rippling from him like heat waves. She managed to smile graciously at the curious glances. "That I bought the pendant here in Herculaneum, when we were children. Alexius, I wanted to keep your name out of this. I am sorry—"

He smiled at her. Yet it was no smile. "It is done, Messi." He looked away to sip more wine.

She claimed a biscuit covered with shrimp and garum from a tray carried by a passing slave. The food barely worked its way down her dry throat. She sipped wine to shove the treat along. Both landed in some crevice of her stomach.

"Is this right?" Alexius asked calmly. "You gave Rose an identical pendant that Balbus had specially made, and that you bought here when you were younger, that…?"

She nodded and smiled at a passing friend.

He nodded as well. "…I said I bought an illegal copy of it at the Max and gave to you as a special gift?"

She sipped wine. "I…I will say that I mixed it up with another piece I bought here."

"I see." He toasted a colleague and his wife as they passed. "Then, to appease Balbus, I will have to prove there are more copies of his pendant at the Max. And to appease your parents, I will find another copy for you." One eyebrow rose as he looked sharply down at her. "Or would you rather I not bother?"

CHAPTER 12

THE TEAM WAS hungry. He could feel it in the reins. Noses pressed to the gate, ready for their break. They wanted this win. He wanted this win. Only days before, Balbus had promised him freedom if he won this race. Zeno could taste the fresh air of Armenia in his lungs. *This win and I'm a free man!*

The racing gate sprung open, and Nane stumbled out into the onrush of the four teams. *Nane?* That wasn't like her. She was the one who jerked her brothers into the race. She steadied and melted into stride, eating ground and dust from the Red and White teams taking the lead.

This was the first of seven rounds around the Circus Maximus. Those two teams didn't have the stamina for seven laps as his blacks did. Nevertheless, he would need all their strength at the end and held his blacks back. It was the Blue team that he worried about. The Blue driver held back as well, letting the team of chestnuts settle into a ground-eating stride.

Fire burned in Vahagn's eyes when he saw the chestnut stallion racing beside him. Amanor and Vanature remained steady. Nane's ears lay flat, and her mane flew straight out in the wind as she stretched to drag her brothers around the narrow end of the spina, the marble island in the middle of the racetrack. Still, something wasn't right with Nane.

The narrow turn at the opposite end of the spina approached. Zeno eased the team out toward the crowd. Like a thunderous wall, the yells screamed for his Green team. "Zeno! Zeno!"

Instinctively, Zeno slowed his horses into the turn and released them out of it. The Blue team pulled even with him. Vahagn bit down on the bit, sending an impatient message through the rein. He wanted the lead from this team. *Not yet, my friend. Not yet. Save your wind.*

Zeno held his blacks for the five turns and then released Nane to drag her brothers through the inside of the White team and then break ahead of the Red. As they neared the final lap, he tightened the reins in his left hand, enough to press the blue chariot into the spina.

Vahagn's ear flicked back as the Blue team disappeared behind him and then crashed into the marble. The Red and White team had to sweep out and around the pile of rubble, which gave him a solid lead.

One turn. One more turn to freedom.

Nane pulled to the center of the track even before he tightened her rein. Her brothers were now in her stride, eating the ground for the seventh and last lap. Dust and sand bit at Zeno's face.

His arms had become mere extensions to the leather in his hands. The reins tied to his waist had ripped through his green tunic, rubbing his flesh raw. His legs braced and shifted for balance for the one last turn. Determination burned in the horses' eyes. They were one with the wind.

The Red's team appeared on Nane's side, matching her stride. He could hear the White team eating his dust. A crash filled the air behind him. The crowd groaned and cheered in the same breath. He knew the White team was no longer in the race. Just the Red team.

He slapped the reins over the black's lathered haunches. The brothers lurched forward in stride with Nane. He leaned even further over the front of the chariot to encourage his four around the sharp turn. Vahagn coiled to make the turn. His brothers gathered as Nane stretched to bring them all around. The chariot slid, spraying sand over the Red team.

Suddenly, the chariot tilted, lifted, spun around. Nane jerked out of stride. She stumbled into her brothers. Then he and his chariot clamored into her hindquarters. Vanature rolled next. Amanor fought for footing and then too collapsed. Vahagn lunged forward, dragging everything with him, and fell a stride later, screaming.

Zeno soared over the mangled mess of horseflesh and thrashing legs. One of Amanor's legs caught in a chariot wheel, snapping it like a twig. The animals' screams were pure pain as the chariot splintered, and as he floated above it all like a god looking down on the earth.

He grabbed the knife at his waist and cut the reins, releasing him from the carnage of hooves cutting the air like an assault of birds. He rolled across Vahagn's thrashing belly to the spina. Pain exploded. The world went black.

CHAPTER 13

A LEXIUS TURNED HIS back on the busy clerks searching for Pomponius's financial reports that the senator wanted to review. The huge sweltering room behind him was awash with the heavy scent of scrolls, the busy sound of flipping abacuses, and anxious whispers.

He leaned against the large, arched window of the dusty record hall of the Tabularium and let his gaze sweep like a bird over the Forum. The plaza stretched below with its painted columns crowned with gold, the colorful assortment of marbled basilicas, buildings, and temples. Everywhere, ornate statues rose amid the steady current of white togas, vibrant colored stolas, and multi-colored tunics. The April air flowed with a cacophony of laughter and voices.

To his left, he saw senators leaving the Curia, the senate house. The men in their purple-bordered togas casually meandering in and out of the senate's tall bronze doors, talking, laughing, and emanating power.

His stomach sank as memories of hearing Balbus say, "I had a special pendant made only for Zeno, exactly like that one. It is curious that you say you bought it at the Max."

In addition, his first and only response he could think of was "I cannot imagine that I would have found the original. Surely."

Then the innocent look on Volasennia's face as she added, "Messalina said she bought it here in Herculaneum."

He could picture Messi explaining herself again. "I simply wanted to keep your name out of this."

Out of this? She might as well have told Balbus they knew all about Zeno and Rosa. Jupiter's balls! Messalina may as well have told them Zeno was the father, and that he knew everything. Why had she done this. Surely, she realized she could ruin his—and her—future? Even if they did not marry, he could not see Messi stooping so low as to ruin his family on purpose.

Fury burned. Well, if Messi wanted the betrothal broken, fine. Except she had to see it done. Until then, he would continue this falsehood that he had given her the necklace and that she had simply mixed the story with another piece of her jewelry she had found in Herculaneum.

Fortunately, Fosco had found a jeweler who could make identical matches to Zeno's pendant to sell at the Max, making it possible that he had bought a copy of the original.

There was no doubt in Alexius's mind that Balbus had informants searching for the vendor who sold him the pendant. He only hoped he had paid the metal smith enough to keep his mouth shut.

"Dominus," a scribe asked suddenly. "We have located the reports. Do you care to see them?"

Alexius walked to the table and scanned the scrolls, noticing that Pomponius's entries were so vague that water seemed opaque in comparison. There was nothing he could do about any of it. Why resist?

"Good work, Meander." He handed the scrolls back to the man. "We still need the report about the grain shipments from Cyrene."

"Yes, dominus."

Returning to the window, Alexius slumped against the arching stones again. He knew his father could arrange any marriage with any other house in Rome if he wanted. However, he did not want to marry just any available female with a large dowry. He wanted Messalina. All he wanted was her trust and hopefully her love. He did not care about her dowry.

Messalina had to see that Hector was only interested in her dowry because the interloper needed it in order to subsist in Rome. Possibly long enough to be noticed among the acting companies. However, there was no doubt that her father would refuse to grant the money to the piss ant in any case.

As much as he had to admit it, it fit Messi somehow that she would change her story, thinking she was protecting him. He should have thought of that. However, the fact Messi failed to tell him galled him.

"Alexius, my boy."

Alexius turned to see Pomponius swaggering into the scroll room ahead of his twenty slaves and a gaggle of clients. The rustling of paper in the large room suddenly grew louder and chatter hummed like agitated bees.

"Good to see you still here, my boy." Pomponius waved at his parade of clients. "Leave us."

The men evacuated as a slave opened a chair behind the man. The senator sat, his stubby, hairy legs flashing beneath his toga. For a brief second, Alexius pictured them between Rosa's spindly legs. It was a gruesome thought.

"Have you found my reports?" Pomponius asked and let a slave wipe sweat from his face.

Alexius looked over to the nearest table. "Meander, you have the reports from Egypt?"

The Greek slave nodded. "Yes, dominus."

"Ah, let me see them." Pomponius waved for the scroll. When they were in his hand, he read over the parchment. "That cannot be right, you fool. Redo it. And do it right this time."

The slave glanced at Alexius. They both knew nothing was wrong with the numbers. And, they both knew there was nothing they could do about it.

A thunder of footsteps climbing the staircase interrupted Alexius's snarling thoughts. He recognized the sound of hobnails on the steps before he heard the commanding voice of a centurion.

"Make way. Make way."

Pomponius looked to the doorway and then up at Alexius for an explanation. Alexius shrugged. What did he know? In addition, if he did, he certainly would never appear to know a damn thing.

Workbenches scratched on floors as anxious murmurs spread like flames. Then a collective gasp sucked the air the moment imperial clerks appeared, surrounded by praetorian guards. A regal Egyptian stepped forward. "Is the chairman of the Committee of Finance present?"

Pomponius rose, squaring his thick shoulders. "Yes. I am the chairman."

"By orders of his Excellency Vespasian Caesar," the Egyptian said with indifference. "I am to collect the financial reports for the last three years and bring them to Vespasian Caesar immediately." He waved the five slaves with baskets forward. "You will see that they are collected and given to us without hesitation."

"I will not!" The soldiers shifted nervously as Pomponius stepped forward as if to personally create a blockade. "I demand to know the reason for this invasion."

The Egyptian's coal black gaze burned into Pomponius's beady eyes. "By orders of Vespasian Caesar, I am to collect all of the records for the last three years."

Pomponius glared at the man, letting soldiers waited for orders. The imperial slaves fretted with their baskets. No one breathed. No one moved.

"Not one of my parchments or ledgers will leave this room until I have talked with the Senate's finance committees. Is that clear?"

"No, dominus. That is not clear." The Egyptian waved to the centurion who stepped forward. "I have orders from Caesar to arrest anyone who does not comply with his demands."

Alexius wondered if the senator was about to explode, and stepped back as the fat man continued. "This…this is absurd! Outrageous, I tell you!" Pomponius pointed a dangerous finger at the Egyptian. "The Senate will hear of this!"

"Your thoughts are of no importance to me, dominus. I have my orders." The black eyes of the Egyptian turned on Alexius, jerking him to attention. "Have everything prepared as the emperor requested."

Alexius nodded to the nearest scribe who began collecting the reports and depositing them in the proffered baskets. He remembered the dinner with Cornelius. Had he said something to Vespasian? Another thought froze Alexius's mind with fear. Pomponius would now need a scapegoat. After all, he had just found and collected all those reports. *Sons of Dis!*

If the fat fool realized that fact, he could—and he would—tie every error to a culprit's tail and Alexius knew he was first in line for that position. Furthermore, if that happened, his election was in the sewers.

The imperial cortege disappeared down the steps, leaving him alone with the scarlet-faced senator and a batch of scribes with nothing to do. His only hope of protection was Cornelius now.

"Out! All of you! Go! Get out now!" Pomponius bellowed. Swiftly, everyone fled the room. Alexius moved to follow.

"Alexius," Pomponius called out as he began pacing before the open windows. His chins waggled in time with his fists clenching inside the folds of his toga.

Alexius stopped at the door and turned. "Yes, dominus?"

"Do you have any idea what happened here?" The man's beady eyes burned with fury.

"Vespasian ordered the last three…"

"No! Not that," Pomponius snapped, waving the air as if words had become gnats. "Why would Vespasian do this?"

"I have no idea."

"Did you see anything strange? Out of place?" Pomponius asked, tossing his fallen toga carelessly back over his shoulder. "In the reports. In the reports, boy."

Alexius shook his head and lied. "No. Nothing."

"Has anyone asked you anything about these reports? Anything?"

"No!" Cornelius had not asked that night at dinner.

After staring long and hard, Pomponius turned to his nearest slave. "I need to warn Julian about this. Find the committee chairman of the legion and tell him I must speak to him immediately. Go."

The small man fled down the stairs.

Pomponius walked to the nearest arched window and was met by a breeze that ruffled his toga. Alexius watched as the man stared into nothingness and then looked back. "Did you by chance mention something to someone, anyone at all?"

Alexius shrugged a lie. "Me? Of course not."

"You are kidding me," Marcus said. "Just like that. They came in and took the financials?"

Alexius had been walking back to his house on the Aventine, the one he envisioned sharing with Messalina, and had found Marcus waiting in the atrium.

"They did," Alexius said, as he tossed the election toga to Fosco. "I can't believe it either."

He glanced around the quiet atrium where he could picture Messalina greeting him with a polite kiss and a smile for Marcus. She would be ordering slaves to get food for them while they settled in the triclinium. By the gods, he wanted that. He turned to the master slave. "Have the cook prepare something. We will be in the summer triclinium."

"Yes, dominus."

Alexius walked past the tablinum where he had hoped one day to be receiving clients and on into the garden tri-clinium where the hot afternoon sun basked. One glance and Alexius realized how tired everything seemed. The house needed more plants, more tables, and maybe a few vases about. He shrugged. It needed... Messalina.

"I bet Pomponius almost popped," Marcus said as he reclined on the nearest couch in the summer triclinium.

Alexius reclined across from his friend and reached for a wine goblet, hurriedly set by the kitchen slave. "I never saw a room empty so fast in my life. A legion could not have moved faster."

"Do you think he is extorting money from the accounts?" Marcus sat his goblet on the center table.

Alexius wanted to say yes. However, he knew Pomponius's men would be asking questions to everyone he spoke to now. Ears would be everywhere. "I don't know."

Marcus leaned forward as if to share a well-known fact. "If anyone knew how to move accounts or money, Pomponius would. Any idea who instigated all this?"

"None." The lie clipped from Alexius's lips. He rested on an arm cushion and searched the newly set tray of cheeses and fruit. "Zeno did not race at the Circus Max yesterday. Why?"

Marcus munched on a carrot. "Because he has been sent north to look for horses."

"For horses? Why?" Such news meant that Zeno was far enough away to keep Balbus from tying him to anything.

"The blacks were killed in an accident in the last race."

Alexius choked on his wine. "Was Zeno hurt?"

Marcus shrugged and reached for his wine. "His arm. I heard the Red team locked wheels with his chariot. Wasn't there when it happened."

Alexius's heart split in half as he remembered the feel of the wind cutting into his face as the blacks charged down the road. Even his hands remembered the power that burned through the reins.

To blunt the pain, he reached for a slice of the baked crust covered with melted cheese and peppers. "What is your father going to do now? Let him train a new team?"

"Father!" Marcus ground a dinner napkin in his hands and tossed it on the table. "Never."

"Then what?"

"What else? Zeno cannot race with a broken arm. He plans to sell him and get another charioteer." Marcus drained his cup. "You know how my father is. Money can buy any winner he wants. He bought Pomponius with my sister, didn't he?"

Marcus was right. Balbus would sell Zeno as a punishment for not winning. "Have you seen Rosa since the wedding?" Alexius asked, waving for the slave girl to refill the cups.

Marcus admired the girl and shook his head. "Father tells everyone she is sick and to stay away. I do not believe a word of it." He stared at Alexius over the cup's brim and started to laugh then choked on the wine. "It is more likely Rosa's been crushed to death."

Cheese churned in Alexius's stomach. "I was asking, because I promised Messalina that I would check on her while I am here. She is worried about her."

"So I hear." Marcus reached for a date. "I will check on Rosa for you and let you know, so you can tell Medusa."

"Messalina."

Marcus grinned. "Maybe I can get a letter from Rosa for her. Is she still in Sicilia?"

"Until last of June."

"Still worried about her running off with Hector and humiliating your family?"

Alexius put his wine back on the table. "I give Messi more credit than that. But, if she does, what can I do?" By the gods, he hoped he was right.

"Go after her," Marcus said. He chuckled suddenly. "Which would be better than being betrothed to her little sister."

Jupiter's cock! That was exactly what his parents and Messi's parents would do. It was the joining of their family that they wanted. He remembered Messalina's little sister wrapping her legs around his waist after the parade. He suddenly felt ill.

Marcus burst out laughing. "My best advice, my friend, is to get Medusa—I mean, Messalina—pregnant as soon as possible. Before she has time to think about anyone else doing so."

CHAPTER 14

RIVERS OF RAIN plummeted down the building walls and gushed through streets, leaving Herculaneum quieter than usual. People huddled by their warm braziers, keeping away from gusty windows as sheets of cold wind heaved loose debris against the curbs and into crevasses. Only the desperate wandered the dusky shadows where the streets were slime-slippery with water.

Carena was one of them. She shivered beneath a boy's leather cloak as she huddled in Messalina's entryway. Should she knock? Would the domina's parents let her keep Paullus? Fear they would not allow that chilled her deeper than the buffeting wind.

Beyond the stoop, the gushing downpours regained strength and created waves of water that funneled into the pedestrian tunnel at the end of the street. Her domina's words echoed in her memory. "Take care of my baby. Please."

Baby Paullus didn't belong to the domina anymore. *He belongs to me.* She had to see to his care as she had for these three months.

Carena eased from Messalina's stoop and clung to the passage wall to keep from being swept down the passageway to the beach. Paullus snuggled to feed. He was hungry, making her hurry down the steps shrouded in the stormy darkness. "Not much further. Not much further."

A dim light gleamed through the slats in one of the boathouses. She stopped at the closed door and pounded on it. "Ruso. Ruso. Open it. Please. Ruso!"

When a worn and scarred hand heaved the door open, Carena slipped inside and looked up at the weathered face of Ignatius. His three-day-old beard resembled a white porcupine.

"Carena?" the old fisherman asked as he dragged her deeper into the boathouse. A simple oil lamp dangled from the arched ceiling, creating odd shadows in the small space. Lobster catches and dank ropes hung amid the thick odors of fish filling the room.

Ruso bolted off the pile of fishing nets. "Carena, is that you?"

Before she could answer, Paullus wailed his fury. Both man and boy stared in shock as Carena removed the angry bundle from beneath her cape.

"Girl, what have you got here?" Ignatius asked, curiously grinning at the familiar sound.

As Carena revealed the red-faced urchin, Ruso's gaze lifted with a million questions. "They abandoned him for the wolves. His name is Paullus, and he's mine." Carena began rocking back in forth to sooth the baby.

"He wails like an emperor," Ignatius said. "There's nothing here. My youngest daughter has a three-month-old child. She'll feed him. Give him to me."

The old man took Paullus from her and cradled him into his weathered arms as if the babe were a precious prize from the gods. "Hush now , if you want something to fill that belly of yours." He covered his own boney back with a well-oiled cape and adjusted the baby close to his chest. He silenced the babe with the tip of his finger and started for the door. "I'll take the babe home. You bring her, Ruso."

Ruso caught the door before it slammed back with the wind and latched it. All Carena could do was stare at the door, feeling the empty pit in her arms.

"I…I saw you, months ago, on the galley going to Sulla's villa," Ruso said as he walked back. His voice was flat with curiosity. "I thought I'd never see you again."

"I am free now, Ruso." She dug in the leather pouch she kept around her waist and pulled out the manumission papers. "I really am. See?" As she offered the rolled parchment, an opal ring fell to the floor.

Ruso motioned to the jewelry as if it were poison. Confusion filled his face. "But your domina married two months ago. They'll be looking for you. For this?"

"No. No, they won't. They don't care." Carena straightened, ready to beg Ruso to help her. He was all she had. Carena shoved the pouch of jewels at him. "The domina Rosa. She gave them to me. You can have all of it, if you will let us live with you."

Ignoring the bag, Ruso stared at the parchment. She knew he couldn't read, but he would recognize the name of Marcus Nonius Balbus and his crest pushed into gold wax. "Balbus signed this?" he asked.

"Look. It's his seal. You…you can sell the jewels. Do whatever you want to with them. Just let us stay with you. Please, Ruso. We need you."

He looked at the ring again. "Under the big nose of the witch? If they find you living with us, they will kill all of us, or we'll become slaves like you."

She went to him, grabbing his wrists. "I'll-I'll stay inside. I'll do your sister's chores. I'll cook, clean. Anything. Please, Ruso."

Ruso studied her. "We have to talk to Papa."

CHAPTER 15

To Messalina. I wish I were there with you in Sicilia, instead of being here in the stink of Rome. Here is another pendant to bring you luck. I hope it does. Marcus managed to see Rosa and said she does look better. She is resting in Pomponius's villa near Ravenna. However, no visitors are allowed visitors. Take care, my swan.

Alexius

IS SWAN. SOMEHOW, it did not seem as repulsive coming from Alexius.

Messalina folded the letter and laid it on the terrace table, stunned that he had written her at all. She dangled the new silver pendant from her hand—identical to Zeno's.

She picked up the letter and studied it again, first one side and then the other, remembering how angry Alexius had been. Until he left for Rome, he had barely spoken to her beyond being polite. She could not blame him for one minute.

She looked at the amber bracelet on her wrist, the one Alexius had brought from Britannia. She had expected a lovely woven bag for her head. However, his small bag contained an amber bracelet, a matching ring, necklace, and earrings. She grinned as she recalled all the wives swelling with jealousy at his welcome home celebration.

The Galerius blue wax seal sweating in the hot sun drew her attention. It looked wrong. She looked closer. The leaping stag had made two spots on the parchment when there should have been only one.

Unless….someone else had already read her letter. Fury ignited. *Her mother.* "Niki, has anyone touched this letter from Alexius?"

"No. No, domina. I brought it straight to you when it came. Your mother wasn't here then." The girl cringed with guilt. "But I had to tell her about it. I had no choice, domina."

Then who? She scanned the letter again. There was nothing to draw anyone's attention. Bona Dea! If they were reading his letters to her, were they reading hers, too?

She thought about what she had written. Nothing really, just asking about Rosa and complaining about being trapped in Sicilia with her family, as well as being bored. But Alexius had to know that their letters were being read.

Just then, her brother blustered into the atrium, bellowing at the slaves, and bragging to anyone nearby about his hunting day. Her brother adored Alexius. Would he help? Messalina stepped into the atrium. "Claudius?"

"I am not late. I sent word," he snapped, enduring the slaves washing his dusty feet and changing his sandals for house slippers.

Messalina walked toward him. "Claudius, I need your opinion about something."

He looked at her with suspicion. Another slave held a bowl of water for him to rinse his face and hands. "Me? You want my opinion?" he asked while wiping his face with a towel.

"Yes." She offered Alexius's letter. "Does this seal look as if it has been opened more than once?"

Claudius wiped his hand on his green tunic, which smelled of sweat after riding horses all afternoon. He took the letter, studied the wax seal, and then spread it open to read. When Messalina grabbed for it, her brother swung away. "My swan?" His eyes sparkled with delight. "How many times have you read this? Twenty?" He snatched the letter farther from her reach.

"Once. Now, give it to me."

"And I believe that," he said, mocking her. "But yeah, it looks opened, at least twice." Brilliance beamed on his face. "You think his mistress read it?"

"No." She yanked the letter away. Did Alexius have a mistress? "Why would anyone else want to read this?"

"I know I would like to, if just to hear the ambrosial words he is using to seduce you, you little swan."

She snarled at the smug grin on her brother's face. Maybe involving Claudius was a bad idea. However, who else did she have? "Claudius, somehow, Alexius has to know about this. And I can't tell him because whoever they are, are probably reading mine too."

"Yours?" he grinned hopefully. "Can I read those too? What do you call him? Stallion? Stud? What?"

"I knew this was a mistake. I knew it." She glowered at him. "Will you help Alexius? Please."

"I guess I could write him," Claudius said with a shrug. "But what if they read my letter because it is from our house?"

Claudius was right. Maybe whoever was reading them was there in Sicilia. She stared at the impluvium for an answer.

"I know." Claudius straightened his shoulders. "I will write Quintus and have him tell Alexius. He is going back to Rome with his family tomorrow, and I think their houses are close."

"What if your letter is read, too?"

"I will make sure mine is not, my swan." Claudius beamed at her. "If you tell me your nickname for Alexius?

"Just tell Quintus. All right?"

"Come on. What is it?"

CHAPTER 16

VESPASIAN'S MASSIVE GALLEY gleamed from the midst of the other sleek, black galleys sweeping through the sapphire waters toward Herculaneum. Three rows of polished, bronze-tipped oars blazed like sparks as they rose and dipped with absolute precision, bringing the regal vessel closer to the pier.

Wives, daughters, and sisters crowded against the marble railing of Messalina's terrace until she felt crushed from the press of silks, jewels, and heavy perfumes. They all wanted to be the first to see the emperor as well as be recognized by him.

Out on the pier, Sulla clasped his hands behind him, coolly watching everything as if the emperor's visit was a common occurrence. Of course, Marcus Nonius Balbus chatted with Pomponius near the spot where Vespasian would step into view. Messalina's father, Galerius, Alexius, and Claudius were also waiting behind these men with all the other important men in the city.

Messalina overheard her mother talking to Antonia. "That is the emperor's galley. Do you see it?"

"Yes, Mama. It is bigger than the others."

"As it should be. It carries the most powerful man in the entire world."

"Will I see him, Mama?"

"Of course, Antonia. But you must behave."

"Can I bring Bru?"

"No. Of course not."

Messalina grinned as she watched the painted eye on the front of the galley turn toward the pier. Ever since Alexius gave Toni that silly dog, her sister took it everywhere with her. It was as spoiled as the little sulking girl in her mother's arms.

Messalina returned her attention to the crowd of those deemed important. Marcus was nowhere in the crowd, nor Hector. While Marcus should be there, Hector would never be. Actors were not included in such things and Hector hated the regal parties anyway. He had complained repeatedly at such elaborate displays of powerful men. Until now, she had agreed with him. After all, this time it was Vespasian Caesar who was arriving in Herculaneum. Something new. Something important.

On the beach, soldiers rose to attention as the imperial galley drew closer. The radiant oars halted and then dipped into the crystal water with a reverse pull, slowing the huge galley. Sailors in blue tunics tossed ropes to the slaves as the galley gently nosed into the pier.

The thump of wood-to-wood echoed to the terraces. Drums thundered on the galley decks. Trumpets sang out. The clarion sound released cheers from everywhere as Vespasian stepped into view.

Messalina's heart thudded with excitement as the man who ruled the world appeared wearing a radiant purple toga bordered in gleaming gold. Even from the terrace, she could feel the power radiating from him.

Balbus greeted him with wide arms and kissed each cheek. The two men laughed, and then Vespasian pounded Balbus's back heartily like a lost friend. He gripped arms with Sulla, and granted Pomponius little more than a brief nod. Women around Messalina gasped. The shun was blatant.

The emperor ruffled Claudius's hair and laughed at whatever the boy said. By the gods, what did Claudius say? Messalina cringed just imagining the possibilities.

She forgot everything when the emperor noticed Alexius. A beaming smile erupted on the emperor's face as he clasped arms with Alexius and leaned forward to say something private. Both withdrew, smiling. As a final gesture, the emperor grasped Alexius's shoulder and gave it a secure hug before speaking to another.

Pride niggled up Messalina's spine as Alexius's name tittered on women's busy lips and men formed into the imperial parade that would move through the city. The parade would stretch to the basilica for the dedications and then to Balbus's house for a reception that night.

As the imperial parade began to funnel its way up the narrow beachfront steps, the garden terrace emptied. Like evacuees, everyone charged for the street where garlands lined storefronts, doors, and balconies. Even donkeys and dogs wore flowers. Throngs of people were everywhere, holding baskets full of scented petals to toss as Vespasian passed. Fortunately, Didius held a small place in the street for Messalina, Antonia and her mother.

Thundering drums and blaring trumpets resounded off the walls in the passageway. Ominous praetorian guards in their black and gold armor appeared with their threatening presence. Priests stoically appeared next. A sweep of envy flowed over Messalina as she watched excited young girls twirling the same ribbon banners to lead the emperor through the streets.

Having led such a parade seemed a lifetime ago and failed to seem important now. Soon, she would be in charge of her own home and slaves. In addition, maybe even carrying a child. Images of living in an apartment building in Subura barely conflicted with living in Alexius's house on the Aventine.

Somber lictors appeared with their rod and scythe bundles. "Make way for the first man in Rome!" one repeatedly yelled. "Make way…!"

Vespasian appeared through the tunnel, and the crowds erupted with tumultuous cheers that drowned out the trumpets and drums. The man waved both arms at the crowd as floating flower petals fell like rain. He was square-bodied and strong. As Alexius said, he did seem to have a perpetual strain on his face that was barely dispelled with his brilliant and happy gaze.

Balbus walked a stride behind, wearing his patronizing smile and waving slowly with one arm. All the other senators and city officials paraded loosely into view, waving or just chatting to each other. Their faces were aglow with sunlight and a sense of importance.

The moment Alexius came through the passageway, Messalina's heart floated to her throat and simmered there. He looked so perfect in that group of men. His gaze found her and caressed her face exactly as it had when she returned from Sicilia. That day flashed in her mind immediately.

It had been an ordinary day when she and her family had returned. Messalina remembered her father's galley settling at the pier just as the imperial galley had done, without the glamour and pomp, of course.

Alexius had been standing on his terrace, waiting for them. When he realized her family had arrived, he vanished like a ghost to reappear, racing down the steps past the busy fisherman. Once the crew attached the gangway, he was there to greet everyone.

She had been clutching the new pendant he had sent her and wondered if he would sweep her into his arms. Instead, he kissed her on the cheek, sending her heart fluttering into her throat.

Her family had turned left on the pedestrian passageway below both terraces to go home, but Alexius nudged her to the right toward his house. She easily complied.

"I enjoyed your letters, Messi," he whispered as they walked through his tunnel. "It was the only pleasure I had in Rome." He stopped her midway, drawing her around to face him. "You were right. Someone has been reading everything."

"So, you knew?"

The corner of his mouth lifted. "Not until Quintus told me."

"Then, do you know who is reading them?"

He smirked. "No. But I will."

If Messalina's smile grew any broader, her blushing face would break, Alexius thought, as he strolled with the rest of the men following in Vespasian's wake. He wanted to pull her to his side and take her with him through the street to show the world she was his. Of course, he could not.

"I am proud to have you at my side," Galerius said.

He looked at his father as they strode in step. "I am proud to be at your side, Father."

His father had only just learned of the emperor confiscating Pomponius's financial records. He failed to seem any more concerned about the event than when Alexius had mentioned the oddity at dinner with Cornelius. By all the gods on Olympus, Alexius prayed his father was right.

As they came to the corner of Zeno's apartment, he saw Felix leaning against a taverna doorway, his arms crossed. Zeno had never returned from his search for another team. As expected, Balbus was spending a treasury searching for the slave. All of it was wasted, so far, at least.

Alexius smiled to the crowds even though the delicate feel of falling flowers had become like a hailstorm of soft pebbles.

CHAPTER 17

"Y OU SAW VESPASIAN talk to that little shit, didn't
you?" Pomponius grumbled as he tried to breathe
and keep up with the rest of the parade of fools.

Sulla leaned closer. "Galerius's son?"

"Of course," Pomponius snipped. "I hear his son is
responsible for Vespasian demanding my reports. In addition, that little mongrel had dinner with your son the last
time he was here. I will see that Galerius's spawn never
makes it to the senate floor."

"Do what you have to with Alexius. But be careful with
my son, or you will deal with me," Sulla said, waving at the
crowds. "Will they find anything in the reports?"

"I made sure very little," Pomponius said, gasping for
breath. "This is insane. Stupid, I tell you. Why do we have
to follow in that fool's wake?"

"Possibly because he is emperor, and you want to be
seen with him," Sulla said, grinning down at his miserable
sweaty friend. "You will not be following him for much
longer, I promise."

Pomponius swabbed his face again, juggling his chins as he did so. "You are certain of that?"

"Absolutely."

The parade stopped near the plaza across from the Temple Augustalus. Vespasian and Balbus stepped from the procession under the thunder of clarion trumpets, pounding drums, and a roaring crowd. Alexius turned, looking for Messalina anywhere in the crowd. He did not see her.

Marcus tapped his shoulder. "My, you looked grand in the parade?"

"Where were you?" Alexius asked. Balbus would be livid over his son not being seen walking in the parade.

"Watching from Murio's tavernas, enjoying a fine glass of wine while you sweated your ass off." Marcus tilted his head. "So, are you going to tell me what His Excellency said to you?"

"You saw that?"

"Of course. Everyone saw that. As well as Vespasian's slight toward Pomponius. Now, everyone wants to know what made you so special to get a private word from his Excellency."

Alexius smiled. "Vespasian assured me I had his vote for the Senate."

Marcus started to make some retort when the ground suddenly shook beneath them. Drums and trumpets silenced. People either froze in place or scattered like rats. Guards encircled Vespasian with oval shields and drawn gladiuses as if they could halt Vulcan's attack.

Then, the tremors stilled, because the god stopped laughing or scratching his ass as some said. Trickles of nervous laughter rippled through the crowds as they began breathing again. Shields parted for a grinning emperor who broke through his protection with a teasing shove.

"Even Vulcan is happy to see me this day!" Vespasian announced. Cheering broke out again as he strode toward the basilica, followed by the train of senators.

Inside the massive space, slaves scurried to set chairs in proper rows for the senators vying for imperial favor. Fosco motioned Alexius to his chair properly placed in the last rows with all the other insignificant men of the honorarium.

Vespasian rose to speak. Alexius's mind went back to the day Messalina and her family returned from Sicilia and how even the gods seemed determined to keep them apart.

He had been surprised to get her letter and had enjoyed knowing she was bored. Until Claudius's friend pulled him aside, he had no idea someone would be reading his mail. He now had his own men searching for this person. They assured him they were close to finding out. Praise the gods, Messalina had noticed, because Alexius had been too busy covering his tracks with the pendant.

Marcus leaned close. "Have you heard one imperial word pouring from the great emperor?"

"No."

Marcus chuckled. "Dare I ask why?"

"No."

Marcus chuckled again. "You will make a perfect senator."

"I hope to."

Senators scowled at them. Nothing more was said.

CHAPTER 18

"MESSALINA CLAUDIA!"

Her mother's high-pitched screech rang through the house.

Messalina sat up on the terrace lounger as the woman raced through the breezeway. "Messi, you have been invited to dine with Vespasian Caesar," her mother gasped. "Tonight. Now, get up. We have so little time, and you must be made ready."

She stared at her mother who seemed about to burst. "Dine…with the emperor…tonight?"

"Yes, silly girl. Alexius wants you with him at Balbus's welcoming party." Her mother waved to hurry. "Niki, get things ready. Messi, please, get up and cooperate this time."

"Alexius wants to be seen with me…with him?"

"Of course, he does."

Her mother grabbed Messalina's hand and started pulling her stunned body from the lounger. "And why not? Messi, just think. Once you are married, you will be doing this constantly in Rome." Octavia looked as if she would faint. "I have never had such a chance, but no matter. Now come. We have too much to get you ready."

By the time Messalina was bathed, oiled, combed, and seated before her vanity, she had managed to comprehend what was happening. Alexius actually *wanted* her at his side with the most powerful people of Herculaneum present. Thoughts of doubt attempted to dispel her growing excitement.

Was this Vespasian's idea? No. The emperor could not know she even existed.

Balbus? She wanted to laugh. She was nothing to Rosa's father.

Rosa? Would she be there with Pomponius?

Or, was Alexius just being polite? Proper? Did he really want her there? She recalled the smile beaming from his face during the parade. The defensive wall she had raised against her betrothed seemed to crack.

"More ocher, Mira," Octavia said.

Her mother's personal slave woman sat the red powder down on the table and reached for the eyeliner. Messalina noticed the flash of disgust in the slave woman's eyes. "Mother, I do not want to look painted any more than I already am. Please." The subtle agreement on Mira's face only solidified Messalina's determination.

Octavia waved for the woman to obey. "Venus forgive me, you know nothing of fashion, Messalina. You will look absolutely pale around the other women. Mira…"

"No." Messalina set her hand over the jar. "Mother, please, for once let me decide for myself."

Attending slaves backed to the walls as her mother swelled with indignation. Messalina met the distress with a cold stubborn glare that seemed to last an eternity.

"Well, then, fine." Octavia looked up at her slave woman. "I leave her to you, Mira. See that she does not embarrass her father's house."

"Yes, domina," Mira said, swallowing a grin.

Once her mother was gone, victory surged through Messalina's veins. After washing her face of her mother's designs, Messalina basked in her new freedom.

"Yes, the sky-blue tunica. I want the tiara. No, not the pearl one, the gold. Those slippers. A little more blue eye shadow."

Her fingernails were buffed, eyelashes darkened, and eyebrows plucked. Her lips smoothed with blushing gels. Her face dusted very lightly with powder. Each touch was met with a glance of approval from Mira.

Slaves drew a white chemise up her body first, and then the sky-blue silk was pinned at her shoulders with small ornate hooks. A silk dark blue, silk belt encircled around her waist, and then a long dark blue silk palla was drawn over her shoulder, swept low in perfect folds around her, lifted up to her left shoulder, and pinned with a pearl-encrusted brooch.

Her hair, now brushed, combed, curled on hot rods—as if there were any need of more curls— was braided and arranged with hairpins topped with delicate golden birds and butterflies. Finally, Mira eased the gold tiara into place.

Another of her mother's slaves approached. "Your mother asks if you wish to wear the blue topaz jewelry this evening."

The blue topazes. Even more excitement erupted through Messalina. "Yes. Yes, of course."

Feeling Mira latch the gold, double-chain necklace with pear-shaped topazes around her neck felt glorious.

Messalina slipped the matching earrings that dangled now on each ear. She expected that, at any moment she would awaken, all would vanish, and she would be making porridge for Hector in some apartment building.

Mira leaned forward and sniffed each side of her neck, each pulse point of her wrist, and the curve of her elbows for the fragrance of lilies that Didius had made for her. Only then did the slave woman truly smile. "You are now ready to meet the emperor, domina."

Messalina's mind froze as she stepped from the garden into the massive atrium. Tears filled her mother's gaze as Messalina walked across the black and white flooring tiles toward her father's tablinum. Her father stood, gawking at her as if she were a stranger. Claudius stopped playing with Bru, fully stunned. Antonia's mouth gaped open wide enough to catch flies.

Only Alexius moved. He stood up from his chair before her father's desk and walked to her, radiant in his white toga and tunic. "Messalina." The sound of her name floated on the gentlest breeze filled with a sweet fragrance of honey.

Alexius enjoyed the expressions on everyone's face as he led Messalina through Balbus's atrium toward the back gardens. All eyes locked on them as if he were escorting Venus herself.

"Welcome, Alexius. Messalina," Balbus said as he and Volasennia hurried forward.

"Thank you for asking us to join you, Balbus. It is an honor," Alexius said as he handed a wine goblet to Messalina and then took one for himself.

"Ah, how could we not invite the imperial favorites? Come, join us." Balbus waved them back through the peristyle garden where other guests milled. He stepped beside Alexius. "I hear great things about your election."

"I am pleased. The election does seem to be going well. Yet, there is always more to be accomplished."

"Receiving recognition from Caesar will help, no doubt," Volasennia added with a proper smile toward Messalina.

Alexius nodded. "May the gods help me not disappoint his judgment, domina."

Introductions were made to the various guests. Sulla and Agrippina greeted them formally. Meaningless talk came from senators of the Augustalus. Pomponius stood by the far railing that overlooked the ravine, alone and ignored.

"I thought Rosa would be here tonight," Messalina asked, as she looked for her friend in the milling throng.

Volasennia sighed sympathetically. "Oh, she is resting at Sulla's villa. She remains quite weak."

"Is it serious?" Messalina asked.

Balbus cast one of his condescending glances. "No. Nothing serious. Pomponius has the best medics looking after her."

Despite having been on that very terrace a thousand times, to Messalina, this seemed like the first. Fear followed with every step, afraid she would embarrass Alexius or herself. Never had so many stared at her…and smiled.

Guests and conversation meandered about the elegant garden until trumpets near the steps sang out and Vespasian appeared wearing a rich red tunic bordered with gold laurel leaves. "Greetings to all," he announced.

His attention danced across the faces before him and settled on Messalina, along with a smile. "Alexius, what a prize you have with you," he said as he walked toward them, parting the sea of onlookers. "How lovely you are, Messalina Claudia."

She bowed properly. "Thank you, your Excellency. It is an honor to dine with you." Alexius's fragrance of sandalwood, sage, and pine drifted close, assuring Messalina of his presence.

"Well, I am sure that once Alexius is elected, I will see you quite often on the Palatine. It will be a pleasure having you." Vespasian claimed her hand, placing it on his wrist to lead her into the garden of statues. "Now tell me, when is the wedding date so I can make plans to attend?"

The most powerful person in the world had just claimed her hand and said he would attend their wedding. "13 September, Your Excellency."

"I do believe I hear a twinge of excitement in your voice, my dear," the emperor continued as they walked. "So many young dominas seem discontent with the choices their parents make for them."

"I am sure their concern is for our happiness." *So many lies lately.* Her parents' concern had nothing to do with her or Alexius's happiness.

The emperor stopped at the foot of Jupiter's statue. The milling guests encircled like an approaching tide. Vespasian motioned for wine. A clever smile lingered on his lips. "I have no doubt that Alexius will make you quite content in Rome, since I intend to see that his election will be very successful."

"He will be most grateful for your support."

"The fact he is working so hard for his success impresses me greatly." Vespasian said, enjoying the wine. "We need more young men like him."

Maybe Alexius was truly working for their future and not just enjoying his time there. And, regardless of what he had done to her in the past as they grew up, she knew how much Rome meant to him—a certainty as sure as the sun rising each day. "I can assure you that Alexius only wants the best for the people of Rome."

The emperor's scowling face brightened considerably. "As you will be the model wife who understands the sacrifice of his position." Vespasian glanced at Alexius and presented her hand to him. "I have kept her from you long enough."

Alexius placed her hand on his arm, resting his palm over her fingers with the comfort of a homing pigeon returning to its nest.

"She is a rare gem, Alexius. Do not lose her or her respect, and I can promise you a most successful career in the Senate."

"I will honor those words, your Excellency." A smile gleamed in Alexius's eyes, tempting her to believe him.

Alexius led her away like a drifting leaf in a pond of jealous smiles and approving nods. He greeted many. Introduced some. She let him deal with everyone, smiled politely, and answered questions as if this were a common occurrence. Fortunately, his hand never left the top of hers resting on his arm supporting her, because her heart had stopped, and her knees threatened to melt.

They found his parents standing by a blue fishpond. Galerius chuckled as he made a small private toast. "You have all but won your election just now, Alexius."

"I take no credit for that, Father. I believe Messi managed it for me."

"You may be right." Galerius's gaze sparkled with pride as he turned his attention to her. "Did I hear that Vespasian wishes to attend the wedding?"

There still was not enough air to breathe even on the terrace. "Yes."

Aurelia beamed up at her husband. "Then, I will arrange for a special invitation." She looked at Messalina. "Or would you prefer to arrange this?"

Messalina's heart thundered in her rib cage. "I think it best you do so. I know nothing about such things."

"Ah, but you will soon enough, my dear." Aurelia drew her away as questions and compliments on the coming election sprang up like weeds around Alexius and his father.

Unlike her own mother who managed to impose herself on every element of life, Alexius's mother remained softer, while still maintaining a commanding presence that Messalina had always felt drawn to. And soon enough, Messalina caught herself chatting, smiling, and complimenting the wives who had gathered around her like bees to honey. She had no more than begun to relax when the dinner gong sounded, and everyone began meandering toward the formal triclinium filled with couches covered with purple for the honored guests.

Just outside this formal dining area were groupings of dining couches draped with green and set according to rank and privilege. Personal slaves stood at the assigned couch, indicating where each guest was to recline. Both Niki and Fosco stood by the loungers placed just below the step into the triclinium—a step below the honored guests.

Messalina followed Alexius's parents and stood beside Sulla, Agrippina, and another member of the Augustalus and his wife. Nothing was touched until trumpets sounded and Vespasian reappeared, escorting Balbus's mother to the honored seating. Balbus and Volasennia followed with Rosa's sister and her husband.

Wine filled the ornate glass goblets. Silver trays of honeyed dormice and softly boiled eggs filled the small, ebony tables placed before their loungers. However, only after the honored guests reclined, did everyone settle on their couches, having their hands washed, could they indulge in the presentations. Slaves scurried about filling goblets. Off by the terrace railing, Pomponius blatantly simmered with fury with a group of little-known senators and their wives. A lute played somewhere.

Messalina gazed around the marbled room where she and Rosa had often played with their dolls or dropped pebbles on the boys racing through the ravine below. It all seemed so strange now, so deliciously foreign. She listened, responded, and ate carefully, feeling the weight of everything pressing down on her like boulders. There was nothing childish about the conversations; even in jest, all words seemed carefully spoken, each measured for its effect.

"Where is Marcus?" she whispered to Alexius. His fragrance drifted over her, luring her closer.

"I have no idea. But he will pay for escaping." His gaze warmed through her. "Messi, I am glad you came tonight."

She had to look away. "I cannot believe I am here. It is all so different."

"Wait until you see some of the houses in Rome." Alexius offered her a fresh strawberry. "Or the imperial palaces."

She accepted the fruit instead of eating it from his fingers even though the thought tempted her. "You have been to the palace?"

Alexius nodded as he ate a dormouse. The delicate glaze of honey lingered deliciously on his lips. "A few times, with Cornelius."

The golden glow of at least a thousand oil lamps blanketed the soft music, spouting poets, floating dancers, and clumsy dwarfs. A fanfare halted everything as the chef's prize appeared, and Messalina's heart died.

On a huge silver platter filled with honeyed fruit lay the roasted neighborhood peacock still wearing its feathers. The cooks had raised the peacock's tail as she had seen a thousand times on her own terrace.

Each morning this bird had greeted her father before flying off for yet another house. Her father had been grumbling about not seeing his little friend lately. She could never bring herself to tell him that ten slaves wearing matching colors now paraded the cooked cock through the dining hall.

Watered wine and food began flowing from the kitchen: stuffed cabbages, red mullets drowning in creamy sauces, lobsters stuffed with asparagus tips, peas to spear with pointed spoons, peppery meats and mushrooms, breads and cheeses. The flavors were more varied than the houses of Herculaneum.

After the meal, Vespasian raised a toast to each man according to rank, and thus started a drinking game among the men he addressed. Pomponius was not included. Following the status established by the emperor, each man rose and individually toasted each man above him up to the Emperor. The match ended with the last man recognized—Alexius.

He rose to toast each of the fifteen men in order up to Caesar himself. Swaying on his feet, Alexius turned to Vespasian. With a heavy drunken sigh and grasping Fosco's shoulder to stabilize himself, he lifted his goblet. "Hail Rome, from a man about to die."

He slumped down beside Messalina, laying there like a wet cloth. The room exploded with laughter. Grinning, Galerius motioned to Fosco to take his son to the lavatory.

"I'll s-see her h-home," Alexius demanded as Fosco and Galerius helped him to the awaiting litter.

Alexius was so pathetically adorable standing there, not as elegant and perfect as he had been all evening. His white tunic and toga draped askew, spattered here and there with blotches of wine. His laurel crown had slipped, and his hair dangled boyishly over his eyebrows. His gaze even reminded her of their guard dog Maximus when he was taunted with one of Antonia's treats. "Messi, my s-swan, may I see you h-home?"

"Fosco will see her home," his father assured with a grin. "And we will see you home."

"N-No. I insist. I insist. I'll...I'll see Messi home... myself." Alexius managed to slide onto the litter and settled beside her. Then he managed to motion to drop the side curtain.

The moment the litter began to move, he propped his head on his hand and smiled down at her with a not so drunken smile. "Did you enjoy yourself, my swan?"

"I thought you were drunk?"

"Not as much as everyone thinks. Still, I do not appreciate the sway of the litter at the moment." He grinned a little carelessly. "Did you enjoy tonight, Messi? I know I did. Because you were here. With me. I have missed you."

He what? No. Did he really? "I only wish Rosa had been here," she said to calm her heart suddenly dancing on her rib cage.

"She will be." Alexius sighed heavily again. "You know we will have many more invitations after the election. After we are married." He studied her. His head slipped off his hand. He repositioned it. "You do want to marry me, don't you?"

She watched the curtains sway with each step. All those years growing up, she had adored him. Then, when he nicknamed her 'Medusa' in front of everyone and her heart had died. She then proceeded to build a wall between them. Tearing that protection down terrified her.

"I don't…"

Before she could finish, his lips found hers, soft and warm, stunning her senseless. He drew back with a grin. "Please, don't run away with Hector. He will cheat on you. He has already, you know." His hand brushed the side of her cheek. "Lizbet. I have seen him with her at the Max."

A spark of anger ignited in her veins. Should she really care? No. Nor, for some reason, that failed to surprise her. The detail actually released her from the idea of running away with Hector now.

Alexius lay back on the cushion and staring up at the blue drape. He rose up on his arm to look at her. "I am sorry…for all the stupid things I did back then. Will you forgive me?"

"No. Never." She fought the grin teasing her lips. However, she may reconsider if he continued to deliciously grovel.

His gaze was half-mast as he continued. "Messi, please. I will not cheat on you, Messi. Never…sons of Dis and Jupiter!" He leaned to the side curtain. "Slow down."

The litter settled on the pavestones.

"I did not mean stop!"

"Yes, dominus," Fosco said from the other side of the drapery. "But we are at the House of Claudius."

"Oh." Alexius melted down beside her, less than victorious.

"Niki." Messalina called. When the girl pulled the curtain aside, Messalina started to stand.

Alexius caught her wrist. "Wait." He tugged her back inside. "Never? You won't forgive me, never?"

She swallowed a giggle and tried to look ever so serious. "Never. Now, go home."

His hand held. "Messi, everything will be just fine. Do you believe me, Messi?"

She nodded, wanting to.

"Good." He lifted her hand to his lips and kissed the back of her fingers. "Good."

The second Messalina entered her bedroom a giggle wiggled its way out of her. She gazed at the departing gift given to all the women—a delicate ivory box—as the entire night danced before her.

Of course, her parents had been waiting for her the instant she came inside. Her mother gushed over the gift box as if it had come from Jupiter himself. She had calmed enough to answer questions that seemed never ending and then escaped to relish each moment again.

Mira stood from her corner chair. "So, it was a good evening, domina?"

"Nothing has ever been more wonderful."

It was almost impossible to stand still while Mira directed slaves to remove her mother's jewelry, the tunica, brush her hair, and wash the make-up from her face.

She almost ordered them not to touch one thing, to let her remain that way forever. Instead, she relished her new freedom from Hector as if bathed clean. The memory of Alexius's hand sliding along her cheek trickled through her with the image of him dropping him back to the cushions with a groan. "Never? You won't forgive me, never?"

She giggled as her night tunic dropped over her head. "Never."

Once freed from the busy hands, Messalina swirled around and around and flopped on her bed. Sleep evaded her. Her mind was too dizzy with details of the night. Still, she replayed each occurrence. First, it was everyone smiling at her…no, at her and Alexius.

She gazed at the hand that had rested on the emperor's wrist—Vespasian! Flesh and blood—the most powerful man in the world! He had smiled down on her as if Jupiter had done so. Their little discussion echoed in her brain…

"I do believe I hear a twinge of excitement in your voice… So many young girls seem discontent with their parent's choices for them.

"I am sure their concern is for our happiness."

"I see that you will be the model wife who understands the sacrifice…She is a gem.

"Do not lose her…"

Messalina sprang to her feet as if splashed with cold water. She was not a model wife!

The single flickering candle seemed to be closing in around her. The air suffocating. She ran out and down the back stairs to the terrace. The silver moon rose brilliant across the restless waves. The diamond stars danced in a black velvet sky. A perfect night after a perfect evening.

It was all a lie. It would not be perfect.

"I am sorry…for all the stupid things I did… I will not, Messi. Never. Please do not run away… You still want to marry me, don't you?"

Did he mean any of what he said? Was he lying? Had Hector cheated on her? After all, he had fooled everyone else, letting them think he was drunk. She turned away from the bay, letting the terrace wall support her. She remembered his head sliding off his hand and watching him prop it up again and his hair sticking up through his fingers. *"I won't, Messi. Never."*

The closest table supported her as she gasped for air. Images of Alexius throughout the night resurfaced like taunting dolphins: when he stood as she came into the atrium, when he was walking behind her and the emperor, when they were eating, talking with guests. His gaze had been brilliant.

She had seen that same expression on his face a thousand times before: when he gave her the amber jewelry at his welcome home party, each time he returned from Rome, when they had returned from Sicilia. She had also seen it throughout the years growing up, right before he…

No. He was drunk. And, the kiss earlier did not count either. Well, maybe it did. Could he really mean anything of what he said? On the other hand, as before, was Alexius just biding time before he crushed her heart again?

She sat. Fortunately, the chair remained in place.

Shadows danced on the terrace wall as Maximus came waddling through the arch, as if to check on her. He nuzzled under her lifeless hand that automatically began stroking the short hairs down his back. Long slow strokes.

"Maximus, I don't know." Tears blurred her eyes as she looked down into the worried brown gaze looking up at her. "What do I do?"

Her answer was one long slurp of a wet tongue along her arm.

CHAPTER 19

ALEXIUS WATCHED MESSALINA and her family climb the hill to Sulla's villa. She bent down to listen to Antonia, displaying thousands of loose curls streaming down her back. Claudius saw him on the terrace and waved. He said something to Messi. She looked up for a brief second and then gazed out at the restless sea.

The way the sunrays lit Messi's face stirred every nerve in his body along with every memory of the previous night. By the gods, he hoped he had not made a total ass of himself. However, he may have because he could not remember anything he had said.

Images of her floated back into his mind- seeing her walk into her parents' atrium, the look in Vespasian's gaze when the emperor saw them together, and the entire gathering of guests turning to one another to whisper. Messalina seemed oblivious to the fact that she had caused such a stir, especially among the women.

That morning, his mother had laughed as their galley crossed to Sulla's pier. "They all but swallowed their tongues."

Alexius sat on the terrace wall, his thoughts returning to the galley crossing. After he and his father had barely returned from the arduous morning rituals with the emperor, Aurelia hurried them to the galley to arrive at Sulla's villa early. She said that Balbus's wife had been working for weeks, garnering contributions from every wealthy house in Herculaneum to help repair the crumbling temples. All those who contributed received a special tour of the villa.

His mother had wanted to donate the bathing tube Alexius had given to his father when he had returned from Britannia. However, his father had refused, which surprised Alexius. He thought he was the only one enjoying the private soaks. Therefore, his mother had contributed a set of silver wine goblets and Egyptian pottery she no longer liked, garnering a special tour of the villa.

Alexius had refused the tour because he knew the villa well enough. He had spent a great deal of time with Cornelius there. Besides, he wanted to wait on the sun-filled terrace for Messalina.

Alexius's heart stopped the instant she appeared on the terrace. His amber jewelry gleamed against her dark green tunica. That wondrous collection of curls poured from behind the silver tiara emblazoned by a large amber jewel.

"Where's Galerius?" Messalina's father asked as he appeared, scanning the line of people strolling about the garden terrace overlooking the bay.

"Mother has him on the tour."

"I pity him."

"Why? You are going." Octavia asked. "Antonia!"

Claudius immediately found his friends and disappeared. Alexius stepped aside for the slaves to remove the litter and found Messalina staring out at the seascape. He joined her. "Beautiful isn't it?"

"Yes. It is," She said to the throbbing water.

Dis! No doubt, he had embarrassed himself last night. Only the gods know what he had said to Messalina. His father had told him what he said to Vespasian.

"Messalina, I—"

"Alexius, my boy, how is that election going?" A man he had never seen before hurried close. "Heard you dined with the emperor last night. That should settle your election, with Vespasian on your side."

"Yes, we enjoyed the evening," Alexius said, hoping that was true. He glanced at Messalina who smiled to the man. "I hope I continue to please the emperor. Thank you."

The man waved more friends over and began introducing them. Alexius managed to listen as if interested, trying to remember their names. Fosco remained behind him in case he failed.

Messalina touched his arm. He jolted as if stung. "I am going to see if Rosa is here." She looked up at him with a gaze that felt deeper than the bay. She nodded to the small crowd around them. "Excuse me, please."

Without even a breath, the group let Messalina escape while entrapping Alexius with their senseless verbiage. As hard as he tried, he could not make sense of what these men were saying, other than they were voting for him. Yes, Rome needed young blood; yes, new blood; yes, whatever blood in the Senate. Jupiter knows how the Senate needed new blood, something to shake things up a bit. Yes to it all.

Marcus appeared on the shaded porch by the balcony. "Ah, there is someone I have to see," Alexius exclaimed and smiled as if they had become lifetime friends. "Be sure to let me know what I can do to help you in the future." He hurried away as if on fire and up the two steps. "Have you seen Messi?"

Marcus nodded. "She is out in the main garden with her friends, talking, I believe, about your evening last night." He nodded. "Did yourself proud, I hear."

Alexius grimaced and then washed it from his face, as another supporter noticed him and assured him that he had gleaned yet another vote. "Where were you last night?" he asked his friend.

"Drunk and passed out on Sabrina's bed, as far from that dinner as I could manage." They both saw people start walking toward them. "Come on, I know a place to hide."

Marcus led him along the outer garden full of herbs and vegetables, obviously plucked clean for the dinner that evening. They passed a wall fountain spewing water into a shallow pool. A few people wandered into the secluded areas off each side, places he would like to be with Messalina instead of Marcus. However, no one was assaulting him with promises and questions at least.

"Well, did you enjoy the night with your betrothed?" Marcus asked as he stopped by the pump house busily whispering water back into the villa.

"Yes. Yet I think I made a fool of myself on the way home." Alexius studied the rear balcony, hoping to see Messalina there.

"The future senator of Rome made a fool of himself? How?"

Alexius slumped against the stonewall. "I must have said something. Messi is barely talking to me."

"I am sure you will get her back into the proper graces." Marcus looked up, curiously. "Mother was impressed. I am not sure about my father. He grumbled all morning about how you and your betrothed were all the emperor could talk about in some way or another."

"I do not care about that right now," Alexius said. He added a serious glance at his friend. "I just want to know what I said that upset her."

Marcus laughed. "I do believe, my friend, you would give up this election to have her."

"I would consider it."

"You idiot. No girl is worth that."

Alexius failed to share the humor. He could still hear Messi bragging to Vespasian about him. "I assure you that, Alexius only wants the best for the people of Rome."

"She is worth it, Marcus. Now excuse me. I have to find her."

"I hope you don't eat too many words…or, at least, may they be sweet."

Thick, flowering vines clung from the second-story arbor over the balcony, filling the air with sweet perfumes. Alexius walked back into the villa from the far end of the long pool where he and Cornelius used to swim laps. People were as dense there as the shrubbery surrounding the many statues that Agrippina had collected over the years. He used to count them from the second-story balcony of the guest bedroom.

He scoured the crowds for Messalina, remembering the night he had found her in Zeno's stairway. This was harder now since women wore every color of the rainbow as they mingled among the dining couches for the evening dinner and auction.

He finally found her staring up at a bust of some Greek. "Who is that?" he asked, drawing her sober attention from the statue.

"Zeno…of Sidon." She looked again at the statue. "I wonder if he is any relation to Zeno."

He drew closer, inhaling her lily fragrance that had carried him off to sleep in the litter. "I suppose it is possible. Messi, I am sorry about whatever I said last night."

She glanced up at him and then continued toward the long impluvium protected by the bronze maidens. "Are you sure you should be?" she asked.

"No."

A small smile teased her lips. It tickled through him. A sense of play relaxed him. Her eyes sparkled before she turned her attention to the busy eels in the water.

"Your eloquent speech last night did seem to please everyone. They laughed for some time."

Fear of ruining the moment clotted in his throat. However, he had to get rid of the misery eating at him. "I had to toast everyone."

She stopped by a huge Grecian urn on a pedestal. "I know."

"Messalina, I know I said some stupid things. I didn't mean anything—"

She looked at him through thick eyelashes. "You truly don't remember?"

He shook his head. "Actually, no. Are you mad?"

She raised her eyebrows and continued her stroll past the bronze maidens. He followed like an idiot. He must have said something ludicrous.

"I know it must have been…outrageous."

She moved on to a fat vase as big as Pomponius.

"Messi, tell me. What…what did I say? Tell me that much." For a breath, he thought she might tell him.

"No. I can't repeat it."

Alexius had become her shadow, seemingly determined to correct whatever he could not remember. Yet she remained stalwart in her resolution to torture him until he did. It itched that he did not mean most of what he had said, or that he was sorry for naming her 'Medusa'. However, watching him grovel was so delicious.

A group of wives fawning for his attention drew Alexius away. What woman would not fawn over him? He appeared too perfect: handsome, attentive, and caring. On the other hand, was he trying to win her vote, as he was those women, giving them his undivided attention?

Well, she knew him. She had grown up with him. She had now seen him imperfect. His hair messed up. Pleading like Max over a treat. Even drunk. Were his confessions more honest that way than if he had said it sober?

After last night, she knew that she did not want to be an actor's wife and live in Subura. She wanted to be like Aurelia, a senator's wife. However, Alexius was not the only one running for the senate. What if he didn't get elected? That thought had occurred to her more than once. Then the question arose, once he had her dowry, would he change?

The old fear crept over her like a fog. If she did not marry Alexius, as before, it would be her parents making that decision for her. Bona Dea! What if it was a fat senator like Pomponius?

Chapter 20

THE FRAGRANCE OF rose floated in the misted air as Alexius directed Messalina though the dining couches where both families were settling. Alexius stretched himself down beside her as her father, mother, and Aurelia reclined across from them. Galerius shared the honored couch with his long-time friends Lucius Calpurnis Piso and his wife.

Instead of listening to Piso's exposition on how his father had sold this very villa to Agrippina's family, Messalina scanned the gathering for Rosa. Excitement pulsed everywhere, in the chatter, dress, and faces of all those invited. It rippled over her. How could Rome be more thrilling?

Alexius adjusted an arm cushion for better comfort. Then his bare foot brushed against her ankle. She flinched at the contact of flesh against flesh. His foot immediately moved away as he continued to answer Piso's questions.

Curiosity tickled a new interest. What if…? She brushed her foot along his ankle. He choked on his wine and looked at her. She met his scrutiny without removing her foot, almost daring him to withdraw. One side of his mouth curled up as he drew his foot closer and returned to the history lesson.

Eating became a delicate exercise when Alexius had decided to play as well. Messalina lifted her wine goblet and smugly drank as her toes raked down the baby soft skin along the top his foot. He nearly choked on the egg.

The sound of two trumpets halted the foot play and silenced the excited chatter. All attention turned to the entrance. Everyone stood for the arrival of the emperor and his guests. Alexius's gaze simmered as he offered his hand to help Messalina up from their couch.

She tore her attention away to the honored triclinium where Vespasian settled with Sulla and Agrippina, Balbus and Volasennia, the witch Viciria, and Pomponius and *Rosa*.

Messalina gripped Alexius's arm. "Rosa! She is here." She wanted to race to her friend and touch her to be sure she was real.

Alexius studied the honored guests with a cool gaze. "She looks better. Stronger since the wedding."

Alexius was right. Rosa did not look as sick or as thin. Messalina's heart leaped in her chest. The ribbon that carried Zeno's pendant now hung around her neck, dangling the pendant below the neckline of her golden stola.

"I cannot imagine what illness she has endured," Aurelia said as everyone resettled on the dining couches. She moved a platter of stuffed dormice and mushrooms closer to Piso as more entrees covered the table before them. "She has lost so much weight."

Piso smiled as he reached for a mushroom. "The girl does seem to have gained some weight. Although she will never carry a child being that thin."

"I believe Pomponius is only interested in her family's name," Messallus said, shifting back on his arm pillow to drink wine. "Since he had four sons by his previous wives."

"Weren't his sons killed in the East under the Flavians' leadership?" Galerius asked as he poked the tip of his spoon into a simmering clam. "These are good."

"Yes. You are right. I believe they were," her father said, munching on a celery stalk filled with olive paste.

"Fine young men. A bit self-possessed, I suppose," Piso said with a sigh. "Nevertheless, good examples of Rome's best youth. Had you met them, Alexius?"

"No, I have not." The abrupt answer came as Messalina caressed her toes along his instep. "How…ever, I heard about them."

She grinned into her wine.

Soft music and waves of trays full of elegant foods continued: stuffed goose, milk-roasted piglets, vegetables simmering in fruit sauces and cheeses, fruits decorated in relishes and coated with honey, and breads folded in shapes of animals and trees, along with an endless parade of slaves washing guests' sticky or grimy hands.

After the sunset, Volasennia's auction began under the glow of thousands of small torches and oil lamps that bathed a golden aura over the evening. The city's auctioneer stood before the formal triclinium as slaves paraded Volasennia's plunder about the portico. When someone bid, a slave shouted toward the auctioneer. There were times the shouts sounded like an avalanche of rocks; at other times, the shouts were like lonely owl calls.

Octavia stunned everyone when she bid against Volasennia for an ornate silver fruit bowl, running up the price to well over the value of a beautiful slave. Piso and Galerius grinned at Messallus as he stared in shock at his wife.

"You can afford it, Messallus," Piso said with delight. "You have another galley arriving soon"

"It will all go to pay for that damn bowl," her father barked back.

Nothing fazed her mother. The women bid like gladiators. Then Octavia shook her head, letting Volasennia gain the prize. "Now, let Volasennia help pay for something for once," Octavia gloated.

Messalina noticed that Rosa had left, which meant only one thing—she was alone somewhere in the villa. "Excuse me, please." She felt Alexius's intense gaze as she slipped back into her sandals and departed.

The melodic noise of the lively auction followed her as she strolled the quiet rooms and found Rosa seated on a bench in the covered walkway and staring into the inkwell of the sea. A gaggle of slaves surrounded her like soft statues. As if called, Rosa turned

Messalina broke into a run, tears bursting the instant she felt Rosa's bony arms surround her. She pulled back to study the marriage part in Rosa's hair and her stola bordered with silver embroidery that signified she was a married woman.

"Rosa. Oh Rosa, I have missed you. They will not allow me to write you. Why? "A million questions fought to be spoken.

"Because they still read everything, Messi. Everything." Rosa brushed Messalina's cheek with a kiss. "I have missed you so much."

Messalina swiped tears from her friend's bony cheek. "Why are they doing this to you?"

Rosa drew Messalina to the bench. Hatred flashed in her eyes. "He is insane, Messi. I hate him. I exist for only one day…the day he dies. It will come, Messi. I know it." Rosa fingered the ribbon dangling around her neck. "I will not let him have this ever again. It is my only hope."

"You can walk with me, can't you?" Messalina asked, wanting to be away from the meandering crowd also escaping the auction.

"Yes, but…" Rosa flashed a furious glare at the hovering slaves. "They follow me everywhere."

They found a bench on the back veranda, not far from the soft sound of the distant pump house shushing water through pipes. Rosa sighed, resting her head on Messalina's shoulder. "Messi, this is the first sense of freedom I have known since that day in September when…" Rosa halted. "I forgot how fresh and clean the air is here."

Messalina remembered feeling the baby move—the baby that was born, exposed, or saved by the gods. "I cannot believe that all that time you were here in this villa, this close."

"I might as well have been in Britannia. At least, it was not filled with his odors, like I have to endure in Rome." Rosa sucked in the fresh air. "I never want to smell garlic or garum ever again." She waved at the slaves to back away. "They try to mask it with oils that only putrefy on his skin. Some days, I simply want to die, Messi. Be rid of this burden."

Messalina glanced at Rosa's belly. "You are not—"

"No," Rosa snapped. A sneer appeared on her face that once laughed with so much life and joy. "He has quit mounting me. He hates me as much as I hate him now. He has his power, and I have nothing."

"You will always have me." She gripped her friend's hands. "Rosa, I miss you. I want to talk for hours, go shopping like we used to, and laugh."

For a long precious moment, they gazed into each other's eyes, reading thoughts. "I want that too, Messi." A once familiar smile emerged on Rosa's lips. "Do you still want to run away with Hector?"

Messalina looked toward the shadows of the distant bay where burning torches on the awaiting galleys dotted the black sea below. "No."

Rosa gasped. "Do you want to marry Alexius now?"

"I don't know. That is why I need you, Rosa. There is no one else to talk to." Messalina stopped to breathe. "Alexius, he has…changed. He is not calling me 'Medusa'. Instead, he calls me his swan. He even said he was sorry about all that he did, even if he was drunk when he said it." She sighed and looked away. "Do you think I can I trust him?"

Rosa gathered Messalina's hand into hers. "Yes. I think you can…now. Maybe you are the lucky one. I heard his election is going very well in his favor.

"Yes, I suppose."

"That is good, Messi. That way we will be in Rome together. I will demand Pomponius let me see you."

Memories of all those times shopping together there in Herculaneum danced in Messalina's memory. "We will go shopping as we used to. We will…"

Slaves swarmed in like locusts when life seemed to evaporate in her friend's hands. "Domina, we will see to her care," a male slave said as he lifted Rosa in his arms as if she was as delicate as porcelain. Another blocked Messalina from following.

She melted back to the bench. They were killing Rosa and there was nothing she could do to save her. Tears poured into her hands.

CHAPTER 21

ALEXIUS FOUND MESSALINA sobbing. The sight of it shredded his soul. He sat on the bench and drew her to him. He had seen Rosa's limp body carried away in the slave's arms.

"He is killing her."

He brushed her face with his palm. "No, Messi. Pomponius would gain nothing if he did. She is tired, Messi. She will be fine."

"She hates him."

"She is not the only one."

Tear-swollen eyes pleaded up at him as guests strolled by. He had to get Messi away from their curious gazes and vicious tongues. "Come with me, Messi," he whispered, drawing her to her feet. "Niki, Fosco, stay here."

The two slaves remained on the veranda as Alexius led Messalina into the back garden surrounded by thick blooming oleander. The air filled with the heavy scents of sea, moss, and flowers. Sounds of pumping water whispered near a tree full of cicadas and tree frogs in full voice. Occasionally, an owl hooted from the overhanging trees. Their footsteps silenced in the soft thyme as he drew her along a pathway into a hidden area with only room for a stone bench. Her large mahogany eyes looked up at him, glistening with latent tears. "I am afraid she will die before—"

"She won't, Messi," he said, drying her tears with his fingers. "Zeno will come for her, soon."

Messalina shook her head, sweeping those curls across his forearms. "No. I heard Zeno's ran away."

"He did." Marcus had told him that before dinner. They sat on the bench as the faint sounds of the auction drifted on the night breezes.

"That may explain the many slaves around Rosa."

He was drowning in the fragrance of lily and the moonlight dancing on her face. "What slaves?"

"They cluster around Rosa like vultures." Messalina looked at the thick bushes blocking the view of the garden walkway. She turned to look at him. "She refuses to take Zeno's pendant off."

Alexius wanted a lifetime to gaze at the small diamonds lingering in Messalina's lashes. "Then she will live, Messi."

He brushed a strand of hair from her face and let his fingers sink into those wondrous curls. "Messi, whatever I said last night upset you. I am sorry. I was a fool."

She studied his face as another tear ran its course down her cheek. She wiped it away. "You really don't remember, do you?"

Alexius shrugged and shook his head

"Do you really want to be with me at all?"

By the gods, what had he said? Alexius sat back and ran a hand through his hair. "Yes, Messi, if I said anything as ridiculous as that, I am a fool."

"Then, you truly want to marry me?"

His heart tripped. "By every god on Olympus, yes."

"Then why did you say that to Vespasian before everyone there?"

He was lost. "What did I say?"

"From a man about to die. Because you have to marry me?"

His gaze ran all over her face for some ounce of humor, some bad joke. "I said that?"

She shrugged. "Somewhat."

"Messi, I would die a happy man if I were married to you."

He could not believe her hand rose to his cheek and drew his mouth to hers. His mind spiraled with need as he feasted, tasting sweet wine and desire. He encircled her with his arms as her hands glided across his shoulders. Her head dropped back, exposing her throat to his lips.

"We have to talk."

"Why here?"

Demanding whispers cut through the darkness. Messalina jerked upright as Alexius pressed a finger to her kiss-swollen lips, both struggling to focus on the voices that rang familiar.

"Because I have to know."

"Know what?"

"When will it happen?"

A man and a woman. Too far away to determine who. And the bushes were too thick to see them.

"Before the Kalendae of July Vespasian will be a dead man."

Messalina's gaze froze on Alexius's face, as Flaccus's words echoed in his brain. *The fool bragged that it would be the Augusta and Cyrenaica who will soon be choosing the next emperor for Rome—"*

"You are sure?"

"You doubt me?"

"Me? Doubt you?"

There was a soft feminine chuckle.

"You shouldn't. Now, we have to go before we are seen."

The night sounds returned to fill the void. Messalina touched his arm and broke his gaze frozen on the thick shrubbery. "Not the emperor?"

CHAPTER 22

A BREEZE FULL OF fragrances from the flower-covered terrace drifted across Messalina's couch. Climbing rose blooms meandered through the arbor above her. Hanging pots of cascading pink petunias, white viburnums, and lavender mallow dripped from their recent watering. Cherry laurel bushes trailed over the railing to the lower sun-filled terrace filled with more pots of sage, basil, rosemary, marjoram, and thyme.

Messalina basked in it all, feeling more wonderful, more beautiful, than she had ever felt in her life. First, the reception, the dinner and then the garden. All night she had relived being with Alexius. She stroked her neck where his kisses still tingled. She licked her lips, sucked in her bottom lip. Even the heavy worry for Rosa lifted, along with the ridiculous idea that someone would try to assassinate Vespasian.

She thought of a million things she and Rosa would do once she and Alexius were married and living in Rome. Every nerve simmered beneath her skin as if he had just stroked her foot with his again.

"Trust him, Messi. Maybe he has changed."

"I would die a happy man married to you."

She felt like a bird ready to take flight. She languished in the sea-green cushion as every sensation Alexius awakened exploded to life again.

"Domina, you have a…"

Messalina turned to the slave and saw Alexius racing toward her. His eyes were aglow with excitement. Her heart soared as he tore the white toga off his shoulders and tossed it to the railing, leaving him in a plain white tunic that came just above his knees, strong legs, strong arms, perfect face with a radiant smile. He was Adonis personified.

"Alexius!" She rose to bolt into his arms, except he was already beside her.

"You have to be the first to know." He grabbed her hands and pulled her down to the couch with him. "I don't believe it myself, Messi."

Except when he had just been appointed to Agricola in Britannia, she had never seen him this excited. "What?"

"Vespasian wants me to return with him to Rome. Can you believe it? The imperial galley. He wants to hear more about Britannia and what I think about the legions there."

He was leaving. Already? The fact drained life out of her. They had planned to go walking into the countryside and spend time together before he returned to Rome. "But…but that means…"

"Vespasian asked me to go. It is…like a command, Messi." Excitement melted from his face as he gripped her hands. "I will be back for the Neptunalia games. I promise."

Messalina pulled her hands free and walked to the lower terrace, seeing the imperial galley resting in the water. "You know I don't care about those games."

Alexius followed, coming close enough that his fragrance surrounded her. Thoughts of entrapping him with her arms about his neck played in her mind. If she rose on her toes and found his lips would he stay? Would that work?

"Messi, you know how important this is to us." He ran his hands down her arms and turned her to him.

She dropped her gaze and watched her orange tunica ruffle against his ankles.

"Fine. I'll stay."

Her gaze shot up to his attention on the distant galley preparing to return to Rome. *He would? Stay?* Vespasian's words about the sacrifice for Rome resurfaced. She faked a brave smile. "Alexius, go. You need to. This is a wonderful opportunity for you." The words fell like rocks falling from her lips.

He leaned on the rail, studying her. "Are you sure?" His eyes again were that deep blue that seeped into her heart.

"Yes." She lifted her chin with the lie. "It will help your election to be seen with the emperor." She slid her hand down to the warm gold cuff that covered his wrist as if she meant what she said and tried to laugh. "I wouldn't probably see you even if you did stay. Someone here would keep you busy."

He pulled from the railing. "Messi, about what we heard last night—"

"No. We need to forget that." She faced him. "Now go. Vespasian is waiting for you." She pushed at his hand away, remembering how it had caressed her face. "Promise me you will find Rosa and give her a letter for me. Will you?"

"Marcus will if I can't."

Niki appeared with a tray of glasses full of sweetened lemon water and sweet biscuits with figs bulging from every side. Messalina motioned to set the tray on the table next to the couch. "Niki, bring my writing material."

The girl nodded and left as Alexius turned to the railing, like a legate, his face serious, his body taut. "Messi, I promise when I return, things will be different. It is just that—"

"I know, Alexius. I understand."

She stepped away from the railing, from him, detaching from her feelings as she had all these years. If she was to be the respected senator's wife, she had to understand the sacrifices whether she wanted to or not. And right now, she did not want to.

An excited crowd gathered on the beach as the imperial galley began its slow retreat. All waved as the brilliant oars began the slow rhythmical strokes, dipping and rising in the azure waters. Alexius searched Messalina's terrace, knowing she would not be one of those waving goodbye.

All he could think about was the night before and her drawing his lips to hers. She had looked at him with stars in her eyes. They died with the news of his leaving with Vespasian. And leaving had torn something between them like a scab that kept bleeding.

Messi was right. He had very little time to spend with her. When they were together, the election, parents, and everything else interrupted them. By the gods, he wished he could stay. If she had wrapped her arms around him, he could never have left her. He would have found some way to stay. At least she understood he had no choice. He had to think about their future, now more than ever.

Behind Alexius, the crew scurried about like busy rats, rolling ropes, and tying last minute cargo down. The gold sail rippled onward on the center mast. It caught a gust of wind and bellied out, heaving the galley forward through incoming waves. Seawater sprayed over the sides, washing the painted eyes on the bow. Mist carried in the air. Herculaneum was disappearing and so was Messalina.

An imperial slave appeared at his side. "Dominus, the emperor has asked that you join him."

Alexius followed the slave to the imperial tent set in the center of the main deck. Six purple loungers faced a broad, ebony table covered with delicious tidbits of cheeses and fresh fruit on silver trays

Vespasian reached for a handful of cherries. "Join us, Alexius. We want to pick that young head of yours about the Britannia."

Sulla and Balbus watched intently as Alexius walked across the thick wool rug to join his father.

Where was Marcus? They had boarded together. Seasick, probably, or pretending to be. Alexius reclined and reached for the one goblet left on the table. It contained chilled wine, which explained the fruity fragrance circling under the awning. "Yes, Your Excellency. All that I know is yours."

"Was it a good experience being laticlavius to Agricola?" Vespasian asked, reaching for a honeyed fig.

"Yes, it was."

Finally, he could get away. Somehow, he had managed to hold up under the barrage of questions about the three legions still in Britannia, about its commerce, and the tribes contending with Rome's presence. The subject had then changed to Germania, offering Alexius the opportunity to excuse himself and search for Marcus, only to find him sea-green with misery.

"Go away."

Back on the deck, Alexius walked about, admiring the view of land in the distance and the way the sun basked golden against the hills, mountains, and small villages. The waves were gentle and soothing.

"Apollo has granted us a magnificent day, has he not?"

Alexius turned as Balbus joined him at the polished black railing. "Yes. As Neptune has fair seas."

Balbus sucked in a deep breath and leisurely released it. "I have sailed these seas in Neptune's rage." He smiled over at Alexius. "It makes you appreciate such blessings as today."

Alexius looked out at the water. The presence of this man irritated like a festering splinter. "Definitely. We endured a major storm coming home from Britannia."

"Yes, I heard about that." Balbus ran a hand across the railing, his bulbous gold citizen's ring gleaming in the sunlight.

Seeing it made Alexius play with his own citizen's ring, the one his father had given him at the age of twelve when he had dawned his pretexta toga for the first time. It was much smaller, but Alexius preferred it that way. While with Agricola, he had heard that the legionaries judged the offi-cers by the size of this ring. The bigger the ring, the bigger the asshole. It seemed to be true.

A light breeze ruffled the senatorial toga around Bal-bus's legs. "You have a great future ahead of you, Alexius." The senator leaned on the railing as the deck dipped into a sweeping wave. "Not many young men receive such an opportunity to bask in the emperor's attention as you have, much less being appointed to the senate so early."

The man's expression reminded Alexius of a cat playing with a mouse. "Something I do not take lightly, dominus."

Balbus turned, rested his hands on the rail, and looked down at the waters shifting past. Soft drumbeats set the pace, commanding the oars to rise and fall with a 'shhhing' sound. The galley heaved smoothly forward.

"There are many pitfalls one must avoid while running for the Senate," Balbus said, as he watched the dolphins jumping alongside the galley. "Those very pitfalls can destroy a man as well as his entire career. And possibly his family's name." He looked over his shoulder. "I am sure you are aware of that, Alexius?"

Alexius's stomach sank to the deck, yet he nodded. "Of course. Life can be very unpredictable."

"That it can." Balbus turned and leaned on the railing, crossing his arms over his chest. "Just how serious are you, about avoiding those pitfalls?" His cold brown gaze searched Alexius's face for any weakness.

Alexius felt the probe and met the man's gaze. "Very serious, dominus."

Balbus smiled, not a friendly smile. "I have always considered you a very smart young man. I never doubted that you would follow your father's example." He gazed up at the billowing sail and then studied Alexius again. "I am sure you have heard that Zeno has run away."

Alexius managed to draw in a deep breath, letting it out slowly, as if enjoying the air. He braced both hands on the rail. "Marcus told me." He moved with the shifting galley and looked across to Balbus. "I am sure you have legions out looking for him."

"Oh, I do. I do." One light brown eyebrow lifted as the penetrating gaze continued its search for a crack. "I was hoping you could remember the vendor who sold you Zeno's pendant. I cannot seem to locate him."

Alexius shook his head and leaned on the railing as a vise clamped around his guts. "The vendors at the Max come and go like the pigeons. Since Zeno broke his arm, I am sure they have forgotten him by now." He studied at the passing clouds. "They are a fickle lot; which I am sure you know. Have you found another team as good as Zeno's blacks?"

Balbus turned to rest both hands on the deck, his knuckles blanched white. "Are you sure Zeno didn't give you the pendant?" he asked, eyes on the water.

"Zeno has given me nothing, dominus." And he had not. He gave it to Messalina. Alexius scanned the arrogant man observing the passing shoreline, biting back a mounting snarl. "What are you trying to say, dominus?"

Balbus dropped his gaze to the moving oars and then looked up with a black hard gaze. "Are you also aware of the cause of my daughter's illness?"

He endured the assault with one as equally hard. "All I know is that Messalina is very concerned about Rosa. She wishes me to give your daughter a letter when we get back to Rome. Will that be possible?"

Balbus blinked. "That is for Pomponius to say. Not me." He rose from the rail and stepped toward Alexius. "And so you know, I do not believe you. I think you do know the cause of Rosa's illness as well as where Zeno has gone."

Alexius stood from the railing, both hands held at his side. "Well, I do not know where he has gone or what ails your daughter. I just know Messalina is very concerned. Fortunately, someone cares." None of which was a lie… at least.

"She is Pomponius's concern now." Balbus returned to the railing with a snide grin. "Were you behind Vespasian claiming the financial records?"

"What?"

The steel in Alexius's voice caused Balbus to startle. The man's black gaze sliced the air between them. More than ever before, Alexius now knew why Marcus hated his father.

"Why would Pomponius think I would be involved with what happened that day? Unless, of course, someone wanted him to think that," Alexius answered. "Or unless Pomponius wants a scapegoat."

Balbus met his gaze as solidly as a hammer. "If I find you are lying about any of this, rest assured that I will see your future does not happen and that your family is destroyed."

"Then I have no worries about my future or my family's honor. Now excuse me, dominus."

Balbus fumed as he watched Alexius walk down the galley stairs. "I know the little piss ant is lying."

"Lying about what?" Sulla asked as he joined him by the railing.

"The necklace. The financial records. Galerius's pathetic spawn knows more than he is saying."

Sulla glanced at the empty galley stairs. "What makes you think Alexius knows anything?"

"Messallus's daughter. Their stories did not match at the wedding reception. Alexius said he gave her the pendant that he bought at the Max, and she said she bought it in Herculaneum. However, I had only one made for the fool to keep him winning." Balbus turned back to the railing. "I say Zeno gave it to that fool to give to Rosa."

"Your daughter has more sense than to sleep with a slave."

Balbus looked at the man beside him. "Rosa? She would do anything to get away."

Sulla gazed at the setting sun. "Then Zeno could be the father."

"He could be. My barn manager recently told me that Zeno was frequently taking Rosa for rides in his chariot, just as he did that little shit." Balbus lifted his gaze to the billowing mast. "So Alexius knows more than he is letting on."

Sulla chuckled. "Prove that, and you will have Alexius as your next charioteer."

Balbus smiled. "Prove that, and I will have Galerius scrubbing my latrine floor with his tongue."

Sulla rested his hip on the railing and crossed his arms. "You could very well have that anyway. More, if things go as planned."

"Yes. I will." Balbus chuckled and looked at Sulla. "It is done. Mother saw to it personally." Both men watched Vespasian stroll to the opposite railing and stare out at the passing land. "Pomponius will be pleased."

"No, he will not be pleased."

"Why not?"

"Because another Flavian takes his place."

"At least for now." Balbus looked down at the dolphins. "It is only a matter of time, Sulla. Only a matter of time."

Chapter 23

MESSALINA CONTINUED TO brush her hair and watch a yellow butterfly flit from flowerpot to herb pot. She was bored. Horribly bored. All she could do these last weeks was go to the baths each morning and shop in the afternoons. She wanted to help Didius make their oils, except he was too busy with the cracks in the walls and porticos that the tremors were causing

She wished Vulcan would calm down. He was destroying cities everywhere in the Campania valley. Not just Herculaneum. The sacrifices and pleas failed to appease. She released a long sigh and started pacing the terrace while brushing her hair.

The butterfly flew over the dividing wall to Alexius's gardens. Since he had returned to Rome, his letters had developed a strange sound to them. Rome stinks. He lost at the Max. He won at the Max. He missed her, wishing he were there in Herculaneum. Nothing more than just flat deliberations. Nothing about Rosa. Nothing about the committees. Nothing.

Her own letters were equally as boring, which was not a grand feat. She was bored and restless. She could never tell Alexius she had seen Hector in Herculaneum. Nor did she want to tell him. Hector no longer mattered.

Instead, all she could think about were those few nights with Alexius that had been glorious. Yet a part of her still waited for that fatal moment when Alexius would break her world apart.

Slapping the hairbrush down on a nearby table, she glanced around the terrace and found Niki playing with a kitten in the breezeway. "Niki, I want to go shopping." The girl jolted to attention as if she were guilty of some crime.

Messalina found her mother lounging in the solarium, munching on cherries that looked sweet. She plucked a cherry from the dish. "I am going shopping, Mother," she said, sucking the sweet meat off the seed.

Octavia sighed and sat up. "I would prefer that you stay. I am expecting a letter from your father today about Claudius's betrothal, and I would appreciate your opinion."

Claudius? Betrothed? She wanted to laugh. Poor girl. "He is only twelve, Mother."

"I know." Her mother gave her one of those frustrated glances. "And she is only eleven. Your father has been approached. It would only be arranged as it was for you and Alexius. The formalities will come later. It is much better if the two families know their children's futures are sure. As you should well know by now." She waved a hand in the air as if to clear it of unpleasant concerns.

Curiosity got the best of her. Messalina sat down on the empty bench nearby. "Who is asking?"

Her mother sighed heavily. "Lucius Calpurnis Piso."

"Calpurnia!" Messalina sat back in shock. "Calpurnia Piso? She is a spoiled brat!"

"Your father is considering her because Calpurnis is an affluent investor in merchant galleys, and he is thinking of sending galleys to Britannia. However, regarding Calpurnia…I agree she is horribly spoiled."

"It would be a life of misery for Claudius. He will howl through the roof if this is arranged." Messalina could not help but feel sorry for her brother and wondered if Alexius had howled through the roof because of her. No. They were barely five and seven when their agreement had been arranged.

She and Alexius had been raised their entire life knowing that they would be married one day. Then, he had simply proceeded to make it his personal and private goal to make her life as miserable as possible and had succeeded quite admirably…until lately. The old fear niggled again, deep in her stomach.

A slave appeared by her mother's couch, waiting until her mother looked up at him. "Domina, there is a messenger with a letter for you from Rome."

Octavia glanced at Messalina. "That must be the letter from your father. Hand it to me." She reached for the folded parchment. "And maybe there is a letter from Alexius as well."

Moments passed as her mother read. The fact that no letters came from Alexius again consumed Messalina's thoughts as she reached for another cherry.

"By the gods! No!" Octavia grabbed her throat as if strangling. "He can't be."

Messalina rushed to her mother's side. "What, Mama? What?"

"The emperor. Vespasian. He is dead. Vespasian is dead," sobbed from her mother's lips as she stared into nothing.

Messalina took the letter from her mother's trembling hand.

> 1 July 79 My beloved Octavia. The emperor is dead. I cannot believe it. Dead. All of Rome mourns the loss. We have to remain in Rome for the funeral and the installation of Titus to the throne, and then we will return home. Mourn and pray for the Empire, my dear. We have lost a great man.
>
> Messallus

Tears swelled in Messalina's eyes as she stared at the parchment. She stared into nothing as her mother was doing. What she and Alexius had overheard had happened. It actually happened. He was a dead man. They should have done something, told someone. But what?

As Alexius said, no one would have believed them, because neither she nor Alexius recognized who was out there. What is more, even if they had, whoever they were would only deny it.

"Has the messenger left?" her mother suddenly demanded.

"No, domina."

"Get him. I want to speak to him."

Her mother sat up as the lanky man appeared, dusty and worn. His face also carried the sad information. "What happened? How?" Octavia asked.

"As I hear, he died in Reate, domina," the man said. "The emperor seemed well enough when he returned home.

Then suddenly, he complained of a fever and died in the arms of his attendant. On his feet, as rumors say."

"A fever?" Messalina asked. "What could have caused such a fever?"

"It is not known, young domina. His physician said it was possibly a chill."

Messalina remembered her father bragging about how unusually well the emperor seemed to be, even with the responsibilities of the empire riding on his shoulders. The man was never sick. He had been glowing with health while in Herculaneum.

Alexius! He had been on board the galley with the emperor. Had he caught the same illness? No. She could not lose him now. Not now. Not this way. "Mama, we have to do something."

Her mother turned to Didius. "Prepare for mourning."

CHAPTER 24

"COME WITH US, *you filthy fool.*"
Guards jerked Alexius's hands forward and clamped the iron cuffs around his wrists. Another shoved from behind, making him stumble outside his house and onto the stone street filled with onlookers.

"Didn't your father tell you, you idiot fool, that helping a slave escape makes you a slave?" someone barked.

Another laughed. "And you thought you would get elected you. You filthy piece of shit."

"No! I did not. I did not."

A soldier's laughter rang in Alexius's ears. "Not what I heard. Throw the cur in the wagon."

Crowds threw garbage at him as the donkey pulled the wagon through the torch lit streets of Rome.

"He is the stench of a low-life latrine."

"And we almost voted for the filthy leech."

"Yeah, you filthy leech, you deserve to be a slave."

The wagon jolted toward the Circus Maximus where a man screamed from inside. "Alexius! He helped me! He knew all about it!"

Alexius knew that voice, but he could not place it. His mind searched helplessly for answers.

The gates opened, allowing the donkey onto the sandy track. Black shadows of the guards lined the way to three lashing posts buried at the nearest end of the spina. Senators filled the stadium, cheering, laughing, and pointing at him.

"He is the one. He helped me! He helped me!"

The voice. It came from the lacerated man hanging from one of the lashing poles.

Zeno!

His father's shredded body hung limp on a second lashing post where three senators waited. Sulla. Pomponius. Balbus. The three turned, and in one voice, announced, "You are a liar, Marcus Galerius Alexius. The Senate and the people of Rome have found you guilty."

Balbus pointed a barbed whip toward the remaining empty post. "Tie my new slave, so I may show him, I am his dominus now."

Alexius burst from his bed and raced to the bedroom window. He threw it open to the cool night air that did little to soothe his mind as the nightmare replayed all too clearly. He saw Balbus, the whip, Pomponius's jowls bouncing with laughter, and Sulla's clever smile oozing across the man's face, as well as the vision of his father's torn, mutilated body. Somewhere in his mind, he heard his own voice. *No! I did not! I did not!*

However, he did know.

Alexius grabbed the pitcher from the nearby table and attempted to pour water into the small glass. His hand shook most of it out. He splashed some over his face and fell back against the wall. Tears choked through him at the image of his father, suffering for what he was responsible for doing. A pain stabbed through his chest. He gasped for air.

"Dominus? Are you all right? Dominus?"

Alexius blinked until he recognized Fosco standing before him. "Yes. No." He had to sit down and stumbled to a stool. Fosco walked behind him and began to massage his neck. The touch stung. "Don't."

He sprang from the looming trap and raced into the garden filled with fragrances of moonflowers. Instead of sinking into hot sand, the cool marble chilled his bare feet. He collapsed against one of the columns and forced himself to watch the trickling fountain, the fish scurrying in the water below, the fireflies flitting over the boxwoods. Stars floated in the black sky. The moon appeared like hope.

Still, he heard the roaring crowd laughing at him and their insults.

Slowly, the nightmare faded amid the songs of the cicadas in the ivy. An owl hooting banished the roar. He managed to simply breathe, until a donkey in the streets bawled in distress, and his insides melted all over again.

It was all so real, so close, and right there in Rome.

Sons of Dis and Jupiter, if anyone found out that he had helped Zeno, Balbus would make him a slave to humiliate and ruin his family. By all the gods of Olympus, the man would force his father and mother to witness him serving him or even beating him in public before everyone in Herculaneum.

Messalina.

That would be another spectacle. A reminder of what happens to her…to any citizen helping a slave run away. Pomponius would claim her and bed her as some masters do their slave girls. Bile rose in his throat at the thought.

All…All he had done was advised Zeno not to leave. Not take Rosa. His own words rang in his ears. *"You are as good as dead if you do…They will be looking for the father to do just that…Let the gods decide that, Zeno."* That was all. That was all.

However, he had encouraged Zeno to wait until he could return. He knew about Armenia. He remembered the pendant around Messalina's neck. *"Let me give it to Rosa."*

And he knew that Rome had expected him to report all this to Balbus. And he had not. However, no one would understand that he had done everything only to reclaim Messalina's trust. No one would believe him.

Tears burned in his eyes as he slumped down on the garden bench. The nightmare had been a message from the gods. He could not help Zeno anymore. There was too much risk to his family, to Messi's family, to her. No more. No more.

"Dominus, a blanket. The night is chilling."

He turned to find Fosco holding a blanket toward him, afraid to come any closer. Alexius forced a smile. "Thank you, Fosco. Bad dreams. Just bad dreams."

"As I thought, dominus." The slave nodded. He parted the blanket enough to sweep it over Alexius's shoulders. It was a comforting, securing gesture. "Would you care to tell me about it? Talking sometimes helps."

"No."

They could torture Fosco to gain the truth because he knew everything, as well as Niki. It was only a matter of time before Balbus would learn the facts, and then Alexius knew he was as good as dead. Or he would wish he were.

"I'll get you some warm tea, dominus."

Alexius nodded and curled into the blanket, leaving one leg exposed just to remember Messalina gliding her foot along his ankle. He searched to remember the smell of her fragrance of lilies. All attempts eluded him.

He had to get away from Rome. He could not endure the smiling, the talking, and the answering questions. He was tired of everyone controlling his life and especially tired of men flaunting power.

He had to get home. He had to see Messalina. He had to hold her. He had to feel her alive in his arms. He had to drink in her fragrance, so soft and soothing, for as long as the gods would allow him to do so.

CHAPTER 25

I F ALEXIUS DID not come home soon, Messalina knew she would go out of her mind. What was he doing? What was happening in Rome? Was being there as miserable as Herculaneum, which remained sad and draped in black? Everyone still wore their funeral clothing as they went about his or her daily tasks, even though the time for mourning was well past the nine days. Few talked, fewer laughed. Some just burst into unexpected tears.

With Niki holding a sun umbrella over her head, Messalina ventured out into the gloom-filled city where even the dogs were quiet. The empty Decumanus Maximus felt more intense from the summer sun burning unusually hot for even July. The street radiated heat like a baker's oven. Aromas of soups and chowders, fresh bread, and sweet cakes drifted in the air. After all, mourners needed to eat and drink.

She saw Felix standing near the stairs that led to Zeno's apartment. He nodded to her as she turned the corner. There had been no word about Balbus finding Zeno. If they had, the news would have burned across the Empire like the news of Spartacus's escape. "Domina?"

Messalina turned to the short, weathered man. "Felix, good to see you."

He walked toward her with an intent look in his eyes. "It is good to see something pleasant about the city for a change," he said, glancing nervously around the walkway. "Are you well?"

"Yes." There was no one close enough to overhear them talking. "We were saddened by the news. Vespasian was good for Rome."

"May the gods bless Titus." Felix cast a direct glance at a few people lingering in the nearest storefront. "Apollo seems intent to melt the city walls today. Would you care to find more shade, domina?"

"Yes. Actually, it is quite hot." She motioned Niki a few paces back as they strolled under the canvas that protected one side of the street. They chatted about the weather, the strange sunrises, restless birds as they passed a cluster of shoppers.

Felix halted beneath the four-way arch near the basilica and Temple Augustalus. He quickly scanned the streets for any who could overhear. "Do you know if the Domina Rosa will be going to the Neptunalia games?" he asked.

"No. If I knew Rosa would be there, I would certainly plan on going."

He checked around them again and faced her, eyes direct as if to promise something. "She will be, domina. Please, give her a message from a friend that he will be coming to visit. Soon." Felix studied her intently. "Will you do that?"

So much was at stake for Alexius. Even for her. All she wanted now was to marry Alexius and shop in Rome with Rosa. She wanted to laugh with her and be happy, as they had once been. However, Rosa would never be happy. Not with Pomponius. The only thing keeping Rosa alive was the hope that Zeno would come for her.

"Yes. I will tell her."

Messalina saw her father's galley settle against the pier. Alexius stood by the railing next to him. Both still wore their black togas. They strode across the beach together and passed the public entry to Balbus's thermae. She had expected Alexius to turn toward his house. Instead, he followed her father up the ramp.

Alexius's gaze finally found hers. She had never seen him so somber. Her insides twisted into knots as she walked back through the garden and heard them enter the atrium.

A sudden cawing came from her father's new peacock. The bird flew to safety to the side portico roof as Messalina stepped through the garden doorway. Alexius strode across the checkered tiles, hands out, smiling timidly. "Messalina." A weakened smile appeared, the moment she let him have her hands. "You look wonderful."

She searched his gaze for some hidden clue to his private misery. "Thank you. However, I prefer you wearing blue really."

The first glint of joy lit his gaze as Antonia ran through the room with her little Britanni dog yapping her heels. Alexius squatted down to greet her sister and ruffle the dog enough to delight it.

"Were you there, Alexius?" Antonia asked in a somber tone, much too old for her age. "Did you see the funeral? The emperor?"

"Yes, Toni. I hope I never do so again." Alexius's voice remained lifeless. Her sister ran off back toward the garden as he stood. Octavia had her father in his tablinum as she whispered questions.

Alexius drew Messalina out onto the terrace railing. Bay breezes blustered against his mourning toga, rippling it against her peach tunica. Fragrances of bountiful herbs greeted them.

"It is still hard to believe," he said, gazing out at the throbbing sea that felt no horror over the death of Vespasian.

"Neither can I."

"I just keep hearing, 'Before the Kalendae of July, his Excellency will be a dead man.'" His gaze scanned the horizon. "Over and over."

"Alexius, I can't get it out of my mind either." Messalina rested a hand on his chest. His latent strength seeped into her palm as his gaze left the unknown and settled on her. His brow gathered with confusion.

"How Messi? The best physicians say he just caught a cold and died."

She shrugged and withdrew her hand. "Maybe he did."

Alexius shook his head. "No. Somehow, they did it."

Messalina looked out at the seascape. "I asked Didius about any flowers that could be poisonous like belladonna."

"Messi, Vespasian had tasters who would have recognized that." Anger festered in his gaze.

"Didius said there is a residue in the ground that was too dangerous no matter how it is handled."

Curiosity struggled with the fury biting in his eyes. "What is it called?"

"Charbon. Didius says it is found in certain dirt."

Curiosity won as he scanned her face for more answers. Or possibilities? She was not sure. "Has anyone recently died here in a strange way?"

Messalina shook her head. "I haven't heard of anyone."

Alexius turned to the railing. His shoulders seemed to wilt as he shook his head. "No one would believe us without proof." He faced her, still looking as helpless as she felt. "There is nothing we can do, Messi. Nothing." He clasped her hands, drawing her closer.

"I wish we could though."

Alexius lifted her hands to his lips, thrilling each knuckle with a kiss. She studied the soft waves in his thick hair. When he looked up, she noticed that the deep wrinkle between his arching eyebrows had disappeared. He led her closer to the dividing wall between their houses, to a corner bench by the potted fichus trees. The shade of the nearby garden room hid them. His mouth found hers, banishing every concern in her brain. He pulled away all too soon.

"I have missed you, my swan. With every breath."

"I missed you. Your letters were—"

"There they are, Bru. You found them."

Messalina drew back, wanting to destroy the little dog jumping at Alexius's leg. To make matters worse, Antonia was skipping down the steps toward them.

Alexius scooped up the pet with his hand. "You little mongrel, I am sorry I brought you here."

"No you're not!" Antonia announced. "I love him."

CHAPTER 26

ALEXIUS QUICKLY DISCOVERED that Herculaneum was just as crowded and oppressive as Rome. Simply walking out his own doors and seeing Balbus's front doors across the street nauseated him. He had to get out, get away to breathe. Fortunately, Messalina was thrilled to go for a journey away from the streets.

Apollo granted them a glorious day to do just that. The sky was void of clouds. Birds soared as if freed from a cage. Even the breezes played about like teasing fools. In addition, Vulcan must have been asleep, because the ground remained quiet.

He and Messalina stepped onto the beachfront near the boathouses where fishermen waved a greeting. A herd of boys raced around the corner of Balbus's thermae like stampeding horses, bringing him and Messalina to a sudden halt. Their lanky brown legs were blotched with mud as were their tunics. Creek water and leaves saturated their hair. How well he remembered such freedom. It seemed a lifetime ago.

Alexius dodged a cliff-hanging tree that dangled out into the ravine's rocky sides where washerwomen busily scrubbed laundry and hung tunics, undergarments, and pants on overhanging limbs. "I remember playing here when I was a kid."

"I know." Messalina ducked under the limb that he held back for her. "You played pirates here."

Her yellow ribbon snagged on a branch and tore from her hair. He handed it back, enjoying the simple smile resting on her lips. However, if he and his friends had seen any girls back then, they would have been captured and tortured.

"You are making that up," he said as he eased around some of the cleaned laundry lining the trees and rocks.

She cast a clever glance at him and then moved through the jumble of rocks that he and his friends had once used for a fortress, as the boys did now

"You, Marcus, Quintus, Albinius. Let me think. And Rudius used this as some kind of galley to catch prisoners. You were Pompey the Great, and you would jump from here into the water. Once, you almost drowned Marcus out there, didn't you?"

"How did you—"

She looked up at Balbus's garden terrace overlooking the riverbed and giggled. "Rosa and I watched everything. There was little we missed."

He did not want to start remembering all the things she might have seen. "Then if you saw everything, where is the best to cross? Here or down there?"

Messalina's gaze danced as she scanned the narrow ravine. "Here."

Unless the riverbed had changed, that was the deepest part of the river. Back then it had been the perfect swimming hole. It was only waist high now but deep enough to carry someone across.

"Think so, do you?" He swept Messalina in his arms. To his delight, she screeched as he strode into the water. "If you are right, you will not get wet. However, if you are wrong, I will not promise what will happen."

"Don't you dare drop me."

He waded deeper into the unusually warm water and pretended to slip. Messalina grabbed him tight around his neck, nearly making the pretense a near reality. He considered letting go and plunging into the water with her. The idea of seeing her sopping wet and furious was so tempting. However, Messi would storm back home, more furious than a hornet's nest, and the day would be ruined.

"Stop kicking or I will."

Currents were strong as the water climbed up his thighs. He dipped her sandals beneath the surface. Messalina screeched and wiggled to his delight. Her arms were nearly strangling him. "Still think this is where we crossed?"

"It is only deeper now. Alexius!"

The sound of Messi crying out his name excited every muscle in his body. He slugged to the other side and set her down on a flat rock. "Still think that is the shallow end?"

"Yes."

"Wrong." He laughed victoriously and pointed up the river. "It is up there, so you didn't see everything, my love."

Did he just call me his love?

Messalina could barely breathe as she climbed through the dense trees, thick bushes, and dark shadows shot with arrows of sunlight. Her breathlessness had nothing to do with the climb.

"We took our captives here," Alexius said as he helped her along a mud-packed trail near a small busy waterfall that poured down the side of the cliff and into a rock bowl. "If we had seen you, you would have been taken prisoner and tortured."

"If you had seen us," she taunted.

Messalina remembered the afternoon that she and Rosa had snuck away from their attending slaves and followed Marcus and Alexius, only to find everyone stripped naked and screaming like Pompeii's pirates. "Except you did not?" she informed with a challenging grin.

He scowled and motioned on up the hill. "We would have seen you."

Alexius had come back from Rome deeper in thought than usual. However, climbing along the childhood paths, the stress seemed to melt away like dew. The sparkle finally returned to his gaze as his smile reappeared.

One thing was absolute though. She and Rosa were never allowed this far from the city walls. Like a sudden dawn bursting from a dark cloud, a meadow opened before her, filled with blooms of yellow, blue, and orange flowers and knee-high grasses. Birds flew overhead, diving into the flowers or sweeping up to the encircling fat pines and narrow Cyprus trees. The air was heavy with fragrances of flowers, cedar, and smoke.

Her feet came to a complete stop as she stared as if what stretched before her as if this were the Elysian Fields. "This is beautiful."

When Alexius turned, the sun fell radiant on his face. His eyes sparkled like blue fragments torn from the sky. "Haven't you ever been this far before?"

She shook her head. "Never."

Smiling, he took her hand and drew her farther along a path cutting across the field. Another path led off toward two small farm huts on the other side of the meadow. Two foxes leaped over the heads of the flowers and bounded into the woodland. Butterflies fluttered everywhere. A yellow one settled on Alexius's dark green tunic still wet from the river.

Freedom filled the air and thrilled through her. She raced away like a zephyr, swirling into the meadow. Alexius charged after her, laughing devilishly. Hearing his laughter made her dodge and run even faster, barely escaping his grasps. She taunted him, punishing him for not believing that she and Rosa could hide from them. Ponies joined the fun, bolting and bucking in a small pasture.

Giggling, Messalina finally let Alexius catch her. They collapsed to the ground, laughing and heaving for air. Alexius was glowing as he rolled to his side and propped his head with his hand. "I can't believe you haven't been here before."

She sighed and realized she had missed so many things while growing up. Herculaneum seemed imprisoned by city walls, as she had been all these years! A blue butterfly landed unnoticed on Alexius's shoulder, fanning its wings. "Father never permitted it."

The insect walked down the fabric covering his forearm. She rolled onto her back to gaze up at the clouds drifting in the fathomless sky. "There are times I think I have missed out on so much." Sighing again, she brushed the heads of the nearest flowers.

"If I could, I would show you the world." Alexius plucked a daisy from the grass and handed it to her. "Would you like to see Britannia?"

She brushed it across his cheek. "Yes."

"Then I will take you one day." The somber expression covered his face like a mask again. "If I decided to become a merchant, instead of a senator, we could go there with your father's galleys. We would see the entire Empire. Would you like that?

What? Alexius not a senator? Impossible. She sat up to study his face. "Would you really want to do that?"

Alexius shrugged and lay back in the grass, staring at the sky. "What is wrong with working with your father?"

He was serious. "Why, Alexius?" She reached for his wrist and found it. "Is there a problem with the election?"

He shook his head all too quickly and pulled away as he sat up, twirling another daisy between his thumb and forefinger. "Cornelius congratulated me for making my first enemies in the Senate."

"First enemies? Who?" A protective rush swept her. Alexius did not deserve this. He did not.

"Balbus and Pomponius." The daisy stopped. "Balbus knows, or thinks I know, who the father of Rosa's baby is." The daisy twirled again. "Pomponius thinks I am the reason the imperial staff took his reports. And I might have been." His lips tightened as he stared at the flower. "I don't know where Sulla stands in all this, but if it is anywhere, it is with Balbus."

Anger snarled every nerve in her body.

He looked up, his gaze blunt. "So, Messi, the chance of me gaining a place in the Senate is dead since they own more than half of Rome. I doubt I will even be able to be on the latrine committee now."

Messalina breathed. Not an easy task. "But…you said Cornelius congratulated you."

"According to Cornelius, if I am any kind of worthwhile senator, this will be the first of many enemies."

She stopped the twirling daisy by resting her hand on his wrist. "Don't you want to win this election?"

"I do. Yes. But…" He started tearing petals from the flower, dropping them before his crossed legs. "Cornelius knows only half the story, Messi. I do know about Zeno. I did tell Cornelius about Pomponius's reports." He stopped, his attention returning to her gaze. "Eventually, they will find out."

She wanted to destroy Balbus. If there was some way. "Alexius, you can't let them take this away from you." She looked past him to the delicate smoke drifting innocently from one of the small huts. "I knew you should not have found me that night. If you had not, you would not be in this mess. It's my fault."

"I am glad it happened, Messi." He stretched onto his side and played the bare stem along her arm. "And I was only concerned about the reports when I told Cornelius. As far as Zeno is concerned, all I have done is keep him from being killed. He chose to run. I did not make him do that."

She scoured his face. Was he trying to convince her or himself? Now she had another reason to hate Rosa's father. The man had tried to destroy his daughter, and now he was planning to destroy Alexius. "Will Titus Caesar grant you his vote?"

"Who knows?"

"Do you really think Balbus can ruin your election?"

He stared at the destroyed flower. "Right now, I don't care. I did not want to run for the Senate right now anyway. I would have preferred just spending time in the Palaestra." He looked at her. "I am sorry, Messi. I shouldn't have told you all this." The bald daisy twirled again. "I just needed to tell someone." He ran the stem along her cheek. "Forget I said anything. I want to see you smile."

She tried, granting him half of one.

"Alexius, I …" She would be involving him more if she told him about Felix. "Nothing. Never mind." She lay back in the flowers and looked at the sky.

"What?"

"It is nothing." The clouds were a funny yellow as they floated over the top of Vesuvius.

"If it is about Zeno, tell me. I have to know."

She turned her head to the most demanding gaze she had ever witnessed. Worse than her mother's. "It will only involve you more, Alexius. I can't."

His gaze leveled on her. "Yes, you can."

"Alexius. Please. I am serious. I don't want you involved in this anymore." She rolled away.

"Are you going to the games?"

She lay back. "Father's informed me that the family will all be going to the games. No excuses. And, he looked at me when he said that. Why do you need to know?"

"Because, if you stay here, so will I."

She stared at him. "You would give up seeing the Valkyrie!"

The corner of his mouth lifted. "To be with you, yes."

"Dominus!"

Alexius turned to see both Fosco and Niki strolling toward them. Fosco held up a basket for an answer. He looked at Messalina. "Are you hungry?"

"Famished."

"Fosco, in the trees, near the stream!" He pointed the way.

Fosco nodded and turned to go as directed. By the time they neared the tree line, a wool blanket lay across a thick patch of wild thyme. Plates of hard bread, sliced peaches, figs, and cheese sat in the center. Fosco held a wine bladder while Niki placed mugs by small bread loaves and honeyed nuts.

"Go eat. We can handle everything here," Alexius said, motioning the slaves away. He did not want either of them overhearing their conversation. Messi already knew more than she should and more that she was not sharing. She had sullied up like a stubborn donkey, as he well knew she was exceptional at doing.

Somehow, he would get her to tell him. In the meantime, just being with her had fed life back into him. He had forgotten everything about the election as he chased after her, listened to her screech, giggle, laugh as she taunted him.

Then the nightmare returned the instant they had fallen among the flowers. The gods had offered him an escape… working with Messi's father. Knowing Messalina would travel with him only encouraged the idea of becoming a merchant. He just had to find a way to approach his father with the idea.

They settled on the blanket. He noticed a bush full of plump ripe berries. "Look." Messalina looked over her shoulder to see where he was pointing.

"Berries!" She bolted to her feet and began plucking the fruit. He joined her, dropping his pickings in her makeshift pouch she formed with her tunica. Stains quickly spotted the fabric.

He plucked an especially large one and offered it to her. "For you, my swan."

She stepped close and took the berry. The touch of her lips on his fingers ignited fantasies. He smashed another berry to the roof of his mouth and lowered his lips to hers, melting his senses entirely.

The moment ended when Messalina released her tunica, dropping the berries around their feet. They squatted down to reclaim them, bumping heads, and burst out laughing. It felt better than good.

"I have never tasted sweeter berries than these," he whispered, offering her another. She took it. Without another thought, he drew her lips back to his and, together, they fell onto the wool blanket. She was sustenance, life, everything he needed.

Breathless, Messalina pulled away, her face glowing. "You are…smashing…the berries."

He rolled away, and she began scooping the surviving fruit to the center of the blanket. "And they are too good to waste."

"So we will eat them." He popped one in his mouth and reached for her. She dodged his hand and playfully flung a berry at him. He snapped it up like a fish, daring her to toss another. One hit his nose, another hit his cheek. The rest he caught, to both of their delight.

They settled back on the picnic blanket. A quiet mood developed, comfortable and natural. He sipped wine, enjoying how the sun played in the waves of her hair as she studied the berry stains on her tunica.

"Messi, I am sorry."

She scowled at him. "It is old anyway." She reached for a slice of cheese.

"No, I mean, I am sorry for all those stupid things I said that night when I was drunk."

He saw her smirk and look across the field. She turned back. A taunting gleam danced in her eyes. "Why do you think they were stupid?"

He set his cup of wine down on his plate and looked directly at her. "Weren't they?"

She grinned. "I didn't think so."

"Well, then, I meant every word." He lifted his cup and drank.

"I doubt that you meant every word."

"Test me."

She studied him seriously. "You saw Hector with Lizbet at the Max?"

"I did. You weren't going to run away with him, were you?"

"No." She gathered her next thought. "Will you cheat on me?"

"Never."

"Do you want to—?"

Laughter giggled out in the sunny meadow, drawing their attention. "You are so big, Paullus, my lovely Paullus." A toddler squealed with delight. "What will I do with you when you get so big that I can't carry you?"

Drawn, Messalina climbed to her feet. Alexius got up and followed her back into the field. He recognized Rosa's slave girl dancing around and around to the delight of a child in her arms. His stomach twisted as he forced his feet to move toward Balbus's runaway slave girl who held Zeno's baby on her hip.

Chapter 27

"CARENA?" MESSALINA CALLED out.

The girl froze as Alexius followed Messalina through the flowers. "D-Domina! I-I didn't know you were here."

Messi drew closer and played with the child in the girl's arms. Its tiny fist clamped onto her finger. "He is beautiful." Her gaze lifted to Carena. "Please. Can I hold him?"

"I…I can't stay, domina. I should go."

"Please?"

Obediently, the girl released the baby to Messalina, who lifted the bundle before her, cooing as the baby squealed with delight.

Messi looked so natural with a child in her arms that Alexius's body ached to give her one.

"Alexius, look at the tiny bells and Cupid's pendant," Messalina said as she toyed with the jewels dangling around the child's neck. "Just whose baby, are you?" she cooed.

Carena fidgeted like a caught deer. "R-Ruso's sister's."

Alexius studied the child. Ruso's family all had straight brown hair and smooth features. This child had sharp features and curly black hair like Zeno. "You care for her children now?" he asked, curling a strand of baby hair around his finger.

"Yes. I'm…I'm free. I…I live here with Ruso. My papers. Here, see." The girl pulled worn parchment from a pouch at her waist. "The… domina Rosa gave them to me."

Alexius accepted the presented paper and studied it, praying they were valid. They were not. He knew Balbus's signature and he should report this. Already, he knew he would not. He forced a smile and handed the roll back to the girl. "I am happy for you, Carena. I am sure Ruso is as well."

"Domina, I have to get Paullus back. I do." Carena fretted pathetically at both of them. "Please. Forgive me. I didn't mean to bother you."

Messalina handed the baby back, brushing its fat chubby cheek with her fingers. Carena adjusted the baby on her slender hip. "Domina? Dominus? Please, don't tell anyone you saw me. Please."

"We won't, Carena," Alexius said, plucking another daisy from the grass and handing it to Messalina to get her attention. She took it, sniffing it thoughtfully as they watched Carena scurry back toward the hut like a freed rabbit.

They walked back to their picnic, only to find Niki and Fosco cleaning things. Alexius leaned against an oak sapling as the weight of what just happened snatched the air from his lungs. "Messalina, those were fake papers."

She stopped by the empty berry bush and faced him. "I know. And, it is Rosa's baby.

The worry in Messalina's eyes confirmed the fact that he would say nothing to anyone. He pulled Messalina close and enveloped her in his arms. She settled against him, her head resting on his chest. He would find a way out of this trap. He only wished he had a string like Theseus in the Minotaur's maze.

Suddenly, Messalina stiffened in his arms and drew away. "Alexius, this never happened."

He brushed her cheek and smiled. "My love, like it or not, I know. However, no one has reported anything to Balbus. And I do not need his gratitude." That was a lie. He continued anyway. "Therefore, until someone else finds her, we will keep silent. The baby? We are not sure the babe is Zeno's. You heard Carena. She says the child is Ruso's sister's. Maybe it is."

Her arms glided around his waist. "Will I see you tomorrow?"

"Cornelius needs me to help him on new case. I can only hope my nights are free, my love."

Over the next week, Cornelius kept Alexius busy by day, and the vigils kept him busy at night. Like everyone else in the city, Messalina had attended the hearings of a slave girl named Justa. She could now argue every detail about the case that Alexius was helping Cornelius oversee.

Obviously, Alexius was born to do exactly what he had always dreamed of—becoming a senator. He would not be happy being a merchant for her father. Now, having to ride in a horrid wagon lurching over road stones toward Pompeii left her ill-tempered and restless.

Why her father decided to go to the Neptunalia games in a pathetic wagon instead of his galley was beyond her. He said the omens were bad. She doubted that. It was more likely that he and Galerius wanted to stop at every village between Herculaneum and Pompeii to look at furniture, which they did. To make matters worse, their wives seemed enthralled with the idea.

Apparently, the world was going to the Neptunalia games to see this much talked about Valkyrie. Was it possible for a woman to equal a man in the arena? Would she fight? Would she win? That was all everyone talked about.

Messalina could not count the number of times she overheard that the gladiatrix had simply been lucky in Rome and that Fabius had underestimated her. However, no such advantage awaited the woman in Pompeii's amphitheater. At least, that was according to the men on the front seat.

If Messalina was not hearing about the games, it was Aurelia and her mother gossiping about Pompeii's plague, Cornelius's new betrothed. Every woman seemed to be shocked that he had betrothed this Faustina Satrius without his father's consent. All knew that Sulla could annul the betrothal, except then he would have to face his son's wrath. That was another matter.

"Well, it was about time this girl turned her father's estates over to a husband," Octavia huffed. "But Cornelius, of all men!"

"Do you suppose she tricked him?" Aurelia asked.

Messalina silently laughed at the comment. Nothing would trick Alexius's friend into anything, much less a wedding.

Messalina continued listening to the women and endured her sister babbling to her blasted dog. "Don't do that," Antonia fussed as she attempted to dress the wiggling dog in doll clothes. "Cara won't like it." She teased a doll before the snapping dog. "No. I told you no. Don't bite her."

"Then don't taunt him."

Antonia scowled at Messalina. "He has to learn."

"You are encouraging him, Toni, not teaching him."

Everyone lurched about like toys as the wagon clunked over some object in the roadway. Messalina focused her misery on Marcus, Claudius, and Alexius chasing after some leather object flaunted as a prize. Seeing them together brought back the memories of them taunting her about her big nose, fat lips, and calling her ugly 'Medusa'.

Each day in the mirror, she still saw the truth of their heckling. Niki caught her scowling at her reflection in her round ivory mirror. "You are very pretty now, domina." *Pretty?* She would never be pretty like other girls who had delicate noses, rose petal lips, arching eyebrows.

Albeit, her freckles had disappeared, and her hair no longer spiraled out of control like Medusa's coiling snakes. However, her cheeks remained large enough to hold up eyes once called bug-eyes by the horseracing trio grabbing for Marcus's water bag.

Alexius had the bag now and was keeping it from the crowd of young men who had joined the fun. He rode like Bellerophon on Pegasus. There were moments he actually made her feel pretty, that he liked what he saw. She wondered if she were simply wishing that to be true.

Claudius had started keeping his insults quiet because he knew she would tell their parents that he had been sleeping with Niki. Nothing would ever silence Marcus.

"I hope you don't love Alexius. And I hope you run away with Hector."

Messalina dropped her attention to her sister. "Why would you want me to do that?"

Her sister wiggled around on the wagon cushion to face her. "Because I heard Papa tell Mama that if you did run away, they would arrange a betrothal with Alexius and me." She focused on the doll in her arms. "I love him, even if you don't."

Alexius and Antonia? Messalina wanted to laugh. However, could not. However, that is exactly what their families would arrange. Regardless of what Alexius wanted. Even though it would grant him six more years of freedom before Antonia was marriageable. Was that why Alexius was being so nice lately, fearing his parents would betrothed him to Antonia? Well, she would not let her sister gloat.

"Enjoy his dog, little sister, because that is all you will get of Alexius. I am beginning to like him."

Instead of sulking, Antonia brightened like a star. "Really? Little Bru, did you hear that! We get to keep him. And I'll get to pick who I marry."

Messalina thought of Calpurnia and Claudius and laughed. "Don't count on that, Toni."

CHAPTER 28

THE WAGON FINALLY meandered through the Herculaneum Gate and into Pompeii where every roadway buzzed from the mass of people arriving for the Neptunalia games. Messalina almost sighed with relief, except that Balbus and his parade of clients appeared as everyone climbed out of the wagon.

"Messallus. I see you made it," Balbus called out as he approached.

"Whatever remains of us greets you, my friend," her father huffed. "We left most of our bodies on the road. I dread the return trip already."

Balbus laughed. Messalina noticed Balbus's gaze darken like a passing shadow the moment Alexius and Marcus dismounted and stepped into view. "Alexius. Greetings."

"Dominus." Alexius's intent gaze was equally direct and dark.

"F-F-Father," Marcus asked. "Where...are w-w-we staying?"

Disgust rankled in Balbus's eyes when he focused on his son. "Have Minus show you." His gaze changed like a chameleon as he turned back to her father again. "Where will you be staying while in Pompeii?"

"Marcus Epidius is still in Athens. We are staying in his house."

"Ah, fine house," Balbus announced as if granting an imperial blessing. "You will be able to watch the games from the balcony."

Her father shrugged. "Have you heard whether the gladiatrix will fight?"

Balbus shook his head. "Rumor is no. We have tried to talk sense into Cornelius to insist that his betrothed allow the female to fight."

"Will he?" Galerius asked eagerly.

"Cornelius says the slave belongs to his betrothed, and he won't meddle." Balbus leaned in with a smirk. "However, if this Satrius girl does not fight her gladiatrix, her family's name will be mud."

"If I hear right," Galerius said, "Sulla won't mind that one bit."

"Nothing would please him more."

"Rosa…and Pomponius?" The senator's name choked from Messalina's throat. "Are they here?"

Balbus turned toward her with a patronizing smile. "Yes. They will be staying with us."

"May I visit her?"

"Ask Pomponius if she is feeling up to it." Balbus waved a dismissive hand. "I won't hold you any longer. We will see you at the games." Balbus started to leave and then turned back. "Oh, yes. I would like all of you to join me in my section for the games." He shrugged curiously. "Unless you would rather watch from Epidius's balcony."

"No better seats would be available than your honorarium seats," her father said eagerly.

"None. I assure you."

"Did you enjoy the thermae?" Alexius asked as he strolled across the back garden to where Messalina sat near a statue of Venus, both bathed in radiant afternoon sunlight.

She looked up from playing with a gray kitten. "It was nice."

"So was the Stabian thermae. Even Balbus had problems getting in this afternoon."

Alexius leaned against the wall and watched the fluffy gray kitten pounce away into the bushes after a butterfly. He wished they could truly be alone. However, busy slaves scurried about the peristyle like ants in a colony. Their parents were reclining in the summer triclinium, and Antonia was playing with her puppy on the other side of the garden. Claudius was likely at the brothel with friends. They were alone as much as they would ever be during the festival to Neptune.

Messalina caressed a nearby rose. "They won't let me see Rosa. A messenger came to say she was too sick." She looked at him, her eyes dark enough for a storm. "I know visiting Rosa would help her."

"It would, I am sure." A wavy strand of Messalina's hair brushed across her breast. He stepped closer, filling his mind with the soft fragrance of lilies floating off her skin. "I will talk to Marcus and see if there is a way that he can arrange something."

The eager look in her eyes made his heart lurch. It dimmed suddenly. "Don't, Alexius. You have risked enough." Messalina got up and walked toward the small bubbling fountain surrounded with rosemary. "I saw how Balbus looked at you earlier."

He followed and dragged a finger along her neck "So did I, my swan." He wrapped his arms around her waist to draw her close. She did not resist. "He can look at me however he likes. All I care about is how you look at me."

She tilted her head slightly, perfect for a kiss. Her lips parted. He bent to taste them. She drew closer, sliding her arms around his neck. His hands sank into the mass of curls as his mind spiraled with the taste of her mouth against his.

Something tugged on his tunic. He looked down at the intruder. Toni. Of course.

"She loves you now. She told me."

CHAPTER 29

TRUMPETERS SOUNDED IN the amphitheater as the official parade entered the arena. When the sponsor's gold chariot appeared, the jubilance of the spectators exploded. Messalina easily recognized Cornelius in his senatorial toga riding next to his betrothed who was elegantly dressed in a brilliant white stola edged equally with gold.

Some said that Cornelius's betrothed, this Faustina Lucia Satrius, had angered the gods because she disregarded their expectations of marriage and family. Therefore, the gods were punishing the valley with tremors that tore buildings down and crippled crops.

That made no sense. This Faustina could not be more than twenty years old and the tremors had been happening for many more years than that. Her father even grumbled that the problems had been going on during his childhood.

However, it was obvious why this Faustina had captured Cornelius. She was stunning. Not only that, gossip sprang from how she dressed. Her silk stola, something reserved only for a married woman, poured smoothly down her body like milk, instead of in layers of cloth. In addition, Faustina had her hair arranged up like a married woman instead of left down and unparted like a virgin. That alone brought on more gasps and heated questions by many around where they now sat.

"So revealing! Indecent, I say!" complained Octavia.

The women around her mother nodded in agreement, everyone except Alexius's mother. She smiled as she watched Faustina step from the chariot and climb to the sponsor's podium not too far away.

What would Alexius think if she dressed as this Faustina? Messalina turned to ask, but he was talking to his father. Everyone had settled in their seats, chatting excitedly. They silenced when the procession of gladiators entered the arena.

Immediately, the crowd noticed the absence of the gladiatrix and a roar erupted. "The Valkyrie! We want the Valkyrie!" The seats vibrated with stomping feet. The insanity grew.

Messalina glanced at Alexius's concerned expression. She followed his attention to the sponsor's box where Cornelius and his betrothed discussed something very serious.

The stands roared with victory the instant that the largest woman Messalina had ever seen burst into the arena. She drove a chariot in a full run, spraying dirt into the cheering audience. Everyone bolted to their feet, taking Messalina up with them.

Two rows down was the only exception where Volasennia proceeded to glare up at the sponsor's box. Messalina followed her glare directed at Sulla's wife Agrippina standing beside Sulla. Why would…

Someone fell into Messalina, knocking her forward. The blundering fool slumped over her. "Amphitheater

Baths. The domina Rosa waits for you," he whispered quite clearly. His voice swiftly changed to drunken apologies. "I'm s-sorry, domina. P-Please forgive me." The man snickered with humor. "Clumsy m-me. I'm s-so s-sorry."

All the men around Messalina shoved the drunk out into the aisle. "Fool! Get out of here," her father bellowed.

Alexius drew her back onto the cushion. "Messi, are you all right?" He sat down beside her, his expression torn between rage and concern.

Messalina tried to make sense of what the man had said. *Amphitheater Baths. The domina Rosa waits for you.* She jerked around to find him, but the man had vanished into the crowd cheering at the first match striding into the arena.

"Messi?" Alexius drew her face back to his deeply worried gaze. His hand brushed vagrant strands of hair from her shoulder.

"Fine. I…I am…" If she were hurt, she could leave. "I…I don't know." She melted against Alexius as if fainting.

"Messi!" Panic flooded through Alexius's voice. "I will take her back to the house." He stood, ready to pluck her from the cushion.

No. Not Alexius. He had to stay at the games. Messalina struggled from his grip. "No. Didius can—"

Alexius swept her into his arms before another word muttered from her lips. Both sets of parents melted with smiles of approval and moved aside enough for Alexius to carry her up the stone steps.

She rested against his chest, something she found all too easy to do. He worked his way toward the vaulted exit and past people moving aside. Once in the tunnel exit, she stiffened in his arms. "Alexius, I am fine. Let Didius and Niki take me back. You will…you will miss the gladiatrix."

He looked down at her, his gaze twinkling with pleasure. "I will miss you more."

"No. You do not understand. You have to." She wiggled to be put down.

Alexius halted outside the amphitheater entrance and finally set her on her feet. Behind him, Didius and Niki followed with a gaggle of vendors closing in like vultures. Her glare stopped them in their tracks. "That fool wasn't drunk, was he?" Alexius asked with a clever grin. "And that was no accident."

"No. Yes. Rosa…" Her gaze flashed up at Alexius. "I will be fine. I am going to…" She looked around, lost. "The Amphitheater Baths. Didius will bring me home." She nudged him to leave. "Please. Go back to the games."

"I am going with you."

Rosa released a nervous sigh as she settled on one of the thermae loungers placed along the wall. Sunlight glared through the opening above and spilled into the small impluvium, glittering the water with sparkling diamonds. Aside from three other women who had chosen not to go to the games, she was alone. She could easily imagine the room filled with people waiting their turn to enter the bathing rooms.

Angry yells and thundering sounds from the amphitheater vibrated across the neighboring orchard and into the shadows surrounding her. She could not help but wonder what was happening at the games.

Pomponius had expected her to attend with him, except she had refused, complaining of yet another headache. This was her only chance to be alone with Messalina. Marco had found out that both Alexius's and Messi's families were coming to the games. He also assured her he would get a message to Messalina. Now, if only Messi could get away.

Rosa settled into the soft cushions. At least, she had one friend. Marco was the only slave who had helped Carena flee with Baby Paullus. He had misdirected the soldiers hunting for the missing slave girl. He had also taken compassion on her without question.

She clasped Zeno's pendant, the one Pomponius had tried to take from her. He still knew nothing more than what Messi had said the day of the wedding…the day her life had turned into this misery.

She looked up the instant Marco walked into the small-enclosed courtyard. He was surprisingly strong for his lanky appearance and early gray hair. He simply nodded to her and strode toward the doorway to the narrow swimming pool basking in the day's heat.

Hope surged. Messalina might be able to answer the thousand questions that hung like baggage on Rosa's heart. Had Carena gone to Messalina? Where was her baby? Was he alive? Did she know anything about Zeno? Where he was? Was he well? She did not dare ask anyone anything. Voices! She heard voices outside the door. Alexius and Messalina appeared in the atrium.

"Messalina! You came!"

They raced together and melted into each other's arms. Messi pulled back with tears streaming down her beautiful face. "I couldn't believe what your man said. We all thought he was drunk."

Laughter rang like pure joy. The familiar sound swelled through Rosa like a current. A deep chuckle drew her attention. "Alexius?" He looked…like a senator. "I am glad to see you."

"And I, you." He came forward to kiss her on both cheeks and drew back, smiling. "You look well."

"As allowed. I hear you are running for the senate?"

Messi looked up to hear his answer. Rosa noted a gleam of pride in her gaze.

"Yes, if the gods allow," he said.

"I pray that they do. Rome needs men with honor like yours, now more than ever."

"Alexius," Messalina said. "Please, go back to the games. I will stay with Rosa. Didius and Niki will see me home after the games. Now, go.

Concern vibrated in Messalina's voice. A rarity toward her betrothed.

"Alexius, tell Messallus that she is with me at the baths, and that I will see that she returns to you after the games."

"Now go," Messalina fretted at him like a wife. "You are missing the excitement."

Smiling, Alexius strode to the door. Rosa turned to Messalina and, once again, hugged her like a lost child. "Messi, I have missed you. I miss everything."

Messalina clasped her face with both hands. The feel of gentle hands rubbing the tears away felt so strange.

"Rosa, I can't believe you are here. It is a dream. You are better. Much better."

Clinging to each other's hands, they moved to the abandoned couch. Niki and Didius appeared stoically at the doorway. Marco crossed the room and drew them away as Rosa absorbed the reality of Messalina being there.

"Yes, Much better, but not well. I will never be well in his house. I hate him."

"Yes. And so do I."

"Messi, has Carena come to you?" Rosa asked, praying the slave girl had, that there was news. She had to know… at least something.

"No," Messalina drew back. "We, I mean, I saw her… in a field just outside Herculaneum. She was twirling a baby in her arms."

It had to be Baby Paullus. Rosa sagged as someone newly freed of a demon. "He is alive, Messi? I sent Carena away with Paullus and my jewels to take care of him." Joy burst through her heart as if reborn. "She has, Messi. She has."

"She showed us…me the manumission papers," Messalina said dubiously. "And said the baby belonged to the girl inside one of the huts."

"Us, you mean Alexius was with you?"

Messalina nodded painfully.

"Did he think the papers were real?"

"He knew they were fake." Messalina released a worried sigh.

"Do you think anyone will find out?" Fear cut through her. "If they do, she may run away." She could not lose Baby Paullus now."

"I hope not, Rosa." Messalina gripped her hands. "Rosa, he looks like Zeno."

"Then you know who the father is?"

"Yes."

"Does Alexius know?"

"Everything."

Rosa studied her friend. She could not believe that Alexius knew about running away with Zeno and had not said anything, as Rome expected of all its citizens. Otherwise, if her father found out Alexius had not, he would not only destroy Zeno, he would ruin the House of Galerius. *Pray the gods will protect Alexius.*

Their gazes fed on each other for an eternity. "I am worried for Alexius, Rosa. The night of the auction, we overheard someone saying that they planned to kill Vespasian. One of them even said before the Kalendae of July that Vespasian would be a dead man. Now he is dead. Therefore, he did not die of a chill. He was assassinated."

Rosa drew up to study Messalina's face. "You heard them say this! Who?"

"We didn't recognize their voices." Messalina's expression pleaded for help. "Who would believe us if we said anything?" She sat back. "And I am afraid that Alexius is in enough trouble. He won't tell me everything."

Messalina was more right than she knew. "Messi, Pomponius thinks Alexius was the reason Vespasian investigated him. He is working to ruin his election. I heard him talking to Father about it."

"Alexius was not the cause of that."

How strange to hear Messi protecting Alexius. Rosa wanted to laugh. "You love him now, don't you?"

"No…Yes." Messalina turned toward the impluvium. "I am not certain if he truly loves me, Rosa. I think it is all part of getting elected or something other than me."

"I could see it in his eyes, Messi." Rosa reached for Messalina's wrist. "He is concerned about you."

Marco stepped beside them, glancing back at the approaching women leaving the thermae. "Domina, would you care to relax by the pool now? It is empty."

"Yes, Marco," Rosa said. "Where are Niki and Didius?"

"Waiting in the changing room, domina."

Messalina could not believe the change in Rosa. Though still too thin and gaunt, she had a new command of life. Maybe she was clinging to the hope that Zeno would come for her and the baby. She never released the pendant around her neck for more than a breath. One hand or the other clasped or fingered it.

Every part of her soul wanted Zeno to take Rosa away and make her happy again. However, that would mean losing her forever. She would never be able to visit her, receive a letter from her, nothing. However, at least, she would know Rosa was happy and free of the men she hated more than life.

After undressing, Messalina followed Rosa into the small round room full of steam, leaving Didius to watch over their belongings. Both sat on the narrow seat on the proffered towel given by the attending slave who poured water in a bowl filled with hot stones. Steam rose to the cupola roof.

Heat soared, almost dizzying Messalina's mind, full of thoughts. Was Rosa right? Could Alexius love her? She did not know what to think and was afraid of the truth. "I can't stand any more. I am going out." Messalina walked from the small room and dove into the tepid pool. Cheers from the games filtered into the marbled thermae.

By the time she had swam the short pool twice, the water had only purified a few of her concerns. It was definite. She did not want Hector near her again. Would the charade evaporate once Alexius's election was over?

Rosa followed her to the pool, only to ease up to her neck in the sun-warmed water. Niki and Marco watched from the pool edge, holding towels.

"What is Rome like?" Messalina asked.

"I don't know. He has ordered the slaves to keep me confined as if I were his Greek wife." Leaning against the pool's side, Rosa swirled the water with one hand while still clinging to the pendant with the other hand. "And I refuse to accompany him anywhere. I have my room. He has his."

"You can't even go shopping?"

"If I wish something, I call for a vendor to come to the house. Nor will he let me do anything to his house. Not paint, not even change the drapes. Everything is exactly as his previous wife had it. And it shall so remain." Rosa reached for Marco's hand and let him lift her from the water. "Come. Let's go to the caldarium."

The intense heat of the room was thick enough to cut. Messalina's mind played while a slave massaged the fragrances into her skin. What it would be like to live with Alexius? She had not really considered that before. Thoughts of decorating his house in Rome niggled through her. Would he let her? She could imagine him admiring her newest adornment—a lounger, a curtain, a new painting. Excitement tingled through her.

However, what if he did not? On the other hand, what if Aurelia demanded the last say on everything she wanted to do to the house? Her world flattened as horribly as it had when he called her 'Medusa'.

"I am going back out to the pool," Messalina passed new members now lounging in the tepidarium and dove into the water. The coolness chilled her thoughts instantly. At least she knew Aurelia was not like that. When Messalina swam back, Rosa was dangling her legs in the water. Before she turned for another swim across, Rosa grabbed her wrist. "Messi, what is wrong."

"Nothing." She did not want to say the words, except Rosa never would let her get away with that. She diverted the subject away from Alexius. "He is beautiful, Rosa. Paullus was happy the day we saw him. Healthy."

"She calls him Paullus?" Rosa asked longingly

Messalina swished her legs in the water. "I hope your father never sees her."

A silence drifted between them as the sound of the crowd roared with delight over some victory happening in the arena. The afternoon air hung with dust. Rosa stared at the sparkling water in the pool. "It is the witch who would recognize her."

"But she never leaves the house."

"Except to go to the temple to Jupiter." Rosa stared off across the sparkling water. "Zeno will come for me...us. I know it. One day, Messi, he will come. Only that keeps me alive."

Chapter 30

BOTH FAMILIES WALKED toward the plaza filled with people from every part of Rome. Messalina heard lutes playing from every direction. As they walked into Pompeii's city's center, dancing girls and boys greeted them, accepting coins for their performances. The aromas of tangy sauces, warm breads, and sweet biscuits hung in the air like fog. Fruits of every color decorated tables. Cheeses and sweet sticks covered tables lining the surrounding portico. Slaves milled about with flagons of wine, ready to fill empty goblets. Talk about the Valkyrie dominated all conversations.

"Alexius, will you take me over to ride a camel. Please?" Antonia pleaded ever so pathetically.

"I will take you, Toni," Claudius said. He and their sister headed toward the slaves leading camels, donkeys, and pigs in circles before Vespasian's temple. Another ride swung children around in a rigged rope swings. Their parents followed, laughing and talking, not realizing that neither Messalina nor Alexius had joined them.

"Alexius!"

They had barely crossed the plaza and turned to see Cornelius and his betrothed walking toward them. The elegant woman at his side was even more beautiful close up. It was no wonder Alexius's friend had fallen for her. A bright smile beamed from Cornelius's face, one that that every girl in Herculaneum had, at one time or another wanted to drown in. Messalina remembered doing so.

"Faustina, I want you to meet Marcus Galerius Alexius and Messalina Claudia." Cornelius announced to his betrothed with pride and turned back to Alexius. "This is Faustina Lucia Satrius, soon to become my wife."

"It is a pleasure to meet you," Alexius said, his gaze sparkling. "Domina, thank you for sponsoring the games. I know such events come at a great expense."

Messalina observed the conversation while she admired Faustina's dark blue stola. Her neckline revealed a taunting cleavage and a strand of pearls and sapphires. So unlike the usual modestly worn by most patrician women. "Your stola is lovely," Messalina said, "It is different."

"It has raised a few eyebrows," Faustina said with a clever grin. "I am head of my father's household and remain unmarried, so I decide on such things as what I choose to wear. However many do not agree with me."

Cornelius chuckled. "I find it quite delightful. Don't you, Alexius?"

"Definitely. I hope Messalina will enjoy such things once we are married." Alexius chuckled to his friend. "However, we may live to regret getting these two together."

Cornelius laughed heartily as he plucked a shrimp from a passing platter. "Hardly. I cannot wait to parade such beauty about Rome."

The stroll continued. "Did you enjoy the games?" Faustina asked Alexius.

"I did. Unfortunately, not Messalina," Alexius drew everyone's attention to her. "Some drunken fool fell on her before the first match."

Concern flooded Faustina's face. "I am sorry. I hope you weren't hurt."

"No. I wasn't," Messalina assured. "I am sorry I missed your games. Everyone is talking about them."

Cornelius smiled "Well then, next year, possibly you could join us in my family's seats."

As they passed tables, people continuously interrupted to thank Faustina for letting the gladiatrix fight. She acknowledged them with a forced smile. Alexius had told Messalina that the games had not gone to Faustina's liking. It was matters best left ignored.

"Your father would have been proud of all that you have accomplished, Faustina," Messalina said, munching on a bread stick plucked from one of the tables groaning from piles of food.

Faustina gazed up at one of the statues of honored men nearby. The statue was of a brilliant stalwart man who definitely resembled his daughter. "I hope he is," she said.

Maybe it was Faustina's pride and determination to keep her father's memory alive in Pompeii that raised Messalina's respect toward his daughter. Rosa held no such respect for her father, which was now fully understood.

She thought of her own father. Even thought he had financed most of Balbus's designs in Herculaneum and helped in the city when needed, Herculaneum would never grant him such a monument, which seemed unfair now. Without the help of the equestrian and freedmen, the patricians would never accomplish any of their grandiose plans for Rome.

A slave appeared.

"Yes, Lorenz?" Faustina asked.

The slave whispered something. Faustina turned to Cornelius, who nodded and turned to Alexius. "I am sorry. You will have to excuse us," he said, "We have something that we must attend.

Hands clasped. Hugs were shared. Alexius sipped at his wine, watching Cornelius and Faustina disappear into the crowd. "What do you think?"

Messalina dipped a clam in a honey sauce from a nearby table. "Faustina is perfect for Cornelius. Yet, it is a shame his father and mother don't agree with their betrothal."

Alexius offered her a cheese stick. "Sulla doesn't like much of whatever Cornelius does, which is unfortunate." He looked out to the crowd. "He is good for Rome."

"Well, if it isn't the first couple of Herculaneum." They turned to see Marcus and Hector staggering toward them, arms draped over shoulders.

"Aren't they just adorable, Hector?" Marcus blustered.

Hector's gaze felt slimy as he scanned Messalina. "You look absolutely scrumptious, my swan. Oops." Hector giggled and turned to Marcus. "I'm not supposed to call her my swan."

"Why not?" Marcus asked.

"Only Alexius can." Hector snickered in Marcus's ear. "She so commands."

Marcus scanned her from head to toe. "Well, she looks good enough to eat, which I'm sure Alexius wants to do. Don't you, my ol' friend? Humm?"

Fury rose like a lion. Messalina remembered the many times that Alexius had fed off Marcus's insidious remarks like this. Her heart hammered in her chest. Would he now?

Alexius slipped his arm possessively around her, which melted her to him. "I think it is time you bothered someone else. The brothel is that way."

Hector drunkenly scanned Alexius then tried to focus on Messalina. "You haven't changed your mind about our plans, have you, my swan. I mean, my love. I mean Messalina?" He giggled again and tried to focus on Marcus. "She doesn't want me calling her any of that. Don't know why. Do you know, Marcus?"

Marcus dropped his forehead to Hector's. "Medusa doesn't much look like a duck anymore. So maybe she has become a swan."

Messalina looked up to see a deadly gaze in Alexius's eyes. His weight shifted as if to step forward. This was so different when he would have joined the insults. People were gawking at them. "Alexius, let's go."

Alexius nodded, his jaw knotting while his steady glare pulsed at his friend. "Like I said, Marcus, the brothels are that way. They are waiting for you."

Marcus toasted them with his cup and slid his free hand down Hector's back. "We must be gone, Hector, before you start to drool again." He turned toward Messalina. "He does so miss you, Med…Messalina. Pines for hours, if he does not see you somewhere in the city. Try as I may, I'm barely able to console him."

Hector giggled to his friend. "She is my Aphrodite, my swan. No, no, no. I can't call her that." He brightened as Marcus dragged him in the direction of the brothels. "Messi, maybe after we run away, I can."

Humiliation burned like a rash. Messalina stormed away. She did not care where, just away. Alexius caught up with her and grabbed her arm to stop her. "Messi, they are drunk."

"That was quite obvious."

"Did you really tell him to not call you 'my swan'?" Alexius asked, grinning curiously.

"Yes." Marcus had never told him?

"I am glad, because I prefer that no one call you that except me." Alexius studied her. "Do you mind it if I call you 'my swan'?" His gaze sparkled with curiosity.

Regardless of how she tried to avoid him, she failed. His face had turned into that all-familiar boyish tease that had destroyed her on many occasions. Yet, somehow, it felt different now. A giggle tickled through her.

"You will anyway, regardless of what I prefer." She walked away.

Alexius raced ahead of her and started walking backwards. "I won't if you don't want me to. But, I will call you 'my love," he pleaded. "Would that be all right?"

He already had called her that, but she liked him asking. She lifted her chin and continued through the crowd. "How can you call me 'your love' when you don't?"

He almost danced alongside her as she walked toward the basilica. "Oh, I do, my love."

"I don't believe you."

She started around him, except Alexius grabbed her by the waist, pulled her into some dark vestibule of the basilica, and further into some dusty back room filled with incense. A silk garment brushed her arm as he pressed her against the wall. A soft sack of something touched her leg. "Alexius? Where are we?"

"The storeroom of Apollo's temple." His voice was husky. "And alone, my love, my swan. Not even Fosco or Niki know where we are."

Before she could say anything, all was forgotten the instant he kissed her. Words, thoughts, and concerns melted as snow dropped on a flame. Her flesh sizzled, hot and wondrous, emptying her mind of all sanity and filling her with a new desire.

Her mind spiraled as she wrapped her arms around Alexius's neck, wanting him to kiss her like this forever. Heat pooled deep and delicious. She gasped when his hand slid under the flounce of her tunica and cupped her breast. He caught the sound with his mouth.

"What do you see in that slut?"

"Opportunity," answered.

Alexius jerked away, his hand covering her mouth. Motionless, they stared at each other and then at the cloth drape hanging over the door and separating them from whoever was out there. Their gazes met with the same thought. *These are the same voices heard in the garden.*

"As well as you and all that is you. Now, kiss me."

Sulla! Messalina looked at Alexius. He nodded.

"No. Not until it is done."

Volasennia! Alexius locked his gaze on her. Messalina nodded.

"How much longer?" Sulla demanded.

"Balbus will last only a few more weeks. What about Agrippina?" Volasennia snipped. "When will you get rid of that bitch?"

"Give me more time. She can't hold out forever."

"And neither can I."

The ground heaved like a bucking mule. Supplies and incense fell. Wooden boxes and pottery jars crashed to the floor. The shelving teetered as rock dust plummeted from the ceiling.

Alexius lifted her in his arms and charged past the curtain and into Sulla and Volasennia charging for the outside doorway. Everyone froze in the small quaking hallway until the floor heaved again, more violently than before. Sulla and Volasennia bolted into the panic flooding the plaza.

Alexius followed, carrying her out into the exploding pandemonium where people stumbled about like drunks. Food servers raced from under the falling portico. Tables tumbled, spreading food into the insanity. Torches and oil lamps swayed in their pegs and then fell, starting fires. The greedy glow of flames roared to life in a back street where screams pierced the darkness.

Messalina turned to Alexius as he watched the frantic crowd. "Alexius, that was them."

He nodded and turned to her "I know. I know. Are you all right?"

"Yes. For now." Her heart thudded like a drum as they staggered for footing. A donkey from the children's rides raced by. Honorary statues rocked as the ground lurched again. The one next to Faustina's father fell, heaving the thick crowd backward like a wave.

Messalina gripped Alexius's tunic. "Alexius, we have to tell someone or Balbus is going to die like Vespasian. Maybe Cornelius—"

"No." Alexius grabbed her by both arms. "Just pretend nothing happened. You didn't hear anything." He looked sternly into her eyes. "Messi, promise me."

"But Alexius—"

"Promise me!" His grip on her arms tightened.

"I promise."

"Do you think they heard us?" Volasennia asked, clinging to Sulla's arm as he dragged her away from the basilica.

Sulla snarled as he watched Alexius and Messalina disappear in the crowd hovering in the center of the plaza. "Every word."

"Then you have to do something."

He smirked. "Trust me. I will."

"What?"

Sulla looked down at Volasennia's inquiring gaze. "If they say one word to anyone, I will see both of them killed."

"Why wait for them to say anything? Why not kill them anyway?"

Sulla shook his head. "Too many people are watching Galerius's spawn."

"Then kill her?"

CHAPTER 31

MESSALINA STARED DOWN at the jar of per-fumed oil in her hand. No part of her wanted to be standing in Didius's work shed, even though the small room smelled of hibiscus and jasmine. Normally, she enjoyed making oils, but now, all she could think about was Alexius. She had not received a letter from him for weeks. Why?

She placed the jar down on the worktable and looked out at the restless bay. After the tremors left Pompeii in shambles, her father said he could not tolerate another bone-shattering trip home by wagon and had sent for his galley to take them back to Herculaneum.

She wished the galley had taken them all away to Egypt or Britannia instead. Volasennia and Sulla's voices kept reverberating in her brain. Before Alexius and their fathers had left to go to Rome on business, Alexius had insisted, "Remember, my love. Say nothing to anyone about hearing anything."

It did not take an oracle to tell her that Alexius was in far more danger than she ever could be. Not only were Pomponius and Balbus threatening to destroy his career.

Now Sulla likely wanted him dead. After all, if Sulla and Volasennia could kill Caesar, they could kill anyone.

Maybe she was in danger, as Alexius had said. Without letters, how would she even be able to guess? She simply wanted the election over and Alexius donning his senatorial toga. For once, she wanted to be in Rome with him instead of trapped there in Herculaneum. She was sure Alexius was not hiding in Rome. Therefore, she was not going to be intimidated by such worries either.

"I can't work any longer. I am going shopping," Messalina said, startling Didius.

He spilled the oil over the table. "Yes, domina, I will go with you as well."

She sighed heavily. "You don't have to worry about me running away with Hector because I am not. He is a fool." The smile on the old slave's face made her blush.

Messalina meandered past the shops shadowed by the street canopy covering the sidewalks. Niki followed close enough with the parasol to share sandals. A heavy sigh escaped Messalina's lips. She truly missed Rosa on days like this.

A new slave, Pollux, followed Didius. Her mother had found the scrawny boy in the slave market and felt pity for him. Her mother bought the child only to discover he ate like a horse and remained as thin as a reed.

New perfume bottles caught Messalina's attention outside the glass shop where she remembered Felix giving her Zeno's note to come to his apartment. She ran her hand over the smooth-colored surfaces of the small jars, recalling how Alexius had found her that night and had protected her, risking his own life. Now, he was still risking everything for her.

Months ago, she would have asked why he would do so. Now she actually relished the idea that he did want to marry her. That he did care for her. That he was trying to make a life for them in Rome. That he would not break her heart again. She warmed with the thoughts.

"You like to buy?"

Messalina looked up at the middle-aged saleswoman. "No. Thank you."

She left the jar and memories and crossed the street to her favorite fabric shop. The instant she stepped into the simmering sun, Niki covered her with the parasol. The summer days were becoming unbearably hot. Even the bay breezes failed to cool anything. Apparently, Vulcan was very busy lately because a day failed to pass without the ground trembling as it just had.

Envy nettled at her nerves. If she were in Rome, she could possibly visit Rosa. However, her father only owned a small apartment in Ostia near his warehouses. She would have no other place to stay in Rome than at Alexius's townhouse, which would be inappropriate. He certainly did not need any more gossip following him while he ran for office.

The vibrant colors in the fabrics drew Messalina. She ran her hand over a mustard-colored cloth the same color of Alexius's tunic the day he left. It had made his hair appear thicker than mink.

"This is a much better color for you, domina," said a young woman who looked much older than her years. She spread delicious linen, the color of raspberries, across the table. "This is much better for you."

Messalina immediately thought of Alexius feeding her berries in the fields when they found Carena with the baby.

She pointed at the teal-colored bolt of linen above the shop-keeper's head. "Let me see that one."

The woman presented the bolt of silk and smiled. "Domina, this one brings out the gold in your eyes."

Designs much like Faustina's began popping through her mind. "I would like to see that green?"

"Yes. Of course." The woman spread the silk ,the color of dark evergreens, between them. She wanted them all. She wanted special designed stolas and pallas that turned heads when she appeared with Alexius. She wanted everyone jealous. Gossiping. Her blood surged with delight.

"I would like enough of all of these," she stated to the shop keeper, whose eyes gleamed with success."

"Domina, how do you wish to have them bordered?"

Borders of a married woman? Yes. She needed to be thinking like a senator's wife. After all, she hoped to be one soon enough. That thought danced through Messalina. "Yes, silver on the green, white on the raspberry, and blue on the teal. Not with the same patterns either. No. I want—"

"Messalina."

Hector? What was he doing here? She turned to the familiar voice that chilled every delightful thought like a bucket of cold water. She looked at the woman still holding the green fabric and turned to Didius. "Have everything arranged to be delivered."

"Yes, domina." The old master slave bowed to her and rose with a scathing glare at Hector.

"Messalina, I must talk to you." Hector gripped her wrist and drew her out into the searing sunlight. "I must beg for your forgiveness for my stupidity."

She wrenched her wrist from his grip and stared, first at the angelic curls framing his face, his soft lips, his pleading gaze. He was nothing compared to Alexius. Her stupidity had blinded her.

"Messi, please say you forgive me." He reached to brush irritating strand of hair that blew across her cheek. "Please, my lovely rosebud."

She flinched back as if violated. "I have to go." She started back into the fabric shop. He caught her firmly by the arm again. "Alexius has a mistress—Sabrina Rufus. I saw them at the theater together before I left Rome. She's the one reading your letters."

Messalina's heart slammed against her ribs. Alexius promised her that he would never have a mistress. "You are lying."

Hector sandwiched her hand between his in a prayerful plea. "I could never lie to you, Messalina. I saw them laughing together. My heart is breaking, but you should know about him before you are married to this mongrel."

She yanked her hand away. "Never lie? What about Lizbet?"

He gasped. "Oh, my love, Lizbet is an actress and I am but an actor. Of course, he sees us together."

CHAPTER 32

ALEXIUS STUDIED HERCULANEUM'S skyline as his father's galley eased closer to the pier. A month from now, the galley and the townhouse in Rome would be his. His parents' wedding gifts. He had already instructed his master slave in Rome to start preparing it for their new domina. However, come September, thanks to Pomponius's slander and Balbus's lies, he may never be able to afford either if his election failed.

He still spent his mornings in the basilicas, talking to all who would listen, hearing voters concerns, and smiling until his face hurt. His hand ached from shaking all proffered hands until his fingers felt like mush. There were moments he wanted to scream, yet he kept reassuring everyone that their concerns were his as well.

"Rise above all things, son. Pomponius is well known for this by those smart enough to see the man's misdirected anger," his father had stated that very morning. Alexius hoped his advice would be enough.

Unfortunately, Titus Caesar had decided not to accuse the fat fool of embezzling funds and, instead, had fined him heavily for the so-called "mistakes" found in the reports. So much so, that Pomponius's villa in Ravenna was now up for sale. The rumor was that Sulla had invited him to stay at the villa in Herculaneum. That was too close for comfort.

Alexius gazed at the massive backdrop behind the city, Mount Vesuvius—shimmering in all its glory. He simply hoped that Zeno was already in Armenia, hiding with Rosa at his side. However, since there were no such rumors of Pomponius losing his wife spreading over the city like lava, that was not likely either.

Alexius rubbed his wrists as if the iron shackles had just been removed. Since the nightmare, he had not been able to wear wrist cuffs and might never do so again. Those nightmarish images rose like ever-present demons. The sound of Zeno's cries struck like hits from a whip. "He is the one. He helped me! He helped me!" He saw his father's lacerated body, heard his mother's screams, and Balbus pointing to the empty lashing pole.

Herculaneum drew closer with each swish of the oars. He stared at Messalina's terrace, remembering his last night patrolling with the vigils instead of being with her. He had told Flaccus everything about what he and Messi had heard in the garden and in the basilica.

"Arrogant ass was askin' for it," Flaccus had said over a cup of ale. "All of 'em are too arrogant for my blood, if you ask me. I'll see to the young domina 'til you return. Mind if I tell Felix?"

The galley lurched to a stop at the pier and the gangway finally dropped. Alexius was off the galley deck like a wounded bear. He bolted across the beach to Messalina's house, ignoring the greetings from the people he passed.

Didius greeted him at the door. "Dominus, how good to see you home. The trip was good?"

"Excellent," Alexius said, "Is Messalina here?"

"Yes, I believe she is in her room. Pollux, go announce that the young Marcus Galerius Alexius wishes to see her."

Alexius's sandals were being replaced when the boy returned. "She says she is ill and isn't up to visitors, dominus."

"Ill?' His heart stopped. Had Volasennia done something? "What is wrong?"

Pollux's scrawny shoulders shrugged as Messalina's mother appeared.

"Alexius!" Octavia hurried toward him, arms out in greeting. They politely hugged. The woman quickly scanned him and smiled. "It is so good to see you. Pollux, go inform my daughter her betrothed is here to see her."

The boy hesitated, glancing at Didius.

"The young domina says she isn't feeling well," the master slave said.

Octavia studied both slaves. "That is strange. Get Alexius something to drink, and I will go speak with her." She turned to Alexius. "I won't be long."

Alexius followed her to the doorway that opened to the manicured gardens and watched Octavia walk up the steps to the second-story rooms overlooking the bay. He would rather be the one checking on Messalina.

However, he forced himself to wait by the garden pool sparkling in the afternoon sun. The water quivered beneath his feet, sending the fish darting under the floating lily pads like flecks of gold.

If the gods had deemed 26 August perfect for Cornelius and Faustina to marry, why did he and Messalina have to wait until 13 September? That did not make any sense.

Not one priest could give him a logical explanation. All he wanted was to get Messalina out of Herculaneum and away from Balbus's family. Flashes of his fantasies of Messalina naked in his bed came to mind.

"She refuses to come down," Octavia said, shocking Alexius back into the present. "She says she has a headache."

Vespasian had chills and fever, not a headache. "How long has she felt this way?"

Octavia shrugged with a scowl. "She went shopping yesterday and seemed perfectly fine then. It is nothing, I am sure." A coy smile appeared on the woman's face. "Alexius don't worry so." She slid her arm through his and began leading him back through the atrium. "She will be anxious to see you tomorrow. I am sure of it."

Worry hung on his heels like lead as he approached the vestibule where Niki lingered near the front doors. She touched his arm as he started to leave. "Dominus, Felix has a message for you. He is waiting across the street from…"

Octavia noticed the girl's chatter and scowled. Niki dropped her gaze and stepped back.

"A message? Across the street from Zeno's apartment? Does that make any sense to you?" Alexius asked Fosco who trailed behind as they walked toward the main street.

"No, dominus. Nor does it make sense the young domina fails to greet you."

"Exactly."

He had enough messages lately. He wanted answers. How much did Sulla, Balbus, and even Pomponius know? Had the emperor died of natural causes or assassinated? Was Balbus a walking dead man? What was wrong with Messi?

When they approached, Felix looked up from watching Flaccus carving something that resembled a toy outside on the tavern's bench. The old centurion slid his knife into its sheath, and stuck the pole into his leather pouch at his feet and stood. "Welcome back, young dominus. Began to think Rome decided to keep ya."

"Good to see you both well. Any news?" Alexius asked as he stepped from the street.

"Only that you need to buy us drinks." The leathery smile lines deepened beside the centurion's eyes. He motioned Alexius into the shadows of the taverna.

"Why would I need to buy either of you drinks?" Alexius asked as he sat on a stool.

"We're thirsty," the centurion said, waving three fingers at the server.

Felix sat beside Flaccus and leaned forward on his arms. "What news is there from Rome?" he asked.

"Pomponius is broke from repaying the treasury. Balbus still hates me. Zeno is nowhere to be seen. Election is tanking if things don't change." Alexius stopped as the ales were set on the table. They drank half, and then Alexius pushed his mug aside to lean forward. "Your turn."

Flaccus must have cut his thumb while carving the toy. Blood smeared along the surface of the green mug as he shoved it aside. "Nothing. Sulla is busy at the Temple, greasin' elbows with all the locals."

"Balbus?"

"Saw that big-headed prick in his litter yesterday near the Temple. Didn't linger long." The soldier glanced at Felix sitting beside him and then leaned closer. "But I'd say he's not up to his usual audacity."

Felix drew his mug closer to his chest. "Guess your betrothed didn't have much time for you, or you wouldn't be spending the afternoon buying us drinks. Am I right?"

Alexius glared at the two smirking faces. "She said she isn't feeling well."

Felix chuckled as Flaccus swirled his ale. "And you believe her?"

"Why shouldn't I?"

Felix stretched his arms, crossed them behind his head, and leaned back on the wall. "She was perfectly fine yesterday. Wasn't she, old man?"

"Yep. Saw her with that actor."

Alexius's blood turned frigid. "That spawn of a slave whore," he seethed as he glared at both gloating men and settled on Flaccus. "What was Hector doing here?"

The centurion shrugged. "Nothing much. Other than stopping to talk to your beloved at Demetri's fabric shop."

That fact did little to thaw Alexius's mounting anger as Felix lifted his cup for a refill. "I will say she didn't look none too pleased to see him, though."

That calmed his nerves a bit. "Not pleased? Why?"

Flaccus drew back for three full mugs placed before them. The girl left with the empty mugs. "Whatever he said seemed to upset her. She marched straight home."

Felix gazed at him with a most pathetic look. "I believe he said that he loves her, and you don't. Maybe a mistress is involved."

Both men continued to drink as casually as if the insufferable summer day was all that mattered at that moment. It was all Alexius could do to keep civil. Hector had better be well on his way to anywhere except Herculaneum. He could use something to pound on right now. "Where is that little prick?" Alexius started up from the bench.

Both men penned his wrists to the table. "Gonna cost ya another round," Flaccus said, grinning far too broadly for comfort.

Alexius sat back down. "Damn it, where is he?"

Felix smiled across to Flaccus. "Love's a bitch, ain't it?"

"Damn you. Where is he?" Every muscle drew like a bow.

"Gone. Left about an hour ago. About the time you arrived." Felix said with an easy shrug. "Musta known you were comin', I'd say."

"So, Alexius, that being the case, with you wantin' to pound in someone's head, I could use you tonight. The vigils have been running thin of late, what with Balbus paying every lout to search for that slave of his. So I'll expect you to be joining us?" Flaccus lifted his mug with a toast and drained it.

CHAPTER 33

NOTHING COULD STOP Alexius from seeing Messalina now. He did not care if his father wanted him to return to Rome to meet with voters before it was too late to undo the damage Balbus and Pomponius were arranging. He had had his fill of spoiled senators and their arrogant attitudes. He certainly did not need hers. In addition, he was tired of groveling for her trust.

The street cleared as he marched toward her door. Either Messalina wanted to marry him or she did not. If she preferred becoming an actor's wife and living in Subura, fine. One thing was certain. Either way, he was going to get the truth out of her today.

Didius stepped into Messalina's open doorway with another bright morning smile. "Good day, dominus."

"I need to see Messalina. Where is she?"

The old man stiffened at the blunt greeting. "Dominus, on the terrace. I will have you—"

"No need." Alexius breezed past and headed to the garden. The new peacock cawed furiously and flew up to the roof. Slaves backed away as he stormed past the ivy-covered arbor. A rainbow array of flowers dotted the terrace like jewelry. He found her reading a scroll in the shade of a large potted fichus tree near the garden room.

She seemed well enough, Alexius thought, as he came down the terrace steps. The color in her face was vibrant. Her gaze was sharp enough to cut marble. There were no suggestions of her having been ill at all.

"I hope you are feeling better."

Messalina set the parchment beside her yellow tunica. "Somewhat."

He bit his lips to control the words burning in his brain. "I came to see you yesterday. You said you were ill."

She turned to a pot of marigolds and began deadheading the blooms. She handed the withered flowers to Niki, who left to dispose of the waste. "I heard Pomponius sent Rosa back to Sulla's villa?" she said, resting back in the cushions as if all was well in the world.

He watched her brush the pollen from her hands. "He had to sell his villa. To refund the imperial treasury."

Messalina rose and walked to the railing. "I am sure that will please Rosa," she said to the bay.

"I don't give a fig what Pomponius or Rosa wants."

"Really?"

He watched the sea breeze blow Messalina's hair over her shoulders. By the gods, she was Venus herself. He could worship her if she would let him. Nevertheless, if she wanted Hector, he would see the betrothal annulled, and she could do as she pleased after the annulment. However, he needed to hear from her what she actually wanted.

"We need to talk."

She turned, studying him like a specimen. "Oh, I agree. But here?"

Eyes and ears were all too available. Slaves were suddenly busy behind them. He could hear Antonia and that damn puppy. "If necessary."

Alexius's blunt words unnerved her. "Is it…that necessary?"

He walked close enough to glare down at her. "Yes."

She met his dark blue gaze, wanting to crumble. No. She would not melt before him. After all, he had everything he wanted, which included a lover, maybe many lovers. Maybe he would finally be honest with her and tell her the truth. That all he had said were lies. That he was marrying her for her dowry. That to him she still was 'Medusa'.

Messalina straightened her shoulders and glanced at the side room where her mother chattered with her sister. "This is not private enough. Is there some other place that would not be so…public?"

The intensity of his gaze wavered. "Zeno's apartment?"

"Fine." She turned to Didius standing in the garden. "I will be going out with Alexius. Niki, stay here."

She walked back through the gardens with Alexius practically stepping on her heels. Fury simmered off him like heat from Apollo's chariot. She claimed her proffered palla from a door slave and covered.

This was it. She was finally going to confront him. She did not care anymore. She was tired of worrying about when Alexius would crush her heart again. Somehow, she had to make her parents let her marry a man who…who did not see her as a gorgon. A man whom she could trust, one who would not lie to her. The doubt that a man so honorable could even exist stung her insides like bees.

Shoppers made way for them as they briskly walked down the busy street in total disregard for each other's presence. A few people nodded greetings and instantly saw that they would not receive any in return. Their good wishes changed to curious glances.

Alexius stopped at the stairs, waiting for her to lead the way up to the apartment. She cast him a scathing glance before she braved the staircase. With each step, her dreams of being a senator's wife faded, dreams that once glowed with promise. Still, if Alexius could not love her, at least the truth would be spoken, even if it came out like puss in a raw wound.

Messalina entered the small apartment and went to the same bench where she had sat an eon ago. Alexius closed the door and went directly to the same window shuttering the blazing sunlight. His green tunic lay smoothly across his broad shoulders. The linen drape of darker green crossed his lean torso and lay on his shoulder. It all displayed a perfect body that any sane woman would beg to know, as she did…or had.

Alexius studied the closed shutter. Images of how he had chased her in the flowery field floated in her mind. His laughter, the way he shared his thoughts. Her heart climbed to her throat. The room shrank. The silence pulsed.

"Alexius, I know you have more important things to do today than be here with me."

"No, actually. You are wrong." He turned away from the window and leaned on the wall, crossing his arms over his chest. "Or is it that you would prefer me to be somewhere else, instead of being here with you?"

His snide words bit like lashes from a whip. "Would it matter what I want?"

"Yes, Messalina. It does matter. In fact, it matters to me quite a bit." He stared at her, expecting her to say something.

She had nothing to say.

"What is bothering you?"

She laughed. Everything was bothering her, especially liars and people who used others for their own gain. "Nothing. Is something bothering you, Alexius?"

His hands opened and closed at his sides, fingers stretching. "Something has bothered you ever since I came home from Britannia. Whatever that is, is bothering me now. So tell me, Messi, what is it?"

"Just tell me what is so important that you race back to Rome every chance you can?"

He looked at her and slid a frustrated hand through his hair. "Messalina, I went back to get elected so we would have a future."

"We? Do you mean you…and me? Not someone else?"

Ridicule radiated from his face. "Who else?"

She braced as the words crawled from her lips. "Who else? Oh, maybe a mistress? Lover?" She waved a dismissive hand between them. "Someone you would prefer marrying other than 'Medusa'?"

His face turned red. His gaze sharpened enough to cut granite. "Did that filthy actor tell you that I had a lover hidden somewhere in Rome?"

"Hector saw you with Sabrina Rufus at the theater. She is the one reading my letters." She endured his scathing glare. "Can you deny it?"

Alexius's hands fisted in the folds of his tunic. "I will kill that filthy piece of shit for this." He sneered across the room at her. "Yes. He saw me escorting Sabrina Rufius to the play at the theater."

His admitted the truth that burned in Messalina's brain like a tumor. She stood to leave. Alexius stepped between her and the door.

"Sabrina is the wife of one of Father's clients. Father wanted to talk to Aquillius about the election and asked me to escort her to the theater so they could talk." He rested back on one hip. "If this lover of yours had paid any attention, he would also have told you that Sabrina left with three other wives and went shopping after the play, dismissing me like a schoolboy. And she is not reading your letters."

Fury swelled like hot lava. "Hector is not my lover!"

"He is not?" His smile twisted. "There are no secret visits with him when I am not here? Or is he just your spy, Messalina?"

"Hector is not my spy. Nor my lover. Didius can vouch for me." She straightened before him. "I have known all along that you would prefer to marry someone much prettier…than I am." Tears burned behind her eyes. "So…so, break the betrothal. I do not care anymore. Then you will be free to marry any one you want to be seen with."

"What?"

"I do not care for your platitudes, Alexius. I know I am not as pretty as Sabrina or…" She waved her hand between them to finish what her brain could not. Because every part of her heart hurt. "Or any other girl in Rome." She could not endure any more. She started around him.

"No, Messi." He caught her by her wrist before she reached the door to escape the crushing blow forthcoming. "You are not pretty."

He admitted it. Defiant tears sprang from her eyes like runaways. She lashed at them with one hand as she tried to wring her arm from his grip. Finally, he told her to her face that she was…

"You are beautiful, Messalina. As beautiful as Venus's daughter."

How could he say that? "You lie."

"No. I am not lying or stating platitudes as you accuse me of. Messi, you are more beautiful than all the girls in Rome."

"Stop lying to me, Alexius. You don't want me."

"I am not lying to you, Messi. And I do want you." He drew closer and cupped her face with both hands. His thumbs swabbed tears that would not stop. "I want to spend my life with you…only you. I love you, my little swan." He kissed her forehead.

His gaze melted her like frost before the winter sun. "You…you don't mean that."

A smile lurked at the corners of his lips. "I mean every word." His hands settled on her shoulders.

"Why?"

He tilted his head slightly. "Because you are beautiful, Messi. Because I can trust you. I know how loyal you are to those you care about, which means a lot to me lately." He shrugged and grinned. "After all, we grew up together." He stroked her hair back from her face with one palm. "Messi, I want us to be together as long as the gods will allow. I do want to be seen with you as my wife. Each and every day. No one else."

A strange new joy dared to spring to life. Every trembling part of her wanted to believe him. He drew her close. Close enough for her to feel his heart thudding with hers. His mouth found hers, kindling something inside her, something delicious.

She drew back, drowning in the blue depths of his gaze. "There…there really isn't anyone else?"

"No one and there never will be, Messi."

She shot a daring glare at him. "You…you don't think I am…'Medusa'?"

"You never were. I was the blind fool." Alexius's face became serious. "But Messi, do you want to be with me. Marry me?"

He was actually giving her the choice? She could not breathe. "If…if I didn't, would you break the betrothal?"

He stiffened and stepped back, dropping his arms. "Yes." He turned toward the door.

She caught his arm. "Alexius, don't…leave."

He looked back over his shoulder.

She dared to close the distance between them. "Alexius, you deserve to be happy, too."

The corner of his lips lifted. "As I said, I want to spend my life with you…only you and I would be, if you wanted to be with me."

"I do. It's just—"

"You are certain of that?" His expression demanded fact.

She rested her hand on the end of the bed to help her remain. "Yes, Alexius. I do not care if you do not become a senator. I just want you to be happy."

Alexius came to her and cupped her face. His warm breath brushed her cheeks before his lips rested on hers, igniting a creature trapped inside her. It rose up from her belly and spread through her. It was warm, delicious, and desperate. Her head tilted to allow him to feast along her neck.

Liquid fire coursed through her as his mouth accepted the offering, melting her flesh. She relished the sensations thrilling through her. She drove her fingers into his hair, allowing them to feast on the lush mink fur. They found their way over his muscles flexing along his arms and across his back. His familiar scent flooded her senses, making her oblivious to everything.

Gasping, she pulled back to see if this was real or a fantasy. There was no fantasy in his gaze. It steamed with the same hot need. In that moment, there was no doubt. Marcus Galerius Alexius was the man she wanted more than life itself. "Alexius. Make love to me…now."

"Messi? N…Now?" choked from his throat. He looked like she had slapped him. "By all the gods, do you mean that, Messi? I mean, here in a slave's apartment?"

Her throat closed because her heart had stopped beating, *He is lying. He does not…want me.* "Why would you not want me here or anywhere? So, it is all a lie!" She jerked away and started for the door.

"Messi, no. No!" He grasped both of her shoulders with desperate hands. "Yes! I do. I do want you, Messi." His hands dropped but not his gaze. "Only, I want it perfect. For you. You deserve that much." He scanned the nearby worn bed, around the simple apartment, and then at her. "Messi, you deserve rose petals covering our bed. You deserve the attention of everyone around you." He struggled to think of more. "It should be as perfect as you are."

Her heart swelled back to life. "Alexius, I don't care about all that. I want us to be real, honest."

An ocean gleamed in his blue eyes. "I will never want anyone else at my side. Only you, Messalina Claudia. Only you, my swan."

To be the man she had chosen meant more than Alexius imagined possible. Yes. He wanted to be the man in her life. Yes. He wanted to give her children and provide for her, dressing her in all of Rome's finest. Yes. He wanted her at his side. Yes. He wanted all that. However, to be the one *she wanted* meant more than all the wealth of Rome. With his life, he would see that she never regretted her decision.

All thoughts…all sanity vanished as Messalina let her tunic slide from her arms and drop to her feet like an offering. How did he deserve such perfection? Milky white skin. Rosy nipples atop mounded breasts. A thin waist tapering to a wellspring of hips. "Messalina, you are …the daughter of Venus."

Her skin flushed rosy red. A timid smile teased the corners of her mouth as she closed the distance between them and brushed the clasp holding the green drape from his shoulder. It fell over her silk tunic. Her brown gaze rose to his as thick as fur. She tugged at his tunic.

He ripped the garment over his head and flung it aside. Messalina was still here, her gaze caressing his flesh. None of this was a mirage.

"And you are the son of Apollo."

By all the gods of Olympus, he needed her in his hands, moving, arching, and begging for release. He caught her hands as she reached to remove his loincloth. "Messi. Wait." As much as he wanted to feel her on his cock writhing with desire and moaning with pleasure, he had to wait.

Fear sprang in her gaze. "Messi," He lifted her in his arms and placed her on the brown wool blanket. "I want to enjoy you."

Her hands starved for Alexius's flesh, for the feel of his muscles shifting across his back, his arms. The silk of his hair coiling in her fists felt richer than any fur. Her skin rippled. Her mind liquefied. Her throat constricted. She could not breathe as his hands brushed her flesh and his lips feasted on every nerve.

Her calf glided along his thigh, relishing its coarse hair. Until she met the leather of his sandals. The intrusion jarred their world to a halt as if stopped by a titan. Alexius halted as if he had hurt her

His grin appeared, allowing Messalina to breathe again. He rose and slid out of his sandals and then lifted her left foot to untie the ribbon of her left sandal ever so slowly. He stroked his thumbs over the instep and lifted each toe to his lips, nibbling on her pinkie toe.

She cried out as lightning seared to her scalp. She grabbed the rough wool blanket beneath her. The sound of his warm chuckle teased her back to the living as he removed her other sandal.

"You are exquisite, my swan, my love. Delicious." He teased each toe with his tongue, taunting her with his gaze.

She could not do anything except let him do whatever he wanted. Anything. Just do not stop. She reached for him.

His body glided over her like a warm blanket and she gathered him in her arms as if she could hold him there forever. If only she could. Only his loincloth separated them. He removed it with a quick jerk, and she felt the hardness of his cock pulsing against her belly. The shock of it trembled through her, stirring her with a strange curiosity that frightened her. Yet she wanted him to make her his. Did she?

She found Alexius's gaze full of questions. "Messi, are you…sure?" He seemed to choke on the words. "Do you… want to wait?"

Yes. No. Yes.

Her body sang with a new need, a need to be complete, to be one with him. Her hips rose as Alexius shifted along her body, lower. Low enough for him to touch her.

Everything inside her welcomed him. Only he denied her, leaving her void, empty, and wanting. He moved lower, taking his mouth down to her neck. His tongue drew small circles over the vein pulsing alongside her throat, dizzying her confused mind. His hand cradled one breast and flicked over her nipple.

Every nerve went rigid. She gasped and clung to his shoulders. "Alexius!"

She felt his smile against her flesh as he suckled the other breast and then ventured lower, over her belly, and lower still until his tongue played in her navel.

Then even lower.

His hand parted her womanly-flesh for his tongue to play between the velvet skin She was helpless with need and pleasure. She was frantic. Her world bucked, lashed, throbbed for more and more. Of what, she did not know. Just more.

"Alexius. Alexius, please."

His name sang from her lips as he played her, drove her farther into madness, until her entire body exploded, and she screamed.

It was the feel of his body gliding over her again, set-tling between her thighs. A newer hunger roared to life as he touched her core. This time with needs of his own. She gazed up into an ocean of hot desire pouring down on her.

Her answer was to welcome him as a long-awaited guest. She felt him break through her and ease inside further like a timid thief. However, he was no thief. Whatever she had was his.

She cupped his face, feeling the bristle of a spawning beard in her palms, and drew his lips to hers. His mouth came to hers as hungry as her own. They feasted, their tongues lashing, their bodies surging together, for more, more. Their bodies moved in unison, a dance she had never known existed, except it was a dance of pleasure and joy, of completeness.

His body ignited something hidden and deep inside her. Even her soul cried out. Every muscle in his body trembled with his release. His deep vibrating moans sang in her ears along with her name. "Messalina. By the gods, Messalina."

Her gaze found his gaze gleaming with joy as his lips curved into a contented smile. One lock of hair curled over his forehead. She brushed it back with her fingers. A smile drifted over her lips with contentment all its own.

"You are beautiful, so beautiful."

Her heart soared hearing those whispered words and she could finally believe each one. It had to be like flying for the first time, catching the air under outstretched wings and knowing they would hold.

"I love you, and only you, Messalina."

"And I only you, Alexius."

He kissed the tip of her nose, each eyelid, her forehead, and suckled an earlobe as he moved to her side, withdrawing from her. "I will never be able to sleep without you now, Messi."

He was right. Messalina rose on an elbow. They were not married. Therefore, he would not be there in her bed every night. To not have him, to not feel his flesh, his hands, his mouth on her would be like living without air. Dreams would never suffice.

"Alexius, we have to find a way to be together."

He grinned deviously. "I will think of something, my swan. I will think of something."

CHAPTER 34

EVERYTHING SEEMED DULL all because of Marcus Galerius Alexius. A smile slid across Messalina's lips as she pictured him naked as clearly as the morning sun. She sank back into the pillows of the terrace couch, thinking of the small scar on his thigh, earned from a skirmish in Britannia.

She now knew every hair on his chest because she had kissed each one all the way down to his groin. She was mystified by his penis, enthralled with his mouth, enchanted with his hands, and the way he made her feel so absolutely glorious. She wanted Alexius with her that instant. Of course, he could not be. He was with his father and clients, trying to make a future for them. Nevertheless, he was now the very air in her lungs, the very source of her existence.

Messalina stretched in the warm summer sun like a satisfied kitten, wishing she were in Zeno's apartment, waiting for Alexius, as she had each afternoon that he could get away. The small apartment had become their love nest, where they enjoyed themselves with absolute abandon as far into the evening as they dared. She made excuses to her mother that she must shop for her dowry, and then gave the task to Niki to buy a basket or a vase, anything.

Alexius always came bearing flowers, sweets, or gifts for her, so she had something more to take home. She moved her ankle so the sun could glint off his latest gift—a silver anklet with a pendant of Venus.

Her mother or father believed every excuse even when she did not come home for a few suppers. Oh, those evenings had been those of dreams. Making love, nibbling food from once forbidden places as he claimed her again and again.

With a lascivious grin that Bacchus would envy, she remembered every nuance of his mouth trailing slowly over her body. Usually, he tormented her with slow playful kisses and tongue-lashings until she knew she was going to climb out of her skin. However, she had discovered she could torture him as well. The banquet continued until neither could stand being apart. It was then that they came together with a mind-shattering force.

A long-tortured sigh escaped with a groan. It had been three days since they had been together, three long, impossible days and excruciating nights. Her body was like a taunt lute string, starving for his caress. Alexius should have agreed simply to meet her at Zeno's apartment instead of coming to talk to her father about advancing the wedding date.

"Alexius, I told you. I knew Father would not change the date to any time sooner," Messalina whispered as he led the way up the street to Zeno's apartment.

Alexius did not need to hear that right now. There was no reason they had to wait any longer. If Cornelius and

Faustina could have their wedding 26 August, they could as well.

He hid a scowl as Niki and Fosco parted the busy crowds in the streets. Everywhere, slaves carried baskets of vegetables, fabrics, garbage, and breads. Litters and sedan chairs worked their way through the street. Dogs barked at hissing cats that braced to scratch eyes out. The ground shook for a few strides, failing to stop children chasing in and out of stores and around fountains.

He had spent the last three nights with the vigils, hoping exhaustion would grant him sleep. It had not. Then, as soon as Apollo appeared in the sky, his father expected him to meet with clients in hope of maintaining their votes.

Cornelius continued to send frustrated messages regarding his excuses for not attending Justa's on-going trial. Reports from Rome said the election campaign was struggling worse than ever and that he should return as soon as possible. He had no idea what Balbus, Pomponius, and Sulla were plotting.

However, right now, nothing mattered more than seeing his future wife stretched naked before him, reaching for him like a hungry tigress, feasting on him as he feasted on her. Regardless of the fact that he could not remember being more tired in his life, he knew he could not feel more wonderful. Because every afternoon possible, he had made love with the offspring of Venus.

All the way to the apartment, he dare not look at Messalina for fear of kissing her in the street in front of everyone. Nor touch her, because every part of his body begged to caress her skin and feel her move in his hands. By the time they came to the stairway, his body vibrated with an absolute need. It was electric like before a storm ready to explode, when hair stood on end. Only that was not what was standing on end right now.

The block-long hallway loomed empty like a narrowing tube ending with a speck of sunlight at the opposite end. Messalina stopped outside Zeno's apartment and wheeled, pinning him at the door with a soul-consuming kiss, desperate enough to sweep his brain of sane thought.

He managed to lift her in his arms and stumble through the doorway. He kicked the door closed behind them and collapsed on the bed. Hands pulled at clothes, baring each other's flesh like starved animals.

"Ahem."

Alexius's heart jerked to a halt. He jolted from the bed as if struck by lightning. "Zeno!"

"Don't let me interrupt," Zeno said with a capricious grin. "Pretend I'm not even here." He waved them to continue. "However, I would appreciate it if all of Rome didn't know I was here."

"When did you get here?" Alexius asked, tugging his tunic straight. He felt Messalina readjusting her tunica behind him.

"You'd know that, better than I would. Felix tells me you have been taking very good care of my apartment. The flowers are nice." Zeno motioned to the three-day-old flowers wilting on the table.

"Balbus's men haven't caught up with you, I see," Alexius said, glancing back at Messalina. She had her tunica adjusted now. He stepped away so she could stand.

Zeno chuckled. "Until now, it's been easy. I spent the time with the legions while they looked for me."

"With the legions?" Alexius asked, stunned. "How?"

Zeno walked to the door and nodded down the staircase at Felix. He latched the door. "The auxiliary took me in as one of their slaves. I just kept my head down, limped, and stuttered while doing their laundry or shoveling their shit." He walked across the room to the window overlooking the street. His clever grin melted as he looked back at both of them. "I've come for Rosa."

Messalina stopped brushing wrinkles from her tunica. "Already? Here in Herculaneum?"

"Not yet," Zeno said. "But she will be. That two-faced, piece of shit father of hers is dying."

"Are you sure of that?" Alexius asked as a guilty sense of relief swept over him. With Balbus gone, his election chances would improve. Still, there was Pomponius and Sulla to do enough damage.

Three taps drew everyone's attention. Zeno walked to the doorway and let Felix in with a tray of bread, cheese, and a flagon of wine. Fosco followed with a tray of sliced peaches and bread bowls filled with beef soup.

"Anything?" Zeno asked Felix.

"Nothing. Quiet and normal. All have been alerted though."

"Good." Zeno motioned toward the table. "Let's eat, shall we?"

Everyone took a place at the table as Fosco and Felix left. Wine was poured, bread torn and dipped into the soup. The warm, rich fragrance filled the apartment.

"How do you know Balbus is dying?" Messalina asked, pushing her bread bowl away.

"Slaves know many things that masters would never dream of knowing." Zeno shrugged. "And I've been told Balbus is a walking dead man just as Vespasian was."

Alexius sat his wine mug down before him. "What do you mean…as Vespasian was? You knew?"

Zeno nodded. "Balbus and Vespasian have slept with a death dust, so I was told."

"You mean *charbon*?" Messalina asked.

Zeno nodded again.

Messalina looked at Alexius. "Then they have killed both like they said they would."

"Messi, we still don't have any proof." A desperate sense of concern climbed up Alexius's spine. "It is their word against ours."

"Who are you talking about?" Zeno asked, his gaze darting back and forth between them.

Messalina tore her attention from Alexius and looked at Zeno. "Sulla and Volasennia. We overheard them say they killed Vespasian and now Balbus."

"I wouldn't put it past either of them." Zeno leaned forward, resting his arms on the table. "Why, is what I'd like to know."

Alexius swirled his wine and studied the man. "Have you heard anything about the Augusta getting special land grants?"

Zeno nodded. "Heard a few talking about it in the bath house. Why?"

"Anything about picking the next emperor?"

"But Titus Caesar is emperor," Messalina said, interrupting the moment.

Zeno turned his attention back to Alexius. "As a matter of fact, I did hear talk about that. I thought like you, domina." He nodded at Messalina. "It made no sense, but they are all arrogant assholes to me."

Alexius adjusted on the bench, his nerves itching like a rash. "I don't know what any of this means either. Flaccus told me this a few months back about the land grants. Then, we overheard Sulla and Balbus's wife saying that Vespasian was a walking dead man. Why?"

Zeno shifted nervously. "Doesn't matter. If they know you recognized them, then I'm surprised either of you are still alive."

Messalina looked at him and then Zeno. "Is Rosa in danger?"

Zeno shrugged. "I don't think so, domina. She won't stay with her parents, which is good. Felix found out she will be staying at Sulla's villa again. I've got a boat waiting to take us to Capri then…" He looked at Alexius. "Then home."

Messalina glanced at Alexius and then looked straight at Zeno. "Rosa won't leave without Paullus."

Zeno sat back. "Paullus? The baby? He's alive?" Hope exploded in his face.

"Yes, "He is safe with Carena in Ruso's hut for now," Messi assured. She gripped Zeno's wrist, setting the slave down again. "It's best you don't go, not yet."

"But—" Zeno looked trapped on the bench.

"If Carena knows you are coming, she could run off," Alexius said. "If so, you will never find her because Rosa gave her fake manumission papers."

Zeno melted as if trapped. "Fake papers?

"She showed them to us," Messalina said.

"And they look real enough," Alexius added.

"I'll get Rosa and then find her." Zeno poured wine for everyone, his hand shaking. "And take Carena with us."

"That would be best for all concerned." Alexius released a pent-up sigh. "How do you plan to get Rosa from Pomponius?"

"That you don't need to know, Alexius. You both have risked enough. I'll tell you this. If the vigils get called to the villa, tell them to take their time in coming."

CHAPTER 35

ALEXIUS HAD JUST closed his eyes minutes before the first rooster crowed. A long miserable moan ground from his lips, reminding him that the wedding day could not come soon enough. He grinned even though the bruise on his shin throbbed from his run-in with his mother's marble bench.

Sighing back into the pillow, he pictured Messalina asleep in his arms only a few hours earlier. The early morning rays had beamed through the room's window and lit her face like a goddess. He could still see her hair stretched across the garden lounger set in the sunroom that had become their wedding bed.

He chuckled, remembering the first night he had climbed the dividing wall between their houses and Maximus nearly attacking him. Messi had barely managed to call the dog off and begged Didius not to tell anyone. The following morning Didius had awakened him from a most glorious sleep. "Dominus, the sun will be rising soon. You should go."

Every night since, he had blindly climbed over the wall and snuck back to his bedroom before the world awakened. However, last night, he stumbled into a bench and nearly woke the dead with him cussing the gods.

Alexius laid an arm cross his forehead, knowing he should return to Rome. After all, he was running for election, something his father grumbled about daily. He would never tell his father that if he did not win this year, he would simply run again next year. How could he leave Herculaneum with a goddess with open arms waiting for him each night?

He stretched beneath the thin cover and submitted again to its comforts. He had not heard anything about Zeno for a week and had only seen Felix at a taverna when he was on patrol with Flaccus and the vigils. Rumors were alive that Rosa and Pomponius were staying with Sulla now. There was no doubt in his mind that Pomponius was still licking his financial wounds after having to sell his villa to pay the imperial fines.

He had kept this information about Rosa from Messalina because she would be determined to see her, and he did not want her going anywhere near that villa. Not until he knew, she was safe.

A knock on the bedroom door broke through his visions of Messalina's hungry body. Just by the look on Fosco's face, Alexius knew it was urgent. "What is it?"

"Dominus, your father wants you in his tablinum immediately."

"Why?"

"I do not know, dominus, other than it is critical."

"Alexius!" His father hurried from the triclinium as soon as Alexius stepped into the garden. "Balbus is dead. He died last night."

Alexius stopped and stared at his father. *It had actually happened.* "Dead?"

His father motioned to walk out toward the terrace. "Balbus said he was not felt well lately." He looked at Alexius. "I cannot believe it was that serious." He studied the swelling seascape and then looked at Alexius. "We have to tell our clients before the city learns of this and goes into mourning. They will be here soon." He turned to Fosco. "Get things ready."

"They are, dominus."

Like a plague, the death of Balbus passed over Herculaneum worse than Vespasian's. Mourning cloth blackened the city streets like shadows in broad daylight. Weeping and groans were heard everywhere.

After the news was officially announced, Alexius followed his parents across the street to pay respects. His father's personal slave knocked on a door adorned with cedar wreaths. Labeo greeted them and stepped back to allow everyone in. The house felt like a mausoleum, cold and empty of life.

Alexius followed his father and mother into the red atrium where Balbus laid on an ornate bier in his finest senatorial toga. All unnecessary furniture had been removed except for the rattan chair where Balbus's mother, wearing her blackest stola, rocked at her son's side. Her hair streamed over each shoulder like long silver snakes. Her moans added to the hired mourners wailing the death from the garden.

Volasennia stood beside her, resting her hand on the old shoulder. She looked radiant in black, even with her hair also loose. After giving Rome three children, and with Balbus dead, Volasennia was considered a free woman. She could remarry or not as she chose. Marcus would have no say over his mother's plans, other than goodbye and good riddance.

"Our greatest sympathy to both of you, Viciria and Volasennia," Galerius said gently. "If there is anything we can do, we would be honored to help."

"Most certainly," Alexius added. He kept his gaze sympathetic and studied Volasennia's imploring gaze.

A delicate smile appeared on her face. "I am grateful that I have the support of the House of Galerius."

Before Alexius could move on with his parents, the witch's hand gripped his wrist like death. Fear ripped through him. "May Jupiter protect you, and may the gods bless your election. You make your parents proud."

"I...I am grateful, domina." Alexius forced his feet to move on to Rosa's eldest sister sobbing quietly into her husband's black tunic. Rosa and Marcus were obviously absent.

Images of Balbus in Alexius's nightmare flashed cold in his veins as he followed his parents into the garden. Relief reared tears in his eyes because that threat no longer had a life. A few noticed him pinching the bridge of his nose and smiled, thinking it was respect to the dead that drew his tears.

Other mourners passed quietly by the bier and clustered in the back garden, leaving behind whispers, tinkling chimes, and the witch's woeful misery. Slaves moved silently amid Balbus's accolades that were whispered through the crowd.

Alexius studied the growing number of faces. Where was Marcus anyway? As the new head of the House of

Balbus, Marcus should be making some effort to make an appearance. He claimed a glass of water and watched for Messalina and her family.

He recognized Octavia the instant Messalina's mother arrived. Her familiar wail flowed in from the street. Messi's father passed the bier, obviously sullen and withdrawn. Claudius followed with Antonia. Messalina followed behind her family as they appeared in the red atrium.

"Messi."

She looked up with a gaze as deep as the bay. "Alexius, he is dead."

"Yes. Very much so," he whispered, stepping alongside her as they followed the procession line past the bier.

Once through the atrium, Alexius led Messalina toward his parents standing near the back wall overlooking the ravine. Slaves brought Octavia a garden chair before she collapsed from grief. Aurelia hurried to comfort Messi's mother. Claudius kept Antonia at their mother's side as Messallus walked toward them.

"Can you believe this? I can't," Messallus said as he waved toward the atrium. "He is dead. Only yesterday, he was walking the streets, assuring everyone that what the tremors tore down, he would restore. What will the city do?" He leaned closer. "I certainly can't do anything until the next shipment comes in."

"I am sure no one will expect anything from you, Messallus," Galerius said. "Few could do what Balbus has done for Herculaneum. We will all have to pool what we have now."

Messalina looked at her father and then Galerius. "Have either of you seen Rosa or Marcus?"

"That little stuttering waste of air should be here," Messallus seethed. "Where is he? After all his father has done for him." The man leaned close. "He will destroy this house. Mark my words, he will."

"Volasennia says Balbus's last wish was to continue on with the celebrations and games for Vulcan exactly as planned," Galerius said, shaking his head.

"Sounds like him," Messallus motioned toward the bier. "I say the man deserves the honor of a triumph and nothing less."

Messalina stopped a passing slave. "The domina Rosa, has she arrived?"

"No, domina, she has not," the slave answered. "The bridge over the north gorge is unstable. They will have to come by water. Their galley will arrive soon, I am sure."

"The bridge is out?" Messallus asked the slave.

"Yes, dominus. The last tremor cracked the supports."

Messallus looked to Galerius. "And who will see to this and the rest of things?"

"The Collegium of the Augustulus will have to," Galerius assured. "We have been talking about adding a day to the games in the Palaestra in Balbus's honor. Then we meet, we will discuss the rebuilding expenses."

Messallus claimed a wine goblet from a passing tray. "I heard the main entry to the thermae is being set up for his cremation. Is that true?"

"I believe so," Galerius said.

"Then, may Zephyr blow Balbus's burning stink toward the sea," Messallus grumbled under his breath.

The people of Herculaneum joined Balbus's funeral parade that wound the city's main streets after the nine long miserable days of mourning. Messalina watched as her father in his black toga, joined the other honored men asked to bear the wax masks of Balbus's family and lead the funeral procession to the basilica.

After eulogies were spoken beneath the gaze of Balbus who was propped on his feet before everyone, the priests of Augustalus lowered him back onto his bier and led the procession to the thermae's main entry, now turned sanctum.

The paid mourners filled the air with their misery. The restless crowd spilled everywhere like a flood: down the walkways, out onto the beachfront steps, and well into the thermae plaza. In the midst of everything, a new statue to the man rose with its arm raised as if beseeching the gods. Before the figure, rose a pedestal topped with an open marble scroll, as if he were to read his request aloud. Below, etched into the marble, were the many honors of Marcus Nonius Balbus, first citizen of Herculaneum.

Messalina drew closer to Alexius's side as Sulla drew attention from the crowd of weeping women, quiet children, and solemn men by announcing in a large commanding voice, "Marcus Nonius Balbus was a great man to Rome. To Herculaneum. To his family. As you know, Marcus Nonius Balbus served Rome as proconsul to Crete and Cyrenaica, returned to Rome to serve her in the Senate, to see that the citizens of Rome—and Herculaneum—were assured of their due. However, if Rome could not meet those needs, this honorable head of the House of Nonius met them himself." Sulla spoke until the weepers howls drowned him out, for which he sympathetically submitted.

Messalina scanned the faces around Rosa who sat as cold as a statue beside Pomponius. She looked stronger in subtle ways, but her body was still too thin. Had she received word from Zeno? Volasennia appeared rapt with attention as Sulla spoke of her deceased husband. Balbus's mother moaned and swayed with grief. Nonia Prima sobbed into her husband's toga. Marcus paced the sidelines of the crowd like a restless lion.

"Enough!" Marcus yelled as he stormed toward the lectern. "Enough of what my grand and glorious father has done for this shit hole of a city."

Marcus took the dais from Sulla who stumbled away in shock. "I will tell you the truth about this man you so grandly honor. You hear from Sulla how he was proconsul to the legions in Africa. No, my dear friends, he was raping them of their wealth and filling his own greedy pockets."

As the crowd gasped, Marcus waved at his dead father, once again, wrapped and laying on the funeral pyre. "I will tell you about the real man," Marcus yelled and then laughed. "Oh yes, people, I faked stuttering because, while my illustrious father was busy sponsoring the games in the Palaestra and rebuilding your city, this man also dominated every facet of our lives. When we shit. When we ate. How we would eat. How we were to act in public. We suffered his decrees so you would admire him—so he could strut about like Jupiter himself.

"While he was smiling down his arrogant nose at you, he was at home beating his family into submission! Beating a child out of his daughter's belly." Marcus pointed at Rosa.

The crowd gasped.

Sulla stood as if to stop Marcus's blasphemous tirade. Senators behind him were ready to follow. However, they halted under the son's glare; a glare bequeathed him by the dead man.

"Ah, his many friends are angered by the truth because they loved him like a brother, ate with him, laughed with him, fucked with him, and shared victories with him as Brutus did Caesar." He swept his hand before the crowd. "While his family hated him."

Volasennia stood. "Marcus, you go too far!"

"Shut up, Mother. You hated him as well," Marcus snarled back and then smiled. "Come, fair Herculaneum, let us burn him, and cleanse the city of lies once believed."

Alexius waited by the seaside railing as the crowd passed the burning pyre, offering Balbus bits of the ritual food and drink, leaving flowers and tokens to the dead man. Worried clients walked away, wiping at tears as they passed. They would not be loyal to Marcus, he thought, noting that a few had already approached his father or Sulla.

He walked over to Marcus feasting on the leftover food. "Have you lost your mind?"

Marcus laughed. "Lost my mind? My friend, I am now blessed with it. See, I don't stutter."

A few people standing close overheard and nodded as if Marcus deserved Alexius's reproach. However, that was not why he was here. Marcus was his friend, and he was destroying his future. "You have lost all of your clients' loyalty. Do you not see that?"

Marcus's face gleamed. "Herculaneum can fall down around your handsome face for all I care. I will never see this city again. Hector and I are going to Greece, once he has your 'Medusa' out of his mind."

Fury erupted in his veins. "Take that spawn to Greece or anywhere, but don't call Messalina that to my face again."

Marcus laughed and leaned close. "You know, I caught her suckling his tongue in the theater garden. If I had not interfered when I did, she would be sucking more than that by now, my friend."

"You are a fool. Go to Greece and may the gods see that you never return." It took every ounce of control not to smash that smug grin on Marcus's face and walk away.

Messalina looked up as Alexius joined her at the railing overlooking the bay. "How could Marcus do this to her…to his family, Alexius?" she asked. "Rosa is devastated. Marco has taken her inside."

"He has gone mad, Messi. By the gods, I want him gone from here. Greece can have him."

Chapter 36

A COMFORTABLE SILENCE SETTLED in the guardhouse. The oil lamp's soft yellow glow cast large shadows on the walls, making everything larger than life. Alexius adjusted his leather cuirass across his shoulders and continued watching Flaccus carve a new piece of wood. The bristles of the red crest of his own helmet brushed his arm as he adjusted his legs into a more comfortable position on the bench. It was nice just sitting and relaxing while he could. In a few hours, he and the vigils would be patrolling the streets as they had every night for the last week.

Balbus's death had sent the city into grief-stricken insanity. Brawls broke out everywhere. If it was not fights, it was the constant tremors terrifying the city like an invisible demon. Tomorrow, Balbus's festival dedicated to Vulcan would fill the city with something to do instead of turning on each other.

"Since ya haven't been to Rome for a while, how's the election coming?" Flaccus asked, absently scratching his ear and then brushing wood chips from his lap.

The centurion did have large ears, something Alexius kept to himself. Those who had commented on them had fled from the centurion's wrath like frightened dogs. Flaccus never forgave them for it either. Alexius emptied his mug and wiped his hand across his lips. "Better. Votes are growing since Balbus's death."

"I'm sure you've spent your time mourning the city's loss and nothing else."

Alexius toasted the centurion. "Most definitely, Flaccus." He sat his ale mug down on the table. "What is that going to be?"

"Toy for one of the street kids." Flaccus brushed more chips off his red tunic and chain mail armor.

Both of them shifted their attention as one of the vigils appeared in the doorway and thrust a folded letter toward Alexius. "Tribune, I was told to give this to you."

Alexius took the note from the boy who was no more than seventeen. Most of the guards were about that same age and had volunteered to get a taste of being with the legion, as he had once believed. No one had told him that being with the vigils was nothing like the legion. In addition, he was not about to tell them either.

"Are the men ready?" Alexius asked as he opened the note.

"Most have shown up."

"Let me know when they do."

"Yes, Tribune." The young man saluted and left the small chamber. Flaccus placed the carving aside. "Never woulda let men get this lazy in the legion."

"In the legion, we could do something about it other than scold them like wives," Alexius said as he started to read. "And this isn't…"

Tonight. Z

"The…legion."

"True. I miss those days. What's in the note?" Flaccus asked.

Alexius stared at Zeno's note, remembering the slave's comment. *I will tell you this. If the vigils get called to the villa, tell them to take their time in coming.*

Dread coated Alexius's insides as he folded the paper. Something was going to happen tonight, far worse than simple street fights. "Would you believe it is a love note from my beloved betrothed?"

"Beloved, my ass. Let's go."

Maybe he should be thanking Zeno, Alexius thought as he tossed the note into the busy flame of the oil lamp, and hesitated to watch the paper blacken and melt. He stood and slid his helmet over his head, tying the cheek guards as Flaccus stuffed his carving and tools back in his backpack.

"Same as last night, Tribune?"

Alexius nodded. "We will meet here, otherwise."

Flaccus would patrol the streets around the theater as he watched the area around the Palaestra. It would garner the necessary time needed to meet up back at the guardhouse.

The night stretched endlessly as Alexius and his guards strolled past houses alive with flutes playing in a few courts. The ground trembled. The music stopped. The world hesitated. Then the flutes began playing again. Nervous laughter followed.

Even the men were quiet. Alexius would have welcomed an Ovid ditty to break the restless tension spawning from the shadows. They had just passed Hector's house when a slave came to a sliding halt before them. "Tribune, there's a disturbance at the dominus Sulla's villa. You have to come."

Alexius closed his eyes to hide the grimace. He turned to Numerius. "Find the others and meet us at the guard house."

CHAPTER 37

ZENO TOSSED HIS leather slave collar, the last of his bread, and the last of his wine onto the small campfire burning in the secluded glen. He peeled the wooden cast off, no longer necessary, his arm and dropped it into the hungry flames.

"Tork Angegh, god of power, god of bravery, god of war, see me through this night," Zeno prayed. "Spandarmet, god of the dead, take the one I send you this night. Judge him for what he is."

He lifted a tablet bearing the name Sextius Pomponius Bestius and tossed the wood into the fire. He knelt, touching his forehead to the warm earth and then rose, kicking dirt over the flames. The velvet darkness enveloped him.

Felix had told him that Marco had been a longtime friend and had watched over Rosa. The faith had remained since the slave had brought the message to him to wait until nightfall before coming for her. There were too many slaves present in the house, and that he would signal when it was safe.

That afternoon, Zeno had watched Rosa in the side garden as she strolled with a covey of slaves around her. His pendant sparkled against her red stola bordered with black. The moment he saw her lift the pendant to her lips, it was all he could do to stay on in the branches of the tree.

Dirty gray clouds whispered across the night sky as the pedestrian door to the main gate opened and a slave rushed out it at a full run. And no one closed it. No one.

Zeno crouched down in the shadows and waited for the next signal to know when Marco had unlocked the doors to the upper portico. "First bedroom on the right."

Sulla's wall surrounding the villa loomed like a black abyss. However he saw the instant that a flame spark in the distant darkness, waving side to side, and then disappearing. Every muscle wanted to run, to close the distance separating him from Rosa. He needed to feel her in his arms, smell her.

He eased through to the thickest shadows, feeling a thorn bush scratch deep in his bare leg. Ignoring the simple pain, he raced to the opened gate and paused to listen. Nothing. Not a sound.

He peered inside the walls, where nothing except more shadows lived, and then ran the short distance to the front terrace to the promised rope dangling from the upper railing. Pain shot down Zeno's weak arm as he climbed to the marble balustrade and dropped silently to the mosaic flooring.

Scents of jasmine greeted him as he flexed his hand and flattened into the dark shadows lingering on the villa wall. A window edge cut along his shoulder blades as he searched for the door handle. Unlocked as promised.

A flute played somewhere deep in the villa as he stepped into the cool marbled hallway where small oil sconces flickered along the ornate walls leading to the double door of a bedroom. On the right.

"I have a headache. Leave me be."

Rosa's voice. She was alive and strong. Pomponius had not destroyed her. A smile eased across Zeno's lips. "I'm coming my love. He won't touch you again."

"You are my wife. I wish you to act as one."

Rosa rose from her chair and glared at the fat blob removing his tunic. The sight of his abundant flesh nauseated her. "I don't care what you wish. I am ill."

"I don't care if you are." Pomponius walked across the thick Persian rug, hands clinching at his sides. "I will have you tonight. You can lay in your vomit if you wish."

Rosa shot to her feet and quickly placed the rattan chair between them. "I am simply your means to my father's money and power. Nothing more." A vase met her hand as she backed up to the trestle table in the corner of the room. "You have what you want. Now leave me be."

"I want what is mine. You."

The graying brown hair on his chest rose and fell as he lumbered toward her. She glanced at all the possible escapes. There were a few, not many. Pomponius was close enough to stop her at the hallway door. Her bedroom door was too far away.

The balcony. She could jump into the side courtyard if she had to. He would not expect her to do that. Death would be a blessing compared to him mounting her again.

She clutched Zeno's pendant. He had become a memory, the only part of her life that had mattered, that had given her joy. Marco had heard nothing of Zeno after the accident. Therefore, he could be dead now. Yet, she still clung to the fragile hope that he lived and would come for her.

"Give me that pendant, wife."

Her fist tightened around the charm like her last breath. He would destroy it this time and make sure she never saw it again. "No."

Pomponius stomped toward her. She ran to another corner. He would tire soon if she could continue to play this game. If she could get to the hallway, he would never catch her.

"You little cunt, you will not run from me this time. I will make the slaves find you and hold you for me."

The bedroom door swung open. A shape of a man appeared in the dim light of the oil lamps. "You touch her, you die."

Zeno! Rosa bolted away from the corner.

Pomponius's hand clasped her wrist and swung her around into his wall of fat. "Slaves! Guards!"

Zeno halted. A smile eased dangerously across his lips. "They won't come. I said release her."

Pomponius's arm clamped across her chest, and his hand snapped her chin upward. "I will break her neck, if you come any closer. I order you to leave." Pomponius dragged her with him toward the balcony.

"No, Zeno. Don't leave me."

Zeno moved deeper into the room. "I said, let her go."

Grappling for footing, Rosa bumped into his foot and then slammed hers down hard on his instep. Pomponius stumbled, letting go enough for her plow her elbow into his fat ribs. Another twist and she was free.

Zeno clutched her arm and flung her toward the pillowed couch. The familiar touch scorched life through her. Yet, she stumbled backward as Zeno charged toward the balcony.

"Guards! Guards!" Pomponius threw the vase at Zeno as he backed and searched for some escape. It shattered by Rosa's foot. "Slaves!"

Zeno dodged the next vase and knocked a thrown chair aside as it flew at him. It slid across the round center table, knocking the pot of flowers over. Water spilled as Pomponius backed to a table by the wall.

"Kill him, Zeno. Kill him," Rosa pleaded. "Or I will never be free of him."

The knife in Zeno's hand gleamed. "Oh, I intend to, my love."

Pomponius charged. A huge grunt echoed through the room as their bodies slammed together as Zeno drove the knife deep into the mass of flesh again and again. Finally, Pomponius collapsed on the rug and lay there, sprawled, arms wide, his loincloth loose between his legs.

The site of Pomponius's fat foot twitching froze Rosa in place. She could not move or breathe. *Was he dead? Was he?*

"Rosa."

The sound of her name surged life through her once again. Hope sang with absolute love.

Chapter 38

ALEXIUS HAD BARELY sat on the bench to stare at the ashes of Zeno's note when Flaccus bolted into the guardhouse. "What is it? What happened?" Unfortunately, the centurion came all too quickly. He wished the soldier had taken his time in getting back, or that a fight had broken out and had stalled him. However, there he stood.

Alexius rose and settled his helmet over his head again, tying the chinstrap. "We have been called to Sulla's villa. A disturbance."

The centurion balked inside the doorframe. "A disturbance. We gotta go out there for that? Isn't the city enough to take care of?"

No part of him wanted to go to Sulla's villa either. However, they had no choice. Sulla was a city magistrate and a powerful citizen of Rome. Alexius faced those gathering in the small room, wishing he had actual soldiers with him. No telling what awaited them. "You six, mount up. The rest stay here and watch the city," he ordered.

The air was sultry and stunk of rotten eggs as he swung up on the small bay horse. Alexius looked at the centurion. "Is the bridge repaired?" he asked as he pulled his cape free.

"Didn't know it was broken," Flaccus said grumbling as he vaulted onto the sorrel horse a little smaller than his. "I really hate these animals. I really do."

Alexius looked at Fosco who waited by the guardhouse doorway. "Find Messi and stay with her."

"Yes, dominus."

He nudged his horse toward overhanging shadows that hung darker than death. This was it. Either Zeno succeeded in killing Pomponius and ending the threat against Alexius's election, or the truth was coming out that he had helped Zeno in everything.

The empty lashing pole reappeared in his mind. More thoughts came of Sulla as a cobra and the other two men as poisonous adders. However, Balbus no longer smiled and that snake was dead. Pomponius could also be the next.

Suddenly, the desire to become a senator erupted with a life of its own. More than ever, he wanted to protect Rome from such men. He wanted Messi to be his wife and bear him a thousand children. He wanted to help those clients who believed as he did.

The horses balked at the bridge, refusing to cross. Everyone had to dismount and lead the animals across. Alexius blocked his mind to the deep ravine below, cut by thousands of streams that had poured off Vesuvius for centuries. He glanced up at the looming mountain shimmering in a strange greenish moonlight and then mounted the restless horse again.

The shadowed walls appeared too soon. As they rode closer, the gates parted, and a man raced into view. "Praise the gods you're here, dominus." The slave turned to the other two slaves behind him and ordered, "Take their horses."

"What happened?" Alexius asked as he dismounted and released the reins to the nearest slave.

"It's the dominus Pomponius and his domina. Come. We'll show you."

Was this simply a trap? "Where is Sulla?"

"Dominus, he's consoling Balbus's domina tonight."

He could almost breathe again knowing Sulla was away. "Stephano, watch the court. Report immediately if you see anyone." He waved to the rest to dismount. "The rest come with me."

They followed the slave across the stone entry to the porch steps. Torches flickered in wall sconces on each side of the doorway, lighting the eerily quiet atrium. Even the impluvium, a black ribbon of water behind the ever-observant maidens, was silent.

"This way." The slave motioned up the wide staircase at the side of the passageway to the elegant garden.

Alexius halted as did those behind him. Anything could be waiting up those stairs. "First, what happened here? Where is everyone?"

"Gone, dominus. The slaves have run, for fear they will be blamed for the murder."

"Murder?"

"Whose?" Flaccus asked from beside Alexius.

"The dominus Pomponius."

Another image by the lashing post vaporized from Alexius's memory. "His wife, where is she?"

"He took her."

"He who?"

"I don't know. We didn't see him."

Alexius almost smiled. Rosa was with Zeno now. With Pomponius dead, so was that threat. The desire to sag against the stair rail raced through him. Resisting, he asked, "Pomponius's slave?"

"I'm his personal slave, dominus." Panic flooded over the man. "Believe me, dominus. We were ordered to stay in the kitchen."

"We, you say everyone…was in the kitchen when this happened?"

"Yes. The master slave ordered us to remain there for the evening."

"He who?"

"Marco. He…he's with Sulla's wife in her bedroom."

Alexius studied the man. "Is he still there?"

"Yes, dominus. But you don't want to go in there."

"Why?"

"Marco will let no one in."

Flaccus nudged Alexius. "One thing at a time, Tribune."

Alexius turned to the men behind him. "You two, stay here. Do not let anyone go up. The rest come with us." He turned to the slave again. "Show us the body."

The slave led them up the wide staircase to the surrounding marble hallway, that he knew ever so well, to a short corridor stretching between two bedrooms.

Alexius scanned the space as they entered. A chair lay on its side as did a table. Both laying amid shards of broken vases. He stepped closer to Pomponius's sprawled body lying in a black pool of blood. "The city council will have to witness this in the morning." Alexius waved toward the fallen drapery. "Cover him."

"Yes, dominus."

Alexius looked out at the balcony to the serene site of the garden and the lazy sea beyond. The night's only flaw lay behind him. He turned to the slave. "I want to see this Marco."

"I'll show you, but he's with the domina Agrippina and won't allow you inside her room."

"He will, if I have any say," Flaccus announced from behind Alexius's shoulder.

Alexius motioned everyone into the hallway. "Numerius, guard this door. I don't want anyone in here until the magistrates arrive."

"Yes, Tribune." The soldier planted himself before the now closed doorway.

The slave led them to the main hall and toward Sulla and Agrippina's bedroom. How many days had he strolled these halls with Cornelius? Too many.

Marco stepped out of Agrippina's bedroom. "Stop there and don't come any closer, dominus. It is too dangerous."

"Don't be a fool, you idiot. Let us pass," Flaccus said, ready to flay the slave with his gladius.

Alexius raised his hand to halt. "Why?"

"There is nothing you can do for her." Marco crossed his arms, glaring at the slave who had brought them. "She is dead."

"Dead?" Alexius asked. Volasennia's final victory. He hoped it was her final victory. Thoughts about Messi flashed before him. He blocked his mind. "What happened?"

"The domina Agrippina was no part of the murder of the senator," Marco said. "This is another murder, dominus. One far more dangerous to everyone."

"Let us make that decision, slave," Flaccus snapped, stepping closer.

"Flaccus, wait." Alexius studied the lanky slave. "First, how did she die?"

"Like the dominus Marcus Nonius Balbus, in her sleep. I have been caring for her." The man lifted his head, a gaze as direct as an arrow. "And I am now doomed to her fate, as you will be if you breathe the same air."

The death dust. Alexius stepped closer. "I have to see her." He had to, even though every particle in his body begged him to flee.

"Then cover your face, dominus, and do not breathe." Marco turned to the slave hiding behind the vigils. "Have water ready for the dominus to wash the instant he leaves. And, dominus, leave your helmet here."

Alexius handed his helmet to Flaccus and swept his cloak across his face. He drew in a deep breath to follow Marco back into the dimly lit room.

His heart thundered beneath the leather cuirass. Tears blurred his vision. His skin crawled as if he had rolled in lice. This was insane. Already his lungs begged for air.

A dim view of the formal garden where the auction had taken place stretched beyond the balcony window. A slow lazy breeze drifted inside and circled the room like a lemur. One candle burned on the vanity where Agrippina lay as if she were only asleep. Marco had already closed her eyes and placed coins on them—money for the ferryman.

Alexius did not have to touch her body to know Agrippina was dead. Dead spirits lurked in the dark corners. He could feel them.

He bolted out of the room, dropping his cloak in the doorway where he scoured his face and hands in the bowl of water held by a slave. Drying his face with a proffered towel, he turned to Marco, who once again guarded Agrippina's doorway. "Take care, Marco." He placed two coins in the man's palm. "Keep this for the ferryman so you may go with her."

Marco nodded soberly. "Beware of the bridge, dominus." He turned and reentered the bedroom, shutting its door.

Alexius nudged the horse into a lope back toward Herculaneum. He had posted two guards to the villa until he could return with the city council in the morning. They had to see Agrippina and Pomponius. He hoped that his report would save the slaves from certain death.

Somehow, he needed to find a way to implicate Sulla and Volasennia in all this as well. But how? He needed to know where they had learned of the death dust. How they got it? By the gods, he needed to find all this out before he faced the magistrates.

The moon had long disappeared from the sky and Apollo would soon be appearing. Meanwhile, Marco's warning burned in his mind as the shadowed bridge appeared in the thick shadows. They had crossed that bridge, and nothing happened. Either it had been restored or it was never broken in the first place. On the other hand, maybe it was not the bridge he had to worry about.

"Be ready for anything."

"Yes, Tribune," grunted from the men with him.

The horses snorted and fretted as they approached the bridge but, at least, were willing this time. As soon as they crossed the ravine, shadows dropped from the overhanging limbs like rocks. One jumped from the surrounding bushes and dragged Alexius from his horse.

Jabbing his elbow into the attacker's gut they both fell to the ground. Alexius rolled and thrust the blade of his knife into the man's neck. Behind him, a man screamed down into the ravine. He turned to see Flaccus by the broken rail.

Leaves rustled behind him. Alexius wheeled around. A knife lashed across his cuirass as he thrust his knife upward and cut through the man's wrist. The attacker's knife and hand dropped as the ground rose, staggering them both toward the bridge.

Cool air rose from the ravine's rim like open jaws ready to devour Alexius, but strong fingers grabbed the neck of his cuirass and lunged backward. Alexius felt himself falling back onto solid ground as his attacker dropped into the cold depths. His scream reverberated off the canyon walls. The ground continued to shake, ripping the bridge free. It collapsed into the looming ravine with the man.

Alexius stared at the black crevice that had reached out for him and tried to breathe. Numerius and Stephano shoved captives toward their small group.

"How many dead?"

Flaccus appeared, wiping his mouth with his arm. "None of *uth*. Two of their*th*. Caught 'em tryin' to run."

Alexius stared as the centurion. "Are you all right?"

"Kicked my front tee*th* out. I killed 'im." Flaccus motioned to the gutted fool lying on the ground.

Alexius turned to the remaining soldiers. "Find out who paid these men. Do whatever you have to."

Flaccus huffed. "Oh, we will, tribune. We will."

CHAPTER 39

FINALLY, THE FOUR captives spilled their guts as fragments of dawn filtered into the tiny hut, stinking of sweat, dust, and fear. Sulla had paid them five hundred denarii to kill him and then Messalina.

Alexius sagged with relief as he stared at the beaten prisoners. His father had said the council was meeting in the Temple Augustalus to appoint a new high priest. Sulla would likely be there. However, if Sulla remained at Balbus's house as the slaves at the villa said, they might be able to arrest him there and escort him to the temple.

"This has to be reported to the city council." Alexius pointed to the three youngest vigils. "You three keep them here until you receive my orders to bring them to the Temple Augustalus. Do you understand? Password is Vesuvius. Do not sleep. Do not fail me."

The young men suddenly stiffened with this very important responsibility. "Yes, Tribune. They will not be going anywhere."

"Flaccus and the rest of you come with me."

Everything that happened replayed in his mind as Alexius strode out of the filthy hut: Pomponius's body, Agrippina's body, the assault at the bridge, hearing the confessions. Since Pomponius and Balbus were no longer threats, he knew this was his only chance to see Sulla destroyed. He had to get this right because his entire future depended on his next steps.

Cheers roared from the Palaestra, reminding him that Claudius was competing for the first time. Every part of him wanted to be there, sitting with Messalina and watching Claudius compete. He knew how much that meant.

A nervous fury began to burn in his veins as he motioned to Flaccus to knock on Balbus's door. Balbus's master slave opened the door, smiling

"Good morning, Labeo."

"Good day, dominus," the old door slave said. "What brings you—?"

A woman bellowed beyond the doors. "You killed my son, you bitch! You destroyed everything!"

Labeo started to close the door. Alexius pressed his hand on the oak to halt it from closing. Flaccus and the other vigils peered in the direction of the yelling.

"You old witch, I have destroyed nothing. Nothing that didn't deserve to be destroyed."

There was a shriek. A vase crashed.

"You murdered my son and destroyed our chance at the imperial throne."

I have to get in there. Alexius shoved on the door and stepped toward the slave. "With the authority of Rome, step aside, Labeo." The slave bowed and stepped back, allowing the vigils to follow him into the vestibule as more accusations roared beyond the garden window of the tablinum

"You filthy old hag! How dare you call me a murderer? It was you who killed the emperor."

Alexius lifted his hand to a stop as the red atrium yawned before them. He glanced at the vigils to be sure they had heard everything exploding in the garden. They had. Astonishment and amusement had flooded their faces.

"I did that, so my son would become the next emperor. That murdering, cunt-loving mongrel of yours promised that Nonius would have the throne if I saw to Vespasian's death."

Volasennia screeched with laughter. "And you believed us, you stupid witch. It was all planned so Sulla could take the throne. The legions in Africa are ready to stand with him. They want Sulla as Caesar, not your stinking blood of a slave."

"I curse the day you came here!"

A swift rustle of cloth and another laugh cut the air.

Alexius motioned his men forward. They raced across the atrium just as the old woman scratched at Volasennia. He grabbed Volasennia as Flaccus caught the old woman who turned rabid on him. Fortunately, the centurion's cheek guards protected his face from her claws.

"Alexius!" Volasennia sagged into his arms, relieved. "Praise the gods, you came. She has gone mad and attacked me."

"Really?" He released her and studied her face flooding with innocence. "Domina, we heard everything."

Volasennia backed away. "No, no. You do not understand. The witch has gone crazy." Her eyes darkened. "Sulla will not allow this."

Balbus's mother spat at Volasennia. "She lies. May Jupiter strike her dead." Her hair straggled over the shoulders of her black stola. Strangely, the old woman did not seem like a witch but more like a broken old woman.

"Did you kill Vespasian?" Alexius asked her.

"Yes. So our family could take their proper place in Rome. We deserve it," the old crone hissed and pointed a long-hooked finger at Volasennia. "Now, my son is dead because she killed him!"

"No, Viciria," Volasennia pleaded. "Do not say this. Think, old woman. There is Nonia Rosa and Nonia Prima. Their husbands. Think of them."

A vicious smile teetered on the old thin lips. "Daughters? What value are they?"

"Where is Sulla now?" Alexius asked, breaking the snarl between women.

"The fool's at the temple," spit from Viciria's lips.

His next words clotted in his throat. He swallowed. "Will you witness before the council and all the gods that she killed Balbus and all that you have said is true?"

Volasennia fell on her knees. "No, Viciria, tell them nothing."

The old woman rose like a clever goddess. "What else do I have to live for? My son is dead because you murdered him. My grandson is crazy." She lifted her face to the warm sun and smiled at Alexius. "I will tell everything to destroy her and her filthy lover."

He had to harvest Sulla's name for the soldiers around him. "Who do you mean, old woman, Volasennia and who?"

"Marcus Cornelius Sulla."

Hearing the name staggered each man accompanying him. Alexius began to breathe again. Now he had to expose Sulla before anyone changed their stories.

CHAPTER 40

MESSALINA STOOD AT the terrace, looking out at the sun shining down on the water. Maybe it was her imagination, but the sun appeared to have a bruised tint. The air was muggy and hot, mixing the fragrances from the blooming flowers and hearty herbs basking in a rotten stench of eggs.

She heard Claudius upstairs, ordering slaves about as if he had become a legate of a legion. For the first time, he was going to participate in the Volcanalia game and was making everyone's life miserable. Her father was gloating impatiently beside his desk in the tablinum, while her mother prepared for her début at the games as the mother of a contestant. Messalina had no idea where Antonia was.

All Messalina could think about was Alexius. Nights without him were endless. She looked up at his bedroom window. It was empty. Where was he? Had he forgotten he promised to come with her to the games?

"Messalina, aren't you ready?" her father asked as he stood in the middle of the breezeway. "We have to go,"

"Have you heard from Alexius?"

"I am sure he will be at the games. Now get ready, or we will be late."

"Papa, you heard Fosco say Alexius wants me to wait here for him. Now go. We will be there before Claudius's match." *I hope.*

Her father's new peacock fluttered down from the portico ceiling and landed near the garden pool, cawing at her. Messalina tossed it some grain as Didius walked toward her with a folded letter in his hand.

"Domina, a message has arrived for you," the old slave said. "It just came."

"Thank you, Didius." She settled on a nearby bench, knowing the letter was from Alexius saying he could not come for her...again. Frustrated, she tore open the parchment.

Messalina, My days and nights are you. I must see your glorious smile one more time. Come to the theater or I will kill myself. I live to see only your smile or I shall not breathe another day. Hector

Messalina stared at the words. How ridiculous. Why? Why would Hector even consider killing himself over her? She read the letter again, feeling guilt pull at her, remembering her letters and telling him how much she wanted him to save her from her betrothal with Alexius. She had even made Hector believe she would run away with him. She had to stop him from this foolishness. He should go to Greece with Marcus.

She studied the distant azure bay. Could she be back before Alexius came for her, or should she stay and wait for him? What if Alexius failed to come in time? She handed

Didius the letter back. "When Alexius comes for me, tell him I am at the theater and will return in time to go to the games."

The master slave scanned the note and looked directly at her. "But domina?"

Messalina sighed with frustration. "Do as I tell you, Didius. I am not running away. I am going to stop someone from doing something very stupid."

"Yes, domina."

Except for a few stores, the streets remained empty. The cheering in the Palestrae made Messalina wish she were there instead of meeting Hector. Everyone must be at the Volcanalia games. Actually, she did want to see her brother win his first wrestling event. She grinned. Claudius would be intolerable if he won. But she couldn't let Hector kill himself. That was ridiculous.

The side door to the theater opened easily enough. Messalina peered inside the shadowy darkness that echoed with emptiness. It was noon and the actors were away, relaxing before the afternoon play.

"Niki, wait here. If you see Alexius, tell him I'm waiting for him." She eased inside, hoping she would find Hector on stage. Of course, he was not.

"Hector?"

The scent of saffron and ginger wafted in the air as she walked up the side steps and felt another essence surround her—she was actually on the marble stage. The opening in the ceiling canvas allowed an unusually dim light to focus on the back wall of the play's setting of arched fronts. The stage curtain lay neatly folded on the edge of the stage between her and the empty rows for the audience. Shadows stretching across the seating beckoned her to sing, dance, or just twirl an invisible ribbon. She even felt the expectant stares from all of Balbus's family statues standing in their niches and on their pedestals.

This was what Hector had talked about. A thrill trickled through her as she twirled about toward a table placed near one of the trap doors. A knife rested on the tabletop. She ran a finger along the glimmering blade laying there so innocently lethal. The afternoon play must be a tragedy.

Cheers from the games filtered through the opening overhead. She really should go. She needed to see Claudius's competiti…."Messi?"

Hector strolled through the backstage door and swiftly crossed to her. He looked radiant in a green tunic and with a fake laurel wreath crowing his head. Nothing seemed as if Hector were about to kill himself. "You shouldn't come to see the rehearsal. That is cheating, my dear." He clasped her hands as if enthralled to see her.

"You…wrote me a note to come. You said…"

"I didn't write you, my sweet. Your note demanded that I find you here."

The stage trembled slightly beneath her feet as confusion misplaced fact. She had not written any note to Hector.

"Ah, how touching. Alexius will appreciate this, I am sure." Marcus appeared from another door at the far end of the backstage. "I wrote them." He sauntered toward the table and smiled at Hector. "And since you can't quit prattling on like a pathetic lover—even though you say you love me—I have arranged for 'Medusa' to join us." He sighed deeply. "I simply can't endure her separating us anymore." He twirled the dagger on the tabletop. "So, before we leave for Greece, 'Medusa' has to die."

CHAPTER 41

THE VIGILS PARADED with an air of importance beside Balbus's mother riding in her sedan chair toward the Temple of Augustalus. The sight drew the attention of people who stepped aside and began following, extending the parade. Curiosity feasted in their gazes and chatter.

Alexius did not know if it was the heat of the midday sun or fear, but sweat ran along his jawline and fed into his neck scarf. His new cape weighed down on his shoulders with each stride, as if to remind him of what he was about to confront. His entire future, his father's name, reputation…everything.

And everything depended on Viciria.

If the old woman did retract her words, there was no doubt in Alexius's mind that he would be riding with the Ferryman, along with Balbus and Pomponius. The council would accuse him of fabricating the stories and paying the captives off to frame Sulla. Nothing the vigils had to say would mean anything.

He studied the old woman, stiff and stalwart, as he assisted her from the sedan chair and helped her toward the closed temple doors. He nodded to the two nearest guards. "You two, allow no one inside. The rest come with me," he ordered and then led Viciria into the marbled hall.

Sulla stood on the apse steps, draped as the newly elected high priest. The golden robes gleamed in the radiant sunlight flooding through the ceiling opening. "On this 24th day of August, I accept this title with great honor and will—" He stopped midsentence to glare at the intrusion. "This meeting is not open to outsiders, and as high priest of the Council of the Augustalus, I demand you to leave immediately."

Alexius scanned the curious gazes of the council gathering protectively around Sulla, his father among them. Every part of him wanted to leave and pretend nothing had happened. However, he could not. Sulla was guilty. His responsibility to Rome, to his future, was to expose everything.

He stiffened to attention. "Forgive this intrusion, your Excellences, but we must—

"—Murderer!" Viciria yelled, pointing her gnarled finger at Sulla.

Senators gasped as if slapped. His father stared at Alexius, confused and suddenly worried as Sulla barged through the group of senators.

"How dare you bring this ignorant old woman here with this false accusation?" Sulla motioned to the lictors lounging along the wall. "Remove them."

Flaccus and the guards gathered between Viciria and Alexius, blocking the lictors' approach.

Sulla rose up to his full glory. "I said remove her!"

"She remains." Alexius met the man's glare as a cold chill cut down his spine. He swallowed something down his dry throat. "Marcus Cornelius Sulla, you are under arrest for assisting in the assassination of the emperor, for murder, and the attempted murder upon the vigils."

Sulla stepped toward Alexius. "You are out of your mind. These are lies! I did no such—"

"You murdered my son! You murdered the emperor!" Viciria yelled. Two soldiers grabbed her before she could charge at Sulla.

Galerius stepped from the restless group. "Viciria, calm yourself. Do you know what you have accused this man of doing?"

Viciria's black stola and palla trembled with rage. "He is the murderer who promised me that my son would sit on the imperial throne if I would see that Vespasian died."

"She has gone mad," Sulla's glare seared over to Alexius "I demand you leave before any further insults are spoken."

"I will not." Alexius swallowed to relieve his parched throat. "What she says is true."

The council turned to each other like hens. Galerius desperately glanced at Alexius and stepped closer to Balbus's mother. "Viciria, did you kill Vespasian?"

"I did. Yes." The woman's eyes shifted to Alexius's father. "For that whore monger." She pointed at Sulla.

"He…he died from a stomach chill. I was there," one council member muttered.

Viciria glared at the man as if he had become a specimen. "He slept with the death dust."

"Death dust?" one of the senators asked and glanced at the other men as if they might understand.

Her old chin rose with pride. "Charbon."

Alexius watched as everyone withdrew from Sulla as if he had suddenly become diseased. They hovered in nervous little groups like scared children, whispering.

"Viciria, surely you realize what you are saying," Galerius begged, open-handed. Alexius had never seen his father this nervous. His toga trembled around his sandals.

The old woman rose up like the goddess Juno and glared down on him. "Before Jupiter and all the gods of Olympus, I swear all I say is true."

One council member fainted. His slaves collected around him as the rest of the council sagged in shock. Sulla wheeled about. "You see. I had nothing to do with Vespasian's death. She admits to murdering the emperor."

"Last night, where were you?" Alexius asked.

"I was—"

"You were with your filthy whore, while your wife died like the emperor, like my son died! Your bitch killed him." Viciria jerked free of the soldier holding her. Flaccus barely held her before she clawed Sulla's face.

"What she says is true." Alexius stepped forward, feeling every gaze burn. "The vigils were called to Sulla's villa last night." Alexius motioned to Sulla. "When we arrived, he was not present. The slaves reported that he was consoling Volasennia and we found Agrippina dead. I have witnessed this myself."

Sulla staggered backward into a few of the lictors. "No. She cannot be dead. She was ill. That was all. Ill."

Alexius kept his gaze directed on Sulla, remembering him with Volasennia that night in Pompeii. "We were returning to make our report when we were assaulted at the north bridge. Those not killed confessed to being paid by Sulla to kill me and my betrothed, as well as all other vigils present."

Galerius lost his footing. The nearest council member caught his elbow. "Alexi…" Galerius corrected himself. "Tribune, you—you have the witnesses? You have proof of this?"

"I do."

CHAPTER 42

"MARCUS, DON'T BE ridiculous. I want to go to Greece with you. I never preferred Messalina over you."

Stupidity swept Messalina like a tidal wave. She backed up, not believing the words she had just heard from Hector. She needed to leave and made steps back across the stage.

"It's obvious you lie." Marcus paced between her and the exit like a panther, as he continued. "You love her more than you do me. Even while 'Medusa' wallows in Alexius's arm, she divides us. I can't have that any longer."

Surely, Marcus would not hurt her. He had to be acting some fool's part in some play he had devised. She glanced at Hector who was standing there as if reprimanded.

Alexius was waiting for her, wanting to go to the games. She needed to go. She needed to go now. Messalina backed along the folded stage curtain. "Marcus, believe me, this is all a mistake. You see, Hector has always cared for you more than me."

The ground vibrated beneath her feet, as Hector brightened. "Messi, my love, don't say that. I will always care for you."

"Hector, I understand. I truly do." She cast him a fake sympathetic smile and eased toward the side door.

Marcus grabbed her arm and yanked her to him. "You are going nowhere, 'Medusa'. You see, as long as you live, Hector will pine for you."

Messalina wrenched to get away. "He will not. Just let me talk to him."

"You prove my point. Why would he listen to you instead of me?" Marcus's hot breath brushed her neck as he dragged her back toward the table.

"Marcus, let me go. Alexius—think what he will do when he finds you."

He laughed in her ear. "I know about Rosa and Zeno. I have all along. I also know I will have Alexius as my personal slave to wipe my ass if he tells anyone anything." Marcus reached for the knife. "Hector, you have to see how much I love you."

Alexius heard the vigils outside, arriving with the prisoners who had assaulted them at the bridge. "Arcadius," Alexius called without removing his attention on Sulla. "Bring them in."

"Yes, Tribune."

With much grumbling and scratching of hobnails on the marble floors, the soldiers dragged the prisoners into the temple. Sweat drenched Sulla's face as he backed toward the apse.

"You are freedmen?" Galerius asked as he approached.

"Yes, dominus, we are," stated the one less bruised of the prisoners.

"Do you confess to an assault on the vigils last night?"

"Yes, dominus, for five hundred denarii, we was to kill the young dominus and all them with him. Then find the domina Messalina Claudia and kill her for 'nother two hundred denarii."

Alexius saw his father flinch, take a deep breath, and then choose his next words carefully. "Who…paid you?"

"He did." The man pointed at Sulla.

"No. No. I had nothing to do with this!" Sulla yelled. "It was all Pomponius's plan. He did it. Find him. He is—"

"Pomponius is dead," Alexius said to his father's frantic gaze.

The weight of the news kept falling on the council members, wilting them like flowers before a fire. As if turned to stone, Viciria remained silent as a statue, her gaze searing at Sulla.

"We found his body last night, stabbed." Alexius met Sulla's glare and continued. "The dominus Sulla was not present at his villa when we arrived. This morning when we arrived at Balbus's house to deliver the report we overheard Viciria and Volasennia argu—"

"His filthy whore!" Viciria snapped. "This filthy pig and his whore want the throne for themselves."

"Where is Volasennia now?" a council member asked as he joined Galerius.

Alexius studied the short senator. "She is under house arrest."

A pause drifted through the marbled room. Alexius's shoulders wanted to sag. He swallowed the lump in his throat as his father scanned all those present.

"You…you saw Pomponius and Agrippina's bodies?" his father asked.

"Yes."

Galerius drew in a deep breath and scanned Alexius's face. "I…I recommend that, until a thorough investigation is made, Marcus Cornelius Sulla must be dismissed from his elected position of High Priest of the Augustalus. Does the council agree to this decision?"

Every senator applauded.

"Any disagree?"

"Then, until all evidence is investigated, you, Marcus Cornelius Sulla, will remain in the custody of Rome."

Finally, Alexius's shoulders could sag with relief. It was all but done.

Flaccus whispered through swollen lips. "Where we gonna put 'im?"

Alexius studied the centurion. Sulla's villa was not a possibility. It was part of the investigation. He certainly could not stay with Volasennia or with Viciria. "August fathers, I ask that you place this man in the anteroom of the temple under guard, until you have witnessed the deaths at his villa and have questioned Balbus's widow further."

Galerius nodded, motioning toward the back room. "Yes. Yes. You may do so."

"Flaccus," Alexius called out. "Take the prisoner to the anteroom and see that the room is locked and under guard at all times."

The sanctum silenced as everyone watched Sulla fight the soldiers dragging him to the anteroom. The door slammed shut and a chair was rammed under the handle.

Then, questions began flourishing like spring mushrooms as everyone vacated the temple. Galerius stepped beside Alexius. "By all the gods, Alexius, I hope you are right."

"I am, Father. There is more you have to know." Alexius dragged his helmet off and cradled it under his arm. By the gods, he wanted to tell him everything, what he and Messalina had heard, what he had seen, what he had known all along. The ground trembled beneath his feet, swaying the water in the nearby fountain.

"We will talk about this later." Galerius turned to a cluster of council members lost in discussing the investigation.

Alexius turned to the vigils stirring about like lost children. "Marcadius, take Balbus's mother home and see the prisoners are—"

A sharp thunderclap split the air.

The ground lifted and jerked.

The sudden movement tossed Alexius against his father. Together, they stumbled toward the collapsing fountain. All eyes froze on a dirty gray plume bursting from the side of Vesuvius directly over Herculaneum. A sudden gust of wind ripped through the street, tearing roof tiles from buildings and tossing merchandise about the street like litter. It ripped Alexius's helmet from his arm, flinging it into the air like a toy.

Then, a horrendous explosion burst from the top of Vesuvius, throwing huge craters and stones into the air. The black blobs arched toward the city as if thrown by Vulcan himself. The ground shifted without mercy, tearing balconies from buildings and collapsing pillars.

Alexius stared at the large black column lifting skyward, catching in the wind, and drifting toward Pompeii.

Messalina!

CHAPTER 43

HECTOR WALKED TOWARD Messalina, shaking his head. "This is unnecessary. Let her go, Marcus. I want to go to Greece with you. Her heart no longer belongs to me."

"Liar." Marcus pointed the knife just under Messalina's rib cage. She flinched when the sharp point broke skin. "You have to see her dead or you will never forget her!"

Tears welled as Messalina froze against Marcus. She did not want to die. *Alexius. Rosa. My family.* She looked at Hector, pleading to him.

Hector shook his head. "No, Marcus. You know I have always loved—"

An explosion lifted the stage like a bucking horse. The trapdoor in the middle of the floor stage banged open, leaving a large black hole. A stage statue collapsed behind Marcus. He whipped about, releasing his grip enough for Messalina to jerk free and bolted to the side steps.

Marcus grabbed the back of her tunica, ripping it. A cold wind buffeted her back as she stumbled. Hector charged toward her as the ground heaved again, tossing both men against each other.

Hector's gaze gaped on Marcus's face as he clutched his stomach and crumpled to the floor. Blood blossomed across his tunic. Marcus stood there, holding the knife dripping with blood. His gaze slithered upward. "You bitch! You filthy bitch. See what you made me do!"

He lunged for her. Hector's hand grabbed for Marcus by the ankle, as another explosion rocked the theater walls. The stage lifted, throwing Marcus backward and through the trapdoor. A heavy cacophony of bronze drums and things collapsing thundered from the bowels beneath the stage. More statues fell or teetered in their niches as the walls shifted. The main arch of the stage background cracked. Like screaming arrows, rocks ripped through the theater awning and bounced onto the seat cushions.

Another odd roar boomed against the walls. Messalina fell onto the shifting marble stage beside Hector's body, curled into itself. "Hector, I'll…I'll get help!"

He gripped her wrist before she could rise. "No. It is too late, my beautiful swan." He laughed and then grimaced. "Can I call you that one last time?"

"Hector, please, let me find someone." She looked to the side door. "Niki!"

He clawed her closer. "Hold me, Messi, as no other death could bring such rapture."

Alexius turned on his father. "Have you seen Messi?"

"She should at the games with her parents."

Alexius suddenly remembered sending Fosco with a message for her to wait for him. By the gods, he prayed she had not listened this time and went to the games with her parents. He and his father joined the frantic race pouring into the streets and fleeing away from the waking monster.

People shoved into them with absolute indifference. His father's personal slave fell beneath the mass of feet. Galerius started throwing people aside to get to the man. By the time they did, the slave was dead.

As Galerius lifted the dead slave in his arms, someone plowed into him. Alexius grabbed him, knocking aside those around his father before he too fell beneath the stampede.

The world had gone insane. Merchandise was ripped from storefronts, then tossed aside. Boxes, vases, amphorae littered every step forward. Flaming bombs ripped through the sky, clambering onto rooftop and then falling into the frantic crowd. Clothing was set on fire. No one paused to throw water on the victim. Only when the person fell was the fire extinguished by trampling feet.

Alexius shoved his father into the doorway of the Palaestra while hordes of people flooded out from the confines. Screams pierced the thundering roar as more people shoved past.

"The upper terrace! It fell!"

"Don't go in there. Everything is falling."

"Messi! She could be in there." Alexius started to shove inside, but his father's hand gripped his arm.

"Don't. What if she's not?"

Messallus barged into sight that same instant and fell back on the wall beside them, ordering his slaves to create a barrier. Aurelia came through the archway. Galerius pulled her to his side as Octavia appeared, clutching Antonia. Claudius trailed behind them all.

Octavia looked at Alexius. "Where is Messalina? She should be with you."

Alexius stabbed his hand through his hair. Why couldn't Messalina be with her family just this one time? "We need to get to your house."

"How in Juno's name will we get there?" Octavia snapped. Her eyes grew wide with panic as she studied the impenetrable wall of frightened flood of humanity before her.

"Follow me." Messalus snared his wife and daughter and motioned to their personal slaves. "Whatever you have to do, do it. Get us home."

"Yes, dominus."

The way was cripplingly slow along the building storefronts, moving with the stream of humanity flooding toward the beach or be crushed beneath feet. Alexius and his father held Aurelia and her personal slave woman between them and simply blended in with the horde.

The only space granting room to breathe came at Hector's house. Everyone eased into Messalina's street clotted with crowds racing for the passageway. Didius opened the door, and ushered everyone inside. With Fosco's help, Didius managed to shut and bolt it to keep the flood from entering with them.

"Messi!"

"Messalina!"

Everyone called for her as they hurried across the black and white tiles and into the massive atrium. Water in the impluvium slushed back in forth in the pool. A table had fallen. Flowerpots had toppled. Vases rocked and fell, spreading dirt as each lolled back in forth with the rippling floor.

Her father wheeled on Didius. "Where is she?"

"Dominus, she received this message to go to the theater and said she would return in time for the games." The slave held out her letter.

Alexius claimed it and read, his guts melting inside him. Hector? Kill himself? Was this some Ovid stupid ditty? Sons of dis, surely not. Messi said she felt nothing for the fool. A million more questions raced through his mind. He blocked them. She was out there in this insanity … alone. He hoped alone.

Panic coated Octavia's face as she read the letter. "No. Surely, Messalina would not do this. She…she would not go to the theater. Not now."

Every breath filling Alexius's lungs wanted Messi's mother to be right but knowing how Messalina cared about everyone, he knew she was there.

"My galley just came in yesterday," Messalus announced with certainty. He turned to Didius. "Gather everyone. We have to leave immediately, or we will never make it out."

"Yes, dominus."

"What about Messalina?" Octavia snapped. "We cannot just leave her."

Determination spawned inside Alexius's guts. "I will find Messi and bring her to the galley."

Claudius tossed his victory laurel aside. "I'll go with you."

Alexius gripped the boy's shoulders. "Get our families to the galley. I will find Messi and bring her there." He looked up at all the worried faces. "I will find her."

His mother shook her head. "We will never make it through the passageway now."

Didius nodded. "She is right, dominus. The passages are impassable. Maybe everyone could go through Balbus's house to the thermae."

Octavia gasped. "But how? We cannot go back around in that panic."

"Go over the wall," Alexius said. How many nights had he done that? "All of you."

Everyone nodded and started toward the rear garden, except for Octavia, "In the name of Juno, I will not climb that wall like a fool."

"You will do whatever is necessary, woman," Messalus barked and shoved her before him.

Galerius turned to Alexius. His father rested a hand on his shoulder. "Find Messalina, Alexius. Bring her to the pier. If for some reason the galleys are gone, I will see there is something waiting for you. Understand?"

Images of his father's trampled slave flashed in his mind, along with the rest of the dead bodies littering the street stones. "Fosco, help Claudius get everyone to the pier."

"Yes, dominus."

Alexius turned, wishing he had his helmet to protect his head from the hot debris and falling rocks. He considered using a pillow. He had no time for that.

His father grasped Alexius's arm, halting him in place. "We will wait for you, son. But hurry. Gods be with you. And remember what I just said."

The top of Vesuvius roared with fury as Baby Paullus screamed. Rosa knew that cry. It was her son, her flesh, her life. She bolted from the horse Zeno had stolen and raced to the girl trailing behind Ruso's family. Carena saw her and then looked about for a place to run.

Rosa tore the screaming bundle from the slave girl's stunned arms. Joy burst inside her to finally hold that which was ripped from her soul. He was beautiful, perfect like Messi said. "Paullus, I will never lose you again."

"Come on, Carena," Ruso ordered. "Father is…" The boy stopped and stared in shock. Rosa now held the baby. Carena glared at her domina. Zeno hovered over both to see the screeching boy. "Come on, Carena."

The girl stubbornly shook her head. "I can't."

Zeno looked at Ruso. "Are you heading back to Herculaneum?"

"Yes, if we can. Father's waiting for us in the fishing hut," Ruso said, shifting the load on his scrawny back.

Zeno nodded toward the only way down to the beach. "The ravine is flooding. You'll have to go across the foot-bridge." The ground shifted beneath their feet, sending the horse into a panic. It broke free and bolted away.

"We have to go to the docks. I have a boat waiting for us." Zeno slid an arm around her waist.

"If we can get to my father's house, we can get to the beach," Rosa said to everyone gathered. "Can we?"

Vesuvius roared again, tossing massive boulders through the air like pebbles and belching putrid fumes down on everything with a shower of ash. Jupiter's lightning flashed through the roiling black cloud. The little group stopped at the small wooden bridge swaying over angry water vomiting through the narrow chasm.

Rosa refused to move and just stared at the angry water roaring below the rope bridge. "No. I can't. No." Rosa tightened her grip on the screaming bundle in her arms.

"You can't make it with him." Zeno tore the child from her arms and shoved her forward. "Go. Go now. We have to get across with the others."

"I can't! I can't." Rosa reached for the baby. Zeno jerked it away from her hands. "Not without my baby."

"You have to. Just cling to both ropes and keep your feet apart." He nudged Rosa forward with his elbow. "You can have him back when we get across. I'll be right behind you. It's our only hope. Now go."

Rosa stepped timidly on the first board and glanced back.

"Don't look back or down until you get over, Rosa. Don't look back. Look at Ruso," he ordered.

Rosa hesitantly shuffled her feet and started toward Ruso waving her toward them. Carena's gaze remained on the squalling child behind her. Zeno inched forward, ignoring the throbbing pain cutting through the arm holding his son. He had to see the woman he loved more than life and his son safe. Whatever it took, he had to protect them from this horror. *His son.* A trickle of joy threaded his soul.

Punishing wind covered them with dirty mist as he inched along behind Rosa. Her hair collapsed down her back and drifted on the wind like a tether that drew him. "Don't look back. Keep going, Rosa. Keep going." His arm burned with pain from gripping the child so tightly, only making his son bellow his own fury. He couldn't lose either of them now. Now or ever. He followed one-step at a time behind her. If the bridge swayed any more, they would be tossed to the roar below.

A gust of wind smacked against the bridge, swaying it precariously. Rosa screamed and stumbled to her knees. A sense of absolute helplessness twisted his guts. He couldn't catch her if she slipped from the swaying bridge and into the gushing water. A vision that cut to his core. "Crawl!"

Ruso reached toward her. "Just a little more, Rosa. A little more. Keep going."

Rosa lunged for the last post to safety and reached for Carena's help from the bridge. The girl's gaze remained riveted on the screaming baby.

The wood slat beneath his back foot cracked, plunging his leg through the bridge. Filthy water grappled to claim his foot. Clinging to the rope slimy with mud, he pulled up to his knees. Rosa stood there, holding her scream with both hands. He couldn't make it with the child. He needed both hands.

"Rosa!"

He nudged the child to her and grappled for the rock ledge, claiming the rock ledge as the bridge tore free and dropped into the roaring water. Ruso clutched his tunic and hoisted him to safety.

The angry mountain spewed clouds of ash over the city, shadowing everything in dark gray. The air thickened with the stench of rotten eggs as the small group joined a throng racing toward the city gates that were now closed. A desperate horde outside pleaded for safety within the walls and away from Vulcan's wrath. "Go around. Go around, I tell you."

Ruso stopped with a glare. "They won't let us in. We have to go around."

Fire burned in Zeno's brain. Felix has a boat waiting to take them to Capri and to freedom. "No. We have to get to the pier," he yelled.

"Get me close enough to talk to the guards," Rosa ordered over the maddening roar. "They will let me through." Zeno began shoving bodies away, opening a path to the gate. Once there, Rosa rose to her full patrician height before the soldier peeping through the slat opening.

"As the daughter of Marcus Nonius Balbus and the wife of Pomponius Beastius, I demand you let me and my slaves pass."

Her words seared through every nerve in Zeno's body as if touch by fire. Yet, the soldier submitted and opened the pedestrian gate. The throng behind them shoved them through and flooded in. Zeno grabbed Rosa and Paullus back against the guard station wall, letting the mass surge over the two soldiers as if they were only rugs.

CHAPTER 44

"HECTOR. HECTOR, I will get help." Messalina felt his life slip through her arms as Hector's gaze went lifeless. "No. No." Tears tore from her soul as she released his body to the stage, where he should be pretending to be dead, but was not. He was dead. And none of this was an act.

Two more statues collapsed into crumbles. The sky lurked greenish gray beyond the shredded awning flapped like a horse's mane in the punishing wind. Fear crawled out of the black shadows and settled around her as if Marcus could climb from the depths of the stage and claim her.

Screams scratched into her consciousness. They were not her screams but those drifting in with the wind from another world. The world outside seemed to have gone insane. She climbed to her feet, tying the torn tunic over one shoulder as the stage cracked. A long streak cut through the marble. Another trap door in the stage burst loose as if opening for her.

Alexius? Where was he in all this insanity. Messalina raced down the shifting steps to the side door, wanting to see Niki. The girl was not there. Then the door slammed shut as if to keep her there. Panic beyond measure rose beneath her skin. No. She could not be trapped there with the dead.

Shoving at the door, it burst open to a frantic crowd stampeding through the street, trampling over bodies as if they were clods of dirt. It was insanity. Why? What was happening? Her gaze lifted to the top of the mountain that now shadowed Herculaneum to witness Vesuvius belching fury from his guts. The sky roiled above the city with angry gray-black clouds. Stones, boulders, and flames slammed into walls, hailed down on people, on anything in the way. No break. No pause. Just fury.

She had to get home. She had to find Alexius.

Messalina eased along the wall, feeling bodies pummel past her. The fabric store beckoned to her. She remembered that store. She had bought fabric for her stolas. The ones she wanted to wear after the wedding. Her heart twisted with the memories as she eased toward the doorway as if it offered safety. Demetri bolted out brandishing a club. "Get away. Get away, you thief!"

"No. No, I am not."

The woman did not hear her, but smashed a pot behind Messalina as it missed her. Another rolling clay vase tripped her attempt to flee from another assault. "Get away from there. Get away!" she screamed again.

Messalina stumbled into the wall of humanity that somehow had claimed her, demanding her to move with it. Bodies clamored into her, knocking her about like a loose rock in a box. An arm slammed into her face. She stumbled and fell. Pain seared through her brain, and the world went black.

Alexius shoved his way through the street thick with bodies pressing their way to the beach. He needed to find Flaccus. Felix. The vigils. Anyone who could help him find Messalina.

He wormed his way between the horde and the store-fronts as his body rebelled. It seemed he had been up forever. Now Vesuvius had erupted with the fury of the gods. Had he angered them or was it over Balbus's death? Why?

Sweat poured as he worked his way to the familiar intersection where Messalina had lashed him with her ribbon in Jupiter's parade. He saw Flaccus shove a man away from Zeno's staircase. "Get out of here, fool. The city i*th* doomed," the centurion yelled.

Alexius fell against the stairway wall where he once found Messalina, an eternity ago. "Messalina. Have you seen her?" A group raced through the long hallway and poured down the steps, brushing past him.

"In thi*th* mob!" Flaccus shook his head, still swollen from the kick in the teeth.

"Flaccus, Messi is out here somewhere. I have to find her. Are the vigils still at the city gates?"

"They'd better be."

"Maybe they can help me find her."

"Worth a try. You…" Flaccus studied him. "Have you eaten *th*ince dawn?"

"No. Not hungry."

"Can't make it if you don't. Come on."

Messalina felt something tugging at her, lifting her. Alexius? Pain jolted through her entire body as she stirred enough to open her eyes to see Felix adjusting her in his arms. "Lucky for you, you fell under that cart. Or you'd be squashed like them." He nodded to the trampled bodies littering the street.

It hurt to think, much less speak. However, she had to get home. "Alexius. I have to find him."

"Not now." Felix wrapped an arm around her waist and studied the approaching stampede. "Hang on to me." He charged across the street and sagged against the temple wall to catch his breath. "I'll get you to Zeno's apartment. Then I will find Alexius and bring him there."

He led her into the block-long hallway that led to the other side where Zeno's apartment was. People scurried past like frightened rats. Alas, Zeno's door finally appeared.

Let him be there. Please, by all the gods of Olympus, let Alexius be there waiting for me. Desperation cut through Messalina like a knife the instant the door opened to an empty room, void of his smile. She sagged onto the bed where every moment they had shared flashed before her. How could he come for her now.? And if he found Marcus's note, why would he? "Felix, I have to go home. He is out there. I know he is."

"You can't. The passages to the beach are blocked with fools fighting to get to the galleys. I'll find him. Wait here until I get back."

He bolted from the apartment, leaving her alone with nothing except an empty existence. Once this place had been the Elysian Fields. Now it was horror. The floor trembled with each step she studied the Decumanus Maximus below, praying she would see him. Concrete flaked off the ceiling in big chunks behind her. Vesuvius roared again, flaming like a large torch in an ever-darkening fury. The flood of desperation locked around Messalina. Everywhere frantic people surged to escape.

Was Alexius one of the trampled bodies she saw? No. He could not be. He was too strong. No. Her body ached as if beaten. Her brain clamored against her skull. The door burst open. Her heart sprang to her throat, only to have it slam down on her guts.

"Messi!" Rosa raced toward her, carrying a bundle in her arms. Zeno held the door for Carena to enter and then closed it.

"Have you seen Alexius? Tell me you have. Please."

Everyone looked at each other and shook their heads.

"He's out there. I have to find him!" Messalina started toward the door.

"You can't go out there. It's too dangerous," Zeno said, stopping her. "We barely made it this far."

Black bathed everything—the streets, buildings, sky—all lost in the abyss. Falling ash made it hard to swallow. The ground spasmed with each precious step. The wind whipped dust and sand in the looming darkness.

Yet Alexius knew that it could be no more than midafternoon. He watched a pack of frantic people trampling over anything or anyone and fighting to get to the beach. He stuffed meat down his throat that Flaccus shoved at him and studied Zeno's apartment window. Something beckoned him to attempt to cross to the staircase again. A mug of ale slammed down on the table, startling him back to the moment. "Drink."

Alexius felt every bite flood into his body, filling it with strength enough to find Messalina in this insanity.

"Know where they went?"

"The theater."

"What in Hade*ths* wa*th* the girl doin' there?

Hector wrote her, saying he would kill himself if she didn't come."

"*Tho*ulda let him."

Alexius toasted the comment. "I will go there. And you check to see if she is…" He almost said trampled in the streets. No. That could not happen. "We can meet at Zeno's."

"Sons of Dis, where is she?"

Alexius had barely made his way to the theater to find Hector laying in a pool of blood on the stage and Marcus's broken body below the trap door. He called out for Messalina, hearing his voice fade in the roar. Nothing. Nothing except the falling stones and pumice peppering the marble around him.

Where are you, Messi? Where are you? Tell me.

He stepped out into the ever-thickening darkness. Fires burned in various storefronts offering little guidance. The hordes were much less now. Here and there, someone would venture from their hiding place as if they were walking beneath a shroud settling over the city.

Desperation clamped like a vise around Alexius's guts. He collapsed on one of the supports of the marble arch near the Temple of the Augustalus. One of the equestrian statues lay in fragments in the entrance of the basilica. Something sparkled in the bushes.

His helmet, caught in the wind. It lay trapped in the branches. He emptied it of ash and pumice and felt his brain sigh once the protection settled over his bruised scalp pummeled by the falling debris. Exhaustion hung on his heels as he made his way closer to Zeno's.

How many times had he entered their love nest to find Messi laying there naked, arms open, smiling as he removed his clothing? "Be there for me, Messi. Please be there," the whispered words poured off his lips.

Yet the door lay open. The bed lay empty. Disappointment edged his concern as he scanned the room and saw a note on the table.

Alexius, come to the pier. I love you. Messi

She was alive. A world lifted from his shoulders.

Messalina's heart sank as she entered the silence of Alexius's dark atrium, made only darker by the looming shroud draping the city. The blue-black walls echoed back at her as she called for Alexius or anyone else. There was no life here. Even the slaves were gone.

"I'll check upstairs." Zeno raced up the nearby steps as Messalina followed Rosa clutching Paullus. Carena clung to the child's blanket as they passed the triclinium. The freshly painted black panels framed in red glared back at her. Even the ash-covered loungers seemed unwelcoming as if they insulted by the falling filth.

"Wait here," Messalina said as she hurried by the statue of the drunken Hercules, past the stags attacking a deer that Alexius liked, to the dividing wall, and climbed on the table that Alexius used to come to her each night

"Mother! Papa! Claudius! Where are you?"

Maximus galloped toward her, barking. He stopped, wagging his stub of a tail. "Where are they, Max?" She barely heard the dog whine over the roar. A hand touched her leg. Messalina startled and looked down at Rosa.

"Zeno says we have to get to the galleys. We can go through my house." Rosa waved back toward the breezeway where Carena now held the baby. "We can get to the beach through the thermae and go down to the pier."

Messalina brushed vagrant strands of hair out of her eyes as she looked past Balbus's sanctum, at the standing statue of the man and at the frantic beach stirring like bothered ants. Out on the docks, guards with drawn gladiuses and raised shields held the desperate pandemonium from racing to the few remaining galleys.

Lighting streaked the starless sky, releasing booming thunder. Beyond the pier, Messalina saw her father's galley bobbing about, riding on the angry waves taking it out to sea.

They left…without me. Muddy rain hit her face like fat tears. Deep booming thunder mixed with the roaring mountain. Walls of waves rose like grimy claws and crashed on the shore. They were gone. All of them. Leaving her there. Why? Was it Hector? No. Please not for that.

Each step back through Alexius's house was precarious as the ground rippled, knocking Aurelia's statues off tables and out of niches. Any other time, she would have stopped to pick up a statue and set it back in place. That life was nonexistent now. She had no one except Zeno and Rosa now.

Fear and sweat pulsed in the egg-rotten air as Messalina held onto Zeno's belt, letting him drag her blindly through the throng to Balbus's doors. Other than Carena's desperate grip on her belt, Messalina was oblivious to the clotted thickness of humans.

Zeno burst the doors open to Balbus's house and the mass of people plunged in with them, shoving Messalina and Rosa against the walls. Pressed there, Rosa suddenly screamed. "Paullus! My baby! Carena." The girl had vanished in the panicked throng. "Zeno, we have to find him," Rosa screamed. "Carena!"

Zeno grabbed her back from the herd of humans and sagged against the wall. "She's gone to the pier. She has to have gone to the pier."

Rosa's frantic gaze shot up to his face. "How do you know for sure?"

"I don't. But where else would she have gone."

"She was just here. I saw her. She wouldn't leave…me."

Messalina clutched Rosa's wrist. "She is not here, Rosa. Listen to Zeno."

Zeno flashed a smile of gratitude. "Rosa, we have to go to the beach, if we want any chance of finding her and Baby Paullus now."

They made their way through the hallway to the thermae and through the rooms echoing with pandemonium of a broken window that now opened to the beach. A whirlwind of people met them. Lightning cut the black sky like long crooked spears painted in greens, reds and yellows.

"I see her.," Zeno yelled over the roaring mountain, screams, and lashing waves.

Messalina searched but saw nothing but the pier blocked by the flat side of the huge shields that rose like a wall. "No more. Not until another galley arrives."

Sheets of lightning screeched through the dirty velvet sky. Deafening thunder pounded the walls as Vesuvius lashed more fury at the city. Alexius stood on Messalina's terrace wall, searching the insanity on the beach. Max waited beside him, happy to have company. "Where is she, Max?"

Ravines on both sides of Herculaneum vomited water and muddy ash as if an aqueduct had broken open. Maybe it had. The bay roiled like a bubbling stew pot. Nothing except a blur of frantic faces filled space between the boathouses and lashing waves.

Cold fear crept up his spine. Messalina was out there in all that and he had to find her, get her out of the doomed city. Then again, maybe it was not doomed. Maybe everything would stop as quickly as it started. Like the earth tremors that shook everyone to the streets, only to stop, and life continued as it always had. Maybe tomorrow everyone would flood back into the streets, laughing.

Vesuvius roared, banishing his fantasy. The stench of rotten eggs belched through the air like a thick fart. Nothing about anything felt certain. In their hurry, the mass could not move. The tunnels were constipated.

Beyond, Messalina's father's galley lurched in the distance. They left? Without us? Without me? His father's words rang in his ears. "We will wait as long as we can…." His father's promise rang in his ears, 'I will find a way for you.'

Movement on his terrace allowed Alexius watch as a thief claimed all he could and then climbed onto the railing. He launched himself over the heads of the entrapped crowd in the passage and came short, only to disappear into the mass that heaved forward inch by desperate inch toward the beach

She was out there. He knew it. And there was no other way to find Messalina other than to jump across to the boathouses as the thief had. He studied the distance from the terrace railing to the rooftops. If he fell short, his fate was the same as the thief.

Somehow, the distance across the passage had grown to the size of a ravine and looked blacker. Alexius's heart climbed to his throat. This would be the longest jump of his life. He had to get airborne, lurch high over the passage to cross the distance, high enough to land at least ten feet down below the terrace to land on the roof tops of the boathouses.

The table he stood on was not enough to give him a chance. He needed more of a ramp, something to make a decent run for it. He saw the lounger Messi had been resting on when he came to confront her about Hector.

Alexius put his cuirass next to his helmet on another lounger and adjusted the sweaty under tunic, as if doing so would help him fly. He tied his sandals tighter and wished he had Mercury's winged feet instead. This was it. He either made it or died trying.

He stood and focused on a direct spot of the boathouse roof. He sucked in a deep breath and blocked the images from his mind of what he was attempting to do. *Fly.* He bolted to a full run up the lounger, onto the table, and flung all his weight at the rooftop. Black air swept around him. Shadows loomed like hungry spirits below. Lightning cracked as he landed, catching one foot on the edge and fell onto the delicious hard surface. Pain screamed down his shin as he rolled and bolted to his feet. His heart thundered with joy. He made it.

Hope of finding Messalina surged as he raced to the opposite edge of the roof. The swarming mass shifted below like beings trapped beneath a black blanket. In the glow of torches moving like fireflies about the beach, he could see the stairs belching people out like a flood of bees escaping a burning hive. People poured from windows of Balbus's thermae. Here and there, a frantic face looked upward, lit by the flashes of lightning. Voices screamed names, searching for someone lost.

Alexius's gaze moved to the pier, invisible now without the flash of lightning. Where are you Messi? Where...

"Alexius!"

A siren call, the one he had been praying to hear rose above the cacophony. He scoured the desperate lives below him and saw Messalina charging through the crowd. He had to wait until she was there below, or he could lose her again by dropping into the swarming mass below.

She stopped directly before the boathouse below him and then he stepped off the ledge and dropped into an eternity. His feet hit the pebbles, and he sank to his knees. Messalina grabbed him. His lips found hers and drank in the thrill of her mouth as his hands filled with the reality of her flesh.

"Alexius, I thought you had left with everyone else." Her voice cracked as she spoke.

"Never, my swan. Never." He caressed her face as life surged inside him. "We have to get to the pier."

"No. They have left without us. We have to go to the boathouses with everyone else."

"Father said he would find a way for us if the galley had to leave. Come on." He saw Zeno and Rosa working through the crowd toward them. "Follow us."

"No. I won't leave without Paullus," Rosa yelled. "I won't leave without him." She broke from Zeno's grip and started back into the crowd.

Zeno yelled back to Alexius. "Go on. Go now. You will find us in the boat houses when you return." He disappeared into the crowd where Rosa had gone.

Alexius clutched Messalina's waist and barged his way toward the pier where waves rose like black clawing monsters that lashed at the shore. A flash of lightning displayed one lone boat tethered to a pole and Ignatius waiting nearby.

The guard's shields rose. "No galleys. Go to the boathouses."

Alexius met the soldier's gaze. "Let us pass. That boat is waiting for us."

The guard looked back over his shoulder and stepped back. Alexius carried Messalina down the stone pier as waves tore at the crumbling sides.

"Couldna stayed much longer, dominus. Water's turnin' to mud." The old man waved at his boat lifting in the waves. "Get her in the bow and help me row."

CHAPTER 45

MESSALINA'S MIND BLANKED the instant Alexius lifted her in his arms and jumped from the pier. Cold black wind surrounded her as they dropped into an angry abyss. The boat heaved upward, catching and tossing them both across the seats. She landed on top of Alexius as he rose to set her into the pile of wet fishing nets in the front of the boat.

As red and white lightning streaked across the roiling green-black clouds and sky, Ignatius released the boat to dance in the crashing waves. Both men slumped onto the middle seat and grabbed oars,

Messalina watched Alexius strain in rhythm with Ignatius as they rowed from the pier, dragging the small craft further out into the angry water. Messalina screamed as the boat rose vertical on a glistening black wall of water and then plunged straight down another monstrous black waves rising like hungry demons.

"Hold on, Messi! Hold on!" Alexius yelled over his shoulder as he and Ignatius pulled at their oars.

Pumice peppered into the boat with the water, pummeling her flesh without mercy. Water crashed over the sides. Again, the boat rose upward, revealing golden specks of burning pumice floating like fireflies on top of the layers of more pumice drifting toward the disappearing beach. The boat slid down into the black depths of another wave as thunder roared Vulcan's wrath.

Alexius and Ignatius pulled with an uncanny rhythm. Occasionally, Ignatius glanced over his shoulder. She followed his gaze and saw her father's galley bobbing and tilting in the bay like a frantic colt newly tethered.

The boat clamored into the galley's side with a hard jolt just as the galley began tilting up and away. It then tilted back toward the boat as if to capsize. Voices yelled down from the darkness. "Grab the net! Grab the net!"

Messalina could not make her hand release the boat rails. Suddenly Alexius launched her toward the reaching hands that grabbed and dragged her over the wood railing, releasing her to the planking like a grain sack. She rolled over, expected Alexius to appear as the galley rail rocked away. He wasn't there. Panic cut her insides as the galley dipped again. "Alexius!" She started for the railing. Hands tossed her back to the deck.

"Stay there, girl." Her father's voice rang in her ears as the crew yanked Alexius over the railing. He stumbled for footing like a drunk. His hands, slimed with blood, grappled for her as she bolted to him.

Another wave crashed against the galley, tossing the galley almost vertical. Alexius lurched backward and slid across the wet deck, tearing him away from her grip. Alexius rammed belly-first into the railing and reached as if grabbing for Neptune. Wheeling his arms, Alexius fought to keep from falling into the abyss beyond.

"Noooo!" She grabbed for anything to keep herself from losing him again. His hand. His leg. His shoe. The wedding vow screamed in her brain. *Where you go, I go.* If the gods took him from her. She would follow.

"Get back, girl!" Her father threw her toward the main mast and then grabbed Alexius's tunic and lunged backward, heaving them both onto the deck.

Indecision dominated the galley's struggle to remain upright. Alexius locked an arm around the mast, pinning her to the wood with his body. "Hold on, Messi. Hold on!"

"Oars! Raise the sail!" Her father's orders towered over the crashing waves and thunder. The leather sail rode up the mast and burst full of wind, heaving the galley away from land. Oars shoved out of portals and the galley floor began vibrating with the desperate sound of drums.

She watched her father riding each shift while he held onto the mast rope. Emotion cracked the wall around her heart. Her father had not left her. He had waited for her, riding this insanity. In addition, he had saved Alexius. Tears blended with the thrashing rain as the galley leveled.

"To the cabin. Now!" Messallus ordered, pointing to a small cabin at the rear of the galley. They staggered through the cabin door just as the galley rocked again and fell together into dry sacks and netting piled in a vacant corner. They lay there gasping.

Messalina scanned the tiny cabin and found Claudius beaming across the small room where Antonia clung to her mother's neck and her squirming little dog. Galerius and Aurelia held onto each other in a corner. Joy blinded Messalina. They were alive.

Octavia stepped from the corner. Her father grabbed her. "Stay, woman. There will be time enough for that once we get to Misenum."

"Are you all right?" The soothing sound of Alexius's voice drew Messalina. His eye was as red as the flashing lightning. Bruises covered his face. She caressed each as if to heal the insult. She wanted to heal it. She wanted to heal everything and make Vulcan's wrath go away.

"I thought I had lost you."

"You almost did." The corner of his mouth lifted with mirth as he dried her face with his bloody hand. He touched the swelling on her forehead. "By the gods, what happened?"

"I fell under a cart. Felix found me."

Behind Alexius's head, the raging storm ripped the leather drape from the window and revealed an avalanche of red fire flooding down the side of Vesuvius like an angry titan. Her scream drew everyone's attention to the wrath plunging directly toward Herculaneum.

Alexius turned and froze. Gasps filled the cabin as fire spew from ravines and spread across the water like oil. Above the city, treacherous bolts of red lightning lashed the black sky like whips driving the gods' fury over the shrouded streets, plummeting it onto houses, bashing everything in its path.

The galley turned toward Misenum, tearing away the horrid view. The oars managed to claim calmer water, no longer blanketed with pumice. They glided farther out where the wind was gentler, and the waves were less vicious.

Alexius tightened his arms around Messalina, drawing her closer. He wanted to be close enough to wear her like skin. How many times had he thought he had lost her?

Messalina turned in his arms. "Alexius, I am sorry. I should not have gone to the theater."

He drew back enough to see her face in the thick shadows. "Did you really think Hector would kill himself?"

"I thought I could talk sense to him. Alexius. Only Hector did not write that note. I should have known that. Marcus did. Alexius, he wanted to kill me to prove how much he loved Hector."

Alexius's guts twisted. "Marcus?"

She nodded. "Hector tried to stop him. Then the ground threw him on Marcus's knife." She rested a hand on his chest. Her gaze thickened. "Alexius, I don't love him. I only wanted to help Hector live. That is all. I love you. Just you." A lone tear coursed down her cheek.

Something settled softly in his soul enough that a contented smile eased over his lips. He enfolded her in his arms. "I love you, my swan. However many days we have left in this world, I want to spend them with you and only you."

CHAPTER 46

ALEXIUS FELT THE oars draw back in the water and the galley slow toward the pier near Misenum. From below deck, Didius ordered the slaves to prepare to disembark. Slaves and other escapees climbed ladders to the deck and sought dry land as quickly as possible. He heard laughter. Excited voices mixed with the orders to prepare to dock.

In the cabin, both families clustered, smiling, talking, touching. Messalina hugged everyone, not resisting anyone's assuring caress. Apparently, the value and brevity of life was apparent not only to him, but to Messalina as well. He hungered for his mother's touch, his father's smile, even Messallus's harsh taunt about saving his ass from going overboard.

"Stick with being a senator, Alexius. You will never make a merchant sailor."

"Pliny's villa isn't far," his father announced. Relief filled his voice. "We can go there until we can return."

Alexius was willing to go anywhere. He hungered for the feel of steady dry land void of the smell of sulfur and where birds chirped. He tightened his arm around Messalina's waist as Claudius bolted across the gangplank and raced up the terraced steps like a freed colt.

The garden terraces on either side of the hill appeared untouched by Vesuvius. Apollo's chariot was rising in the distance. Here, the stars glistened as the early morning approached. Yet, pitch black suffocated Herculaneum and coast well past Pompeii as far as Stabianum. Nothing except for the burning speck of fire on top of Vesuvius could be seen. The only other reminder of the horrors was the faint smell of rotten eggs.

Alexius waved Fosco to go up as he helped Messalina over the stone steps. After being tossed about on the waves, the land felt odd.

Messalina's hands gripped him like death. "Alexius! Look!"

Alexius turned as an angry black cloud rolled toward them like a rejected predator. Screams filled the morning air as panic spread like a disease across faces watching the avalanche of horror gliding across the water. Zephyr's wind ripped the galley from the pier, sending it into the rocks as if determined to bring this horror across the bay. Lightning lacerated the sky as Vulcan sought his revenge on all those who had escaped.

A sulfurous black fog churned across the pier as Alexius dropped, taking Messalina down with him, pinning her behind a terrace wall. "Cover your face, Messi. Don't breathe." The stench thickened, blistering hot and angry like a bully showing off its power. It lingered as if looking for another victim and then drifted away on a breeze.

Dawn, again, peeked curiously in its wake. Nervous laughter filtered along the terraces as people stood, gathered, and coughed. Fresh air filled his desperate lungs as

Alexius moved to climb to his feet. His back did not seem broken, just numb from feet using him to flee up the hill.

Messalina rose with him and ran her hands down his arms. "Alexius, are you all right?"

He slumped on the terrace wall. "Yes. Are you?"

"I am fine."

He was not sure he wanted to move. He glanced at the bay where the sun broke from disappearing gloom to gleam down on the pumice and ash floating in the water like a dirty blanket. However, the black shroud remained over Herculaneum like a drape drawn across a stage.

"Alexius! Messalina!" Calls drew his attention up the hill to where both families stood, gathered close, searching for them. His mother pointed at them. His father nodded and finally smiled. Antonia disappeared behind her mother, probably looking for that damn dog. Claudius looked triumphant. Messallus looked stalwart, even though tears streamed down his round face as he nodded at his wife's chatter.

EPILOGUE

B LINDED BY THE saffron veil, Messalina reached
for the two bowls held before her by a priest. The
heat of the burning oil lamp drew her left hand, and the
chill of the water greeted her right. The instant she touched
both with her fingertips, "Feliciter!" "Talasio!" resounded
around the atrium.

Before the eyes of friends and family, Alexius lifted the
orange veil from her head and kissed her passionately. He
drew her to his side and faced everyone. "I present to you
my wife, Messalina Claudia."

Alexius's voice rang out through the atrium of her new
home. Her mother and father beamed beside Aurelia and
Galerius who grinned at each other. Antonia was scold-
ing one of Little Bru's pups. Claudius looked pompous in
his toga pretexta, one that matched the toga Alexius now
wore—pure white with a broad purple stripe along its hem.

Messalina gazed at the many faces, missing those not
there: Niki. Felix. Carena. Baby Paullus. Zeno. Rosa. They
were faces she would never see again, but would never forget.

A deeper sadness threatened. Nor would Rosa ever feel the growing child inside Messalina now. She drew closer to her newly-elected husband and senator, the only one who knew. The child was their treasured secret, at least for now.

Alexius had assured her that if the child were a girl, her name would be Marcia Galeria Rosa. If the babe were a boy, it would be Marcus Galerius Alexius Zeno. However, for now, life could hold no more bliss than standing next to Alexius and feeling his arm holding her close.

~Fini~

Author's Note

MY FIRST VISIT to Herculaneum was unbelievable. There I was, standing on a solid wall of the sixty-five feet of volcanic concrete, overlooking the houses of Messalina and Alexius. I knew, as I stood there, that this concrete shelf should have been the water of the bay as it was when Herculaneum thrived. Now I gazed at the city of Ercolano stretching above these ruins.

And behind it rose the volcano, Vesuvius—very much still alive.

It seemed impossible that this hazy blue volcano could create so much horror. Nevertheless, there it was—Vulcan's forge as stalwart as it has been for thousands of years. Yet until 24 August 79 A.D., many believed it to be a mountain. No one could believe this monster would bury an entire valley with its wrath.

I hope I have taken you, dear reader, back to this rich and beautiful city when it was alive and throbbing with life, love, and power where you could meet those who lived in this ancient resort town called Herculaneum.

As I did, I hope you do walk through Herculaneum's main street, the Decumanus Maximus, as Messalina and

Rosa had, along the various shops that once bore a covered awning to protect the shoppers from the burning sun. I remember turning the corner to the steps up to the remains of a second-story apartment. (Zeno and Rosa's, Messalina and Alexius's love nest) However, nothing is left of the second floor. It was wiped away in the pyroclastic flows that buried everything with all six surges of volcanic vomit.

Mingled all among these shops and homes were the houses of the rich who vacationed or lived there to get away from another ancient city—Rome. I bequeathed the House of Stag to Alexius and the House of the Mosaic Atrium to Messalina. These remarkable beachfront homes overlooked the bay waters of Naples and not at the wall of volcanic concrete where I stood.

Marcus Nonius Balbus, the first and most powerful man in Herculaneum with his family, did live in The House of Telephas. This elegant home conjoined to Balbus's private thermae—the Suburban Baths—that was opened only to those who paid membership to bathe and relax there. He truly did die right before Vesuvius erupted. His memorial still stands outside the public doorway to his bathhouse directly below Alexius's terrace.

Balbus had three children: a son also named Marcus Nonius Balbus, two daughters named Nonia Prima and Nonia Secunda whom I have nicknamed Rosa, his actual wife whose name was Volasennia (I couldn't make that name up if I tried) and his mother Viciria. They were all actual people who lived in this history. Their statues were found in the basilica, including equestrian statues of Balbus and his son who, for some unknown reason, wears a scowl on his face.

Across the street from the basilica was the Temple to Augustus, where a man's skeleton was found face-down on a cot in the back anteroom. A chair had been jammed under the door handle to lock him in. Nor could he crawl out the narrow window on an outer wall. Who he was and why was he trapped there; I could only wonder? (Sulla, maybe?)

I granted another infamous villa to Sulla and Agrippina—the Villa of Papyri, so named because of the scrolls found in a library. This villa remains mostly buried, however the uniform sticks of wood that turned out to be ancient rolls of papyri are now in the process of being deciphered. One such scroll was unrolled to reveal the floor plan of this magnificent villa.

J. Paul Getty bought a copy of the floor plan and built a magnificent replica of it in Malibu CA, USA. It is open and free to the public—The Getty Villa. I have visited this exquisite place and highly recommend it. Do not miss it if you are ever in Los Angeles.

Herculaneum's theater remains buried. However, this was Herculaneum's first discovery when it was tunneled into for a well. Apparently, in 1708, while digging, workers broke into the theater and discovered the first remains of this buried city. Treasure hunters and archeologists have flocked there since and continue to chip away at this concreted city.

One find was the Palaestra. At noon on 24 August 79, spectators were attending the games, watching swimmers competing in the intersecting swimming pools, where a five-headed hydra fountain spewed water on the contestants. All around the swimming pools were the young men competing in various sports. Of course, this sports-center was filled with concrete; however, the hydra fountain has been carved out and stands in a niche in this volcanic wall of vomit.

Vespasian actually did come to Herculaneum during his trip to Campania right before his shocking death. He had come to see what troubled this fertile valley and returned to Rome and died shortly after. According to Suetonius, *"Vespasian visited Campania and caught a slight fever. He hurried back to Rome to Cutiliae, his summer retreat near Reate where he made things worse by bathing in cold water and getting a stomach chill…he almost fainted after a sudden violent burst of diarrhea, struggling to rise, muttering that an Emperor ought to die on his feet and collapsed in the arms of the attendants who went to his rescue."* (Penguin, p291)

The death dust, 'charbon', an ancient name for anthrax (Merriam-Webster Online), lingers in the soils of southern Europe. "If inhaled, this poison has similar characteristics as a stomach flu or the common cold and continue to severe breathing and shock and is usually fatal." (CDC.gov.)

Vespasian was a very health- conscious man with a strong constitution, so it was odd to me for him to have died suddenly. Could there have been a plot to kill him? There were plenty of powerful families who hated the taxes that Vespasian garnered to restore the imperial treasury after Nero's extravagances.

I could not resist using these facts in my story as well as the five-headed hydra spewing water over Alexius and Marcus as they raced one another. However, while perusing this ancient city, what staggered me the most was seeing a human skull in one of the fishing huts.

It gave credence to all those writings and pictures that I found while researching—the thirty-foot boat found washed ashore with a man holding an oar (Ignatius?), the centurion missing his front teeth and wearing a backpack of his carving tools found face-down in the street (Flaccus?)

However, of all these pictures, the most powerful was the fourteen-year-old girl's skeleton protecting a baby in her arms. Researchers determined that she was pretty, had been poorly fed, or had been sick as a child. Her bones, too, were worn. She was likely a slave. Yet, the babe she protected wore "little bells and a pin shaped like a cupid" and was likely a patrician's child. Who was she? (Carena holding Baby Paullus?) In addition, there were so many others who died that horrid death simply trying to flee Vulcan's wrath. (Rosa and Zeno?)

I am grateful to all the research done as Joseph J. Deiss wrote about in his book *Herculaneum-Italy's Buried Treasure* and Pliny the Younger's account of this tragedy. I must thank Dr. Jim Murowchick (Department of Geo-sciences-Professor at the University of Missouri-Kansas City) for his help in understanding volcanoes and for telling me about the centurion's remains that opened my eyes to this city. All mistakes are mine and not intentional. My only attempt is to bring life back to a magnificent time and place where people laughed, loved, cried, played, and prayed. And still do.

My greatest concern is that this all could happen again. Vesuvius is still alive.

FOR THE FAMILY
COMPANION SHORT STORY TO
THREATENED LOYALTIES

BY J F RIDGLEY

You met 'the witch' in *Threatened Loyalties*. Have you ever wondered how a woman could become so heartless? Find out in my companion story to *Threatened Loyalties* that tells Viciria's story of how such a gentle creature could be changed forever.

CHAPTER 1

"PACK YOUR THINGS. You're leaving."

I stared at my husband's back, not truly understanding what he was saying. Lucius Quintus Rufius had said nothing of me going on a trip or going anywhere until now. He was usually the one leaving to attend to the Senate's demands or the demands of his three apartment buildings in Subura. I typically remained in our country villa to see that it was run properly and to care for our sons.

However, he had been especially cold and aloof this last week, even with our two boys who bore their father's name…the same name. The eldest was Lucius Quintus Rufius *Gullus,* for his cocky attitude. Water drizzled lazily into the impluvium pool as I nursed our two-month-old son Lucius Quintus Rufius who hadn't claimed nickname yet.

I shifted in my chair in the atrium. It wasn't my place to question why Lucius had been acting this way until now.

"And, why am I leaving?"

Lucius continued to stare through his tablinum window at the sun-filled garden. He just stood there by his desk. One hand rested on the polished oak corner. He was a tall man, lean, and stiff. His aquiline features were made sharper by the afternoon shadows.

"Viciria, your father is here. He waits for you outside."

Papa? Why hadn't he come in? It made no sense that he would be made to wait outside. I looked at the door slave whose gaze avoided mine.

"See my father inside."

"No." Lucius swiftly turned and motioned to Marta, my personal slave, standing behind me. "Get your domina's things removed from this house."

This had gone far enough. I stood up from my chair and handed our child to the slave woman. The boy immediately voiced his fury at being removed from my breast. I covered and then faced my husband who refused to look at me even as he stepped into the atrium.

The ever-present divide between us seemed to be expanding. Not in the five years, since my father granted him my hand in marriage, had I felt any warmth from this man.

"For how long am I to be gone, may I ask?"

His gaze raked my face like claws. "You will not be returning, Viciria."

I melted back into my chair. *How was this possible?* Lucius couldn't be moving me back to my father's house in Nuceria. This was where my children were. Where they lived. Where I lived.

"Why…will I not be returning?" I gasped. "This…This is my home."

Lucius's jaw knotted. A snarl tempted his lips. He bit it into submission. "Your home is with your father now, who can do with you as he sees fit. I no longer care." He flung a hand to the air as if to brush a gnat aside. "The divorce is final and your dowry has been repaid. Now, go."

What divorce? I knew nothing of a divorce. Why? The world around me shattered. Surely, Lucius wouldn't take my sons from me. My beautiful sons.

I flew at the man to clutch the shoulders of his tunic. "Lucius, why? What have I done to deserve this? By all the gods of Olympus, tell me."

He peeled my fingers away and gripped my wrists. The corner of his straight lips curved up in humor. His gaze gleamed down on my face. "You? What have you done?" He shrugged. "Nothing."

About the Author

I love the ancient world. Even after years of researching and many trips to the sites of my stories, I am still fascinated by what I find for my next story. I love bringing this world to life in my award-winning stories of power, greed, violence, and love.

Be sure to stop by my website to discover more about my stories and hopefully sign up for my newsletter so you never miss what's coming next.

http://www.jfridgley.com

I would love to hear from you so drop me a note at **jfridgley@jfridgley.com.** And a review would be soooo appreciated.